Praise for *The Grand D...*

W9-BXZ-577

"*The Grand Dark* is a miracle of the old and the new: a tale of Weimar decadence that is also a parable for our New Gilded Age. . . . It's a fun and terrifying ride, gritty and relentless, burning with true love and revolutionary fervor."

 —Cory Doctorow, author of *Radicalized* and *Walkaway*

"Kadrey has written for us a beautiful nightmare—one that's often eerily familiar—showing a theatrical world set on the edge of war, and losing itself in the shadows of brutality and oppression."

 —Chuck Wendig, *New York Times* bestselling author of *Wanderers*

"Stunning. The hard, spare, considered voice that's driven Kadrey's gonzo supernatural noir has been honed to a deft Kafkaesque edge. Unsettling and dreamlike, seductive and bleak, the jaws of *The Grand Dark* gape to devour you."

 —Max Gladstone, author of *Empress of Forever*

"Artisanal gene mod and robots and coal dust and a big middle finger to the oligarchs, plus bicycles!"

 —Kevin Hearne, *New York Times* bestselling author

"Wildly ambitious and inventive fantasy from an author who's punching above his weight in terms of worldbuilding—and winning."

 —*Kirkus Reviews* (starred review)

"A constant underlying tension makes the city's powder-keg agitation visceral, and the individual neighborhoods and their residents are well wrought."

 —*Publishers Weekly*

"*The Grand Dark* is more than just another reliably strong outing from a veteran writer. It's the work of a major science fiction/fantasy creator going way out in a limb in the effort to wholly redefine himself, all while crystallizing what's made him great."

 —NPR

"[For] readers who like morally complex characters and enjoy their fantasy on the dark side."

 —*Booklist*

THE

GRAND

DARK

THE
GRAND
DARK

RICHARD KADREY

HARPER Voyager
An Imprint of HarperCollinsPublishers

To Drexel and Conan,

both of whom should have been

around a lot longer

HarperCollins books may be purchased for educational, business, or sales promotional use. For information, please email the Special Markets Department at SPsales@harpercollins.com.

Harper Voyager and design are trademarks of HarperCollins Publishers LLC.

A hardcover edition of this book was published in 2019 by Harper Voyager, an imprint of HarperCollins Publishers.

FIRST HARPER VOYAGER PAPERBACK EDITION PUBLISHED 2020.

Designed by Paula Russell Szafranski

Frontispiece © Ethnic Design / Shutterstock

Library of Congress Cataloging-in-Publication Data has been applied for.

ISBN 978-0-06-267252-0

20 21 22 23 24 LSC 10 9 8 7 6 5 4 3 2 1

There were a few short, wonderful years of euphoria when the slaughter was over. Of course, nothing had been settled and we knew it but, in its own way, watching the cataclysm hurtle toward us made the madness of the wild time even sweeter.

—Günther Harden, *Cocaine and Bullets: My Lost Years*

CONTENTS

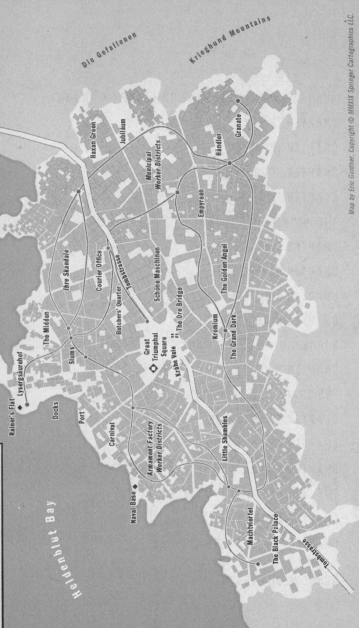

LOWER PROSZAWA

Die Gefallenen

Krieghund Mountains

Haxan Green

Jubiläum

Granate

Händler

Municipal
Worker Districts

Empyrean

Ihre Skandale

Courier Office

Tombstrasse

The Golden Angel

The Midden

Butchers' Quarter

Schöne Maschinen

The Ore Bridge

Kromium

Slums

Great
Triumphal
Square

Krähe Vale

The Grand Dark

Lysergsäurehof

Rainer's Flat

Docks

Port

Carnival

Armament Factory
Worker Districts

Little Shambles

Naval Base

Machtviertel

The Black Palace

Tombstrasse

Heidenblut Bay

Map by Eric Gunther, Copyright © MMXIX Springer Cartographics LLC.

CHAPTER ONE

THE GREAT WAR WAS OVER, BUT EVERYONE KNEW ANOTHER WAR WAS COM-ing and it drove the city a little mad.

Near dawn, Largo Moorden pedaled his bicycle through the nearly deserted streets of Lower Proszawa. It was exactly one week since his twenty-first birthday. Fog from the nearby bay and smoke from the armaments factory left the center of the city looking like a flat, ashen mirage. As Largo sped over the Ore Bridge, the edges of Gothic office buildings, dwellings, and cafés coalesced into view. Streetcars gliding atop silent magnetic tracks in the street and above, old church spires—shadowy outlines a second before—solidified and were gone.

At the bottom of the bridge, where Krähe Vale crossed Tomb-strasse, a line of Blind Mara delivery automata sat waiting for the crossing signal to change. Some of the larger contraptions—the Black Widows carrying machine parts for the factory—resembled wrought iron spiders the size of pushcarts, while the little tea and breakfast Maras were wooden bread boxes decorated with wings and carvings of flying women. Largo was tempted to veer into the line of machines and kick over one or two of the smaller ones. He knew that someday soon the Maras were going to put human couriers like him out of business. Each time he thought about it, a little wave of panic bubbled up from his stomach because, aside from a strong set of legs, the only things Largo possessed that were worth money were his bicycle and an encyclopedic knowledge of every street and alley in the city.

To Largo's surprise, while the crossing signal still read HALT, one of the little winged bread boxes crept past the other Maras and whirred quietly across Krähe Vale. With a mechanical rumble, a squat, armored juggernaut carrying soldiers sped around a corner and crushed the bread box under its metal treads without slowing. All that was left of the little carrier were a small motor sputtering blue sparks, splinters, and a flattened sandwich. Largo hadn't eaten for a day and the sight of food made him hungry. Still, he smiled. Indeed, the Blind Maras would put him out of business one day, but not today, and not for many days to come. When the signal clicked to PROCEED he guided his bicycle through the remains left in the intersection as the rest of the automata split up, carrying their goods all over Lower Proszawa.

The clock over the Great Triumphal Square—renamed, perhaps a touch optimistically, after the war—showed that it was just a few minutes before six. Largo had spent far too long in bed that morning with Remy, his lover, but it was so hard to leave her. He bent over his handlebars, pedaling faster, knowing all too well that being late at the beginning of the work week was a good way to have Herr Branca snapping at you until Friday. Worse, it could result in a humiliating dismissal.

The edges of the plaza were coming to life. Bakers laid out loaves and pies in the windows of their shops. The newspaper kiosk attendant by the underground tram station cut open piles of tabloid yellowsheets full of political intrigue and reports of the previous night's murders. All-night revelers wandered through the square, still jubilantly drunk from the evening before. Along the gutters, purring piglike chimeras cleared the street trash by devouring it.

Beyond the edges of the plaza, prostitutes flirted with men in strange masks made of steel and leather—Iron Dandies, they were called, but never where they could hear it. They were war veterans considered too disfigured to be glimpsed by the city's ordinary citizens—Largo among them. He'd heard that if you stared too long at a Dandy he'd rip his mask off, giving you a good look at his mutilated face. Seeing a Dandy that way was considered bad luck.

Bad luck or no, the truth was that Largo didn't *want* to see what was under the masks or think about how the wounds, or the war itself, had happened. He just put his head down, pedaled harder, and arrived panting at the courier service as the plaza clock rang six.

Dropping his bicycle next to those of the other couriers, Largo ran up the stairs to the office and made it inside before the head dispatcher, Herr Branca, noticed his tardiness. He lingered at the back behind the other messengers so that his supervisor wouldn't see him sweating.

Herr Branca was a burly man, one of the strange sort who seemed to have been born old. None of the couriers knew his age, but depending on the season and whether he'd shaved or not, they guessed it to be anywhere from thirty to sixty. He wore the same thing every day: pinstriped pants, matching vest, and a white shirt with an old-fashioned starched collar that he left open except when visiting their superiors. The bottom button on his vest was always missing. This could mean only one of two things: that Herr Branca was an eccentric who cut the bottom button off all of his vests, or that a second vest was beyond his means. No one at the service took Branca for an eccentric, so that had to mean their supervisor was so poorly paid that his choice in clothes was no better than the couriers'. This possibility always depressed Largo. He liked being a courier, but if Herr Branca was his future, perhaps it was time to make other plans.

But what?

Different futures weren't easy to come by in Lower Proszawa.

As he did every morning, Branca leaned heavily on a standing desk, shouting names and the addresses where couriers were to go while old, battered Maras handed them whatever documents or parcels they were to deliver.

When Branca had called most of the morning's deliveries and the room was nearly empty, Parvulesco, Largo's closest friend at the service, gave him a worried look as he carried a parcel out the door. Largo shrugged. Maybe Branca had seen him come in late and was keeping him back for a good talking-to. There was nothing to do but wait and endure whatever was coming. Parvulesco mouthed, *Good luck*, before heading out.

Soon, everyone else had been given an assignment and it was just Largo and Herr Branca. The supervisor didn't look up for two or three minutes as he took his time filling out a small pile of paperwork. As the seconds ticked by, Largo imagined all sorts of scenarios. A simple dressing-down. Having his pay docked. Maybe he'd even be fired. He stood still, hoping to not draw attention to himself, but after a couple more minutes passed he couldn't stand it anymore. He cleared his throat.

3

"Do you have a cold, Largo?" said Herr Branca. "If so, kindly keep your distance, as it would be inconvenient for me to be ill at this time." He spoke quietly. Branca always spoke quietly, no matter the topic or circumstances. The couriers joked that if he were an executioner, you'd never know he was there until your head was on the ground.

"No, sir. It's nothing like that. I was just wondering if . . ."

"If I noticed you come in late, then hide in the back like a cockroach from the light?"

"Yes," Largo said. "Something like that."

Herr Branca looked up wearily. "Rest easy, Largo. While you were tardy and more than a bit insectile in your earlier behavior, you're not going to be fired.

"In fact, you're being promoted."

Largo frowned, afraid he'd misheard his supervisor. "Promoted?"

Branca set down his pen and sighed. "You're aware of the word, aren't you? It's a verb meaning 'to advance in rank.' 'To ascend to a higher position.' Must I explain it further?"

"No, sir. It's just that . . . it's a bit unexpected."

"Quite, especially considering your less-than-cordial relationship with the clock," said Branca. "That's going to have to stop. Do you understand me? This promotion brings new responsibilities, and promptness is one of them. Can you handle that?"

"Yes, sir. I can."

"Very good. Now stop cowering at the back of the room and come up here so I can explain the lofty position to which you have ascended without having to shout."

Largo was still wary as he approached Herr Branca's desk, waiting to find out that the promotion was a mistake or a cruel joke and his supervisor was going to fire him after all. Branca was looking over more papers when he reached the desk and once more Largo couldn't help himself.

"Why?"

"Why the promotion or why you?" said Branca without looking up.

"Both, I guess."

"Did you happen to notice König was not with us this morning?"

König was the company's chief courier, a tall, handsome man just a few years older than Largo. "No, sir. I didn't," he said.

Branca tugged at his collar. "I didn't expect so. But it's true nevertheless—he wasn't with us. And it's likely you won't see him again here . . . or anywhere else," Branca said. "He's been arrested by the Nachtvogel."

Largo didn't say anything for a moment, still not sure whether Branca was playing him for a fool. König was a nobody, as were all the other couriers at the company. Why would the secret police take away a nobody?

"You saw it happen? I mean, they arrested him here?"

Branca nodded. "Right where you're standing now."

Largo looked at the floor, not sure what he was expecting to see. Then, feeling foolish, he looked back at Branca. "I don't understand. What would the Nachtvogel want with König?"

"I have no idea because I didn't ask, an attitude I advise you to emulate should you ever find yourself face-to-face with them."

Largo took a step closer to his supervisor and said very quietly, "What were they like?"

Branca cocked his head for a moment as if looking for the precise words. "Men. They looked like men. Very serious men."

"That's it?"

"Except for the horns and hooves. And their long, forked tongues, of course," said Branca. He made a face at Largo. "Don't ask silly questions, boy. They were citizens like you or me. And before you ask one more idiotic thing and I'm forced to reconsider your promotion, I'll tell you this. I heard one significant word as they were putting König in irons: *anarchist*. Personally, I never took the man for a political extremist, but there you are."

Largo shook his head. "I wouldn't have guessed. I mean, he never talked about politics. It was always about money, his girlfriend, and work. The same things we all talk about."

"Would you expect an anarchist to shout slogans from the loading dock at lunchtime?" Branca said. "And as for his talk about money, well there you are. More than one good man has been turned to crime by dreams of easy cash. Don't let that happen to you. You've been given a rare opportunity. Use it wisely."

Largo nodded, his earlier fear giving way to feelings of guilt at his good fortune. Good fortune that came on the back of—no, not a friend, but someone like him, at least, someone he knew and moreover had nothing against. He felt a little queasy, but then he straightened. Branca was right. This was an opportunity, and a promotion would mean more money in his pocket. With luck, there would be enough that he wouldn't ever feel hungry again at the sight of a crushed sandwich in the middle of the street. He thought of Remy and his mood lightened slightly. He couldn't wait to tell her about it after work.

Branca leaned on his desk to get closer to Largo. When he spoke, his voice was quiet. "The reason I've told you all this was to impress upon you the importance of your new position. It's a great embarrassment for the company to have one of its trusted employees hauled away in chains. If the news got out it would be very bad for business. Therefore, we must redouble our efforts and do everything we can to keep up the company's good name. Do you know why?"

"Because we're grateful to them for the opportunities they've given us?" he said.

"Don't be naïve." Branca tapped his pen on his desk. "Because you and I are utterly disposable. Never forget that."

"I won't."

"Good. Now, welcome to your new position, chief courier."

"Thank you, sir."

Branca held out a hand to him. When Largo shook it, he was surprised by the force of his supervisor's grip. He'd never seen Branca move more than a step or two in any direction, so it was a shock that there was any strength left in his large body. And what an even greater shock to hear the man's concern for his own position. It didn't exactly make Largo like the old fossil any more, but he couldn't help feeling a bit of sympathy to hear someone Branca's age refer to himself as "utterly disposable."

"Does the promotion mean that I'll be spending more time in the office?" Largo said.

Branca let out one grunting laugh. "God help us all if it did. No, you'll continue your normal duties, making deliveries and picking up goods, but you'll be doing it in parts of the city that you're not used to—including some of its most prosperous districts. That's why I chose you. None of the other rabble here know Lower Proszawa as well." He paused for a moment, then said, "Also, you seem generally honest, which is important. Some of the parcels and documents you'll be carrying will be worth considerable sums of money. Can I count on you to do your job honorably and intelligently?"

Largo was a little shocked by the question. No one had ever asked him anything like it before. "Yes, sir. Of course," he said.

"Good. I thought so. Here are some forms for you to sign to make your promotion official," said Branca. He handed Largo a stack of papers, then dropped a leather box about ten inches long on top. "And here is a new tool of your job. With luck, you'll never need it."

Largo took the papers to a nearby table, set them down, and picked up the box. Turning it over in his hands, he found a small brass lock. With just a little pressure it popped open. At first, Largo wasn't sure what he was looking at. It was made of a dull gray metal. There were holes in it that were clearly meant for his fingers. He put them in and felt a sort of metal grip against his palm while the rounded loops over his knuckles were studded with spikes. He pulled the strange object the rest of the way out of the box. It was a knife. A trench knife from the war, with blood channels down the blade and brass knuckles over his hand. Largo looked at Herr Branca.

"Sir?"

His supervisor glanced at him. "You wear it in a harness under your coat," he said. "Understand, with every job comes certain liabilities. Your promotion will bring you new respect and a larger salary. Unfortunately, it will also make you a target."

"Oh," Largo said. He hesitated for a moment, not liking the word *target*. However, he shook off the feeling and reached back into the box, pulling out a tangle of worn leather straps and clasps. The harness, he guessed. "I don't know how to put it on."

The old man nodded. "I'll show you. Welcome to your future, Largo."

Having Herr Branca strap him into the harness was an embarrassing experience. The couriers were all required to wear black suits and ties while making their deliveries. Years before, the company had given them a clothing allowance to make sure they remained clean and tidy on their rounds. However, the allowance had stopped during the war and never been reinstituted. Largo's one suit was of cheap wool and barely thicker than paper. Worse, the seam had split along one side of the white shirt he'd worn that day, so it was held together with safety pins. To his credit and Largo's relief, Branca said nothing about any of that as he wrapped the harness around the young man's back and shoulders so that, with his jacket on, it and the knife were entirely invisible. Largo moved his shoulders and twisted this way and that, feeling tight and uncomfortable.

Branca said, "How does it feel?"

"Strange. But not bad. I'm sure I'll get used to it quickly."

"See that you do. Keep it on whenever you're on your rounds. If I were you, I would also wear it coming to work and going home at night."

Largo looked at Branca gravely. "Do you really think it's that dire? I've traveled these streets all my life and except for places like Steel Downs and the docks, I've never felt myself to be in much danger."

"Well, you are now. And not just from street bandits. There are young men in this very company that you need to keep an eye on."

"You can't mean that, sir. Who?"

Branca went back to his desk and pressed a button on the side, summoning a small Mara. "Andrzej. Weimer. They're both convicted criminals. Did you know that?"

"No, I didn't."

"Their convictions weren't for violent offenses—otherwise the company wouldn't have taken them on. But management likes to hire a few unfortunates every year as a show of good faith in the government's rehabilitation efforts."

Largo shrugged. "If they're rehabilitated, then what's the problem?"

Branca shook his head. "Largo, you can't afford to be this naïve anymore. I said their *convictions* were for nonviolent crimes. God knows what else they did before they were arrested. Do you understand?"

"I think so," Largo said, touching his elbow to the hilt of the knife under his coat. He didn't like Andrzej or Weimer, but saying so might cause trouble. "Still, we're all friends now. Of a sort."

"I'm glad to hear it. Let's hope that Dame Fortune smiles upon you and it remains that way."

Largo didn't say anything. It was a lot to take in all at once. A promotion. Herr Branca's speaking so frankly to him. A lecture on the dangers all around him. Plus, he hadn't had a dose of morphia since the previous night. A chill was building inside him and he was afraid that if he was stuck in the office for more than a few minutes, his hands might begin to shake.

Sure enough, Branca said, "You're looking a bit pale. Are you all right?"

"Fine, sir. It's just a lot to think about."

"Think at lunch. Right now, you have your first delivery." From the Mara, Branca took a wooden box about the size of the one that had held the knife and tossed it to Largo. "The address is on the parcel. You know the area, I believe?"

Largo checked a slip of paper affixed to the box with red wax. It was a street in Haxan Green. He drew in a breath, wondering if this was some kind of test. Unpleasant as he knew the delivery was going to be, he wasn't going to let that stop him. "Yes. It's at the far end of Pervitin Weg, where it crosses the canal."

"Very good. Not the best part of town, but not bad for a first run in your new position." Branca took a leather shoulder satchel and tossed that to Largo too. "Keep your new deliveries in that. It's old and if you think the stains inside look like dried grease, they are. It's the type of bag used by many of the workers at the armaments factory. A nondescript way to haul your cargo and perhaps save your hide. Do you have any questions before you go?"

"None," said Largo. "Thank you again for the opportunity, sir."

"Stop thanking me and stop saying 'sir' all the time. That's for the others. Not the chief courier."

Largo's bones felt icy. He needed to get away. "All right," he said, having to choke back a reflexive *sir*. "Before I go out, do I have time to use the toilet?"

Branca went back to doing paperwork. He didn't look up when he spoke. "Use the toilet if you need to. Better now than being arrested for pissing into the canal."

Largo put the box in the shoulder bag and started out. His hands were beginning to tremble.

"One more thing, Largo," said Branca.

He stopped nervously midstride. "Yes, sir?"

"Your chum Parvulesco. Keep an eye on him too. He's never been arrested, but he has a most colorful reputation."

"Thank you. I'll remember that," said Largo before hurrying out of the office and down the hall to the employee toilets. Once inside, he locked himself in the farthest stall from the door. His cold hands shook as he pulled the bottle of morphia from an inside pocket of his jacket. Earlier, as Branca had taken it off him to fit the harness, he'd been nervous that his boss would discover the drug. Now Largo couldn't care less. The only thing that mattered was the bottle.

He unscrewed it, drew a portion into the rubber stopper at the top, and squeezed three drops under his tongue. It was one more drop than usual, but these were dire circumstances and he needed the relief an extra drop would give him.

Within seconds, the blizzard inside him began to calm and he felt warm again. The muscles in his shoulders and back unknotted. The tension in his jaw eased so that he wasn't tempted to grind his teeth, which, along with the shakes, was one of the sure giveaways of morphia addiction.

Not that any of that mattered now. His nervousness over the promotion and Branca's paranoid warnings meant nothing. His stomach settled as his hunger pangs vanished. He felt wrapped in safety even as he thought again of the humiliation of staring hungrily at the sandwich in the street.

Never again.

Never.

Again.

Remy's beautiful face swam into his head and he couldn't help but close his eyes. Just for a second.

And drifted back to earlier that morning.

Remy was in bed, wrapped in a sheet. She turned the pages of a script with one hand and smoked a cigarette with the other. Largo was in the little kitchen of her flat making tea for them both. It was still dark outside. They hadn't slept much the previous night.

While he waited for the water to boil, Largo took a step out of the kitchen and called to her. "Is there any cocaine left? I could use a bit to help me wake up."

Remy glanced at the bedside table. "Not a speck."

"Damn." He leaned back against the wall. "It's your fault for keeping me up so late."

She didn't look up from her script. "Yes, dear. I distinctly remember you saying how much you wanted to sleep as you took my clothes off."

The teakettle whistled and Largo turned off the burner. "If only I could have found your pajamas, none of this would have happened."

"Hush," Remy called. "I need to learn this script."

As the tea steeped, Largo went back into the bedroom and lay down next to her. "Please. You don't need any time. You memorize those things in a flash."

She stubbed out her cigarette. "You think so?"

He laid his head sleepily against her shoulder. "No question. It used to take you days. Now it seems like you have a new script in your head by the time you finish reading it."

"I hadn't really noticed."

Largo yawned. "You learn the words and blocking faster and better than ever. Are you doing something different?"

Remy shook her head. "Nothing. But I've felt better since the doctor gave me a shot. Sharper. More clear-headed."

"What kind of a shot was it? I could use one."

"Vitamins, I think."

As he went to check on the tea, Largo said, "You haven't had one of your attacks in a while."

"That's a relief. Now leave me alone. I have to work."

He poked his head out from the kitchen. "You're quite sure there's no more cocaine?"

Remy playfully tossed a pillow at him. "Finish making the tea and be happy I don't push you out the window for interrupting my work."

Largo froze in the doorway. "Work . . ."

He lurched to his feet in the bathroom stall, realizing he'd nodded off. He checked the address on the package one more time and left the building through the loading dock so that he didn't have to pass Herr Branca's office again. Promotion or not, he'd had enough of the old man's scrutiny for one day.

Outside, the fog had begun to lift somewhat, but the sky was still gray under the smokestacks of the armaments factory. A light mist fell as Largo pedaled along Tombstrasse, making the air smell fresh and clean. With the welcome promotion, good air in his lungs, and morphia in his blood, Largo felt better than he had in days.

THE CITY. THE AIR.

From *Noble Aspirations and Hard Realities: Life in Lower Proszawa* by Ralf Moessinger, author of *High Proszawa: A Dream in Stone*

A haze, perpetual and gray, hangs over much of Lower Proszawa, like a murder of crows frozen in flight. Below, the coal plants that dot the city smolder and roar, roiling black ribbons of soot into the atmosphere. There, they're caught by the wind and distributed throughout the city. The dust settles everywhere, on the rich and poor alike. Of course, the wealthy have the means to sweep their streets clean, as if soot wouldn't dare venture into their districts, griming the windows and tower rooms that overlook the roofs of the less fortunate.

But even the rich can't entirely keep ahead of it. The dust invades homes, offices, and churches, drifting down chimneys, snaking through cracks in window frames and under doors. The outdoor cafés and markets that display fruits and bread in the open air employ troops of ragged children armed with horsehair brushes and dustpans to wipe every surface clean. They throw the soot into the sewers, where it mixes with the city's waste and drifts out to sea in a black tide that stains the hulls of fishing boats and smuggler ships alike a uniform gray. People call the color "city silver" and laugh it off because what else is there to do?

Thus, the citizens of Lower Proszawa have learned to live with the dust, even be amused by it. Of course, in the post-war elation that's gripped much of the city, almost everything is amusing. Besides, it rains frequently and when the clouds part, the streets are washed clean, if just for a day or two.

Rain or shine, however, the power plants are nothing compared to what truly fills the skyline. Dominating much of the city are the cluster of immense foundries and assembly lines that make up the armaments factory. Unlike the streets, it is never completely clean. The coal dust clings to its sides and roofs. When the rains fall, they leave strangely beautiful ebony streaks and rivulets down the exteriors of the buildings, making the factory look ancient—like a mountain range that has been rooted to the spot forever.

Districts such as Kromium and Empyrean are kept pristine by cleaners who work in clouds of filth. Ironically, in some ways these workers are the lucky ones. While they go about their jobs, the crews wear surplus gas masks left over from the war. That means that for a few hours every day, they breathe air cleaner and sweeter than that of even the wealthiest industrialist or banker. Still, not everybody has the means to cope with the gray air so easily. It is a particular problem in the Rauschgift district.

Among the people I interviewed for this piece, Frau Mila Weill's story is typical of the area. She lives in a cramped apartment with her children and grandmother. Herr Weill died suddenly from the Drops a few months earlier, leaving Frau Weill as the sole breadwinner. There are many explanations for the Drops among the ignorant class in these poorer districts: that foreigners from the southern colonies put it in the food shipped north or that chimeras that gobble trash in the gutters spread it with a bite. Frau Weill saw her husband die in agonizing convulsions and wonders if that is her fate too. She has a chronic cough, which is typical in the area, and it has advanced to the point where there is often blood in the sputum. Unable or, perhaps, afraid to go to one of the city's hospitals for the indigent, she relies on the advice of her grandmother. The old woman tries to comfort Frau Weill using the only tools she has: folk remedies from the ancient past. She assures Frau Weill that she merely has a "touch of Rote Lungen," and that "thistle-root tea will clear that right up."

Frau Weill wants to believe her grandmother, but no amount of tea helps her condition. Each day, the red marks on her handkerchief grow. During one of our interviews she confessed that she had thought about finding someone—anyone—to marry so that he would be obliged to care for her family after she was gone. (There was an awkward moment in that day's discussion when I suspect she considered asking me.) Though she still uses her grandmother's tea remedy, she continues to believe that her condition is really an early stage of the Drops. However, she has formulated her own theory: that the disease isn't spread by foreigners or chimeras. Frau Weill believes that it comes from the very air.

Spurred on by what can be seen only as a new urban folk belief, one morning Frau Weill took some of the household money and attempted to buy a gas mask from one of the cleaners in Kromium. She says that he laughed in her face. To make matters worse, the conductor on a tram asked her to get off, as her coughing fits were disturbing the other passengers. Since then, she remains at home, waiting for what she believes is the inevitable. Frau Weill keeps a constant watch on her arms and legs, certain that someday soon the convulsions will come. As our final interview came to a close I once again had that sense that she was on the verge of proposing marriage, and I was obliged to leave more abruptly than is my normal fashion.

Whatever the truth is about Frau Weill's condition, we must agree on one point—that the "city silver" air in Lower Proszawa is as much a defining characteristic of the place as prewar High Proszawa's clear blue skies. While the high city was known for its universities, museums, and sprawling stone mansions, the swirling gray gusts of the low city represent progress, industry, and strength. And while those things might inconvenience some, the power plants that fuel the place and the armaments factory that keeps all of Proszawa prosperous and safe are national treasures every bit as much as the high city's more traditional elegance.*

---

* Just before publication it came to my attention that Frau Mila Weill had passed away, not from the Drops but from some other lung ailment. It is to her that I humbly dedicate this piece.

CHAPTER TWO

WHILE THE TRIP TO HAXAN GREEN HAD BEEN FAST AND PLEASANT, HIS ARrival in the old district was decidedly less so. Largo hadn't been in the Green in years and the place was grimmer—and grimier—than he'd ever seen it.

The Green had once been a fashionable district where wealthy families from High and Lower Proszawa enjoyed their summers, spending many nights at the enormous fair at the end of a long pier. But the pier and fair had collapsed decades ago and were now nothing more than a pile of waterlogged timbers festooned with canal garbage and poisonous barnacles that killed wayward gulls.

The derelict homes that lined the broad streets had once sported gold-leaf roofs and sunny tower rooms that gave the inhabitants views of both the High and Lower cities. Now the buildings were rotting hulks, the gold leaf long gone and the roofs crudely patched with wood from even more run-down habitations. Most of the lower windows were blocked with yellowsheets and covered with metal bars from fallen fences. Few had any glass to speak of. The addresses of the old homes had all been chiseled away. This was by design rather than neglect, though. Only those acquainted with the district could find any specific dwelling. Fortunately, Largo knew the Green well.

He chained his bicycle to the charred skeleton of an old delivery Mara outside one of the tower blocks. Skinny, filthy children played war in the weed-strewn yard, throwing imaginary grenades of rocks and dirt clods at one another. The children stared at Largo for only a moment before going back to their game, but he knew their eyes were on him his whole way into the building. He checked his pocket to make sure he had a few coins so there wouldn't be any trouble later.

He walked up three flights of stairs littered with stinking, overflowing trash cans and sleeping tenants too sick or drunk to make it all the way home. There were holes in the walls where old charging stations for Maras and wires that provided light for the halls had been torn out, the copper almost certainly sold to various scrap yards along the canal.

Without numbers identifying the individual flats anymore, this could have been a difficult delivery, but through long practice, Largo knew how the apartments were laid out—even numbers on the north, odd on the south—so he found his destination without trouble.

Out of habit, Largo straightened his tie before knocking on the door of the flat, then felt foolish for it. A straight tie was the last thing that would impress Green residents; it might, in fact, make them hostile. But it was too late now. He'd already knocked.

A moment later an unshaven man wearing small wire-rimmed glasses opened the door a crack, leaving the lock chain across the gap. "Who the fuck are you?" he said.

Largo took the box from his shoulder bag and said, "Delivery," in a flat, indifferent voice. Saying anything more might invite suspicion. Speaking any other way definitely would.

The unshaven man tilted his head, taking in Largo and the box. His hair was gray and thin. There were scabs on his forehead near his hairline. It looked like he'd been picking at them. "Where's the other one?" he said.

It took Largo a second to understand that the man meant König. He shook his head. "He doesn't work there anymore. It's just me now."

"Huh," said the man. "You're a bit pretty for this neck of the woods."

Largo straightened, feeling the knife under his jacket. His sense for the mores of the old neighborhood was coming back to him—as was his hatred for them. He knew what would come next from the scabby man and how he was supposed to respond, and the cheap game brought back frightening childhood memories. He said, "Fuck off, my fine brother. I grew up by the canal on Berber Lane."

"Did you now? You've cleaned up since then."

"My compliments to your spectacles." Largo loathed the ritual posturing of the Green, and he'd hoped never to have to do it again.

Yet his promotion had brought him straight back to this awful place. It wasn't an auspicious beginning for the new position. He pressed on, holding up the little box and waggling it up and down. "Do you want it or not? I don't have all day."

The man was starting to say something else when a piercing scream came from somewhere in the flat. "Wait here," he said, and closed the door. Standing in the hall, Largo heard more screams through the door. Questions and images flowed through his head. Had the scabby man kidnapped someone? Was someone—a woman, he was sure it was a woman—being beaten in another room? Or was she dying in childbirth? The next scream wasn't just a wail, there were words: "Now! Now! Now! Now!" Largo dug his heel into a splintered part of the floor as it dawned on him that he recognized the screams.

It was someone deep in the throes of morphia withdrawal.

He looked at the box. There weren't any markings to indicate its origin. He wondered if it was medication from a hospital. He was sure Herr Branca wouldn't send him out on his first delivery with something illicit. It must be medicine, he told himself.

A second later, the flat's door opened again. The man stuck out a grimy-black hand and grabbed for the box. "Give it to me."

Largo took a step back out of his reach. He got the pad and pencil from his bag. "You have to sign for it," he said.

The man's hand dropped a few inches. "Please. I need it now."

"Not until you sign." Largo knew the rules of the Green. If he backed down now it would be a sign of weakness, and if anyone was watching the exchange it would put him in danger. He gave the man a hard look even as he felt a few beads of perspiration on his forehead.

"Wait," said the scabby man. He closed the door for a moment and when he opened it again there was a pile of coins in his hand, including two small gold ones. "Take it."

"Are you trying to bribe me?" he said, a little surprised by the offer.

There was another scream from the flat. Largo felt like a heel for continuing to play the game, but he knew he had to.

"It's a tip," said the man. "For your trouble and my earlier rudeness. Only *you* have to sign the form."

Largo looked at the money. Whether it was a bribe or a tip, it was the largest amount of money anyone had ever offered him for a delivery.

There was another scream, this one more violent than the others. Largo grabbed the coins from the man's hand and gave him the package. "Good luck," he said, but the man had already slammed the door shut. Largo put the coins in his pocket and looked at the delivery form. There was no name on it, just the address.

Perfect. My first delivery as chief courier and I've already committed an offense that could get me fired.

With no other choice in the matter, Largo signed the form *Franz Negovan*, the name of a boy he'd known growing up in the Green. He was anxious and angry as he left the building, thinking that if all of his deliveries were like this, he wouldn't last long as chief courier.

Downstairs, as he expected, the children who'd been playing war earlier were clustered around his bicycle. A dirty blond girl of about ten sat on the seat and looked at him with eyes that were forty years older and harder.

"We watched it for you," she said. "Made sure nothing bad happened to it."

Largo had been through similar shakedowns before and had known this other ritual of the Green was coming. When he'd been in similar situations as a child, when he'd had little to give or trade, the result was usually a beating or his running as fast as he could—and his bicycle being stolen or destroyed. These were only children, but in the Green, age didn't mitigate danger. Fortunately, now things were different. He hoped.

He reached into his pants pocket and came up with some of the coins he'd brought from home and a few from the gray-haired man—all silver. He'd put the gold ones in his jacket. He said, "And you did an excellent job, I see. Here's something for your trouble."

The girl accepted the coins and counted them carefully. When she was done she nodded to the other kids and hopped off Largo's bicycle. As soon as they were across the yard, the girl distributed the money to the other children and the war game resumed without missing a beat. Largo unchained his bicycle, dropped the lock into his shoulder bag, and pedaled slowly back down the route he'd taken earlier. As much as he wanted to speed away from the misery and memories of the Green, he kept to a moderate pace. To go faster was something else that he knew would show weakness. There were many unspoken but universally understood rules in the district, and he'd learned them all the hard way. The one odd thought that struck him as he pedaled

20

away was that if, as a younger man, he hadn't left Haxan Green, a hard-eyed little girl like the one at the tower block could have been his daughter. It made him think of his own family.

Largo had grown up with his parents in a decaying mansion by the canal. His father had a wagon and a sick horse that he'd probably bought under the table from an army stable. Father rode the wagon all over Lower Proszawa looking for scrap to sell and, like Largo, making the occasional delivery. Largo's mother panhandled and picked pockets in the street markets around the Green. Largo had been a pale, scrawny child, and his parents had been very protective of him. Maybe too much, he thought now. He was always cautious and nervous around confrontations. Even his encounter with the scabby man, as well as he'd handled it, left him feeling slightly ill, which was humiliating.

Because no one had been home during the day to take care of him, Largo went with his father on his rounds. His mother worried about taking a small boy to some districts even more dangerous than Haxan Green—kidnappings were frequent and children were often sold off to fishing ships along the bay or pimps in the city. To protect the boy during his rounds, his father put him in a wooden crate up front in the wagon. It was through the air holes in the side of the crate that Largo first learned Lower Proszawa's winding streets and alleys.

Later, he would become an expert while running from gangs wielding chains and knives or bullocks looking for his parents. Of course, he'd never admitted any of this to Remy. It was too embarassing. Besides, she talked as little about her family as Largo did about his, and it made him wonder if she had secrets too.

On his way back to the office, Largo was delayed by a caravan of double-decker party Autobuses. The city's merrymakers always grew more boisterous in the days before the anniversary of the end of the Great War. Buses and street parties were some of the few places where the upper and lower classes mingled easily because each had the same goal—a gleeful obliteration.

When Largo returned to the courier office, Herr Branca was waiting for him.

"And how was your first foray into new territories?"

"Excellent. It went very well," Largo said.

Branca glanced up from his paperwork. "I'm glad to hear that.

21

König was seldom so cheerful when returning from Haxan Green."

Largo smiled but wasn't sure it was entirely convincing. "That's too bad. As for me, I found the building, delivered the parcel, and made my way back without any problems."

"Good. And there was no trouble with the client?"

Largo's stomach fluttered for a moment as he thought of the forged receipt. "None, sir. Our meeting was both cordial and efficient."

Branca chuckled. "Efficient. Again, something I've not heard about the Green before," he said. Then he became more serious. "Tell me about the client. What was he like?"

The question took Largo by surprise. Herr Branca had never asked him about a client before, let alone one as peculiar as the gray-haired man. "He was just a man. An old man with gray hair and spectacles."

"How did he appear to you?"

"Sir?"

"Was he in good health? Happy? Apprehensive? Was there anyone with him?"

Largo considered how best to answer the question. "He was surprised that I wasn't König, but when I explained that he had moved on—I didn't mention the bullocks, sorry, the police. After that he accepted the package without incident."

Branca looked Largo up and down. "And was there anyone with him?"

"Yes."

"A man or woman?"

"I'm not sure. I think a woman. But the person was in another room and I couldn't see."

"Of course," Branca said, and Largo wondered what that meant. He started to say something but Branca cut him off.

"What was his condition? Dirty? Clean? Did you see his hands?"

"No. I didn't see his hands." But he recalled that that wasn't true. The gray-haired man had tried to grab the parcel. "Well, I did. But only for a moment."

Branca scribbled something on his papers. "Were his hands dirty, by any chance, especially the fingers?"

Largo thought about it. "I suppose they were, a bit. His fingers, I mean. A bit black."

Branca held out his hand. "Let me have your receipt book."

Largo handed it to him nervously.

His supervisor looked at the signed form for a long time. "And this is his signature?"

Quietly, Largo said, "Yes, sir."

"I don't see any smudges or dirt. Anything to indicate his dirty fingers. You're sure they were blackened?"

Largo nodded. "Yes," he said, then quickly added, "I held the book for him. He didn't touch it. I'm sorry if that was against procedure."

Branca tore the signed page out of the book and put it with the papers on his desk. Then he put the book in a drawer. "Not against procedure at all, Largo. However, in the future it would be best if the client was in possession of the book when they signed it. Please remember that."

"Of course. I will," said Largo, relaxing a little. It seemed that Branca's preoccupation with procedure had kept him from examining the signature closely enough to recognize Largo's handwriting. But he couldn't help being curious. "If I may ask, sir, was this client special?"

"How do you mean?" said Branca, leaning casually on his desk.

"I mean, will I be questioned like this after each client? It's no bother, you understand. I just want to know if I should pay special attention to them."

"It's always good to pay attention to clients," Branca said, distant and officious, "especially for a chief courier. And no, I won't interrogate you like this after each delivery. However, this was your first in your new position, so I thought it best to go over it carefully."

"I hope I performed satisfactorily," Largo said, hating himself because it sounded like groveling—and he had been sounding like that the whole day. Still, his position was tenuous enough that it seemed better to err on the side of caution, especially with Branca, who had dismissed other couriers as if swatting a fly.

"You did fine. But from time to time I'll be asking you about other clients. A new procedure from management. Quality control and all that. They may wish to conduct interviews with some of them to see that we're staying on our toes. I'm sure you understand."

"I'll make sure to pay more attention," said Largo.

"Very good." Branca gave Largo a new receipt book, then pressed the button on his desk that called a Mara. It brought out a large green folder that looked as if it might contain papers. "The address is on the front. You'll find this delivery a bit less colorful and more posh than your last one. The Kromium district. Do you know it?"

"Very well."

"Good. Herr Heller is an important client, so get there quickly. After this delivery you may go to lunch. And take your time. As chief courier you get a full forty-five minutes. Do you know why regular couriers only get thirty?"

"Because we, I mean they, are in such demand during working hours?"

Branca shook his head. "It's to keep them from drinking too much and getting into trouble. It's assumed that there will be no problems like that from the chief courier."

"No, sir. I never drink on the job." Largo wondered if Branca had caught sight of the morphia bottle in his jacket.

"Very good. I myself am accorded the luxury of sixty minutes for lunch. See? You and I are more and more alike."

Oh god. What a miserable thought.

"I'll do my best to live up to the company's standards."

Branca waved his pen at him. "Get going. I have papers to deal with," he said. "Oh—and Largo? There's no need to sneak out the back this time. The door you came in through is the shortest way out."

Largo hurried away, surer than ever that Branca knew his secret. But if he did, why would he have given him the promotion, and why would he cover for him now? It didn't make sense. In any case, there was nothing he could do about it right then. He'd just do his job, and sort this out when he had time. He thought then about Rainer Foxx. His friend was older and understood more about the real world than Largo felt he ever would. He sometimes imagined what life might have been like if Rainer had been his brother back in the Green. Maybe he wouldn't have grown so afraid all the time.

He'll know what to do. I have to talk to him soon.

Largo checked the address on the envelope, stuffed it into his shoulder bag, and pedaled away from the office as quickly as his legs would carry him.

Of course, Herr Branca had been right about the Kromium district. Its bright, wide streets, quaint cafés, art galleries, and cinema gave the place an open and pleasant atmosphere—the exact opposite of Haxan Green. Largo thought that if all his deliveries were to districts so violently in opposition to each other he might suffer whiplash.

The streets in Kromium were named for various metals, and the deeper you traveled into the district, the more valuable they became.

They began at Boron Prachtstrasse, then Tin, Copper, and Iron. Alloys such as Bronze and Steel crossed the pure metal streets. The address Largo was looking for wasn't among the loftiest metals such as Platinum, Osmium, and Iridium. However, it was still quite respectable and, he thought, it had a much more poetic ring to it than the more precious streets.

The Heller mansion stood near the corner of Electrum and Gold. Largo leaned his bicycle against a wrought iron gate twisted into elegant nouveau curls. He didn't bother locking the bicycle this time. With luck, he wouldn't have to worry about that again for quite a while.

The mansion's front door was decorated with a sunburst made from a dozen precious metals. Even under the overcast sky, it shone brightly. Like many doors in the district, this one was solid steel—not for security reasons, but to keep within the aesthetics of the neighborhood. Rather than rap on the thick metal door with his bare knuckles, Largo used the gleaming rose-colored knocker. It was heavy and slightly dented on the underside. Gold, he thought.

I wonder how long that would last in the Green?

A moment later, a maid in black brocade and a small white bonnet answered the door. Before Largo could have her sign for the envelope he heard a woman's voice from behind her. "Who is it, Nora?"

"A courier, madam. With a package for Herr Heller."

A moment later, an elegant red-headed woman in an arsenic-green gown appeared beside the maid. "I'll deal with it, thank you," she said. The maid curtsied and disappeared into the house.

A mechanical din boomed from the street as a driverless juggernaut rolled down the prachtstrasse. It was festooned with flags and large photochromes of the war dead. Patriotic music blared from speakers mounted on the front and sides of the juggernaut and the songs echoed off the buildings as it passed.

Frau Heller made a face at the behemoth. "Those things clatter by day and night. Of course, we all supported the war. I, myself, lost a cousin in the trenches of High Proszawa. But must we be reminded of the unpleasantness at all hours?" She looked at Largo.

He shook his head in agreement. "No, madam. It seems like a great inconvenience."

"Do these dismal little parades go through your neighborhood too?"

"No. I've seen them in the Triumphal Square and some of the business districts, but not where I live."

"You're a lucky young man," said Frau Heller. When she turned back to Largo her radiant smile faltered for a second, then recomposed itself. "What an interesting jacket," she said. "Wool, is it?"

Largo was tired of clients commenting on how he looked, but he smiled back at the woman. "Yes, madam. Very comfortable on cool, gray days like this."

"You have a lighter one for the summer, then?"

"Well, no, but with my new position—"

"Silk," she said, cutting him off. "You'd look much better in silk than wool."

"I'm not sure I can afford silk, madam. But thank you for the suggestion."

"Try one of the secondhand shops along Tin and Pinchbeck. Some of the servants' families sell their clothes when a family member dies. I'm told there are some wonderful bargains."

Largo looked at Frau Heller, trying to grasp her meaning. At least in the Green he knew when he was being tested, but here he wasn't sure if he was being mocked or given what this woman thought was truly useful advice. However, it wasn't his place to ask or be offended by anything a client said, so he replied, "That's most helpful of you. I'll be sure to stop by very soon."

"Here, this might get you started on your way to manly splendor," said Frau Heller. She plucked the envelope from his hand and laid a gold Saint Valda coin on his palm, equal to almost a week's wages.

"Madam, I couldn't," he said.

"Of course you can and you will. What's your name?"

"Largo. Largo Moorden."

She looked him up and down and smiled. "You're a handsome young man, but I don't want to see you here in wool again, Largo. You'll frighten the neighbors." She laughed as she signed his receipt book. Once she'd handed it back, her eyes shifted to a place over Largo's shoulder and she frowned. "Oh dear."

He turned to look and saw a small group of Iron Dandies in the street. They often followed the patriotic juggernauts, carrying small flags and begging.

Frau Heller called one of them forward and handed him a few coins, though they totaled less than she'd given Largo.

"Thank you, lovely lady," said the man in a grating, tinny voice through a small speaker embedded in his scarred throat.

"You're very welcome," said Frau Heller. "God bless you for your service."

She watched as the ragged procession of wounded soldiers continued on, limping and swaying on crutches behind the juggernaut. Without looking at him she said, "Were you in the war, Herr Moorden?"

Largo wasn't used to being addressed so formally. However, he had a lie prepared for just such occasions. "I'm afraid not. You see, my elderly mother was quite sick at the time—"

"Ah. Your mother. Quite understandable," said Frau Heller, cutting him off again. "I only ask because my husband is one of the heads of the armaments company, and I wondered if you might have used one of his creations."

Largo became nervous. Most people stopped asking questions after he mentioned his mother, and he didn't have many lies prepared to follow up. "No, I'm afraid I didn't have the honor in this war."

Frau Heller laughed lightly. "Perhaps you will in the next one, then." *The next one?*

Largo felt a little jolt of panic. There were always rumors of war in the north, but did Frau Heller know something? He ached to ask her, but knew to keep his mouth shut.

"Don't be a stranger, Herr Moorden," said Frau Heller, and she gave him a wink.

Not quite sure how to respond, Largo smiled and put the Valda in his jacket pocket with the other gold coins. He wasn't sure exactly what had just happened, whether Frau Heller had flirted with him or insulted him. However, he now knew he had a price for any similar future encounters.

One gold Valda and you can say anything you like.

As he got on his bicycle he laughed, thinking how odd the wealthy were, understandable only to themselves and others of their particular species.

Riding out of Kromium, he turned and pedaled past the secondhand shops at Tin Fahrspur. The encounter with Madam Heller had been interesting, but not enough to convince him to spend his newfound wealth on a coat to please a woman he'd probably never see again.

The sky darkened and a light rain fell on his way back to the office. Along Great Granate, one of the city's new automaton trams slid by silently, guided by magnetic rails laid beneath the paving stones. Largo grabbed a protruding light fixture on the rear of the tram and let it pull him all the way to the Great Triumphal Square. There, Largo used some of his remaining silver coins to buy a steak pie from the bakery he'd passed earlier that day. None of the other couriers ate lunch in this part of the plaza and that was fine by him. His new deliveries had put him in a peculiar mood.

He ate his steak pie, wondering if his parents had ever tasted steak in their whole lives.

When he'd been a boy riding in the crate in the scrap wagon, his father had sometimes told him about his adventures scavenging the city for goods to sell. One story that always amused Largo was that he would sometimes steal scrap from one foundry, drive it across town to sell to another, then steal it back in the night and resell it to the first. His father always laughed when he talked about it, and, in his little box, Largo laughed too.

What Largo's father never talked about were his special deliveries. They could happen any time of the day or night and anywhere in Lower Proszawa. Over his mother's objections, his father insisted that Largo come with him on the special trips because, he said, "The city at night and the city during the day are different beasts and you need to make friends with them both." There was one particular delivery that Largo never forgot, no matter how much he drank or how much morphia he took.

It had been late afternoon along Jubiläum, a long way up the stinking canal. There was a small crowd buying fish and meat from the moored boats. Soon after they arrived, Largo's father had handed an envelope—not unlike the one Largo had just given to Frau Heller—to a man dressed in much finer clothes than Largo normally saw in the district. Once his father had turned over the envelope, though, he and the well-dressed man got into an argument. His father shouted something about being cheated out of his payment and when he grabbed the envelope back, a group of other men, who had been lounging on cargo crates nearby, rushed him. A scuffle broke out. Unlike scrawny Largo, his father had been tall and strong and he knocked two of the men down without any trouble. But three others were on him like a pack of dogs. Before Largo understood what was happening, he saw a flash of silver. The men ran away and his father lay on the ground bleeding from a knife wound in his side. Largo cried for help, but the people in the crowd just stood and stared before going about their business.

Later, Largo's friend Heinrich said that the knife had probably pierced his father's lung. It took what seemed like hours for him to die, and the whole time he wheezed and gasped like a fish suffocating on the banks of the canal at low tide.

No one called the police because that wasn't done in the Green. People brought his mother back from the market and she took Largo home to their squat. Neighbors buried his father in the garden of a stately home that was once one of Lower Proszawa's more elegant brothels, but that was the end of the community's involvement.

His mother seldom let him out of her sight after that. She taught him to keep quiet and not upset people. At first, Largo, who'd felt so free by his father's side, fought with his mother about being locked in the house. He felt more confined there than he'd ever felt in the small crate on the wagon. One afternoon, while his mother was at the market, he'd sneaked out of the house.

It was winter and his breath steamed in the damp air. Largo ran to find Heinrich, who, he knew, would be by the stables, where the children often played. When he arrived, Largo found Heinrich surrounded by a gang of older boys from the Green. Largo crouched behind one of the stable doors so they wouldn't see him, and was frozen there as the scene reminded him of the same one his father had endured. One of the gang demanded that Heinrich give them his heavy winter coat, and after some shoving and punching, he did it. Once they had the coat, he tried to run, but one of the boys hit him with a chain. He continued to beat Heinrich as the other boys kicked and hit him with pipes they'd hidden under their clothes. Once the gang had run off—and only then—had Largo crept from the stable to his friend's side.

Heinrich lay in a pool of sticky blood. There was a crack in his forehead where part of his skull had caved in. Largo shook him and, stupidly, yelled his name. Across the road from the stables was a stand of withered trees, and the gang that had beaten Heinrich had been there, well within earshot. They came racing out, heading straight for him. Though Largo was small, he'd always been a fast runner. He darted away from the stables into Haxan Green's back alleys and side roads. The boys chased him for what seemed like hours, but Largo kept ahead of them, ducking through basements, out through coal chutes, and doubling back on himself through the complex web of streets.

The sun had been going down when he finally managed to get home. Luckily, his mother hadn't returned from the market yet. One of Largo's chores in the evening was to start a fire in the old cast-iron oven so that she could cook them whatever she'd stolen that day. Instead, Largo hid in his room scouring Heinrich's blood off his hands in a washbasin. After that, he didn't fight when his mother told him to stay inside. He instead spent his time with old maps of Lower Proszawa he found in the attic, tracing the routes he'd taken on rides with his father and learning by heart the layout of the brilliant city, formulizing his paths of escape but also dreaming of life on those other streets.

After lunch, Herr Branca didn't question him about the delivery in Kromium. He simply gave Largo another assignment right away in one of the few parts of town Largo didn't know well—Empyrean.

It was one thing for a young man in shabby clothes to ride through Kromium without attracting too much attention. After all, that district wasn't just for stuck-up bluenoses. It housed famous artists among the higher metals, along with scandalous bohemians within the lower alloys. Empyrean was different. Many of the best families from High Proszawa had migrated there during the early days of the war. It was a neighborhood of marble palaces, gleaming steel towers, and luxury flats in high-rises with facades of emerald and vermilion bricks imported from halfway around the world. At night they glowed brighter than the moon, and the people inside shone down on the rest of the city even brighter.

It was to one of those glowing buildings that Largo brought his last delivery of the day. At first, the uniformed doorman didn't want to let him into the building and even tried to take the package away from him. When Largo wouldn't let him, he threatened to call the police.

"Please don't do that," said Largo reflexively.

The doorman continued to stare at him. "Let me see your identity papers," he said.

Largo took them out and reluctantly handed them to the man. He hated himself for doing it, but this was Empyrean, not Haxan Green.

I can't just bluff my way through this. If the police came, he knew that it would be a scandal for the company. He might get demoted for it, or even fired.

The doorman made a great show of studying Largo's face and comparing it to the photochrome on his papers. Eventually the doorman said, "I'll need to speak to your superior to allow you into the building."

Feeling deflated, Largo grudgingly gave him Herr Branca's caller number at the courier company. The doorman went into the lobby and picked up a gold-and-sky-blue enameled Trefle. It looked a little like a candlestick with a mouthpiece at the top. Twin listening pieces were attached to the base with thick green wire. It took him a full minute to get an operator to put the call through, and then it took several minutes more for Herr Branca to convince him that the "cheeky scarecrow" with a box under his arm was a legitimate courier. Finally, the doorman relented and let Largo inside.

"Go up to floor fifteen and come right back down again," said the doorman. "I'll be timing you. Take too long and no voice on a Trefle will save you from the bullocks."

Largo wanted to say a lot of things to the doorman, but he knew that the call already guaranteed him a dressing-down by Branca, so there was nothing he could do about the officious prick at the door, the bullocks—any of it.

The lift he rode up in was larger than his flat, and with its crystal chandelier, golden fixtures, and pearl floor buttons, more opulent than most of even the well-off homes he often delivered to.

On the fifteenth floor he knocked on the door, hoping desperately that whoever opened it wouldn't be as chatty as the gray-haired man or Frau Heller.

Largo got what he wished for.

When the door opened, he took out his receipt book, hoping to get business over with quickly with a servant. What greeted him instead was an elegant Mara. It was almost as tall as he was and decorated with silver and bright gems, by far the most spectacular Mara he'd ever seen. "May I help you?" it said.

The voice startled Largo. When most Maras spoke, the sound was small and tinny, but this Mara's speech was soft and melodious. He pressed the parcel and receipt book forward.

"Delivery," he said.

The Mara bent slightly, its eye lenses adjusting to take in Largo and what he carried. After only a few seconds' hesitation, the Mara took the box and set it down gracefully on a nearby table. Yellow-sheet scandal tabloids were piled high there and a few had fallen to the floor. A week's worth of papers, at least. From another room, Largo heard laughter and music swelling from an amplified gramophone. The residents of the flat were having a party. He looked back at the pile of yellowsheets.

Has it really been going on for a week? Is that even possible?

As his pondered this, the Mara came back and held out its hands for the receipt book. He handed it to the machine without looking at its face. That was the most disturbing thing about the situation. The owners had placed a steel-and-leather mask on the Mara's head, the kind worn by Iron Dandies. Largo didn't think he could loathe Maras more, yet here he was staring at this monstrosity. He wondered how the owners had obtained the mask and what had happened to the Dandy who'd lost it. He thought of Rainer and wanted to snatch the mask off the automaton but knew that it would guarantee a beating from the police when the doorman called them. In the end, he took back his book and the Mara slammed the door in his face.

While waiting for the lift, Largo saw something he'd missed on his way up. Set into the wall was a large fish tank holding a colorful variety of chimeras—custom-made mutant creatures favored as work animals by the municipal services and pets by the well-heeled of Lower Proszawa.

Speckled black-and-white eels covered with long spines wriggled among a school of transparent bat-like fish. A pink lizard *thing* pulled itself across the bottom of the tank with bright red tentacles. Largo tapped the glass lightly with a fingernail. Ever since childhood, when a pack of wild hound-like chimeras had terrorized Haxan Green, he'd been fascinated by the strange creatures.

A gray starfish lifted from the bottom of the tank and affixed itself to the glass directly in front of him. As he leaned in close to get a better look, the starfish twisted its limbs and torso into a startlingly accurate imitation of Largo's face. As he watched, the pink lizard crept up from behind and attacked it, dragging the twitching starfish to the bottom with its red tentacles and devouring it. Largo pulled back in shock. He shook his head—that was the one thing he could never understand about so many chimeras. If people could make them in any shape and with any temperament, why were they so often ugly and savage?

I would make only beautiful ones.

Pieces of the dead starfish floated to the top of the tank.

On his way out of the building, the doorman wanted to check Largo's pockets to see if he'd stolen anything. Despite being afraid for his job, this was too much. When the doorman reached for him, Largo shoved him back against the building and jumped onto his bicycle. As he pedaled away, he was sure he could hear the doorman cursing him all the way out of Empyrean. He couldn't help but smile.

THE SECRET FETE

From *A Popular History of the Proszawan Underworld*
by Stefan Kreuz

Der Grandiose Kanzler had been an elegant establishment before the war, serving some of the finest food and wine in Lower Proszawa. However, it had fallen on hard times and closed for good after the owner embezzled the remaining funds and eloped with one of the serving girls. A series of lawsuits kept the place shuttered since then.

But not out of business.

Now dubbed Der Fliegende Schwanz, it was a thriving speakeasy on the edge of the Pappen district, where it served the best bootleg whiskey, cocaine, and morphia in the city. Der Fliegende Schwanz was mainly a working-class establishment, but members of the gentry would sometimes visit when they were in the mood to slum for an evening. They were always welcomed with open arms because they had better pockets to pick than the usual rabble.

The bar was a merry place most nights, fueled by drugs and the ubiquitous postwar delirium. It was a gathering spot for war veterans, workers from the armaments factory, laborers from the docks, and prostitutes to drink, tell stories, and make love in the bar's immense but empty wine cellar. Musicians played for coins all day and night. There was dancing and laughter, but seldom any fights, which was unusual for an underground saloon, with its heady mix of alcohol, drugs, and sex. Perhaps the reason the bar sidestepped so much random violence was a special sort of entertainment it offered its patrons.

A makeshift ring stood at the center of Der Fliegende Schwanz. At the top of each hour two or more Maras—freshly stolen, their functionality modified—fought gladiatorial battles to the death. Most of the purloined Maras came from bluenose families in the city's most expensive districts, so watching them beat each other with clubs was doubly entertaining. Bookies took bets on the battles and liquor sales always went up because the winners bought the losers a round and the losers bought even more rounds to soothe their aching egos. And the music never stopped. Neither did the laughter, the lovemaking, or the drip of morphia under happy tongues.

Around midnight each night, everything in the bar stopped and the patrons sang obscene, drunken versions of patriotic songs. Many of the men were veterans and had fought in High Proszawa, so after the singing they played a game in which they spat streams of alcohol at photochromes of the Chancellor and the Minister of War nailed to the wall. The players stood behind a line on the floor and the one who came closest or hit the chromes the longest drank free for the rest of the night.

Der Fliegende Schwanz never closed. The party never stopped. The delight never ebbed. Every night was a holiday and every morning a feast. And if, on some nights, the crowds got a bit out of control during the Mara fights and started breaking bottles and glasses, who cared? Like the Maras, they were stolen. Everything was fun and nothing mattered because everyone knew that sooner or later the cannons would boom again and nothing would be fun and everything would matter.

Until then, there was always time for one more drink or one more kiss or one more drop under the tongue.

CHAPTER THREE

WHEN LARGO RETURNED TO WORK, HERR BRANCA SHOWED SOME COMPAS-sion by not bringing up the call from the doorman immediately. His only acknowledgment came when Largo turned in his receipt book. Branca said, "We're going to have to do something about your appearance."

Largo touched his rain-soaked suit and looked at Branca. "Sir?"

"Your clothes. We can't have the chief courier roaming the streets looking as if he's just escaped the penitentiary, can we?"

"No. I suppose not."

"Good. I'm delighted that you approve."

"But I didn't think my clothes were that bad."

Branca filled in some figures on a form. "What you think about these matters doesn't concern the company."

"Of course," said Largo, feeling like a prize pig on the auction block. "I didn't mean to overstep."

"Never mind. I've arranged that you will soon receive a certain sum of money with which you will purchase clothes and shoes that look a bit less like you stole them from a . . . what was the word the caller used?"

"Scarecrow?"

"Yes, that's it. As you saw today, some districts don't appreciate the working classes begriming their streets. Arrogant bastards. When you've acquired your new wardrobe, I'll want to see it. Under no circumstances will you wear the clothes except on company business. Is that understood?"

"Completely." Though both knew full well that he was lying.

"Good. Now to the important part. Seeing as how you're an adult apparently capable of feeding and bathing yourself, please tell me that there is no need for me to accompany you on this excursion."

Quickly, Largo said, "No, sir. Not necessary at all." The thought of Herr Branca hovering around him as he tried on pants was horrifying. He remembered what Frau Heller had said. "I even know where to go."

"Thank heavens. It's the little mercies that help us sleep at night, don't you agree?"

"Entirely," said Largo, not quite certain what he was agreeing with.

"That will be all today. I'll see you tomorrow promptly at six, yes?"

"On the dot, sir."

"Very good. And you're still saying 'sir' too much. Work on that."

"I will," he said, once more having to choke back the word *sir* and happy that he managed it.

When he left the office, he saw some of the other couriers gathered around the loading dock, smoking and talking. Weimer passed around a flask, making a great show of it that he wasn't letting Parvulesco have a drink. Andrzej was the first to notice Largo approaching. "If it isn't the Lord High Chancellor himself," he said. "Good evening, Your Lordship. How lovely of you to grace us with your presence."

A few of the other couriers laughed. Others just glared at Largo. He'd been through enough for one day and wondered if he could leave through the back exit and avoid Andrzej's nonsense. However, he'd already been called out in front of the couriers and knew there would be trouble if he didn't answer in kind. There was nothing to do but speak as if he were still in the Green. "What's up your ass, my fine brother?"

"You. You're what's up my ass," Andrzej said coldly. He was five years older and a head taller than any of the other couriers. "König isn't gone a day and you're in there mincing around with high and mighty Branca, trying to steal his job."

"I didn't *steal* anything. When Branca gave me the job I was as surprised as anyone. I was even late this morning, for shit's sake."

Parvulesco grabbed Weimer's flask, took a quick drink, and tossed it back to him. Weimer, whose right arm was a simple wood-and-steel prosthetic, fumbled with it in the air and finally dropped it.

He claimed to have lost his real arm in the early days of the war, but no one believed him. When asked where he had served, he could never name the same company or regiment twice. Plus, he didn't have a Red Eagle medal, something all wounded soldiers received. Worse, while drunk one night, Andrzej had told the others that someone else's name was carved into the underside of the prosthetic, all but saying that Weimer had stolen it. It had been an amusing story at the time, but Largo had never trusted either of them since.

"König is going to kick the guts out of you when he gets back," Andrzej said. "We've all seen you brown-nosing Branca. He'll know you stabbed him in the back."

"Like Weimer knows you told us about his arm?"

Weimer lowered the flask. "What did he tell you?"

"Nothing," said Andrzej. Then to Largo, "Shut up."

Largo wondered if this was why Branca had warned him that morning. The problem was that if he was attacked, he knew he couldn't use the knife. It would be his word against Andrzej's and he wasn't sure how many of the other couriers would side with him against the bully. Besides, he had to admit that after today, more than ever, he was afraid for both his safety and his job. Still, Largo was pleased by the image of Andrzej on the business end of his brass knuckles, even if he knew that he couldn't do anything but reflect the bastard's arrogance back at him.

Luckily, he didn't even have to do that.

"Fuck off, you loudmouth," said Parvulesco. "You would have taken the job and laughed in König's face when he got back. Besides, from what I hear, König won't be coming back any time soon."

"What do you mean?" said Weimer. "Where is he?"

"Yeah. Where?" said Andrzej.

Parvulesco dropped the butt of his cigarette and crushed it with his boot. "From what I hear, and unlike certain people who like to play at being tough, König has joined the army to fight the northern hordes."

No one said anything at first. Then Andrzej made a disgusted face at Parvulesco. "You're a liar and just as much Branca's whore as Frau Moorden over there."

Parvulesco lit another cigarette . . . and then casually flicked it so that it bounced off Andrzej's cheek.

The big man screamed and danced back, batting at his face. Largo and the other couriers laughed. When Andrzej regained his composure, he charged at Parvulesco, who jumped and easily rolled onto the loading dock. Andrzej, on the other hand, had to rush up the stairs at the end of the dock—where he almost ran face-first into Herr Branca. Andrzej stopped just before crashing into him.

Branca said, "Enjoying the evening air, are we, Andrzej?"

He took a step back and his shoulders slumped. "Yes, sir. Just sharing a smoke and a chat with the boys."

"Running with a cigarette can be bad for your health." Branca looked farther down the loading dock. "Don't you agree, Parvulesco?"

"Yes, sir," he said. "Very much. I was about to point that out to the lads when things became a bit . . ."

"Boisterous?" said Branca.

"Yes, sir. Exactly. But you needn't worry about that. We were all headed home. Isn't that right, boys?"

There was general agreement among the couriers that they were, in fact, all heading home at that exact moment.

"Then I wish you all a good evening and expect to see you all here bright and early tomorrow. I'm led to believe that it will be a busy day."

"Thank you, sir. I'm sure we're looking forward to it," Parvulesco said.

Branca turned his head downward. "And you, Andrzej? Are you looking forward to a busy day's work?"

The big man smiled up at his supervisor. "Very much. Busy is always better than bored. Right, sir?"

"And employed is better than unemployed," said Branca. "Good evening, gentlemen. Have safe journeys home."

The group broke up without another word.

Parvulesco and Largo rode out through the employee gate together. Largo got close to his friend and said, "Where did you hear that König had joined the army?"

Parvulesco looked at him in shock. "I just made it up. Do you know where he really is?"

Largo looked straight ahead, shaking his head slightly. "I shouldn't say. It's too dangerous."

Parvulesco veered his bicycle closer and spoke in a mock-conspiratorial tone. "Come on. You can't say something like that and leave me to wonder forever. Give me a hint."

"I can't."

"Look, if it's dangerous, shouldn't you share at least some of the information with a friend?"

Largo looked at him. "You're trying to make me feel guilty."

"Yes. That's exactly what I'm doing."

They rode on in silence for a few more minutes as Largo considered what Parvulesco had said. He wondered if he didn't owe his friend, who'd just stood up for him, some special consideration. Looking straight ahead at the road, Largo said, "König was taken away by a pair of black birds."

For a moment, Parvulesco looked as if he didn't believe him. "The Nachtvogel? You're not serious, are you?"

"Believe what you like," Largo said. "But you didn't hear anything from me on the matter."

Parvulesco looked at him gravely. "Shit. Do you think that means they'll be watching the rest of us?"

"It wouldn't surprise me," said Largo. "And thank you for standing up for me back there."

Parvulesco smiled. "Any day I can goad that walking pile of boars' balls is a good one."

Largo laughed and Parvulesco said, "I won't whisper a word of what you told me to anyone."

"Thank you."

Parvulesco looked thoughtful. "To change the subject to something a bit happier, you know that with your promotion you have a good chance to make some extra money."

"You mean the tips? I know. Isn't it great?"

"I'm not talking about that," said Parvulesco. "König said there were other ways, but the prick would never say what. So keep your eyes open for money falling from the sky."

Largo was intrigued by the idea, but annoyed at König for keeping the secret to himself. "He didn't give any hints about how or what to look for?"

"Not a one."

Something occurred to him. "How do you know about it? Did everybody know about it but me?"

Parvulesco let go of the handlebars and rode that way for a few minutes. "I'm probably the only one. I caught him with a pretty prostitute by the girlie cinema near the docks. That's when he told me and gave me a few coins to keep my mouth shut."

König wasting his extra money on prostitutes struck Largo as the height of stupidity. There were so many better things to spend your money on, he thought. *Like Remy.* "I'll be sure to be on the lookout for opportunities."

"Good. And when you find one, you'll owe me a beer."

"Done." They slowed when they reached a fork in the road. As Largo steered away, he shouted, "Good night. And thanks!"

Parvulesco veered off in the opposite direction, calling, "Say hello to Remy for me."

"And hello to Roland for me," Largo replied.

With the image of Remy's face in his head, Largo rode to his dismal flat in record time.

He lived in a third-floor walk-up in the Rauschgift district, more commonly known as Little Shambles. While his building was superficially cleaner than the one he'd entered in Haxan Green, the stairs and halls nevertheless reeked of cooking fat and rotting vegetables. Layers of wallpaper flaked from the walls, revealing generations of decorations, like geological layers. Red and white peppermint stripes lay atop a beige pattern of waterfowl, which revealed flocked turquoise squares. Largo's flat was at the end of the hall near the shared bathroom, which was both a blessing and a curse. If he was careful, he could be first to wash and shave in the morning, but it meant that he had to listen to everyone else on the floor groan with dawn hangovers and curse the lack of hot water.

He opened the three locks that secured his flat and went inside.

Without turning on the lights, Largo went to the tiny kitchen and turned on the small Bakelite wireless Remy had given him the previous Christmas. Tinny dance music, all trumpets and drums, filled the flat. Through the small living room, he went to an even smaller room that housed a loft bed and a wooden writing desk that Largo hardly ever used for its intended purpose. The desk, with its numerous drawers and cubbyholes, functioned mainly as his dresser. He stripped off his clothes, hanging his damp suit from the underside of the loft bed, before turning on the light. More than the smells in the hall or his cramped quarters, it was the light that drove Largo mad.

The lone bedroom bulb hung from the ceiling by a thick cord. It flickered twice before fully illuminating. The light it gave off was a yellowish white that made Largo think of piss or cheap cheese. It covered everything, including him. He couldn't comb his hair in the morning without feeling slightly dirty. Remy, of course, loved it. On the nights she'd stayed there she said it was like swimming in egg custard. Largo always smiled at the description, but he died a little inside each time he heard it.

The reason for the piss light and the perpetually black skies over Little Shambles was simple: the coal-stoked power plant on the next block. You couldn't escape the stink and it covered all the streets and windows with a fine layer of soot. So different from Remy's flat in Kromium's artists' quarter, which was powered by cool and lovely plazma. Her wireless was twice the size of Largo's and the lights throughout her rooms were as bright and white as new-fallen snow. As he dropped the small coins and the Valda into a tin box he kept under his mattress, Largo debated with himself.

With my new position and the prospect of more tips like today's, there's only one question: New clothes or a new flat? If the company is going to supply me with a new suit, maybe I can think about rooms in Dolch or even Geschoss. No coal in Geschoss.

It was a wonderful thought until reality hit him. A flat in Geschoss would cost easily more than double his current rent. And yet . . . it was sure to come with a private bath. That alone might be worth the expense. As much as his custard-colored flat amused Remy, rooms in Geschoss would really impress her. They would make him seem more serious and substantial, and less of a frazzled boy. And, just maybe, perhaps a new flat would be enough that she'd even consider moving in with him.

But that's a long way off. One Valda and a couple of small princes aren't going to get me far. I need to cut my expenses and save every penny. It's only the essentials from now on.

Which made him think of morphia.

It had been hours since he'd fortified himself and he was beginning to feel the lack of the drug. He took the little bottle from his jacket and put two drops under his tongue. The effects were immediate and heavenly. He dropped to the rickety wooden desk chair and let his head fall back. When it came to cutting expenses, morphia wasn't an option. It was the only thing that made the squalor of his rooms and the monotony of his job bearable. What else was there to cut down on, then? But his mind was already drifting, softened in morphia's gentle warmth. He'd worry about expenses in the morning. Now there was nothing but bliss, and soon there would be Remy—another, even better kind of bliss.

On his way across town, the coal-powered streetlights of Little Shambles gave way to the plazma illumination of Kromium. Where Copper Weg crossed Bronzegasse, a Black Widow carried a load of machine parts to the armaments factory. With his general hostility toward Maras and his frustration at the confrontation with Andrzej, a delicious thought came to him.

Largo knew that interfering with the armament factory's business was a jailing offense and could get you a sound beating by the bullocks. Still, after checking the street twice for police, Largo sped along in front of the Widow and, while passing a shuttered greengrocer, kicked a trash can into the street. Under its load, the burdened Mara was too slow to sidestep the obstruction. One of its front feet came down on top of the can and pierced its side such that the can became stuck on its leg. The Widow stumbled drunkenly this way and that, trying to kick the can off. Before he turned off Copper Weg, Largo looked back and saw that a crowd had gathered where the great black spider was still hopping in the street. They smiled and applauded the contraption's improvised dance routine.

That's one for our side, he thought. He was sure Parvulesco would have agreed.

The marquee for the theater—his destination—lay a long block ahead, but it was still bright enough to light the whole street. With the morphia in his system and the theater just ahead, whatever memories Largo had of his strange day faded away.

Of course, the Grand Dark wasn't the theater's real name, but it was the one everyone knew it by because its real name was a mouthful. Over the box office, the marquee proudly shouted its true name to the whole district.

<><><><><><><><><><><><><><><><><><><><><><><><><><><><><><><><><><><><><><>

THEATER OF THE GRAND DARKNESS

Dr. Krokodil presents
Elegant Butchery
Sensual Slaughter
Voluptuous Demises

The top of the marquee was sculpted into the upper jaw of a great steel reptile. The lower jaw surrounded the doors and thrust several feet over the street. The pointed teeth along each jaw glowed a bright plazma white. For the patrons, entering the Grand Dark was a gleeful surrender, a leap down the gullet of an alluring monster.

Largo chained his bicycle near the back of the theater and Ilsa in the ticket booth waved him inside. He crept through the lobby and slipped between the red velvet curtains into the performance area. The first play of the evening was already under way.

He found a seat in the last row and sat down. The Grand Dark specialized in Schöner Mord, little productions of violence and depravity performed by life-size puppets controlled by actors backstage in galvanic suits. The dolls required no crude strings, but were instead powered by nearly invisible wires along the floor furnishing the watts needed to make them seem almost alive. They moved with fluid, eerie grace, like a three-dimensional zoetrope brought to life.

The night's first production was called *The Boudoir Phantasm*. It was a fiction in which the ghost of a murdered wife possessed the body of the husband's new bride and killed him with a cleaver, the same way he'd killed her. When the new wife came out of her hypnotic state and saw what she'd done, she threw herself from the boudoir's window to her death, much to the delight of the murdered bride. It was a simple tale but elegantly produced. In fact, the run had been extended for two weeks. Since the end of the war, spiritualism was all the rage in Lower Proszawa, so ghost stories were very popular.

When the play ended, Largo wanted to rush backstage and tell Remy what a wonderful job she'd done as the murdered bride, but she never liked to socialize between plays, so he remained in his seat. Normally he would have joined the other patrons in the lobby for a smoke or a drink, but he was thinking about expenses again, so he stayed where he was. Besides, it wasn't as if the show had stopped completely.

The small band that provided the soundtrack for the plays performed during the intermission for tips—and the Trefle numbers of elegant gentlemen and ladies they might meet for trysts later in the night. An evening of murder in the Grand Dark was known to get even the stodgiest patron's blood up. And the drugs helped, of course. By intermission, the air in the theater was heavy with hashish smoke. In the dark corners of the lobby, men and women snorted cocaine together and kissed in groups of two and three. It was a condition of the tension that gripped the city: after the horrors of the Great War, grab as much pleasure as possible before the next, inevitable conflagration. Largo felt a stab of jealousy watching as other theatergoers with money spent it on such pleasures and indulged in them so deeply and openly.

As he pushed himself down into his plush seat, his hand touched something hard stuck between the bottom cushion and the armrest. Curious, he dug down and pulled out a small vial of white powder. Largo looked around to see if anybody had noticed him. Satisfied that no one had spotted his good fortune, he opened the vial, dropped a few grains onto the back of his hand, and sniffed. The sudden rush of energy and sense of well-being confirmed that he'd stumbled on someone's lost cocaine. He screwed the top back on the vial and quickly stuffed it into his pocket before anyone saw him. It would be a special treat he could share with Remy after the night's final performance. Between the gold coins and now the cocaine, the strangeness of the day seemed to have finally been balanced out. He leaned back in his seat, tapping his foot to the music, relishing the bitter taste of the cocaine as it dripped down the back of his throat.

The second play of the evening began fifteen minutes later.

The Erotic Underworld of Blixa Konstantin was a tale of sex, murder, and political revolution lifted from a lurid yellowsheet story—at least, the murder and revolutionaries had been cribbed from the sheets. The sex, Una Herzog—the Grand Dark's owner and chief auteur—had added herself. Finding the erotic in even the most depraved stories was one of her specialties.

The production was straightforward. Blixa Konstantin, a dedicated anarchist, was betrayed to the Nachtvogel by his lover, Eva. To spice up the story, Una added an affair in which both Blixa and Eva were secretly seeing the same woman—a simple but lusty shopgirl— shifting the story from one of bland political treachery to a lovers' triangle gone terribly wrong.

And keeping everyone rapt in their seats.

While Remy had played the vengeful bride in the first play, in this one she was Eva, because being murdered was one of her greatest talents. She'd studied dance and acrobatics as a girl and was able to contort her body into strange and grotesque positions, which made her death in doll form all the more disturbing and exciting for the theater's patrons. Largo was always mesmerized by her performances. He loved Remy for herself, but her talent made her dazzling.

As the curtain finally went down on the still and bloody puppets, the audience erupted into a standing ovation. Some of the patrons shouted for the players to come out and take a bow, but Una strictly forbade it, afraid that seeing the humans behind the dolls would break the spell of the performances. She insisted that the puppets were the stars, not the actors. Since she paid everyone's salary, they were quick to agree.

As the theatergoers filed out, more drugged and happier than ever, Largo finally made his way past them to the rear of the theater. The effects of the cocaine had worn off and he wanted to show Remy his find.

Backstage, the theater's dressers helped the players out of their galvanic attire, skintight aluminized suits studded with wires and small switches that covered the entirety of the actors' bodies. Largo caught sight of Remy at the far side of the stage, slipping a bit wearily into her dressing room. He started her way but was stopped by Una, who maneuvered in front of him and put a hand on his chest.

"Largo, how are you this evening?" she said. She was an inch or two taller than he was, but carried herself so that she seemed even larger.

"Fine. Thank you."

"What did you think of the plays tonight? You know it was poor Blixa Konstantin's last hurrah. His sordid little tale is being retired for a newer, even more exciting story. Would you like to know what it is?"

At that moment, there was nothing Largo wanted to hear less than one of Una's new obsessions. However, since she was Remy's employer, politeness seemed the best course. "Yes, please," he said.

She got closer and showed him a yellowsheet clipping with a bold headline and an illustration of a human head mounted on what looked like a Blind Mara. The headline read MAD SURGEON MELDS HUMAN AND MACHINE INTO A CREATURE OF DIVINE HORROR.

"Can you believe it?" said Una. "Some lunatic put a corpse's head on a Mara and used galvanics to animate it. Only for a few minutes, you understand, but that's long enough to make a wonderful story for the theater, don't you think?"

Largo had to turn away from the illustration. Looking at it made him queasy. "It's perfect. A surefire hit."

Una folded the clipping and put it in a pocket of her brocade bustier. "It will be when I'm through with it. *Imagine* a mad scientist constructing a lover from machine and flesh. There are so many possibilities. I can't wait to write it."

Largo hesitated, then said, "You don't think it might be just a little far-fetched . . . ?"

Una looked at him as if he were a little dim. She said, "Stranger things happen every day. Science and lust? Who says they can't be intertwined?" She patted him on the shoulder as if he were a small dog. "But I'm keeping you from your lady love. Go and see her. She's going to make a brilliant monster for her scientist lover."

"Thanks. Lovely seeing you, Una. I can't wait for the new play." But she had already moved off, distracted by a player complaining that his suit was giving him electric shocks. Largo used the moment to duck into Remy's dressing room.

She was naked when he went in, toweling the sweat of the performance off her body. Her hair and eyes were dark, and her body was as trim as an athlete's. Largo was fairly certain that if they ever had a fight, she could easily overcome him, a fate to which he wasn't entirely averse.

When she saw him in the mirror, she ran over and threw her arms around him, kissing him hard and for a long time. When she pulled away she said, "What took you so long getting here? I thought you'd forgotten about me." She handed him the towel and turned around. Largo began wiping the sweat off her back and legs. She laughed and pulled away for a second when the towel tickled her thigh. Then she leaned against his chest.

"It was Una," he said, bringing the towel around to wipe her front. She pushed herself into the thick material when he reached her breasts and he lingered there as her hands wrapped around his and she dug her nails into him. "She was telling me about how she wants to cut off your head and turn you into a Mara."

Remy threw the towel away and guided his hand down between her legs, where she ground against his fingers. "I know. Isn't it wonderful? Science, lust, and death. The cornerstones of the world!"

"That's only three cornerstones," he said, nipping her shoulder. "Aren't there supposed to be four?"

She sighed and said, "You're right. I left out one. Morphia. You brought some with you, right?"

With his free hand, he took the cocaine vial from his pocket and held it in front of her. "Look at what else I have."

Remy spun around, kissed him, took the vial, and pressed it lovingly between her breasts. Her smile was both wicked and silly, like a naughty child's after she'd been caught stealing sips of the adults' dinner wine. He loved seeing her in such a delighted mood. "What a treat. But we'll keep it for later, all right? We're going to a party at Werner Petersen's house. Do you know him? He's a great arts patron."

Largo's heart sank a little and the desire from a moment before evaporated. He always felt clumsy and drab around Remy's artist friends, and his clothes were pathetic. But maybe more cocaine would help his mood. He took the vial back and dropped it into his jacket pocket.

Remy pressed against him and cupped his groin in her hand. In her silkiest voice she said, "Morphia, please. Now, please."

Her hunger helped to lift his mood once more. He kissed her lips when he took out the bottle. Remy grinned as she closed her eyes and opened her mouth. Largo put two drops under her tongue. Then she snatched the bottle from his hand and did the same for him. They kissed, letting the morphia mix and melt their bones at the same time. A moment later, Remy let her head fall back. "Why is it so necessary for people to get dressed when they go out? I feel too wonderful for clothes. Why can't I just go like this?"

"You'd certainly be the hit of the party," said Largo. She shivered when he touched her nipples. "But I'm afraid we might both be arrested on the way. Besides, it's cold out. You'd freeze your poor toes."

Remy dropped down into a chair by the dressing table. "All right, I suppose for the sake of my toes I'll put on shoes."

Largo went to the clothes stand where her dress hung from a padded hanger. It was black silk and opaque for the most part, but with a flower pattern down the front that revealed glimpses of her skin and the flesh-colored brassieres she favored. He held it up before her and said, "Come on. I'll help you put it on."

"Fine," she said. "But I'm not wearing anything under it. I plan to fuck you quite violently when we get home and there's no point in wearing anything that will get in the way."

"A bold fashion choice, but one I heartily endorse."

Remy stood and held up her hands as Largo slipped the dress over her and zipped her up in the back.

"Can you see my tits?" she said, standing in front of a full-length mirror mounted behind the dressing room door.

"Quite well," he said.

"Good. I want everyone to be jealous of you tonight. Some of the people who will be at the party are quite delightful, but you know how it is with rich art benefactors. A lot of their friends are more prudish than a country priest."

"Trust me, you'll make them forget their vows," said Largo. "But I'm not so sure about me."

"What's wrong?" said Remy, turning and touching his cheek.

"Look at me. My coat has holes at the elbows and my shirt looks like someone stole it from a corpse bound for Potter's Field."

"But you look adorable that way. My handsome waif with the lovely cock."

Largo looked at her and said, "Am I how you go slumming?"

"Don't be silly," said Remy. "I love you for you, and because you're not like the jaded snots I work with. Pretty boys from rich families who expect the world to open its legs for them. I know that you've worked for what you have, and that makes you better than them."

Largo kissed her when she was done. Remy had saved the day after all, the way she had so many times before. "Thank you," he said. "But I still look like a scarecrow."

Remy waved away his worry as if it were nothing and ran her fingers along Largo's jaw to his lips. "Your coat is perfect. Some of the artists will be wearing much worse. Everyone will think you're a famous painter or poet. As for the rest, wait here."

Remy left the room and came back a moment later with a pressed white shirt with mother-of-pearl buttons down the front. "Where did you get that?" Largo said.

"From the doll that plays Blixa. This is one of his extra shirts. Try it on. I think it will be perfect."

Feeling extremely foolish, Largo stripped off his shirt and slipped on the new one. Earlier he'd been tempted to wear the knife and harness to amuse Remy, but now standing foolishly in her dressing room in doll clothes he was glad he hadn't. Remy buttoned the shirt for him. "You look wonderful," she said. "It's like it was made for you."

"The collar is a bit tight," he said.

Remy rolled her eyes at him. "Practically everything women wear is too tight or too loose or too hot. Welcome to our world," she said.

Largo gave her a small bow. "Then as one lady to another, shall we go?"

Remy took his hand and led him to the door. On the way out, she swatted him on the rear end. "Lovely ass, Fräulein."

"Am I to suffer all the indignities of a woman tonight too?" said Largo.

"We'll see," said Remy. "I think you'd look darling in lipstick, but not false eyelashes, so you're safe for the moment."

"It's the little mercies that help us sleep at night."

She cocked her head and looked at him. "Pardon?"

They went out the backstage door and Remy hailed a Mara cab for them.

"It's just something Herr Branca said at work today," said Largo. He left his bicycle chained behind the theater and held the door for her as they got into the cab.

"No," said Remy firmly. "I forbid you to talk about him or work. This is a night for fun, not worrying about the cares of stuffy old men."

"I agree completely," said Largo as Remy spoke Werner Petersen's address into a small Trefle mounted in the back seat of the cab.

"Thank you," said the Mara in a static-filled voice. It whirred to life and sped off. Largo put his arm around Remy and she rested her head on his shoulder. While he was still nervous about the party, the morphia helped him to not care too much.

A CURSED PLACE

From the profile "The Theater of the Grand Darkness" in *Ihre Skandale*

It seems entirely appropriate that the land where the Grand Dark sits was once known to the area's residents as "Ein Verfluchter Ort": a cursed place.

A boardinghouse once stood where the theater is now. Among the house's long-term residents was Otto Kreizler, the serial killer better known as the Brimstone Devil for his habit of burning his victims alive. In the year it took the authorities to track Kreizler down, he murdered at least thirteen people. After a short trial, he was hanged and his body was buried in an unmarked prison grave. Still, it seemed that the Brimstone Devil hadn't finished his work, since soon after his death the boardinghouse where he'd once lived burned to the ground, killing three people.

After the boardinghouse burned, the land stood vacant for some time. Since the area was known as an entertainment district for the lower classes, the first building to occupy the spot was Kammer des Schreckens, a wax museum of horrors depicting famous historical murders. This was later expanded to include a small cinema specializing in illicit erotica, thus adding to the area's already dire reputation. Still, the Kammer drew steady business, so local cafés and merchants didn't complain.

During the Great War, stray bombs leveled every building on the street—except for the Kammer. However, during those years of social repression and heavy censorship, the authorities eventually forced the theater to close.

Una Herzog, along with her business partner and lover, Horst Wehner, purchased the Kammer just a few weeks before the armistice was signed. Wehner is acknowledged to be the Dr. Krokodil in the theater's name, but little else is known about him, as he disappeared soon after the site was rechristened the Theater of the Grand Darkness.

Like Wehner's, Una Herzog's past is shrouded in mystery. It is rumored that Wehner had been a spy during the war and might have been killed on one of his assignments. It's further rumored that Una was credited with seducing one, and perhaps more, enemy officers and obtaining vital war plans. A darker version of the story goes on to say that, having grown weary of Wehner's secrecy and possessiveness, Una convinced one of those officers to arrange for his murder.

Of course, this remains mere conjecture.

Una has stated publicly that the Brimstone Devil's murders were her original inspiration for the Grand Dark. She'd already seen Schöner Mord—short one-act plays of murder and depravity—while abroad and believed strongly that she could bring the form home to Lower Proszawa.

While the theater went through renovations, Una's theater troupe performed in the nearby ruins of bombed-out buildings, giving the productions a level of verisimilitude never before seen in the city. Even with the area's unsavory reputation, the plays brought in viewers from all over Lower Proszawa, and the theater was a success from its early days.

There is one question that certain critics and conspiracy theorists always come back to when discussing Una Herzog: Where did her puppets originate? No other theater in the city had them and few people had seen similar appliances outside of the military and large corporations such as Schöne Maschinen. Whatever the truth, the strange stories swirling around Una have only enhanced her enigmatic reputation and added to the otherworldly luster of the Theater of the Grand Darkness.

CHAPTER FOUR

THE MARA CRUISED THEM PAST BRIGHT CAFÉS, RESTAURANTS, AND DANCE halls. The music was frantic, the crowds laughing and boisterous. Though they were moving through Kromium, Largo knew that the streets in Little Shambles were just as wild. It had been this way since soon after the armistice was signed, an endless frantic party.

Largo frowned when he saw Petersen's home. It was nothing more than a large but old-fashioned Imperial mansion—a great granite-and-marble box meant to show off old money. He expected more from an art patron.

Remy paid for the cab and Largo held the door for her. He could hear music, and shadows flitted by the bright windows. "What a mausoleum," he said.

"What?" said Remy, adjusting her hair in the cab's side mirror.

"The house. I didn't expect your friend to live in such a dull old place. It's not a home. It's a bank vault."

"If it were a bank vault he might have made it himself. His family supplies most of the steel to the government so they can make the little bombs and tanks they're so fond of."

"I suppose rich codgers like that have to keep up appearances," Largo said. He turned to Remy. "Which makes you and your friends his attempt at radicalism. At least he has good taste in vices."

Remy kissed her index finger and pressed it to Largo's lips. "I'm *your* vice, dear. As for Petersen, I'm here to drink his champagne and smile prettily so he'll shower more of those lovely war profits on us poor, deluded artists."

She looped her arm around Largo's as they went up the long walkway to the mansion. Maybe it was the morphia wearing off, but Largo's self-consciousness returned. He held his free arm straight at his side, hoping that the holes in the elbow wouldn't show. This would be so much easier, he thought, if he really were a failed poet or an aspiring musician. He wasn't even sure he could lie well enough to pass himself off as either to justify his shabby clothes. The best he could hope for was that everyone would already be so drunk and drugged that it wouldn't matter what he said.

A tall servant Mara, like the one in Empyrean, greeted them at the door.

"Lovely to see you," it said, and ushered them inside. Seeing the automaton did nothing to improve Largo's mood. Still, he forced himself to smile. The last thing he wanted to do was let Remy down in front of these people.

A large Proszawan flag on the wall directly across from the front door caught Largo's eye. He supposed it was there to signal patriotism during uncertain times, but festooned as it was with balloons and tinsel, the flag looked more like something that would be up in the back of the Grand Dark as a joke. Next to the flag was a winding marble staircase lined with ancient tapestries and flowers in golden pots. Below that was a white grand piano. A man in a tuxedo played something light and fast, but Largo couldn't pick out a melody over the sound of an amplified gramophone in the next room. Remy took his hand and led him inside.

The living room was enormous, the largest Largo had ever seen. The ceiling was two stories high and the large windows overlooking Heldenblut Bay were each a single pane of flawless glass. Almost everything in the room was white, except for the sofa and chairs, which were a vivid crimson.

The room was crowded with guests and heavy with smoke. Young couples in tuxedos and evening gowns and older men with waxed mustaches mixed easily with artists in clothes that were no better than Largo's. However, he noted that the artists were comfortable and wore their garb stylishly. Seeing the shabby artists made Largo feel better and more determined to relax and at least appear at home in his rags.

Remy waved to a group of about eight people across the room. She tugged Largo to an oversize chaise longue where Lucie, another performer from the Grand Dark, had fallen asleep on her side holding a full flute of champagne that, miraculously, hadn't spilled. Remy sat down next to Lucie and pulled Largo down beside her. She reached across the sleeping woman and gently plucked the champagne from her hand. "Lucie won't mind," Remy said, and downed the whole glass.

Her artist friends, reclining on the floor atop pillows and draped on the sofa, laughed. Largo recognized Enki Helm, the blind painter who worked in the absurdist Xuxu style more, Largo suspected, out of luck than talent. There was Bianca, an aspiring opera singer whom Largo liked and who—famously—was discovered while singing for pennies in the streets. Baumann was there too. *Of course* he's *here.* He was a young up-and-coming film actor so handsome that Largo wanted to slap him. Instead, he smiled at them all and they raised glasses or nodded in response.

"Where have you been, Remy?" said Baumann, not even acknowledging Largo sitting beside her. "The evening couldn't properly start without you."

Remy said, "I could say that I was working, but really I was waiting until you were done with your boring stories about which society ladies you're sleeping with."

Baumann sat up in feigned indignation. "My affairs are never boring, and my stories even less so."

"That depends on how many times you've heard them," said Bianca. "Really, you must bed either more of these old fraus or fewer more-interesting ones."

"Does anyone else have love advice for me?" said Baumann. "How about you, Largo? You've charmed lovely Remy here. What's your secret?"

Largo froze. He couldn't think of a thing to say to the bright and witty group. Luckily, before his silence became awkward, he was saved by a Mara that approached the group with more champagne. During the minute or so it took for everyone to get a glass, Largo had time to think. "I'm just the right size," he said.

"What does that mean?" said Enki.

"For her to dress."

Remy laughed, spilling champagne onto her lap. She took a napkin lodged under Lucie's arm and wiped herself off, saying, "It's true. He is the absolutely *perfect* size. Do you like his shirt? It belongs to Blixa Konstantin, the tragic victim in our second show."

Bianca gave a snorting laugh and fell against Enki. Hanna, a biological artist who designed custom chimeras for Lower Proszawa's richest families, tugged open Largo's jacket and ran her fingers teasingly over the shirt.

"It's lovely material," she said. "If you were to die tonight you'd make a gorgeous cadaver."

Remy took Hanna's hand away from Largo's chest and placed it on her own. "And what about me? Would you sneak a feel of my corpse?"

Hanna placed another hand on Remy's breasts. She said, "Alive or dead, you always look good enough to eat." Remy gave her a dainty kiss on the cheek.

"Already on to necrophilia, are we?" said Strum, the poet. "Or is it cannibalism? And barely eleven o'clock."

Hanna sat down on a pillow at Remy's feet. She looped an arm around one of Remy's legs and one around one of Largo's. He looked at Remy and she clinked her champagne flute against his. He didn't know what that meant, but he smiled as if he did, wishing they could sneak off together and take more cocaine.

Lucie said, "Strum was telling us about his new epic poem. What was it called again?"

"*The Sailor's Call*. It's all empire and blood and sacred duty. Complete garbage."

"Then why did you write it?" said Bianca.

"Because it paid more than my last two books combined," he said in an attempt at a joking tone. "There's art and there's keeping a roof over one's head. Sadly, in those moments, the roof always wins."

"How sad for you," said Hanna.

"If only you enjoyed the rain more," said Baumann. "Then you could look at a roof as a luxury."

"True," said Strum. "It's my fault for being born a poet and not a duck."

A few of them laughed, but most smiled politely. Largo felt a pang of pity for the man. Seeing a respected artist forced to betray his gifts made him happy that he had no such ambitions. Before he could dwell on it, a shout cut into his thoughts.

"It's Frida!" Bianca said, pointing across the room to where an elegant woman in furs and a salmon-colored gown looked this way and that. "She must have married that Baron she's been after. Frida!"

yelled Bianca. The woman waved her over. Bianca and several other members of the group got up and went to her.

The only ones left around the chaise were sleeping Lucie, Remy, Largo, Hanna, and Enki.

"A Baron," Enki said contemptuously. "The very class that's ruining this country. They'll drag us into another war before any enemy does."

"Please don't start a tedious screed, Enki," said Hanna. "Can't you see I'm trying to seduce these young innocents? You'll put them right to sleep."

"They're already asleep," said Enki. "So are you. So is everyone in this room. I'm telling you, we're heading for a catastrophe."

Largo had never heard anyone speak with such passion about politics before. Well, he had, but only for a few seconds. *He sounds like one of those cranks standing on a chair in the Triumphal Square, condemning both the upper classes and the bourgeoisie. If he hates everyone, though, who is he speaking to?*

"We must organize and resist the ruling class's bloodlust," said Enki. "Take up arms, if necessary."

"Arms?" said Remy. "I used to think your speeches were scandalous fun. But if you insist on being arrested for treason you'll have to do that alone."

"I thought you were smarter than the others, Remy," he said. "But you're just another dullard artiste."

Largo stared at Enki, angry but torn, wondering if it was his place to speak up to someone so prominent in Remy's artists' circle. Finally, he couldn't stand it. "Don't talk about her like that. She's right. You *are* a bore. And I've never liked your paintings. They're as pretentious as your politics."

Remy laid a hand on Largo's back and Hanna gave his leg a squeeze. "Good boy," she said. Slowly, Largo settled back onto the chaise. It felt good to speak up, but it left him confused. Had he made a terrible mistake that would ruin Remy's reputation with her friends?

Enki said, "Largo to the rescue, so eager to attack a blind man. I wonder how brave you'll be when the bullocks come knocking on your door?"

"Why would they do that?" Largo said.

"Do they need a reason?"

What the hell does that mean? he wondered, before Branca's comment about König came back to him. "*It's likely you won't see him again.*" Largo's day had returned to being strange.

As he considered that, the other members of the group came back with Frida in tow. Bianca had the elegant woman's fur draped across her shoulders. "You might want to keep your trap shut for a while, Enki," said Hanna. "The vile ruling class is almost upon us."

Frida greeted Remy and Hanna like old friends, and gave Largo a peck on each cheek when they were introduced. She and Enki studiously ignored each other.

"How is everyone?" Frida said.

"Still sober," said Hanna. "So, in a word, tragic."

Frida made a complex hand gesture at one of the servant Maras.

"At once, ma'am," it said, and left the room.

She winked at the others. "A little secret I learned from the Baron. It's not necessary to even talk to them," she said. "We'll have more drinks momentarily."

Largo couldn't help noticing a chimera—a long snakelike body with a miniature wolf's head—with its fangs buried in the Mara's leg so that the automaton limped. *More ugliness*, he thought. He wondered if the chimera was one of Hanna's creations. He'd ask her later, if he got a chance.

"While we wait for our champagne . . . ," said Frida. She reached into her purse and took out what Largo thought at first was a tube of lipstick. Frida unscrewed the top with great care, tapped out some powder onto her hand, and sniffed it up. Then she held out the tube to the others. "Does anyone care to join me?"

The cocaine made its way quickly around the group. No one tried to hide what they were doing because many other partiers were doing the same thing. Even Enki took some of the powder. Largo wondered if he was trying to fit in or was simply a hypocrite. *With luck, I won't spend enough time with him to ever know.*

On the end of the chaise, Lucie sat up and looked around sleepily. "What happened to my champagne?" she said. Everyone in the group laughed. No one replied because Frida handed her the tube and Lucie squealed with delight. She snorted a copious amount of the powder and looked at Remy in surprise. "When did you get here?" she said.

Remy put an arm around her and pulled her close, saying, "You're a goose."

In a few minutes, Baumann presented the group with hashish

cigarettes, which they also passed around. Riding the blissful high of the cocaine and hashish, Largo disliked the too-handsome actor a little less.

The cigarettes made their way around the group once, then twice. The third time Remy puffed one she doubled over in a coughing fit. Lucie and Baumann laughed together. Largo patted Remy's back, hoping it would help clear her lungs. It didn't.

"My god, she's turning blue," said Bianca. Hanna spun around and looked up at Remy's face. She pushed Lucie and Largo off the chaise and laid Remy on her back. She was limp.

"We have to get her breathing properly," Hanna said. She tilted Remy's head back and breathed into her mouth.

Frida touched Baumann's shoulder. "Do you know Dr. Venohr?"

"Of course."

"Bring him here. Quickly."

Baumann jumped up and disappeared into the crowd, which remained oblivious to Remy's situation. Largo held Remy's hand as Hanna kept forcing air into her lungs. When, in a few minutes, she began to breathe on her own again, everyone relaxed. But it didn't last long. Remy began to shake. Her arms bent up to her chest and her fingers twisted into claws. She grimaced and Largo had to hold her legs to keep her from kicking herself off the chaise.

Hanna looked at him. "Has this ever happened before?"

"Once or twice," he said, "but never this badly."

"Was she taking drugs those other times?"

Largo shook his head. "No. We were perfectly sober."

"Does she take medication for it?"

"Not that I know of."

After subsiding for a few seconds, Remy's convulsions came back stronger than ever. "Oh my god," Bianca whispered over and over like she was praying.

A moment later, Baumann returned in the company of a bald, bearded man in a tuxedo. Dr. Venohr gently pushed Hanna away from Remy so that he could look into her eyes. "How long have the convulsions been going on?" he said.

"A few minutes," said Largo. "They've never been this bad before."

"I'm afraid they have, but she didn't want you to know about them," said Dr. Venohr.

Largo stared at the man. "You've treated her?"

"I've known Remy her whole life. I'm an old friend of the family."

Largo wondered what else Remy hadn't told him. But all he could think about right now was whether she was truly ill.

What if she's dying?

"Can you help her?"

Dr. Venohr opened a small black leather bag he had with him. "I believe so," he said, and filled a syringe with a clear liquid from a small bottle. Tilting Remy's head to the side, he injected the fluid directly into her jugular vein. Bianca continued repeating "Oh my god." It was annoying, but no one bothered to stop her.

With the shot, it took only a few seconds for Remy's convulsions to subside. Her arms and hands relaxed. Her legs stopped shaking. The grimace faded from her face. It looked almost as if she were asleep.

Largo said, "Is that it? Is she all right now?"

"For the moment," said Dr. Venohr.

"Should we take her to a hospital?"

"That shouldn't be necessary. But we should get her home. And she mustn't be alone tonight. I assume you can stay and watch her?"

"Of course. For as long as it takes."

"Good," said Dr. Venohr. He packed the bottle and syringe in his bag. "I'll call for my car. Can someone help you bring her to the door?"

Hanna and Baumann both volunteered.

Dr. Venohr got up and went to call his car. Largo pulled Remy up from the chaise. Hanna got on the other side and together they lifted Remy to her feet. Baumann went ahead of them, making an opening in the crowd. When they reached the door, Largo said, "Could someone find her coat? I don't want her to get cold." Frida, who had followed them, gestured to a Mara. It bowed and moved off. When Dr. Venohr's car pulled up outside, they bundled Remy into her coat and laid her down in the back seat. Largo got in with her. Dr. Venohr got in the back on the other side and checked her pulse.

"Don't worry," said Frida through the open door. "She'll be fine now that the doctor is here."

Hanna said, "I'll call tomorrow to see how she is."

"Go," Dr. Venohr told his driver, and they sped away.

They rode in silence for what felt like a long time. Largo kept an eye on Remy while Dr. Venohr periodically checked her pulse. Finally, he nodded. "She's stable. I'll give you some pills for her. With the injection, she should sleep through the night, but you aren't to leave her side for any reason."

"I won't," said Largo. Then, "I—I don't have any money to pay you."

Dr. Venohr waved a dismissive hand. "Don't be foolish. As I said, I'm an old friend."

"Thank you." But he did feel foolish, and embarrassed. He felt like he needed to say something more, but he wasn't sure what. "I notice you have a human driver. I thought someone in your position would have a Mara."

Dr. Venohr frowned. "I practically live with Maras all day and night at the laboratory. I don't need them bothering me at home too."

"You don't have *any* Maras at home?"

"None. Don't misunderstand me. Maras are lovely devices and invaluable to my work, but there are times when I prefer the company of humans or to be left alone."

"I understand. I'm not all that fond of them either," said Largo, thinking of the dancing Black Widow. He wished he could tell Remy about it. He knew it would make her laugh.

They fell silent again until Dr. Venohr said, "I hesitated to bring this up earlier with Remy's friends present, and I don't want to alarm you, but I'll need to take some of Remy's blood before I leave tonight."

"Why?"

Dr. Venohr sighed. "Have you ever heard of what laypeople call the Drops?"

Largo stiffened. People talked about the Drops all the time in Little Shambles, though he'd never seen a case himself. Supposedly, perfectly healthy people could be walking along the street, fall into a seizure, and be dead in an instant. Largo had never believed the stories, but now they made him afraid. "Yes, I have," he said.

"There's a slight chance—and I must emphasize that it is slight—that Remy's convulsions are brought on by the virus that causes the Drops." Dr. Venohr looked at Largo. "Tell me, does Remy buy goods on the black market? It doesn't have to be anything large. It could be as small as a piece of jewelry."

"I don't think so," said Largo. "I'm sure she would have mentioned it."

"Excellent. Many black market goods are brought here from the ruins of High Proszawa. These goods can be contaminated with traces of the plague bombs dropped by the enemy during the Great War. The petty scavengers who loot the ruins are putting us all at risk."

"Oh," said Largo. "I had no idea." He could barely understand what was happening tonight. He looked at Remy. The possibility of her dying was absurd. Impossible. Still, he gripped her hand tighter. "She had a shot recently. She said it was vitamins. Could that be the problem?"

Dr. Venohr said, "I'm aware of the injection. An associate of mine gave it to her. It has nothing to do with her current condition, I assure you."

"That's a relief," said Largo, feeling as lost as ever.

The doctor checked Remy's pulse again and said, "As I was saying before, even in the face of plague, life plays its jokes and presents us with little ironies."

"What do you mean?"

The doctor looked at him. "Have long have you been addicted to morphia?"

"I don't . . . I mean, I wouldn't . . ."

"Come now. I'm not a police officer or your mother. I'm merely asking as a physician."

"Perhaps a year," said Largo quietly. "Though I'm not really addicted. I just, Remy and I, we just like it."

"Of course. Of course."

Largo leaned closer to the doctor. "How did you know?"

"It's your eyes. Morphia affects the shape of the pupil. It's very subtle. You have to look for it. Don't worry, people on the street, your employer, even most police officers are unlikely to notice unless you go too far."

"Thank you for the advice," Largo said. "But before, why did you say there were ironies?"

Dr. Venohr chuckled to himself. "Because it appears that morphia may give users a certain amount of immunity to the plague virus."

"That's good news, then. Remy uses morphia too."

"As much as you?"

Largo sagged against the back of the car. "No."

"There you are," said Dr. Venohr. "Continue to addle your senses, young man. Morphia might ruin your life, but it just might save it. That's what I meant by irony."

Largo looked out the window. "We're almost there."

When they arrived, Dr. Venohr helped Largo walk Remy into her flat and get her into bed. The doctor took a blood sample from her arm and placed it in his bag. On his way out he said, "Remember: do not leave her alone. I believe that Remy has a Trefle?"

"She does."

Dr. Venohr took a card from his pocket and gave it to Largo. "You may reach me at this number day or night."

"Thank you, Doctor."

"I'll see myself out," he said. "Oh, and one more thing."

"Yes?" said Largo.

The doctor laid a finger along the side of his nose. "Don't tell anybody about our little chat regarding the plague. We don't want to start a panic, do we?"

"Of course not. I won't say a word."

"You have some morphia with you, I take it?"

"A little."

Dr. Venohr took a vial from his bag and set it on a gilt end table. "Here is a bit more. I don't want you fainting tonight or being tempted to leave to purchase more. Of course, if anyone asks, you did not obtain this from me."

"I appreciate it, Doctor. We both do."

"Don't appreciate it. Merely stay alert. Remy should be fine by morning. I'll call then. Good night."

"Good night."

Largo sat down by Remy's bed. The chair had a straight back and was uncomfortable because Remy didn't buy it for sitting in. She used it as a place to drape her clothes when she got home from the theater. However, recently she'd bought a broken full-size Mara and used it like a dressing dummy. Now the chair belonged to Largo's clothes when he spent the night. Tonight, though, he remained fully dressed and listened to Remy breathe. Every minute or so he touched her chest just to feel her heartbeat.

Remy's flat was how Largo imagined all artists lived or, at least, wanted to. In her bedroom was a large framed poster from the Grand Dark. It was for a show called *Cannibal Nuns of St. Maria*; Remy's first starring role had been that of the mad mother superior. The floor was covered in exotic, though worn and sometimes moth-eaten, carpets. The carpets were covered in shoes, clothes, magazines, books—whatever Remy had become bored with and couldn't be bothered to put away. In the living room was a large, comfortable black sofa—a gift from a wealthy admirer. Because of that provenance Largo hated sitting on it, but he never mentioned it. By the window was a cage with a parakeet inside. The cage was covered at this hour and the small bird was asleep.

The walls were crowded with paintings and photochromes of friends. There was even an Enki painting hanging over the mantel. Largo disliked it, but less than the sofa. Since he was blind, Enki painted by feel, using his hands instead of a brush. He'd grab fistfuls of oil paint, then dab and splatter them across images of older artists and political figures. *Trying to appear radical and dangerous*, thought Largo. *Just like all the other Xuxu artists, thinking they can bring down the government with a few paintings and posters.*

To Largo, Enki's paintings looked like drop cloths you might find in a child's bedroom. Still, the man's work was well thought of and his paintings were in great demand. Largo suspected that the canvas over Remy's mantel had been his clumsy attempt at seducing her. Despite his defensiveness when it came to Remy's admirers, in Enki's case he just smiled.

She would never fall for something so obvious.

The lamp next to Remy's bed lit the room with a pale white plazma glow and reflected off her porcelain Trefle. Largo thought of Rainer, whose old Bakelite Trefle wasn't nearly as impressive. It was going to be a long night standing watch over Remy, and Rainer was older and smarter.

Maybe he'll know something about Remy's condition. And after that ridiculous party I wouldn't mind hearing a friendly voice.

Largo touched Remy's chest and felt her breathing steadily. When he was satisfied she was stable, he took the Trefle into the living room. Removing the handset, he waited for an operator. When she came on, he spoke Rainer's number and waited. There was a click as the connection was made and then a soft purr as Rainer's Trefle rang. Largo let it ring twenty times before hanging up.

He's probably on the roof with his damned telescopes. Is there a meteor shower tonight?

He looked out the window, but the plazma diffused any light he might have seen streaking across the sky.

He went back into the bedroom and sat down, but the little chair immediately began hurting his back again, so Largo kicked off his shoes and climbed into bed with Remy. He lay down next to her with his hand over her heart and stayed that way until dawn.

ABOVE THE CITY

An excerpt from the *Diaries of Gräfin Beatrice Henke*[*]

It was a few minutes after ten in the evening. Or perhaps it was eleven. They'd lost track of time.

The airship moved along Lower Proszawa's southeast border in a light rain. Buffeted by cool crosswinds, it turned slowly, tracing the eastern border over the Krieghund Mountains, heading north. The ship swayed in the updrafts from the somber peaks, but settled again as soon as it reached the open fields of Die Gefallenen.

None of this, however, was of any interest to the partiers in the ballroom, who were focused on Greta, the Chancellor's wife's niece—entirely naked and eating a slice of honey cake with her hands as she fell into Orlok's lap. A handsome man with long ginger hair, he was the singer in one of the city's most popular dance bands. Greta mashed the cake into

---

[*] Readers will notice that the entry is written in a fictive style, as were a number of other entries in Henke's diaries. It is believed that these tone shifts were her attempt to shield the activities and identities of some of the participants, including herself. We cannot wholly identify many of the players here except, perhaps, for the inquisitive "Helene," who is almost certainly Henke. It is also believed that the "Petersen" mentioned here is Werner Petersen, the well-known financier and arts patron.

his face and proceeded to kiss it off as the rest of the party laughed.

"Lucky Orlok," said Gustav. "Another rich little bird lands right in his lap. What is his secret?"

"Don't whine," said Petersen. "You had your chance with her."

"But I'm merely a poet. Not a musical god. All of my little birds flit away in the slightest breeze."

Greta leaned away from Orlok and pulled Gustav over by his tie. She mashed the last of her cake into his face and began kissing him too. The three fell into a pile on the lounge's silk pillows.

The gathering had begun as someone's birthday party, but around the end of day three it had turned into something else. What, no one knew yet. Perhaps it would become clear after another day or two.

For now, though, people were interested in doing everything they could to feel anything . . . or nothing. The languid hedonism in the ballroom. And the foggy boredom in the airship's forward observation deck. It was a greenhouse full of exotic plants, wrapping around the front of the craft. Helene watched as an industrialist named Frölich pried open one of the side windows and threw out a full champagne flute. "For my customers," he said, giggling drunkenly. Soon, others were throwing things—food, plants, articles of clothing. Whatever they found amusing. Helene watched them from a bench by herself, growing bored with these people, their dull games, and the surroundings. She was wondering if there was some way that she could get off the airship without the others knowing when the small squirrel-like chimera that Frölich kept in the breast pocket of his jacket leaped to the floor and ran away. Instead of chasing his pet, Frölich and the others laughed as it disappeared from sight. Without thinking, Helene jumped from the bench and ran after the poor creature.

She soon found it cowering along one of the interior walkways. Picking it up, she cooed until it stopped trembling. When she heard boring Frölich heading down the corridor behind her, Helene didn't hesitate to push through a door marked *Authorized Personnel Only*.

Once inside, she found herself on a bare metal gangway in the true interior of the airship. The craft's skin stretched over and around her. *It's like being swallowed by a great silver whale*, Helene thought. Along the ribs that kept the ship's skin taut, an army of robin-size Maras scuttled up and down, occasionally darting out onto the skin to mend small holes. Brief bolts of white-blue plazma shot from a central shaft to the ribs, jolting the little Maras with power. Instead of being scared, Helene was delighted by the interior lightning storm.

"Fräulein?"

Helene jumped at the sound of the man's voice, almost dropping the little chimera. She turned and found herself face-to-face with a tall, ruddy man in the white uniform of the ship's crew.

"I'm very sorry," she said. "I'll go back with the others."

"There's no need for that," the man said. "The Kapitän saw you rescue your little pet and sent me to invite you to see the control room. Only if you like, of course."

It wasn't a hard decision, as Helene had no desire to return to the tedious decadence of the party. She stroked the little chimera and said, "Thank you. I'd love to."

The man made a small bow. "I'm Leutnant Dietze. Please follow me."

As they went down a short flight of metal stairs, Helene told the Leutnant her name.

"It's delightful to meet you, Helene. The control room is right through here," Dietze said, opening a door for her.

It was a whole different world in the control room. A crew of six men and women nodded at her when she came in. The floor rumbled and the noise of the engines was like thunder. Helene looked around, startled by the sound.

A gray-haired man in a uniform with gold stripes on his shoulders approached her. "It is a bit loud, isn't it? But you get used to it," he said. "I'm Kapitän Siodmak. Welcome to my ship . . ."

"Helene," she said quickly. Like the Leutnant had, he made a small bow, but he didn't extend a hand as she expected. She realized why when she looked closer. Both of his arms were mechanical, intricate contraptions of wood and metal. When Helene looked at the rest of the crew again she realized that many of them also had artificial limbs or eyes. War veterans, she thought. To keep herself from staring, she turned back to the Kapitän and locked her gaze on his eyes.

If he noticed her shock, he didn't let on. "Would you like to see how we pilot the ship?" he said.

"Very much," said Helene, gripping the little chimera nervously.

Kapitän Siodmak swept his mechanical arm toward an intricate control panel that took up much of the room. Helene approached it tentatively. A complex array of dials, switches, gauges, and levers covered the console, which was strangely shaped. Instead of the hard lines she expected, the control panel was somewhat rounded, with small pipes that looked like veins running along the top and sides. The panel appeared vaguely organic to her, which wasn't nearly as startling as what she saw under a glowing dome in the forward center of the console. There was a large knotted mass of what looked like pink tissue. It pulsed slightly with each bump and turn of the ship.

"Is that . . . ?" she said.

"A chimera?" said the Kapitän. "Why, yes, it is. It's why I'm able to chat with you. Our little friend here can pilot the ship for short periods and even set course for us. In case of emergency, it can help us land, but I don't recommend the experience. It's usually a bit bumpy." The crew chuckled quietly at that.

Before she could stop herself, Helene said, "Is that what happened to your arms?" The moment the words were out of her mouth she went pale, shocked by her own rudeness. "I'm sorry. I had no right to ask."

The Kapitän shook his head. "It's perfectly all right. And yes, that is what happened."

"In the war?" she said.

"Yes."

"I'm sorry."

"There's no need. I was happy to do my duty."

Feeling awkward now and wanting to leave as soon as possible, Helene said, "Thank you very much, Herr Kapitän. I've truly enjoyed meeting you and your crew."

However, before she could leave, the Kapitän said, "Actually, I was hoping that you could help us for a moment."

She looked at him and wondered if he was mocking her for her impertinent question. "I don't understand what you mean," she said.

Siodmak pointed out the window at the front of the room. "We'll be turning into an area with more airships soon. We like to warn them of our approach with a signal flare. I was wondering if you'd like to send it up for us."

Helene smiled. "You're not making fun of me, are you?" she said.

The Kapitän shook his head. "Not at all. It's a simple procedure and quite pretty to see. But, of course, if you're not interested—"

"But I am. Really."

"Then step over here, please."

Attached to the bulkhead was what looked like a pistol grip connected to a long tube that led outside the ship. The Kapitän took a brass cylinder from a small box nearby and loaded it into the tube.

"Is that the flare?" said Helene.

"Yes. There's a small chimera inside."

Helene frowned. "The flare is a chimera?"

"You'll see," said the Kapitän. He cocked the hammer on the gun and stepped aside.

Helene approached the gun nervously and wrapped her hand around the grip. It was bulky and slightly cold—probably, she thought, from the outside winds coming down the metal tube. She looked at Siodmak and said, "Now?"

"Whenever you like."

She pressed Frölich's little pet to her chest and squeezed the trigger. There was a loud *whump* as the flare shot up and out of the ship. A few seconds later, it burst into purple flames. The chimera was like a fiery bat, flapping its wings as it climbed into the sky. Helene craned her neck to watch it go. A few seconds later, there was a bright flash of light as the bat exploded above the dense clouds overhead. Then something fell from the sky—a thousand small, burning points of light, like a rain of diamonds.

Below the ship, the clouds parted for a moment and Helene could see the edges of the city and her home, Empyrean. For the first time in a long while, she felt at ease. Forward in the ship, Frölich and some of the older men would be talking about steel production and plazma stores for the army. But here, between the ground and the burning clouds above, there were no worries. No talk about the restless poor or war. Helene never wanted to see the city again. She wanted to explode in the sky and rain down on the world like burning jewels.

Eventually, though, she thanked the Kapitän, the Leutnant, and the rest of the crew and made her way forward again. After delivering the little chimera back to Frölich, Helene went into the greenhouse observation deck and found the window he'd pried open earlier. In a few seconds, the freezing wind numbed her face. It would be so easy, she thought, to step out into the sky like the little bat. Helene wondered how far up she could go if she jumped as hard as she could . . .

The rain grew heavy, though, and soon she closed the window and returned to the party. Helene found Greta still wedged between Orlok and Gustav on the pillows. She and Orlok were making love, but drunken Gustav had fallen asleep. Helene pushed him aside and kissed Greta as Alex pulled her down to join in the fun.

CHAPTER FIVE

DR. VENOHR HAD BEEN RIGHT. WHEN REMY WOKE UP IN THE MORNING SHE appeared to be fine. She didn't even remember getting sick at the party.

"It was very frightening," Largo said. "You scared everybody."

Remy patted his cheek. "You don't have to worry about me, silly boy. I'm not going anywhere." Before he could say anything, she looked down at herself and then at Largo. "Why are we still dressed?"

"I told you. You were sick. Dr. Venohr and I put you straight to bed."

She tilted her head and looked at him. "I don't mean why are we *dressed*. I mean why aren't we *undressed*?" Remy pulled her dress off and threw it on the chair. Naked, she began to unbuckle Largo's belt as he quickly unbuttoned his shirt. He barely got it off in time. Remy tugged his pants down over his thighs and climbed on top of him, guiding his cock inside her. Together, they rocked and thrust and scratched each other's bodies. Largo was amazed that this was the same woman he'd carried home comatose the night before. However fragile she'd seemed then, that was all gone now. This was the Remy he knew. His Remy. And she dug her nails into his chest as she made a few last violent thrusts down onto him before holding still and squeezing him with her thighs. He laughed. Her strong, athletic body held him in place. He couldn't have moved if he'd wanted to. Finally, Remy relaxed and fell heavily on top of him.

Still breathing hard, he said, "Well, that was unexpected."

"Because I'm such a delicate flower?" said Remy.

"Because you were as dead-eyed as one of your theater dolls last night."

"I trust I've convinced you that I'm not about to collapse like an old hausfrau or deflate like a balloon?"

"I pronounce you fit enough to fight an ox."

She kissed him just as the bell in the Triumphal Square rang the half hour. Largo sat up and looked at the little clock on Remy's bedside table.

"Shit," he said. "I have to get to work."

Remy rolled off him reluctantly and said in a joking whine, "I want to prove to you how well I am again. Can't you be just a little late?"

"I'm sorry. I can't. Herr Branca promoted me to chief courier, and he can take the promotion away just as easily."

Remy sat up on her elbows. "Why didn't you tell me? We could have celebrated."

Largo pulled on his pants and shoes. "The party was celebration enough."

"We'll have to do something tonight."

He looked around for his shirt. "Damn. The only shirt I have is the one from the theater. I don't have time to get one of mine. Is it all right if I wear it today?"

Remy lay down on her stomach and waved a hand in his direction. "Go ahead. They'll never miss it."

"Thank you."

"We must at least have some morphia together before you go."

He shrugged into his coat and said, "That sounds lovely." From the gilt table, he picked up the little bottle Dr. Venohr had left the night before. He tossed it to her. "That's for you."

"Ooh," said Remy, pressing the bottle to her cheek. "This will last a while. Where did you get it?"

"A friend," said Largo. He went to the bed and knelt down next to her. "Now hurry. I really have to go."

Remy opened the bottle and squeezed out a drop under each of their tongues. When they kissed, Remy held Largo's face fast in her hands. When he felt the first effects of the drug, he pulled back and gave her a last peck on the lips. "Now I really have to go."

Still naked, Remy followed him through the living room to the door. As they kissed once more, Remy's Trefle rang. She ran to pick it up.

"Dr. Venohr. How nice of you to call. No, I'm fine . . ."

Largo closed the door. It was then that he realized he'd left his bicycle at the Grand Dark the night before. In theory he could take a Mara cab there, but he'd left his tip money at his flat. There was no choice. He took a breath and knocked on Remy's door. She opened it a moment later, still undressed.

"Are you the rent boy I sent for? Hurry inside before my lover finds out," she said breathlessly.

Largo smiled tightly at the joke. "I'm sorry," he said, "but I left my bicycle at the theater and I have no money for a cab or the tram."

Remy went to her purse and brought back a few bills, which she held just out of his reach. "Take this. But just remember that I'm going to make you and your cock earn every penny of it tonight, you tart."

This time Largo's smile was genuine. He took the money, kissed her, and ran out of the building, where he hailed a cab. "The Theater of the Grand Darkness," he said. "And hurry please. I'll pay extra."

"No need, sir," said the Mara.

Largo sat back as it took off through the foggy morning streets. *That was humiliating, asking for money*, he thought. *At least there will be more tips today so I can pay Remy back. Then it will be payday soon. But I can't go on like this if I'm going to convince her to move in with me.*

Largo wondered about Remy's health and whether it had been a good idea to leave her with a full bottle of morphia. He decided that as soon as he had any tip money, he'd call her from a public Trefle.

There was nothing to do but stare out of the window as the cab made its way through the city. Chimeras ate street trash as usual. Drunken couples weaved their way home, also as usual. Posters covered the sides of tram shelters. Ads for the cinema. Antigovernment broadsheets. A faded sign for a performance by Anita Mourlet, billed as the Madonna of Depravity. Largo sighed. It was all so ordinary and dull. And slow. He wondered what time it was.

When the cab finally stopped in front of the Grand Dark, Largo tossed the money Remy had given him to the Mara and dashed out. Thankfully, his bicycle was where he'd left it behind the theater. He unlocked it and sped off to work.

He stayed off the main streets because he knew that they'd be crowded at that hour. He went down trash-strewn alleys and cut through the ruins of buildings that had been hit by stray bombs during the war. Largo went all the way out to the bay and pedaled down the causeway where ships were unloading. Fishermen and scowling dockworkers stared at him. He ignored them as usual—while the route was longer, the empty streets meant he could make up a lot of time.

He steered back onto city streets in the butchers' quarter. Blood pooled on the cobblestones and ran in little clotted rivers down to the sewers. There was a small plaza nearby where old men and young boys had carts where they cooked meat from the shops and sold pieces of it on long yellow skewers. Normally Largo could find a shortcut through it, but today he found the far end blocked—by, of all things, a traveling carnival.

It was promoting its arrival in the city with a small impromptu show. Since it was in the butchers' quarter, clowns juggled raw chunks of meat while pretty women acrobats swung from the old coal gas lamps that lit the plaza at night. A large man in a tiger-striped suit barked orders in a guttural foreign language at a half dozen catlike chimeras as they leaped in the air and came down on their front legs. *They're perfect*, Largo thought. *Just the kind of creatures I'd make.*

But they're making me late.

The happy crowd pressed in around the performers. There was no way for him to get through to the exit, so he turned the bicycle around and went back the way he'd come. All he could do now was go around the butchers' quarter onto the main streets and hope that traffic was clear enough that he could make it to work before six.

Just as he reached the exit, a woman screamed and a man yelled, "Get back!" For a moment, Largo thought they were shouting at him. His first instinct was to get away from whoever was bellowing at him, but when he looked back he saw a man on the ground writhing in convulsions. By his heavy state-issued coat, the mask hiding his face, and a few medals on his chest, Largo identified him as an Iron Dandy. The man's contortions were much worse than Remy's had been the night before. He arched his back so far and hard that it broke, the crack echoing off the plaza walls. His shoulders rolled and his head looked like it wanted to twist itself off his neck. But worse than that, the soldier's arms and legs snapped and bent back at odd, unnatural angles. People shouted for a doctor, but no one would approach the sick man. Even those who'd never seen the Drops knew what it was and no one wanted to risk becoming infected.

Finally, the Dandy's neck cracked and his head flopped back and forth like a dying fish. Blood oozed from his mouth. However, the more Largo looked, the less certain he was about what he saw. What came from the Dandy's mouth wasn't red.

It was black and thick and smelled like scorched oil.

"Don't get it on you," someone shouted, and the crowd moved farther back. Largo felt sympathy for the soldier, but he couldn't waste any more time. He was starting to ride away from the scene when someone grabbed him from behind.

"Where do you think you're going?" said the police officer. He was about Largo's height, with dark lanky hair that fell into his hard eyes. His black uniform had three silver stripes near the cuffs. *A bullock Sergeant*, thought Largo. The officer had a fistful of Largo's coat in one hand and a truncheon in the other.

"Nowhere, sir," said Largo. "I can't think of anywhere else I'd like to be on such a beautiful morning."

The officer looked up at the fog- and smoke-choked sky, then back at Largo. "What a clever young man you are," he said. "Wait here."

The Sergeant left and came back with a man in a long gray coat. He was much older than the Sergeant and very thin, with sharp protruding cheekbones. *An undercover bullock.* Largo despised ordinary police, but this covert one frightened him. Could he have signaled the Sergeant to grab Largo?

The undercover officer wore thick rubber gloves and held a large rolled-up sheet of paper.

"Do you know what this is?" he said.

"I have no idea," said Largo.

The officer let the poster fall open. It was something political. There were strange symbols in one corner. In the center was a burning Proszawan flag being held by a caricatured figure Largo assumed was a politician.

"I'm Special Operative Tanz," said the undercover officer. "What do you know about this?"

"Nothing," said Largo.

"Really? They're all over the city. Are you claiming to have never seen one before?"

"I'm not very political, sir."

Tanz and the Sergeant glanced at each other. The Sergeant said, "What's your name?"

"Largo Moorden."

Tanz said, "That man back there is a radical. An anarchist. How do you know him?"

"I don't," said Largo.

"You were trying to run away," said the Sergeant.

"No, I wasn't. I was going to work."

"You told me you had nowhere else to be."

Largo gave the Sergeant a tentative smile. "It was a joke, sir. I was nervous."

"Nervous?" said Tanz. "About what? Because you knew you'd been caught with a fellow conspirator?"

This was everything he feared, everything he'd been taught to avoid growing up in the Green. He tried to relax and keep his voice steady.

"No. I've just received a promotion and now I'm going to be late."

"Who would give a fool like you a job?" the Sergeant said.

"Besides spreading sedition," said Tanz, "what is it you do?"

"I'm a courier, sir. I deliver documents and packages."

Tanz gave him a look as he rolled up the poster. "What a fine way to distribute propaganda. What's your supervisor's name?"

"Herr Branca."

"His full name," said the Sergeant.

"That's all I know."

The Sergeant made a disgusted sound and spit into the bloody street.

"Didn't we arrest a Branca the other day?" said Tanz. "He was making bombs in his mother's attic. The poor woman had no idea she was harboring a madman."

Largo looked from one man to the other. He knew that no matter what he said, the police would find a way to turn it against him.

"That couldn't be Herr Branca," said Largo. "He's an upstanding supervisor at the company."

"What's the company's name?" said Tanz.

Largo told them. As soon as he said it the officers looked at each other.

"The Nachtvogel," said the Sergeant.

"Yes. They have their eyes on your place of work," said Tanz.

"I swear to you, sirs, I've done nothing wrong."

The Sergeant grabbed him and roughly patted him down. He reached into an inner pocket of Largo's coat and took out a small bottle. "What's this?" he said.

"Medicine," said Largo. "A doctor gave it to me."

Tanz unscrewed the top of the bottle and smelled the contents. "What's the doctor's name?"

Largo's throat went dry. He wished Rainer were there to tell him what to say. He'd been in the army. He knew how to deal with bullocks.

"That's what I thought," said Tanz. "What should we do with him?"

The Sergeant rapped the truncheon against his hand. "An anarchist *and* a drug addict? At headquarters they'd feed him to the dogs."

"Please," said Largo. He looked around and for a moment considered riding away, but that would just confirm the police's worst suspicions. "I'm sorry about the morphia. But I'm not a criminal or an anarchist. I just want to go to work."

Tanz looked over his shoulder. A group of men in thick gray rubber suits with hoods and gas masks were putting the dead veteran's body in a sealed box. Armed Maras patrolled the edge of the crowd, keeping bystanders back.

"You're lucky," sneered the Sergeant. "We have bigger fish to fry than you."

"Go to work, Largo Moorden," said Tanz. "But we'll be checking up on you and your Herr Branca."

The Sergeant said, "You're lucky it's just us. Consorting with a criminal radical like this—people much worse than us would be interested in that."

The Nachtvogel.

Largo couldn't help himself, though. He said, "I wasn't associating with him. He was sick. I was trying to get away."

"You make *me* sick," said the Sergeant.

"Get out of here," said Tanz.

It was 6:15 before Largo arrived at the office. Other couriers were already filing out with parcels and letters. Some grinned and a few sneered at him, knowing what was waiting for him inside. Andrzej bumped his shoulder into Largo's on the way out. "What happened to you?" said Parvulesco. "Branca asked about you twice."

Largo shook his head. "I'll tell you later." His friend gave him a pat on the arm and went to his bicycle.

Margit was the last courier to come out of the office. She was small and blond and wore her hair short like a young boy's. Because it was rumored that she preferred women romantically, some of the other couriers teased her constantly. Her eyes were covered by glasses with round dark lenses. Largo lightly touched her elbow. "I need to speak to you," he said.

She raised an eyebrow at him. "About your funeral? Herr Branca has it planned out. We'll all be attending."

"I need some morphia," Largo whispered.

Margit looked around. "I don't have any with me. Maybe at lunch. Do you have cash?"

"I will by then."

"See that you do," she said sternly. "I can't give credit anymore. Even to you."

"Don't worry. I'll have money."

"At lunch then." She turned and went to her bicycle. Largo looked at the door to Herr Branca's office, took a breath, and went inside.

Branca glanced up at him when Largo entered the room. He made a great show of capping his pen and setting it down on his desk. "Thank you for joining us this morning, Largo."

"I'm very sorry I'm late."

"I thought we discussed this. As chief courier, you have to be an example to the others."

"Yes sir. I understand, but the bullocks, that is, the police wouldn't let me go."

Branca frowned and came around his desk. "The police? What did you do to attract their attention?"

"Nothing. There was an incident in the butchers' quarter and I was trying to leave."

"What kind of incident?"

"A man was ill. It might have been the Drops."

"How dramatic," said Branca. "Why did the police think it was necessary to question you?"

"They accused me of being the man's accomplice."

Branca stepped closer to Largo. "Accomplice? Accomplice in what?"

"They said he was an anarchist."

Branca opened his eyes wider. "And are you?"

"Sir?"

"Are you an anarchist?"

86

"Of course not."

"That's good," said Branca. "I can't abide seditionists and neither can the company."

"There's something else . . . ," said Largo.

"Well?"

"I'm afraid they might come to talk to you."

"*Here?* You told them where you worked?"

"I had no choice."

"I see. I assume they searched you? What did the officers say when they discovered your knife?"

Reluctantly, Largo said, "I didn't have it."

Branca looked at the ceiling. "Where is it?" he said.

"At home."

"I see. You didn't go home last night?"

"No. I was with a sick friend."

"Of course," said Branca. He looked thoughtful for a moment. "Perhaps it was a lucky thing, this sick friend of yours. If the police suspected you of a crime they might have misconstrued the knife."

"Do you think it's safe for me to continue wearing it?"

Branca clasped his hands behind his back. "You must make a choice. Which is the greater fear: the police, or losing your job and possibly your life?"

"I want to keep my job. And my life."

"A wise choice. See that you don't forget the knife again."

"I won't."

"All right. Enough of this nonsense. You have deliveries to make," said Branca. He went back behind his desk.

"Then I'm not fired?"

"We'll see. I'm not happy about the police incident, but I applaud you for your honesty." Branca looked at a few parcels stacked on a battered wooden worktable. He picked up one and weighed it in his hands. "This will do nicely. I suspect you'll wish you had your knife with you this morning."

Largo looked at the package and wondered what was inside. He tried reading the address, but it was too far away. *Is the old bastard just giving me a hard time or sending me off to get killed?* he wondered. "I'll get the knife during my lunch break," he said.

"Another wise choice," said Branca. "Tell me, does this sick friend of yours have any other friends?"

"Yes. Many."

"Then perhaps one of them can visit tonight so that you won't be tardy tomorrow."

Largo shifted his weight from one foot to the other. "It won't be necessary. She's much better now."

"I'm nearly fainting in delight," said Branca, handing the parcel and an old shoulder bag to Largo, who took them and started out.

"Largo," said Herr Branca.

He stopped and turned around.

"I approve of your shirt. It's good to see you dressing a bit more professionally. I should have the money for your clothing stipend tomorrow. That's all."

Largo nodded to Branca and went out to his bicycle. He was excited at the prospect of having some decent clothes to wear. However, when he read the address on the parcel the excitement evaporated.

I was right.

The prick wants me dead.

Machtviertel had never really been a neighborhood, merely a collection of coal power plants, warehouses, and rail hubs. The plants produced power for much of the western half of Lower Proszawa, but its location had been chosen primarily to provide an endless source of heat and electricity for the armaments factory. However, when it switched to plazma power many years earlier, that left a surplus of coal in the district and more workers than it needed. Yet no one lost their job. The government kept the trains coming and let the coal pile up. They calculated that it was better to pay the workers than let them sit idle. And so the coal continued to grow. The coal continued to burn. And thus Machtviertel became a walled city within the city, ringed by a moat of filth.

Smoke from the coal towers blanketed the district in perpetual darkness. A thick crust of carbonous dust covered everything. Around the active buildings, workers left black footprints in their wake. By the warehouses where trains offloaded their cargo, there were great ebony dunes that turned to thick mud in the rain. Machtviertel had a hellish reputation in the city, partly for the environment, but also for its inhabitants. People lived in the older, disused power stations and warehouses. There was a saying in Lower Proszawa: "Those who live in Machtviertel are insane. But those who seek them out are madmen."

CHAPTER SIX

IT TOOK LARGO ALMOST AN HOUR TO BICYCLE THERE. HE STOPPED BESIDE the largest of the abandoned power plants, commonly known as the Black Palace. When it had been built, the dynamos' home was a showcase for Lower Proszawa's strength and ingenuity. The smokestacks rose one hundred feet into the air and the stonework on the front of the plant had been carved into old mythological scenes. At the top, giants pulled iron from the ground and molded it with volcanic fire. Lower and at street level, smaller spirits and artisans molded the iron into metal towers and wires, spreading light and power to a darkened land. Now, however, the Black Palace was a crumbling ebony hulk of sooty stone and rusted beams in a bleak field of coarse weeds.

Largo chained his bicycle to the base of a collapsed light tower. A murder of crows huddled a few yards away. They lifted off at the sound of his chain on the steel, cawing and circling overhead, black bird-shaped holes against an obsidian sky. He looked up at the building, sure that if Herr Branca wasn't trying to get his throat slit, then the delivery was his supervisor's way of telling Largo that he'd been demoted to the point that he'd spend the rest of his days delivering God knew what to Lower Proszawa's most desolate wastelands.

Maybe I'll be lucky enough to visit High Proszawa's plague pits. Perhaps I'll even get hazard pay. Then I'll be able to afford a new flat and Remy can visit me there as I die of every foul disease known to man.

The address on Largo's parcel was for an office on the Black Palace's fifth floor. He squeezed through a junk-filled gap where the towering front doors had once stood. The building was absolutely silent and as he climbed the stairs Largo began to wonder if the delivery was some kind of sick joke—the company sending him far into the outlands on a pointless trip to remind him that he was lucky to have a job at all. At each landing he became less scared, instead finding himself growing *angrier* at the idea that the trip might be for nothing. Maybe his fellow couriers were above him in the building, waiting for him to knock so they could all laugh in his face.

Andrzej would love that.

On the fifth floor, Largo found the office under a cracked skylight so caked with coal dust that the dim light that made it through a few open areas came down in gray shafts. He held the package under one of the light patches and read the address one last time. Yes, he was at the right door. But the building remained utterly silent. It was strange. In the worst hovels in Haxan Green, there were always sounds of life, even if it was just rats in the walls. The silence of the Black Palace was what Largo imagined being walled up in a tomb must be like.

He went to the office and raised his hand to knock, but instead pressed his ear to the door. No—there *was* a sound. Low and rhythmic. Not the sound of voices or people, but the steady sound of a machine. Now Largo's nervousness returned and he missed having the knife under his coat. His options were limited, and a quick look around showed nothing he might use to defend himself. He either had to turn tail and run, losing his job—and almost certainly Remy—or he could knock. In the end, he had no choice.

He knocked.

Nothing happened for a moment. But when he listened again, the sound of the machine had stopped. Before he could lean back from the door it swung open suddenly. Largo jumped back in surprise. The man in the doorway was as tall as Andrzej, but much larger. He wore a filthy sleeveless undershirt that revealed bulging arms and a barrel chest. His black beard was going gray and his greasy hair was combed straight back from his forehead. But as massive as everything about him was, it was his eyes that caught Largo's attention. They were yellow, as was his skin. *Jaundice*, he thought, and quickly tried to remember if he'd ever heard about yellowed skin having anything to do with the Drops. He didn't get to think very long before the man spoke.

"Who are you?" he said in a deep, rasping voice. "I haven't seen you in the Palace before." The big man wiped sweat from his face with a green bandanna that hung loosely around his neck. His shirt was soaked through and there were large patches of glistening red on the front. To Largo he looked like a thief preparing stolen meat to sell on the black market. *But who would run a butcher shop this far out, even if it is a crooked one?*

Largo stood up straighter and held out the parcel. "I have a delivery for this address," he said. The room behind the jaundiced man looked empty except for the angular shadow of something distinctly machinelike on the back wall.

The man's eyes narrowed. "I'm not expecting anything," he said. Turning, he shouted into the room, "Is anyone expecting a package?"

To Largo's surprise, several voices answered at once, men and women. A woman's voice said, "Who's it from?"

The big man gestured at him. "Who's it from?"

Largo said, "I'm sorry, but there's no return address."

Footsteps echoed as someone else came to the door. A woman said, "Let me see," and pushed the big man out of the way.

Largo leaned forward when he saw her, surprised.

"Margit?" he said.

She froze and stared at him. Her voice was angry. "What the hell are you doing here? I told you I'd see you at lunch."

"I know, I know. I'm here because of the parcel." He held it up, as if it were all the explanation needed.

"You know this whelp?" said the jaundiced man.

Margit patted him on the arm. "It's all right, Pietr. Largo is a friend from work."

"One of your customers, I suppose? An addict?"

"No—shut up. Look at him. He just uses for fun, like a lot of people. Isn't that right, Largo?"

"Yes," he said quickly. "Just for fun." But he was already feeling a chill from the lack of morphia.

"What's he doing *here*?" said Pietr, menace creeping into his voice.

Margit took the parcel from Largo's hands and looked it over. "This is the right address. Someone must have sent for it."

"That's madness," said a man Largo couldn't see. "No one would do that."

"You can't speak for everyone. They're not all here," Margit said.

"To hell with this," Pietr said. He snatched the parcel from Margit, pulled out a stiletto, and cut open the wrappings. There were six

93

large jars inside, each one a different color. The big man pulled one out and showed it to Margit. "Ink," he said.

"Yes. I can see," said Margit. "It has to be one of the others. We do need more ink."

"I don't like it," growled the jaundiced man. "Maybe we should keep him here until everyone arrives."

"I'm telling you, Pietr, Largo is no one to worry about," said Margit. She turned to Largo. "You should go now. Please don't tell Branca you saw me."

"Of course not," said Largo. "I take it you're not here making a delivery, are you?"

Margit gave him a thin smile. "Hardly," she said. She reached into a pocket of her coat and pressed a bottle into Largo's hand. "Forget what you've seen here. All right?"

"But I have to tell Herr Branca something. And someone needs to sign for the package."

Pietr and some of the other unseen people laughed. The big man took Largo's receipt book, scrawled something in it, and shoved it back into Largo's hands. Margit said, "That should be enough for the old bear."

Largo looked at the signature. It was an indecipherable scrawl of loops and slashes. "It looks fine," he said. "But what are you doing here?"

"None of your business," a voice yelled from the back, while at the same time the jaundiced man said, "Trying to educate fools like you."

"I don't understand."

Pietr disappeared for a moment and—after what seemed like a whispered argument with whoever else was inside—came back with a piece of paper. He thrust it into Largo's hand. The ink was still tacky and some smeared on Largo's fingers. There was a small target symbol in the bottom right corner. "Here," said the big man. "Now the audience is over." He started to close the door, but Margit caught it.

"I'll talk to you later," she said. "By the gate. After work."

"I'll see you there," Largo said, still confused by the scene.

For the first time Pietr smiled. His teeth were dark and stained. "Be careful that the crows don't peck your eyes out, pup," he said, and slammed the door shut. Largo pressed his ear against it and heard shouting voices on the other side.

Largo didn't linger to hear what they were arguing about. He shoved the paper Pitr had given him into his pocket and ran down the stairs.

He composed himself as he got to the ground floor, however, knowing that like the Green, Machtviertel wasn't a place to show fear. He'd missed his chance with the people upstairs, but he could at least appear unconcerned to anyone outside.

But then Largo remembered the bottle Margit had put in his hand.

He took it from his pocket. It was morphia. A bottle of it as big as the one Dr. Venohr had given him at Remy's. He stood in a shadow by the stairs and stared at it happily. He quickly unstoppered it and put two drops under his tongue. Almost immediately, the chills left him and a gentle warmth moved through his muscles and bones. *Pure morphia*, he thought. *Not watered down. Magical.*

Feeling much better, he put the receipt book into his shoulder bag and made his way out of the Black Palace to his bicycle. As he unchained it, the crows shuffled and cawed at him, utterly unafraid. But with the morphia in his system, so was Largo. He rode swiftly back toward the courier depot.

On his way out of Machtviertel, however, Largo had a coughing fit so violent that he had to stop on the side of the road. When he blew his nose with a handkerchief, what came out was as black as soot. As good as the morphia made him feel, he was still relieved to put Machtviertel behind him.

It was a long ride back to the office.

CHAPTER SEVEN

HERR BRANCA SET DOWN HIS PEN AND APPLAUDED MIRTHLESSLY WHEN Largo arrived. "The prodigal son returns, and in one piece. Did you receive a warm welcome in Machtviertel?"

"I was greeted with open arms. At least by the crows."

"And the people?"

"They were more reluctant, but I successfully delivered the parcel."

"Merely reluctant?" said Branca. "I hadn't heard that shyness was common among the denizens of the district."

"Maybe 'shyness' isn't the right word. They certainly weren't used to receiving deliveries."

Branca leaned on his desk. "What were they like, your reluctant customers?"

Largo thought carefully about his answer. He'd formulated a story on the ride back, but the morphia let his mind drift and now he couldn't remember much of it. "There was a man and woman. An old couple. They didn't want to come to the door at first, but I talked to them until they were reassured that it was safe to accept the package."

"That was very professional of you. It was just the two of them then?"

"As far as I could see."

Branca put out his hand. "Do you have your receipt book?" Largo handed it to him and he looked it over. "That's quite a signature. Is it the man's or woman's?"

Even light-headed from the morphia, Largo remembered the most basic rule of lying: stay as close to the truth as possible. "The man's. It is a bit of a mess, isn't it? His hand shook a bit as he signed it."

"That explains it, then. I take it there was nothing else interesting or notable at the Black Palace?"

Largo looked at his supervisor. "You've been there?"

Branca placed the receipt book in a desk drawer. "Many times," he said. "I wasn't born behind this desk, you know. I made my share of deliveries when I was your age."

Largo tried to picture a young Branca riding a bicycle through traffic, cutting around pedestrians, cabs, and speeding military juggernauts. It was like something from a dream of flying—very strange and extremely hard to believe.

"I'm sure it's changed since you were there, but it was my first trip so I'm not sure what qualifies as unusual. Perhaps if I go back sometime—"

He immediately regretted saying it. *What if the bastard takes it as an invitation to make me the company's representative to the hinterlands? I'll have cancer in a year and no tips to show for it.*

Herr Branca turned his head and looked at Largo from an odd angle. "Did you hurt yourself on the way back?" he said.

Largo looked down at himself. "I don't think so."

"Your hand is bleeding."

Damn, he thought. He wiped his fingers on his coat. "I'm fine, sir. It's just a little ink."

"Ink from what?"

Damn again. Why didn't I wash my hands on the way in? he thought. It was the morphia, of course. He promised himself to be more careful in the future.

"Just something I found on the street on the way out of Machtviertel. To tell you the truth, I didn't even read it."

"Do you still have it?"

Largo felt stuck like a butterfly with a pin through its middle. If he said he didn't have it Branca would ask why he didn't say that in the first place. And what if Branca searched him and found the paper *and* the morphia? That would be the end of all his dreams. Besides, he didn't really owe them anything—although thinking about Margit made him feel a bit unsure. Still, he couldn't think of any alternatives, so he gave in. Largo patted his pockets, trying to look calm and composed. He smiled when he seemed to discover the paper in one of them, and reluctantly handed it over.

Branca opened the sheet and scanned it slowly. "Did you read this?"

"No, sir. What does it say?"

"Seditionist trash," said Branca. "You say you found it on the ground?"

"Yes, sir."

Branca turned the paper over and looked at the back. "It's remarkably free of dirt. And the ink was still wet when you found it? I can't say I'm surprised. Machtviertel is swarming with radical hotheads. It's all the dust, you see. It addles the brain."

Largo nodded, trying to look as if he agreed completely. "That makes sense."

Branca looked back at the paper. "You should be careful about what trash you pick up in the future. Your policeman friend—Tanz, I believe, is his name—was here earlier. After the incident this morning, I can't imagine what he'd think if he found this on you."

Just hearing the undercover officer's name made Largo tense. The sweet calm of the morphia all but disappeared. He thought about the Sergeant and what he'd said earlier. *"An anarchist and a drug addict? At headquarters they'd feed him to the dogs."*

"I see what you mean. I'll be more careful in the future."

Branca wadded up the paper and threw it in the trash. From a desk drawer, he removed a new receipt book and handed it to Largo. "For this afternoon's deliveries."

Largo was putting the book in his shoulder bag when something occurred to him. "Excuse me. This book is new, as was the one you gave me this morning. If you don't mind me asking, will I always get new receipt books?"

Branca held out the previous receipt book so that Largo could see the red stains along the edges. "This one is soiled. We can't have our customers signing dirty books, can we?"

"No, of course not."

"I'm glad you approve." Branca took out a pocket watch and checked it against the office clock. "You had a long ride this morning. You may take an early lunch so that you can go home and fetch your knife."

"Thank you," said Largo.

"And wash that filth off your hands before you contaminate another book."

"Right away, sir."

Branca picked up a Trefle that sat on the side of his desk and waited for the operator. He flicked his wrist, waving the back of his hand. "That's all, Largo. You may go."

"I'll be back soon."

"How delightful."

Largo went to the employee toilet near the loading dock and washed the red ink off his hand with a coarse bar of gray soap.

With the extra time, Largo was tempted to have another drop of morphia, but he couldn't afford to be foggy-headed again. He checked an inside pocket of his coat and found the vial of cocaine. It was just small enough that the Sergeant hadn't found it earlier, especially after he'd been distracted by the morphia. Largo thought it over and decided to use a little powder when he was back at his flat. It would sharpen him up for his afternoon deliveries and still leave enough to share with Remy in the evening.

With those warm thoughts, the morning was already fading away.

When he reached Little Shambles, the traveling carnival he'd seen earlier in the butchers' quarter was there, giving another impromptu performance. Largo hung at the back of the crowd at first, not watching the show but looking at the people, scanning the ragged mob for the police. When he didn't see any he got closer—but stayed on his bicycle in case he had to get away quickly.

The performers were the same ones he'd seen in the morning. Keeping with the habits of Little Shambles, the clowns didn't juggle meat this time but bottles of beer and whiskey. The beautiful acrobats did tumbling runs in the dirty street. There were some contortionists he'd missed earlier, bending themselves in unpleasant ways that reminded Largo of the convulsing man. Not wanting to relive that moment, he went around to the far edge of the crowd, where the chimeras were performing.

The tiger-suited man was there, barking orders at the small cat-like creatures. Now Largo finally got a good look at them. They were hairless and had large, comical ears. The bare skin along their sides and legs changed colors as they went through their routines. At one moment they were striped with purples and at another spotted red. When they ran and jumped, they pulsed with a dozen colors, as if fireworks were going off under their skin. *So beautiful*, he thought. *To be able to create such things.*

He could have spent all afternoon there, but he needed to go to his flat, have lunch, and get back to the office without being late for once. It was heartbreaking to leave such beauty behind for something as mundane as another round of idiotic deliveries, but when he remembered the cocaine in his coat, it wasn't quite as depressing.

After pedaling the last few blocks, Largo ran up the filthy stairs to his flat and locked the door. He put the harness and knife on first, got his bag, and then went to the tin box under his mattress and took a few coins for lunch and a Trefle call. Before he left, he laid a short, thick line of cocaine on the back of his hand and sniffed it up. At the bottom of the stairs, the rush and sense of well-being and beauty were overwhelming. Largo took off on his bicycle, thinking of Remy naked in her flat, her skin crawling with light and colors, catlike and perfect.

As the ride progressed, however, he began to worry. What if she'd had another attack?

He stopped at a crowded little café called Fräulein Sabel, where the couriers often had lunch. Several of them were there when he arrived, including Parvulesco, who pointed to his beer, asking if Largo wanted one. He shook his head and pointed to the public Trefle on the back wall. Parvulesco nodded. Largo made his way through the crowd and put a couple of coins into the slot on the Trefle's side. An operator answered and Largo gave him Remy's number. After a dozen rings he hung up. She never let the Trefle ring more than two or three times. That meant that either she was sick or she had gone to the theater. When the Trefle returned his coins, he put them in again and had the operator connect him to the Grand Dark. After a few rings, Ilsa answered. Largo waited while she found Remy and had to put two more silver coins into the Trefle so that the operator wouldn't end the call. A moment later Remy answered. The cocaine and the sense of well-being had worn off and it was a relief to hear her voice.

"I'm fine, darling. You shouldn't be such a goose."

"Honk, honk," he said.

She laughed. "I do have one bit of bad news, though."

"What's that?"

"Una wants us to put up the new show sooner than anyone expected, so I'll be stuck here doing rehearsals all night."

Largo scratched his head and looked back at the other couriers. Half of them were drunk—which was normal—and the other half were looking at him in disgust. All except Parvulesco. "That's all right. I understand," he said, disappointed but happy she would be with people who would look after her.

"We'll celebrate your promotion tomorrow."

"That sounds like fun. I might stop off later and see Rainer."

"Give him my love. And Largo?"

"Yes?"

"Honk for me one more time."

"Honk, honk," he said.

"I love you, goose. See you tomorrow."

"Tomorrow."

When he started out of the bar, Andrzej and Weimer shouted, "Honk! Honk!" Energized by having survived Machtviertel and hearing Remy's voice, Largo casually spun and kicked the table, knocking bottles in all directions and spilling beer on both of them. Their yells of surprise followed him as he walked—not ran—out quickly. Parvulesco and a few of the others laughed. Largo was already on his bicycle when Andrzej and Weimer came running out of the café. He knew he'd pay for it in some way, but he couldn't resist shouting, "Honk! Honk!" as he rode away.

With the last of his money, Largo bought a skewer of meat from a cart and ate it while riding to the office. None of the other couriers were back when he arrived.

As he went inside, Branca checked both his watch and the office clock. "Will wonders never cease. You're early."

"I hope the shock isn't too great," said Largo.

"I am taken aback, but will endeavor to survive, thank you."

Largo walked to Branca's desk and said, "Am I off on another adventure this afternoon? Perhaps the South Pole or the swamps of one of the southern colonies?"

Branca laced his fingers together and looked at him. "Careful, Largo. Not everyone here has as vivid an imagination or as fanciful a sense of humor as you."

Largo realized that he'd been speaking to Herr Branca the way he would to another courier. The worst Andrzej could do was break his nose. Branca could ruin his life. Largo took a step back. "Sorry, sir. I just had an altercation with some unpleasant characters and I'm still a little . . ."

"Overwrought?"

"That's a good word for it."

"Do you have your knife?" said Branca.

Largo opened his coat to show him the blade in its harness.

Branca said, "Did you show it to these ruffians?"

"No. It didn't occur to me."

"Why not?"

"I'm not sure," said Largo.

"Were they people you know? Were they people that perhaps *I* know?" Branca stared at him.

Largo looked at the floor and shook his head. "I doubt it, sir."

"Oh well. These things happen. In the future, though, you might consider at least revealing your weapon. I've found that the possibility of a sudden, violent end has a mollifying effect on even the most enthusiastic bully."

"That sounds like good advice. I'll remember it."

"See that you do." Branca went through the papers on his desk before speaking again. "Now, as to your possible expedition to the South Pole, I'm afraid I'm going to have to disappoint you."

Largo shuffled his feet, hoping he hadn't bought himself another punishing assignment.

Branca turned his eyes up from the papers and looked at him. "No little joke this time?"

"No, sir."

"Good. Now, I did have you scheduled for a rather important delivery this afternoon, but the parcel has been delayed, so you'll be doing it bright and early tomorrow morning."

"Might I ask where the important delivery was going, sir?"

A Mara brought a letter from the back room. Branca made a note of it and set it on his desk. "If you must know, the armaments factory," he said.

"Schöne Maschinen?"

"The very same."

The factory had dominated the landscape of Lower Proszawa for as long as Largo could remember. Its belching smokestacks dictated whether there was sun or days of perpetual gloom. It occurred to Largo that in all the years he'd stared at the factory, he'd never seen anything but Black Widows, juggernauts, and supply trucks enter or leave the place. No people. Tomorrow, though, he would do it on his bike. The idea made him feel very small. And yet the prospect of seeing the factory's interior was exciting—and one more thing he could tell Remy tomorrow during their celebration.

Largo spent the rest of the afternoon making deliveries to the wealthiest areas of Kromium and one to the Empyrean, where his new shirt seemed to make him acceptably invisible to both doormen and the local police. After Machtviertel, it was a dull way to end the day, but at least these customers gave proper tips, and by the time he rode back to the office his trouser pocket was heavy with silver and small gold coins.

When he handed in his receipt book Branca barely glanced at it before setting it aside. He said, "I have some good news for you."

"What's that, sir?"

"Our superiors have approved the stipend for the purchase of clothing more suitable for the chief courier." Branca took a white envelope from a desk drawer and handed it to Largo. "I trust you remember our earlier conversation. These are clothes to be worn only when you are making deliveries or conducting other company business."

"I remember," said Largo.

"Good. I hope you also remember your promise that I will not have to accompany you when you make your purchases."

"Absolutely. I have a friend who works in the theater. She has a good eye for costumes, that is, clothing. She can help me."

"Interesting," said Branca. "What theater, may I ask?"

"The Theater of the Grand Darkness."

Branca's eyes narrowed. "I've never attended any of their productions, but I've certainly heard about them. Are you sure she's a suitable advisor?"

"Completely. She herself doesn't dress like her characters. In fact, she was the one who suggested I wear this shirt today."

Branca considered that for a moment. "That is more encouraging. Very well. Have her advise you, but remember that we aren't looking for gigolos or ballerinas. You'll be representing the company, so simple, professional attire is what you want."

"I'll explain that to her. Don't worry. She'll do a good job."

"Good, because if you come back dressed like a buccaneer or a limp-wristed dandy, the price of the clothing will be deducted from your salary."

"I understand," Largo said, wanting to get away from Branca and his lectures. "We won't let you down."

The older man murmured, "It's not a matter of letting me down. It's not letting *yourself* down. It's a good motto to follow both in business and in life."

"I'll remember that," said Largo, doing his best to look thoughtful while imagining the bastard falling down a very long flight of stairs.

Branca glanced at the clock. "With the Schöne Maschinen delay there are no more deliveries for you today, and as most of the other couriers have finished their rounds, you may go."

Largo's mouth went dry at the phrase *most of the other couriers have finished their rounds.* That probably meant that Andrzej and Weimer were lurking around somewhere. Perhaps it was time to take Branca's advice and reveal his knife. Still, it was a hard thing to imagine doing. The threat would only enrage Andrzej more, provoking an attack. With the police already on the watch for him, Largo wondered how stabbing another employee would appear to them.

"Good night, sir," Largo said. He left the office but not the building, instead going to the employee toilet, where he splashed water on his face. He knew he could run, but with bullies like Andrzej there would always be tomorrow and the day after that. Besides, he'd promised to meet Margit after work. He was anxious to hear her explain the scene in Machtviertel.

The more he thought about Margit, the more nervous he became about the flyer he'd given Branca earlier in the day. What if the police came back and found it? It would be bad for him, of course, but with company records they could trace it back to the Black Palace and Margit. It was obvious that she was mixed up with radicals, but it was becoming just as obvious to Largo that he didn't want to be the cause of her going to prison.

He knew what he had to do.

Largo walked by Branca's office as if he were leaving. When he saw that the old man wasn't there, he went to the wastebasket and started pulling out trash, piling it on the floor next to him. When he was almost to the bottom of the basket he heard someone clear his throat behind him.

"Are you looking for something in particular, Largo, or have you simply developed a passion for trash collecting?" said Branca.

Largo didn't bother looking back but began refilling the wastebasket. Worse than being caught was that the flyer wasn't with the other papers.

He stood up and said, "I'm sorry, sir. I thought I might have dropped something in the trash on my way out."

Branca continued looking at him in his usual probing, disapproving way. "I'm afraid that the morning trash is gone and currently resides in the large receptacles by the loading dock. They're quite easy to get to if you'd care to spend the rest of your evening burrowing through filth."

Largo stood and brushed dirt off his trousers. "No, sir. It wasn't that important."

"What was it? I can keep a watch for it in case it wasn't taken away properly."

Largo wiped off his hands and edged his way around the room to the door. "It was nothing, really. Just a trifle."

"I see," said Branca. "In that case, good night once again—and for the last time, I hope."

"Good night," said Largo, and he hurried outside to his bicycle. As he got on, he debated one more time whether he should run or keep his promise to Margit. Finally, he decided that running wouldn't do anyone any good. As he waited by the gate he pressed his arm against his side. Though he knew it was too dangerous to use the knife— *Damn bullocks*—the pressure of it on his ribs was reassuring.

To Largo's surprise, Parvulesco leaned out from behind a nearby delivery van. He came over a moment later and offered Largo a cigarette. Though he wasn't normally a tobacco smoker, Largo accepted it. Parvulesco tapped a cigarette for himself, lit Largo's, and then his own.

"Why are you hanging around this dung heap?" said Parvulesco.

"I'm supposed to meet Margit," said Largo.

"What would Remy say?"

"Ha," he said, rolling his eyes.

Parvulesco laughed. "By the way, that was marvelous, what you did in the café today. Andrzej and Weimer came in from lunch smelling like a saloon pisser. Branca didn't take it well."

"I suppose Andrzej is looking for me?"

"With murder in his heart, I'm afraid."

Largo looked around. "I suppose I deserve it. What do you think? Should I run?"

Parvulesco put an arm around Largo's shoulder. "Stay here with me. You'll be fine."

Largo raised an eyebrow at the smaller man. "You're going to protect me from that mad gorilla?"

Parvulesco smiled. "That's *exactly* what I'm going to do."

Largo had no idea what his friend was talking about, so he smoked and waited for Margit and what seemed like an almost inevitable beating. He'd barely finished his cigarette when Parvulesco said, "Here they come."

He looked over his shoulder and saw Andrzej heading his way with Weimer and several other couriers.

"Waiting was stupid," said Largo.

"Not for this," said Parvulesco.

The approaching couriers all grinned, except for Andrzej. As he got closer and saw Parvulesco, however, a mean smile spread across his broad face.

"There they are, lads, a couple of sodomite sisters. Having a post-bugger smoke, are you?"

Weimer and the others laughed. Naturally, thought Largo. The rules are the same everywhere: the leader laughs and so do you. The laughter appeared to encourage Andrzej to continue. Largo looked over his shoulder, calculating his chances of running from the mob. They weren't good, he decided. And showing fear at this point would just make things worse.

"I wonder which of them gives it and which one takes it up the ass?" said Andrzej. "But no. Now that I say it, the answer is obvious. Parvulesco is a prancing fawn, but Largo is the type who would enjoy the taste of dirt when he gets his ass in the air in an alley." Andrzej looked back at the others. "Should we help them out, boys? Give them what they like best, a good cocking? We could drag them into one of those trucks."

As Andrzej said the word *trucks*, a large man appeared from around the side of the delivery van where Parvulesco had been waiting earlier. He wore leather pants and jacket, and while he wasn't as tall as Andrzej, he was half again as broad and all of it was muscle.

"Look," said Andrzej. "It was a threesome they were having. Well, the more, the merrier. He can go in the truck with the others—"

It was clear to everyone from his tone that Andrzej had meant to go on longer, but he was stopped when the man from the truck drove a heavy boot into his midsection. Andrzej fell with a wheezing groan. As soon as he was on the ground, the truck man began kicking him in the ribs and groin. He stopped just long enough for the disoriented Andrzej to roll onto his back in an effort to crab-walk away. With that, the truck man dropped his weight onto Andrzej's chest and punched him in the face until blood flew from his nose and mouth.

"Don't stop, Roland," called Parvulesco calmly. "His face isn't nearly as ugly as his heart yet."

When Weimer took a couple of steps toward his friend, Largo got between him and Roland. He opened his coat, making sure that Weimer and the others saw the knife. Weimer stopped in his tracks. He looked from Largo to Roland, who was back to kicking the now-immobile Andrzej. "Please," said Weimer. "He's going to kill him."

"Don't worry," said Parvulesco. "This isn't the first time Roland has had to educate an idiot. He knows when to stop."

The big man kept kicking. Largo looked at Parvulesco, who said, "Roland, dear, I think he's learned his lesson. Don't you?"

Roland stopped midkick and looked at Parvulesco. His teeth were still bared and Andrzej's blood was splattered down his shirt and leather jacket. He looked down again to Andrzej. Roland prodded the prone man with his boot. "If you think so," he said. "They can take him away." He pointed at Weimer. "But *he* has to apologize to you and Largo first."

Weimer looked back at the other couriers for support, but no one stepped forward. He looked down at Andrzej, then to Roland, and said, "I'm sorry."

Roland put a hand to his ear. "Are you a mouse? Say it like a man so everyone can hear you."

Weimer frowned, took a breath, and in a louder voice said, "I'm very sorry. Can I please take Andrzej away now?"

Roland shrugged. "I'm done with him for now," he said, and gave Andrzej one last kick in the ribs. As Weimer and the few remaining couriers gathered around and tried to get him on his feet, Roland grabbed Largo and pulled him over to where Parvulesco waited, a lit cigarette in his hand. Parvulesco kissed Roland lightly on the lips and made a face. "You're filthy," he said.

"It's your fault. You didn't tell me that Andrzej character was a bleeder."

Parvulesco held up the cigarette and said, "Open." Roland opened his lips and Parvulesco placed the cigarette there. Roland took a couple of puffs and put his arms around Parvulesco.

Largo didn't realize how scared he'd been until the feeling began to subside. "Thank you," he said. "I don't know what would have happened if you hadn't been here."

"It was a hell of a coincidence, wasn't it?" said Roland.

Parvulesco said, "He's right. This was in no way an ambush."

Largo smiled with them. "Mere happenstance," he said.

"Now you get it," said Roland.

"Then I thank providence *and you*."

Roland made a face and held out his hand. "Stop thanking everybody and let me get a better look at that fancy blade of yours."

Largo unhooked the knife from the harness and handed it to Roland. He looked it over while Parvulesco oohed and ahhed. "A wicked toy," Roland said. He slipped his hand into the spiked knuckle grip and slashed the air a few times. Largo took a step back. The big man sighted down the blade, weighed it in his hand. Finally, satisfied, he gave it back to Largo.

"It's a beautiful thing. What will you take for it?" said Roland.

Largo snapped the knife back into its harness. "Believe me, if it was mine I'd give it to you. But unfortunately it isn't. It belongs to the company."

"What?" said Parvulesco. "Who gave it to you? Not Branca."

Largo gave him a look. "I was as surprised as you."

"Did he say why?"

Largo held up a hand and let it drop to his side. "König had it before me. Apparently all the chief couriers have it. Something about how the valuables we carry make us more vulnerable."

"You're a target now," said Roland.

"That's the way he put it too."

"He's probably right. You should let me show you how to use that thing."

"You'd do that?" said Largo.

He put his hand on Largo's shoulder. "We sodomite sisters have to stick together."

Largo touched his pocket and felt the weight of his tips. "I think I owe both of you drinks. As many as you can hold down."

"Thanks for the offer, but another time," said Parvulesco. He looked at Roland. "This one needs to go home and scrub little pieces of bully out of his teeth."

"I'm offended," said Roland. "I didn't bite him once. But now that you bring it up, I'm sorry I didn't."

"I think Herr Andrzej and the others understood the message. No need to resort to cannibalism."

"Yet," said Largo.

Roland pointed at him. "See? He understands."

Parvulesco got his bicycle and pulled Roland away with him. "It's time to go, dear. Have a good night, Largo."

"Thank you again."

As he started to leave, Largo heard a roar from behind the truck Parvulesco had appeared from earlier. Roland, on a heavy motorbike, sped out around it, towing Parvulesco on his bicycle. Largo watched them go until the sound of the motorbike's engine died away. As he got on his own bicycle, it occurred to him that Margit had never arrived.

Or maybe she did and was scared off by the fight.

In any case, there was nothing he could do about it now. He would speak to her at work tomorrow.

As he rode away, the knife tapped lightly against his ribs. He thought about how he'd shown the thing to Weimer but had made no move to take it out. Between Andrzej's brutal threats and seeing Roland charge at him with no thought of backing down, Largo replayed the scene over and over again in his mind. He took it apart and put it back together again in different ways, with different outcomes. Roland's charge didn't work. He was attacked and killed by the other couriers and Largo did nothing. Largo himself was taken down by the mob. Andrzej found Largo's knife and used it against Roland and Parvulesco. Largo ran away before anything happened. Or Largo stayed and was killed with his own knife.

The two constants in these alternate versions of the events were Andrzej's confidence and Largo's lack of it. It was one thing to mime strength, as he'd learned to do, but it was another to have it in your blood.

Largo's hands shook as he rode home. When he reached the door to his building his stomach cramped with tension. He had to stop and lean against a wall. For a few seconds it was hard to breathe. Grasping in his pocket, he pulled out the vial and put two drops of morphia under his tongue, waiting what felt like forever for them to take effect.

Over the next few minutes, his fear lessened and the cramps subsided enough that he could walk upstairs to his flat. Largo's hands still shook and he fumbled with his keys, but by the time he got inside and turned on the piss-yellow overhead light he could breathe again. He was still angry and scared, but the fear had transfigured itself into something hard and bright.

Next time, he thought. *With Andrzej or any of the others—if it comes down to it, I won't flash the knife.*

I'll use it.

THE REFUGEE ROAD

From *A Young Person's Guide to the Great War*

In the days leading up to the Great War, when rumors ran rampant, High Proszawa's wealthiest families began the trek south. Not long after, the rumors reached a fever pitch, with stories about devastating battles and atrocities along the northern front. After that, the flood of affluent refugees doubled. The most prosperous families left their mansions and estates in the care of their loyal servants, while others were forced to sell them off for a pittance.

After moving to Lower Proszawa, High Proszawa's elite began buying the city's most desirable properties at a furious rate. Whole blocks of chateaus and ancient manor houses were snapped up overnight. Because most of the city's industry had been conscripted into the war effort, few new homes were being built. Property prices exploded to the point where the middle class and the poor (including the servants left behind in High Proszawa) who followed were pushed into refugee areas in the least desirable districts of Lower Proszawa.

After the war, some of the middle-class families recovered, but the poor remained exiled in run-down districts near the wharves and industrial areas. And while the price of property dipped in the early postwar days, it never returned to its prewar levels. Partly this had to do with the disappearance of a number of neighborhoods due to stray bombs. Regardless of the reason, with land prices still high, many of those houses were never rebuilt. Rather, developers simply razed the few standing structures, paving the way for new mansions and luxury tower blocks. Within a year of the armistice, Empyrean doubled in size. Even some of the well-off exiles who'd sold their assets during the early war panic found it difficult to afford their opulent lifestyles. Many families who'd managed to hold on to some of their wealth moved into neighborhoods such as Kromium. This created a rivalry between the districts that was jovial on the surface, but could quickly turn ugly, shattering friendships and family alliances that had lasted generations.

The middle and lower classes settled in Granate and similar districts. The less lucky, especially refugees from the south and the foreign colonies, had to retreat to the worst areas, the docks and the Midden. Exiles with manual work skills who spoke Proszawan could sometimes find work in Machtviertel, where they could pool their resources and rent humble workers' quarters, but those were few and far between.

This situation led to the first of a series of worker uprisings, which we will examine more fully in later chapters. However, it should be noted that many manual laborers, such as road builders and miners—workers with limited skills—resented that Maras were performing the low-wage jobs they coveted. Worker Maras in the streets were routinely stolen or ripped apart and burned. There were even break-ins at the Mara factories, where rioters destroyed production lines. Soon, the angry mobs went after chimeras, killing many of the street cleaners. In two notorious raids, the mob released bitva war chimeras in the wealthy districts. It took days for the authorities to round up the animals. During this time, Empyrean was impassable and residents were forced to remain indoors for several days. The servant Maras they sent out into the chaos to bring back food seldom returned. However, the riots were eventually put down by armed Maras, police, and volunteer soldiers returned from the front.

In the wake of this insurrection, rumors began to spread about the refugees. Many from the frigid northern colonies carried their religion with them, which included rituals involving the skulls and bones of certain tundra deer. After the riots, these artifacts were turned into tales of human skulls by the yellowsheets, which also spread stories of kidnapping, human sacrifice, and disease.

Today, the only outward displays of these old beliefs are in the board games refugee children play using small bones, coins, and other odd objects. Because of their obscure nature and nefarious reputation, the games are said to be favored among unscrupulous gamblers, criminals, and smugglers, and should be avoided at all costs by law-abiding citizens.

CHAPTER EIGHT

RAINER FOXX LIVED IN LYSERGSÄUREHOF, A SMALL SQUARE IN THE POOR-est part of Little Shambles. The streetlights hadn't worked there in years and being situated on the shore of Heldenblut Bay, it was per-petually cold and dripping with sea spray, as if a tidal wave that had swamped the area earlier in the day had just receded. Normally Largo would be wary of bicycling into an unlit part of the district, but Ly-sergsäurehof was so cold and dismal that rats and missing cobble-stones in the street were more worrisome than criminals.

The building where Rainer lived was four stories tall and had once been the office of a shipping company. The company was long gone, but the building remained—at least, for the moment. With each loud footfall or door slam, Largo half expected the old wreck to come tumbling down.

There was no proper lock on the front door. Instead, there was an intricate webbing of rebar and wires. It was like a combination lock. Move this bar, pull that wire, and so on. Do it right, and the web slipped easily away from the entrance. Do it wrong, and any one of Rainer's many booby traps would go off, maiming the interloper. Largo had been to the building many times, but still lived in dread of dropping a slippery wire or sneezing at the wrong moment and find-ing himself impaled on a length of rusty metal or hoisted into the air by a loop of wire around his neck. Tonight, despite his shaky hands, he managed to get into the building unscathed.

He yelled as he trudged up the four floors to Rainer's flat. "Hello! It's Largo. I've brought some food."

The door was open when he reached the fourth floor. He went inside and was relieved by the warmth from the small fireplace. After a brief hug, Rainer motioned for him to come to the large bank of windows that overlooked the bay. The area was crowded with Rainer's collection of telescopes and spyglasses. Largo looked down for some activity in the water, but Rainer pointed at the sky. It took Largo a moment to see what his friend was gesturing at.

The land across the wide bay was sunk in darkness and had been so since the end of the war. It was the southernmost tip of the High Proszawa forbidden zone. The land lay a scorched, lifeless ruin and Largo couldn't figure out why Rainer was so insistent that he look at it. Over the bay a few small airborne Maras flew in crisscross patterns, their wings beating furiously. Largo turned to Rainer. "Night patrols looking for smugglers. What's special about them?"

Again Rainer pointed toward High Proszawa. "Look past them, at the city itself," he said, the sound coming from the speaker horn on a nearby wireless. His voice was less grating than those of most Iron Dandies, but the low amplification made him sound ghostly and far away.

Largo stared across the bay. If there was supposed to be anything there, he couldn't see it. The flying Maras didn't help; the winking lights on their underbellies were very distracting . . .

Then he saw it. A single faint flash of white light, as if an eye had blinked once over the dead city and vanished.

"Did you see?" said Rainer.

"Yes! But . . . what was it?"

"I don't know, but it's not the first time I've seen life across the bay."

Largo laughed once. "*Life*? There's nothing over there. Just a handful of lunatic looters in the ruins."

"*Hnn*," said Rainer, a sound Largo didn't know how to interpret. Hoping to change the subject, he pulled a white bag from his pocket. It was still warm from the bakery and marked with spots of grease. "Spiced meat pies," he said. "I know how much you like them."

"Thank you," said Rainer, patting him on the arm. "My pension from the government is late and I've been running low on provisions."

"I can give you some money. I'm getting good tips these days."

Rainer waved a hand at him. "Thank you, but no. The check will be along any day now." As he said it, he went into the small kitchen and brought back plates, napkins, and a heavy fork for himself. They sat down at Rainer's dinner table—an ornate partner desk abandoned by the shipping company. The wood had warped in the dampness, so nothing on it would lie flat. Glasses and bottles tended to slide off the edge, so Rainer and his guests never drank during meals.

Largo put a meat pie on each of their plates and waited for his friend to prepare his. Rainer was a few years older than Largo and had been a soldier, and a decorated one at that. He had a Red Eagle medal for his wounds and a silver Knight's Cluster for his heroism at the Battle of Liebzeit Valley. It was there that Rainer had lost most of his face. Shrapnel had left deep scars across both cheeks, as if he'd been slashed repeatedly with a saber. His nose was missing and his mouth was a soft angular slit. But his eyes had been spared. They were light blue and in his ruined face, they stood out even more dramatically than before he'd been wounded. He was the only Iron Dandy whom Largo had ever seen with his mask off, and the guilt for his own cowardice during the war knotted his stomach every time they were together. Though he was hungry after a long day's work, Largo left his food untouched while Rainer prepared his.

He used the heavy fork to mash the pie into a soft paste. When he was done, he shoveled a small forkful into his ruined mouth. Rainer was one of the lucky Dandies who had enough of a tongue left that he could still taste food. "It's good," he said through the wireless.

Largo bit into his dinner and said lightly, "I know. I think the baker makes the best pies in the city. I can bring you more if you like."

"That would be nice." They ate in silence for a few minutes before Rainer said, "What have you been up to? You're dressed better than your usual rags. Did Remy find that shirt for you?"

Largo shook his head. "Would you believe it? It belongs to one of the puppets at the Grand Dark. You should come with me one night. I can get us both in for free."

"Thank you, but no."

"Why not? You can't sit up here alone forever." Largo looked around Rainer's flat. The part of his friend that survived from before the war—the clever part who'd built the webbed lock on his front door and made his voice come from the wireless—still believed in science and engineering. Visitors entering his rooms could see it immediately by the collection of star charts, telescopes, and other optical instruments that stood by the windows. The part of Rainer that concerned

Largo was the part that had emerged since he'd locked himself away and become obsessed with spiritualism. The walls were covered with spirit photos and posters of famous clairvoyants. Nearby tables were stacked with books on ghosts and various spirit boards, including an electric model that shocked you if you tried to move the platen on your own. Largo knew that electric boards were expensive and he wondered how much of Rainer's pension money he'd squandered on it.

After a few more bites of pie Rainer said, "Who says that I'm alone?" He pointed to the boards with his fork.

"Rainer, please," said Largo.

"You're right. It's rude of me, trying to entangle you in my personal obsessions."

"It's not that. I just worry about you spending your life listening for voices that, even if they exist, cannot possibly speak."

Rainer nodded but didn't look up from his plate. Largo wondered if it was he and not Rainer who was the rude one.

I shouldn't dismiss his beliefs so easily. Rainer's life is so small these days. Stargazing and ghosts are all he has left. And he was a soldier. He doesn't need mothering. He needs me to listen and be a friend.

Largo started to apologize, but Rainer spoke up first. "Tell me about yourself. It's been a while since we've had dinner. How are you?"

"To tell you the truth, exciting things are happening, but before I go into that, would you mind . . . ?" Largo took out the bottle of morphia and held it up so that Rainer could see. "It's been an eventful day and I could use a bit."

Rainer stopped eating. "Do you have a few drops to spare? My allotment is almost gone and sometimes at night the pain keeps me from sleeping."

"It's too damp in here. No wonder you ache. You need to move somewhere dry."

"I wish it were that simple. What I really need is a skull not held together with screws and wire."

Again, Largo felt a little spasm in his stomach. "Of course I have some to spare," he said. "You go first. Take as many drops as you like."

Rainer accepted the bottle and squeezed five drops into his mouth. Largo was both impressed and worried. *That's more than I've ever taken at one time.* He watched for signs of an overdose as Rainer handed him back the bottle. Largo put two drops under his own tongue. He continued to watch his friend, but Rainer seemed fine.

If that's what he's using these days, no wonder he's running low.

Largo set down the morphia so that Rainer would know it was available if he needed more. But the moment he let go of the bottle, it slid to the edge of the table and Largo had to grab it before it fell. He tried to set it down two more times before both men laughed and he had to put the bottle back in his pocket.

"Let me know if you want more," he said.

"Thank you," said Rainer, "but I'm feeling much better. Now, tell me about the exciting things you mentioned."

"It began just yesterday," Largo said. "First, out of nowhere, I was promoted to chief courier."

"Congratulations. We need to have a drink to that."

"Thank you." Largo told Rainer everything that had happened, from his promotion to his trips to Kromium and Empyrean, his strange visit to the Black Palace, and, finally, the fight with Andrzej.

"Roland is a good man," said Rainer. "We didn't serve in the same regiment, but friends in the trenches would sometimes relay stories about other soldiers from Little Shambles. He was wounded in Liebzeit Valley too, you know."

"I knew he served, but I didn't know he was wounded. He offered to teach me to use my knife."

"He'll do a good job. I'd offer to teach you myself, but I've lost all sense of fighting. These days, the war seems like nothing more than a strange, bloody dream."

"Maybe that's good. Maybe it's better to forget," said Largo.

"I don't want to forget. I just want more control of what I brought back with me."

Largo looked around the room. "Do you mean ghosts? Is that what the boards are for?"

Rainer said, "Ghosts, yes. But they're far away. What I really want is more control of my mind. My memories. Everything in the past runs together. The doctors say it's the nature of my wounds. Psychological trauma and other nonsense. Apparently I didn't just lose my face but also my mind."

"You seem fine to me."

"And who'll vouch for *your* mind?" said Rainer, and they both laughed. In the warmth of morphia, it was easy to do. "How is Remy?"

"Wonderful," said Largo. "She's rehearsing a new play tonight. She's becoming the top actress at the Grand Dark. Really, I wish you'd let me take you one night."

"Perhaps. Let me know if they do a play about the war."

"I'll suggest it to Una."

"Marvelous," said Rainer. Having finished his food, he moved from the dinner table to the flat's sitting area. Largo followed him. They sat across from each other on twin sagging sofas, more castoffs from the shipping company. One of Rainer's extra masks was on the table between them, upside down so that it looked like a metal bowl. It was full of ash and a single hashish cigarette. Rainer lit it, puffed, and passed it to Largo. Largo sucked in the hashish lightly, knowing he still had to bicycle home later. Out of the corner of his eye, he could just see the winking lights of the Maras fluttering over the bay. When he turned to look at them Rainer said, "There's something going on in High Proszawa."

Largo passed the cigarette back. "You mean the flash of light earlier?"

"That and other things. The lights aren't always the same. Sometimes they flash, like tonight. Other times they flit to and fro like fireflies. Some seem to move along the ground. Perhaps even under it."

The morphia and the hashish made Largo sleepy. "They're just lights. Probably reflections from passing ships or the Mara drones flying along the shore."

Rainer sat forward, his elbows on his knees. "But why would Maras fly over a graveyard in the first place?"

Largo shrugged. "Searching for looters?"

"They'd be easier to spot in the bay, where lights from the city reflect on the water."

"Then what?"

Rainer opened his hands in a gesture of unknowing. He puffed the hashish. "One possibility—one that you'll possibly agree with—is that it's the enemy probing for weaknesses through the plague zone."

"Let's all hope it's not that," said Largo. His head had fallen back against the sofa. He raised it and looked at Rainer. "What's the other possibility?"

Rainer pointed at him with the cigarette. "The one you don't want to discuss."

"Ghosts?"

"Dead soldiers. Dead civilians. Refugees gassed in their hiding places. All the missing and presumed dead. There's more than a million of them lying just across the water."

This time, Largo was careful not to dismiss the idea. "Have you spoken to them?" he said, laying a finger on a spirit board at the end of the table.

"I'm not sure. I think so. Recently, I was certain that I'd contacted an old comrade-in-arms, Holger Gotho. But I'd been in pain earlier and had taken quite a dose of morphia."

Largo nodded, as if he were listening carefully instead of simply worrying about his friend. "What did Holger tell you?"

"Nothing," said Rainer. "It's not important."

"That's not fair. You brought up the subject of ghosts and now you don't want to talk about them? What did Holger say?"

Rainer pinched off the lit end of the cigarette and placed the remainder on the edge of his mask. "Holger said, 'We're burning. They're burning us.'"

Largo frowned. "What does it mean?"

"I don't know," said Rainer. "Certainly, the enemy dropped incendiary bombs, but those were mostly on ships at sea."

"Then what?"

Rainer stared at the ceiling. "At first I thought that Holger might have died on a naval transport, but then I remembered he stepped on a mine during a reconnaissance mission."

Largo didn't say anything and the silence hung in the air between the two men. After a few uncomfortable minutes, Rainer said, "Maybe you're right. Maybe I am going mad."

Largo sat up. "I never said you were going mad. I simply said that you should get out more."

Rainer went to the windows and looked across the bay. "I can't now. Something is happening. I have to keep watch."

Largo got up and went to where he stood. He said, "I understand."

Rainer turned his scarred face to the stars. "You do?"

"I was wrong to dismiss your beliefs earlier. We all believe in something, seen or unseen, and we have to follow it wherever it takes us."

Rainer looked at him. "What do you believe in?"

Largo thought for a moment and could come up with only one thing. "Remy."

Rainer laid a hand on his shoulder. "Thank you for coming tonight."

"I'm glad I came too," said Largo. "But now I should be going. I have to be at work at six."

"Come back any time. You're always welcome."

"Thank you." As Largo walked to the door, he stopped at the living room table and set down the nearly full bottle of morphia Margit had given him. "This is for you. Do you have a jar I could use? I'll need just a few drops until I see Remy tomorrow."

Rainer went into an adjoining room and came back with a small medical vial about one-quarter full. "This is all I had left before you arrived. Please take it."

"Thank you," Largo said. He put the vial in his pocket just as the Trefle rang. Rainer picked up the handset, holding the speaking end up to the horn of his wireless.

"Hello?" he said. He sounded uncertain. Largo suspected that he didn't get many calls, certainly not at this time of night. A moment later, Rainer turned in his direction. "Remy. It's good to hear your voice. How are you?" Rainer listened for a moment and said, "Why yes, I'd love to come see you perform some night."

As surprised as Largo was that Remy was calling Rainer, hearing him offer to leave his flat and venture out into the world was even more surprising. It was a lie, he knew, so his surprise was mixed with a deep sadness.

"You have excellent timing," Rainer said. "He's still here." He handed Largo the handset. When Remy spoke it was difficult to make out her words.

"What?" he said. "Speak up. What's all that noise?"

"It's a party," Remy shouted. "It's Ilsa's birthday and Una is throwing her a surprise party. You have to come down."

"That sounds like fun. I'll be there as soon as I can."

Remy said something else, but he couldn't make it out, and then the Trefle went silent.

"It sounds like you have another appointment," said Rainer.

"It's a party. I'd ask you to come . . ."

"But you already know the answer."

"Yes."

"Then let's leave it at that. It was good seeing you, my friend."

"And you," said Largo. He gave Rainer a brief hug and went down to the street. He removed and reset the webbing without incident but remained worried about his friend. Should he have given him so much morphia at once? Worse, with all the talk about ghosts, was Rainer genuinely losing control of his senses? As he pedaled away, Largo promised himself to come back to Lysergsäurehof more often.

When he arrived at the Grand Dark, Largo could hear the sounds of laughter and singing all the way out in the alley beside the theater. The stage door was unlocked, so he went inside to the joyful melee.

He didn't get two steps in before someone threw their arms around him from behind and kissed him on his cheek. He turned to find Ilsa clinging to him, deeply and happily drunk. "Thank you so much for coming!" she shouted to be heard above the din, then she kissed his other cheek. In fact, Largo barely knew Ilsa, but clearly on her night everyone was a dear, close friend.

"Happy birthday," Largo shouted so that she could hear him.

"I didn't know that you even knew when my birthday was," she said. "It's so sweet of you."

He didn't dare tell her that Remy's call was the only reason he'd come, so he said, "None of us would miss it for the world."

Ilsa wore a long beaded sea-green dress that was a bit too big for her. She had to keep pulling the straps back onto her shoulders so that it wouldn't fall off. Largo was certain that it belonged to one of the puppets, so he felt a secret kinship with her. *We are the puppet people*, he thought. *Eternally in debt to our mechanical betters.*

"I'm sure I saw Remy here a moment ago," said Ilsa. She pulled him through the crush of bodies toward the performers' dressing rooms. It looked to Largo like the entire theater staff—including performers, the band, the lighting and sound crews, and even the carpenters and electricians—were pressed together in the small backstage area. He stepped on a lot of toes and jostled several people with drinks before he spotted Remy a few yards away.

When they arrived, Remy was chatting with one of the male performers, whose name Largo could never remember, and Volker, who oversaw both the carpenters and electricians and generally kept the theater running. Una was just behind them, talking earnestly to Jünger, who was in charge of maintaining the puppets.

As they drew closer Ilsa said, "Your delivery, madam." Remy smiled and drew Largo in close for a long kiss.

Ilsa sighed. "It's my birthday and there's no one who wants to kiss *me* like that."

Remy stroked her cheek. "It's your night, my dear. The Grand Dark is at your mercy. I wager there are many people here tonight who want to kiss you."

Ilsa looked around. "But how am I supposed to know who?"

Largo shrugged. "It's obvious. Kiss everyone."

Ilsa's smile was wide and excited. "Do you think I can?"

"How will you know until you've tried?" said Remy.

Ilsa laughed once and kissed the performer Remy had been talking to, and Volker as well. "This is fun," she said drunkenly.

"Well, don't stop now," said Remy. "Look at that sea of unkissed lips."

"I don't know. It would take a long time," Ilsa said uncertainly.

"Then you'd better get started," said Largo.

She laughed at him and Remy, then plunged into the crowd, first kissing the pretty blond singer in the band, then each of the other musicians, before they lost sight of her.

"I've never seen her so happy," said Remy.

"I've never seen *anyone* that happy," Largo said. Then he added, "Except perhaps you when I find a fresh bottle of morphia."

Remy put an arm around his waist. "Can you blame me?"

"Not at all. I feel exactly the same way."

"Exactly the same way about what?" said Una. She and Jünger had come over and stood next to them. They startled Largo, who didn't have a lie prepared. However, Remy didn't hesitate.

"True love," she said. "You can't go looking for it or track it down with logic. You just stumble across it, and there it is."

Jünger nodded knowingly, but Una laughed a silent laugh and shook her head. "You children. You think love is all romance and parties. That it never wanes or sours or that you won't spend every day wondering just what it is you've gotten yourself into."

"Then it's not true love," said Remy, sounding somewhat less merry than she had a moment before. She squeezed Largo's arm.

"My grandmother explained it simply," continued Una, seemingly oblivious to the change of mood she was causing. "She and my grandfather met many years ago, when he returned from the First Eastern War. He had been a soldier and looked dashing in his uniform. She said that they spent their first three days together in bed.

126

But, at the end of the third day, they ran out of food and wine and were confronted with a decision: which of them would dress and go to the market and which would stay home and drag all the trash to the stinking bin out back? It was their first fight. She said they went back to bed after she returned from the market, but it was little things like that—the realities of the world—that ripped holes in their so-called true love."

Largo put a hand over Remy's. "That won't happen to us," he said.

"Are you so sure?" said Una. "Which of you is to be the master or mistress of refuse for the rest of your lives?"

Largo looked at Remy, not sure how to answer. He was about to volunteer for the position when Remy said happily, "Neither of us. I'll sell a necklace or two. Our Blind Mara will do it for us." She looked at Largo. "See? Crisis averted."

Una leaned closer to her. "And when you get old and ugly like me? How many automatons will it take to make you happy?"

Remy looked puzzled. "You can't possibly mean that," she said. "You're not old or ugly."

"There's the other secret of love. Our hearts don't age at the same rate as the rest of our bodies. You can be old on the inside long before you're old outside."

Jünger gazed into his empty glass. "The night has taken a decidedly somber turn."

Largo nodded. "Don't worry about us, Una. We'll be fine. Until our Mara appears, the trash duties will be all mine."

Una ignored him, her eyes locked on Remy. "Just don't let your gentlemen admirers know about your current infatuation. Those jewels and baubles might not keep coming forever."

"It's not an infatuation," said Remy sternly.

Before Una could respond, Ilsa came back to them. Her skin was flushed and her lipstick smeared. She was perspiring a little. "My, kissing everyone is harder work than I thought," she said. "I need another drink. Does anyone else?"

"No, thank you," said Remy, looking down at the floor.

Ilsa put a hand on her shoulder. "Are you all right? Everyone seemed so happy a minute ago."

Remy smiled at her. "We're fine. Just a little tired."

Reaching into her pocket, Ilsa pulled out a folded sheet of paper.

"This will make you feel better. A boy gave it to me outside when I was smoking with the band. It's very funny." She handed it to Remy, who frowned when she opened it. Largo looked over her shoulder. It was a pamphlet. On the cover was a collage of the Minister of War made from money, liquor bottles, and guns. It reminded Largo of some of Enki's work, but he would never do anything this blatant. It was clearly someone imitating his style. Inside the pamphlet he read the usual down-with-the-government-and-war-profiteers nonsense.

When she saw the cover, Una snatched the pamphlet from Remy's hand. She looked it over and crumpled it up. "Revolting," she said. She told Jünger, "There was a police car around the corner earlier. If it's still there, give this to the officers. I won't have this trash near the theater."

Without a word, Jünger took the pamphlet and headed to the stage door.

When he was gone Una said to Ilsa, "Could you identify the boy if you saw him again?"

Ilsa shook her head nervously. "It was very foggy. I was surprised he could see us well enough to give it to us."

Una pursed her lips in disgust. "These people should all be deported," she said.

Seeing Una's anger, a small group had gathered around them. "Where should they go?' said Volker.

She smiled. "Why, to High Proszawa, where they can't hurt anybody," she said. The group laughed and toasted the idea. Ilsa looked sullen, her birthday party ruined by politics. Out of politeness, Largo laughed along with everyone else, but the mention of the police made him extremely uncomfortable. Still, he smiled.

A puppet, his strings pulled by those around him.

Remy leaned her cheek against Ilsa's and put an arm around her, trying to get her back into a party mood.

"Come," she said. "Shall we go kiss some beautiful strangers?"

Ilsa smiled up at her. "Really?"

Remy looked at Largo. "Care to join us?"

"You have fun," he said. "I'm going to get a drink."

He watched them disappear into the throng. Largo knew that under other circumstances he should be jealous of Remy going off to kiss the handsome theater crowd, but his immediate concern was the morphia in his pocket. He didn't want to throw it away, but at least in the fog he had a chance if the police stopped him on the way out. But he promised himself that he wouldn't do anything until the last possible moment.

When he found the little bar, Una was there as if she'd been waiting for him. As he poured himself a drink, she pointed to Remy and Ilsa gliding through the crowd, kissing men, women, and each other for everyone's amusement.

Una held her glass out to Largo. He didn't want to toast anything with her but, as always, out of politeness he clinked his glass against hers. "To true love," Una said. She drew out the phrase so that the sarcasm couldn't be missed. He didn't turn around to watch Remy and Ilsa because he knew that's what Una wanted. Instead, he excused himself and found a quiet corner where he took two drops of morphia.

Later, when he asked Remy if she wanted to leave she walked him to the door. "Of course I do," she said. "But Ilsa and Una will be upset if I go in the middle of the party. Why don't you go home and get some rest? We'll see each other tomorrow."

He nodded, disappointed about so much, even as they kissed in the fog beside the Grand Dark. Before he left, she hung on to his sleeve. "Was it all right what I did with Ilsa? Going off with her like that?"

"Of course," said Largo. "You cheered her up. I could tell."

"Good. You're the only one I ever really want to kiss."

"And you're the only one whose trash I want to take out."

Remy laughed. "Maybe instead of a Mara, I should get us a pretty little concubine."

"I think Ilsa might volunteer after tonight."

"Ilsa is drunk and would agree to almost anything, I think. Which reminds me. I ought to go back and check on her."

"That's true love," said Largo, smiling.

Remy blew him a kiss. "I'll see you tomorrow."

As he rounded the corner by the coal power plant a block from home, something hit Largo broadside, knocking him off his bicycle. His first thought was that a driverless Mara had lost itself in Little Shambles and was turning corners blindly, trying to find a way out of the district. But that couldn't be right. If he'd been hit by a Mara, wouldn't he be unconscious? And in a lot more pain? He was a little dizzy, but both his arms and legs felt fine. When Largo opened his eyes, he looked straight up into the angry black clouds that billowed from the power plant smokestacks day and night. Every now and then, a star winked through a hole in the roiling darkness. Then the clouds were replaced by a face, but not like any he'd seen before. His first thought was that he'd fallen and was being helped up by an Iron Dandy. But the face wasn't hideous, just—strange. There was something about it that reminded him of a horse, but also of a large dog. And it seemed to have small antlers. It sniffed at him and its great gray tongue licked at its nose and lips. Someone nearby was shouting, and the sound grew louder by the second. The strange face looked toward the sound and shuffled back a few feet. Now Largo could see that he'd been right. Whatever it was had a long, vaguely horse-shaped body, but it seemed to stand on pairs of very human-looking legs. At the sound of another shout, the creature ran gracefully into a vacant lot full of coarse black shrubs. Largo tried getting to his feet but was knocked down again by a speeding herd of running— *somethings*. These, however, he recognized immediately. They were the catlike chimeras from the carnival, mostly small ones but a couple big enough to leave him on his ass and dizzy. They all ran into the lot after the horse creature. Largo looked around, afraid for a moment that he'd gone as mad as Rainer, and whoever had been shouting rounded the corner.

It looked as if the whole carnival had come to his rescue. Roustabouts and dancing girls, strong men in leopard skins and lion tamers in red jackets and jodhpurs ran to him. A spangled dancing girl and a red-headed clown with a purple nose got to him first and pulled him to his feet.

"I'm so sorry," said the dancer. "Are you hurt?"

"I don't think so," said Largo. "Were those all chimeras? I've never seen any that big before."

"Yeah, they were a few of the bigger bastards. Sorry," said the clown gruffly.

The dancer used her hands to dust off Largo's clothes. "One of our trucks broke down and they escaped."

"Are they dangerous?" Largo said.

"You're the one flat on your arse," said the clown. "You tell me."

The dancer shot the clown a look of exasperation. "They're not dangerous at all. Just scared. Did you see which way they went?"

Largo pointed to the vacant lot. "Over there. It was too dark to see much after that."

The clown ran back to the rest of the carnival workers. "He says they went into the bushes. Come on," he shouted.

Largo's head cleared and his balance returned quickly. The dancer stopped brushing him. She was pretty, he thought. Tall and blond, though her hair was slightly askew, so it might have been a wig. Her face sparkled with glitter. "Nice shirt," she said.

"Thank you. My girlfriend gave it to me. Loaned, actually," he said. Then in a moment of mild panic he added, "Is it dirty or torn?"

The dancer took a step back. "No, it looks fine enough to be buried in."

He relaxed a little. "Oh, good. Remy won't murder me."

"Is that your girlfriend?"

"Yes," said Largo. "She's a performer at the Grand Dark."

The dancer smiled and said, "I'm a bit of a performer myself. You should come to the carnival and see me dance."

"Thank you, but I'm trying to save money right now."

The dancer raised her skirt over one leg and pulled two tickets from under a spangled garter. "Here you go. On the house, partly for being such a help and partly for not calling the bullocks on us."

"I wouldn't do that," Largo said. The dancer pushed the tickets into his hand and ran into the vacant lot after her friends. Over her shoulder she shouted, "I'm Nico. Bring your lady friend to see me dance. I'm not as wild as the tavern girls or nude as Anita Mourlet, but I'm very good. You can find me in the big tent every night."

As she disappeared into the dark, Largo said, "Thank you, Nico. We'll come and see you." He pulled his bicycle upright and checked it over to make sure it was undamaged. It seemed fine. But he didn't ride the last block home. Between the morphia, the hashish, and being knocked on his head, he'd had enough of riding for one night. When he made it to his flat, he barely got his clothes off before falling into a deep sleep in which he dreamed about Rainer and a ghost battalion riding a herd of huge chimeras with human legs into the plague zones of High Proszawa.

Largo had never seen him so happy.

EUGENICS

Final Report to Schöne Maschinen Board of Directors, Personnel Injury Incident C39–01, Eugenics Hold #6

Franck von Krell has worked with eugenics for many years, first in the underground pens in building 2 at Schöne Maschinen, and again in the army during the Great War. He received a severe leg wound in the early days of combat and was sent to the rear echelon. However, due to von Krell's knowledge and enthusiasm, he was able to remain in the army training bitva eugenics for duty at the front.

When he started working with eugenics, he'd been assigned to raise and train docile hausmeisters, a doglike breed the municipal authorities used to clean the streets by eating trash and detritus. After his promotion to Senior Aufseher in Hold #6, he oversaw the full range of eugenic species.

When not attending to supervisory duties, he mainly worked with bitva eugenics because, he said, they took him back to his war days. Von Krell is skilled in socializing the whelps and teaching the young ones basic commands. During this period of training, he was able to wear his ordinary work overalls and gloves. However, several employees testified that when working with grown bitvas, he wore the required body armor, along with a steel mesh face mask and helmet. Von

Krell's specialty was training his bitvas to be vicious enough to kill, yet disciplined enough to show restraint when given the proper command. It should be noted here that it was not von Krell's actions that precipitated the incident in Hold #6, but those of a careless underling.

Unter Vorgesetzten Solveig Kuhlne has stated that late spring is the most difficult period in the bitva pens. In fact, workers have been known to falsify excuses for not going in. Allergies are a common excuse. Others claim injuries. Over the years, some have even claimed mental disturbances, especially the so-called "bomb shock" from the war. Testimony shows that von Krell has dealt quickly with such shirkers and layabouts.

"You're lucky to have these duties," he reminds the staff. "Do you not imagine that there's a line of willing young workers ready to take your place? Dismissal from Schöne Maschinen is something that will haunt you the rest of your days. No one will employ you and you'll remember until your dying day the opportunity you've squandered."

It was in late April, the height of eugenic mating season, when Incident C39–01 occurred. While cleaning the pens, Leopold Rabus, an apprentice with a spotless record, was foolish enough to get between two full-grown male bitvas that were fighting over a female. Though he was dressed in body armor, two adult bitvas were more than the young man could handle. According to witnesses, the bitvas cornered him and managed to bite through one of Rabus's gloves, whereupon the presence of blood only intensified their attack.

When von Krell was called to the pen, Rabus was on his back and unresponsive. Through years of experience, von Krell immediately recognized that the eugenic specimens Rabus had interfered with were the specially bred Giftig variety.*

When von Krell found him, Rabus was seconds from death. Von Krell summoned a group of armored security Maras but, to his credit, he didn't wait for them. Instead, at great personal peril, he entered the pen armed with only a cattle prod and a tranquilizer pistol.

Using the prod, he managed to move the bitvas away from Rabus, but von Krell had trained the animals well. The original two bitvas were joined by two more. They went into a battle formation, backing the two men against the wall on the far side of the pen. With voice commands, von Krell managed to stand down two of the bitvas. However, the ones that had tasted blood were beyond voice command control. He managed to shoot each of them with a tranquilizer, but as they were now in full attack mode, the drug merely slowed them. Despite this, witnesses testify that von Krell stood firm and protected the young apprentice.

When the bitvas made a final charge, one managed to rip through von Krell's armor and bite the leg he'd injured in the war. Ironically, this might be what saved his life because, having lost sensation in the limb due to his injury, von Krell was able to keep a cool head and continue to fire tranquilizers at the eugenics until the Maras arrived. Once they'd secured the animals in a fenced enclosure, it should be noted that von Krell used his antivenin injector not on himself, but on young Rabus, thereby saving his life. By the time a medical Mara administered antivenin to von Krell, he was unconscious.

Due to his heroic actions, he was moved to a private medical unit usually reserved for managerial staff. On his second

---

* For those not acquainted with this rarely used breed, their bite is not only ferocious, but carries a neurotoxin that paralyzes and eventually kills their victims.

day in recovery, Baron Hellswarth himself came to von Krell's bedside to thank him for his dedication to the corporation and his young apprentice. As a gesture of appreciation, the Baron personally promoted him to Oberaufseher, head of the entire eugenics training program.

According to medical reports, von Krell healed quickly and he even joked with the staff about reenlisting in the army. However, he was quick to reassure everyone that the comment was merely a joke. He told his physical therapist that he knew his work with eugenics at Schöne Maschinen would be an even greater contribution to the war effort than he could make as a soldier.

Since returning to the Eugenics Department, von Krell has enacted a series of safety reforms, even consulting on the design of new armor for the workers. Also, no apprentices are allowed in the adult pens without being accompanied by an experienced eugenics worker. Along with a longer, more thorough training program for apprentices, he has mandated that all eugenics personnel carry at least two antivenin injectors at all times.

According to all reports, Franck von Krell remains an exemplary Schöne Maschinen employee and should be considered an example to others.

END Personnel Injury Incident C39–01 Report

THOUGH HE WAS STILL SORE FROM HIS ENCOUNTER WITH THE RAMPAGING chimeras the night before, Largo arrived at work a few minutes early. Herr Branca made a great show of checking the clock and his watch, even pressing his ear to the latter to make sure it was running correctly.

"I see that you're taking your duties more seriously today, Largo. Let me be the first to congratulate you."

"Thank you, sir. I won't be late again."

Branca looked him over. "I did notice, however, a certain limp in your step when you came in. Will you be able to complete your rounds today?"

Largo shifted the weight off his left leg, which still hurt from the previous night's fall. "I took a small tumble last night, is all. It won't affect my work. In fact, it's quite a funny story—"

Branca cut him off. "Were you drunk?" he said.

The question caught him off guard. While he'd been a bit woozy from the morphia and hashish, he'd not had a single drink, so he was able to say, "Absolutely not," with a straight face. "What happened, though, was quite remarkable."

"I'm sure it was and will make a fine tale for your memoirs; however, today all I care to know is that your faculties are at one hundred percent. Do you remember why?"

Largo shifted his weight again, this time out of nervousness. "I'll be visiting the armaments factory."

"Schöne Maschinen," said Herr Branca. "Use its proper name for accuracy's sake, if not as a mark of respect for its contributions to our well-being."

"I will, sir. Schöne Maschinen."

"Very good. And you've said 'sir' twice since coming in. That will be enough of that for today."

Largo kept his mouth shut.

Branca grunted. "Tell me about your clothes," he said. "The shirt I recognize from yesterday. It's looking a little drabber today, so let's do something about that."

"Of course. I have the money you gave me."

"Meaning you'll be purchasing new clothes today?"

"Directly after work."

"Very good." Branca looked Largo up and down. It made him uncomfortable, but he was getting used to it, so he was able to stand perfectly still.

Branca said, "The shirt is passable, as are the trousers, though just barely. But the jacket—have you taken up bear wrestling recently?"

Largo looked down at himself. "No, but I know the right elbow is ripped a bit. It has to do with the incident last night. Anyway, I'll get new clothes tonight, so it won't be a problem tomorrow."

"But it's today that worries me. Take the jacket off and hang it on that hook over there. I'll be back in a minute," Branca said.

Largo did as he was told, feeling like a schoolboy hanging up his uniform after class. It wasn't a pleasant sensation. A moment later, Branca came out of his office with a clean jacket folded neatly over one arm. "Put this on," he said.

Again, Largo did as he was told. The jacket was much cleaner and in much better shape than his own. There were no holes or missing buttons, just a slight fraying at the wrists. However, it was at least a size too big. The sleeves came halfway down over his hands. "It's very nice," he said, "but I'm not sure it fits."

Branca stood before him with his arms folded. "Stand up straight and push your shoulders back a bit." Largo did as he was told. Indeed, standing that way, he filled out the jacket a bit, but he felt ridiculous, as if he were pretending to be a toy soldier. "Much better," said Branca. "It will do for today."

Resigned to his awkward wardrobe, Largo looked it over some more. The fabric was good. Wool, but in better repair than his own jacket. In all, it was much more comfortable than what he was used to. When he touched the breast pocket, he felt a stitched crest and that stopped him cold.

"Whose jacket is this?" said Largo.

"It belongs to the company," Branca said. "Why do you ask?"

"Didn't König wear something like this?"

Branca looked at some papers on his desk. "Not something like it. Exactly that jacket itself. Is that a problem?"

Wearing König's clothes and knowing how the other couriers felt about him taking his job made him shrink a little. He said, "Isn't it bad luck, don't you think? Considering what happened to him?"

Branca didn't look up. "The Nachtvogel didn't arrest him for his sartorial taste. They took him away because he was a dangerous anarchist. I don't think you should worry about wearing his jacket. Sedition isn't like catching a cold. You have to seek it out."

"Of course. That makes sense," said Largo, still feeling like a grave robber.

In ones and twos, the other couriers came into the office. Every one of them looked at Largo in König's jacket. None tried to hide their anger or contempt, but no one said a word. Not after what had happened to Andrzej. Parvulesco came into the office last and stood next to Margit. He took one look at Largo and had to suppress a laugh. He gave Largo a quick thumbs-up before turning his attention to Herr Branca. Their boss waited a minute, checked the clock and his watch again, and then turned his attention to the couriers.

He said, "I note the absence of Andrzej this morning. Does anyone have word of him?" The other couriers shook their heads and looked at one another, feigning innocence. "As I thought. Well, gentlemen, *I* have news. He will not be joining us today or for many days to come, if at all."

"Oh? Why is that, sir?" said Weimer. "Has he taken ill?" A few of the couriers snickered at his stilted performance.

"That's enough of that," said Branca, eyeing the room. He turned his attention to Weimer. "It seems that an accident befell Andrzej last night. He was found behind a truck in the lot out front with considerable injuries. From the state of his body, he might have even been struck by one of the delivery vehicles. Or it might have been something deadlier."

"Deadly?" said Parvulesco, playing along with the game. "How so?"

Branca said, "From the state of his numerous broken bones, it's possible that Andrzej has succumbed to the Drops."

Even though they knew better, just the sound of the word sent a murmur through the room. Weimer was the only one who didn't say anything. Instead, he stared fiercely at Largo. For his part, Largo pretended to look at Herr Branca and not notice Weimer's death glare. He put his hands in his pockets, making sure to push back the side of the jacket to reveal his knife. Weimer turned back to the front of the room.

Branca was going on as if nothing had happened. "Let us keep Andrzej in our thoughts and prayers in the coming days, shall we?"

There was a general murmur of agreement.

"And, of course, let's watch out for our own health, as the Drops are said to be quite contagious. For instance, it might be best to avoid groups of you gathering together by the loading dock," said Branca. After a moment he added, "This goes for the front gate too. Let's avoid gathering there after work, shall we?"

Heads nodded and some of the couriers whispered, "Yes, sir."

He knows, thought Largo. *But who is he covering for with the ridiculous story about the Drops? Possibly himself?* Largo hoped that was the case. An assault on one of his couriers while he was in the office wouldn't look good on his record.

"Enough of that gloom and doom," said Branca. "It's time to get to work. Line up to receive your parcels."

The couriers did as they were told and a few battered Maras rolled from the back room, distributing boxes, cardboard tubes, and letters. After receiving their deliveries, the other couriers left, some shooting glances at Largo but most looking straight ahead as if he weren't there. Parvulesco winked as he went by. "See you at lunch?" he said. Largo nodded and shooed him away.

With the couriers gone, the Maras left the room. Herr Branca took a receipt book and a smooth wooden box from a nearby table and handed them to Largo. As he put them in his shoulder bag, Branca said, "I don't need to remind you that this is your most important delivery yet, do I?"

"No, Herr Branca."

"Good. Here is how things will proceed. When you arrive at Schöne Maschinen, you will be buzzed inside. You are to give the parcel to no one but Baron Hellswarth himself. Is that understood?"

"Completely."

"Good. Now, here is the other thing to remember. Depending on the Baron's mood and schedule, you might be dismissed immediately. If that is the case, come back here as quickly as you can and tell me everything that happened during your trip."

"I will."

"There is, of course, a second possibility. If the Baron is in a different sort of mood, he might want to talk to you."

"About what?"

"About anything that crosses his mind," he said in a peeved tone. "The weather. What you had for breakfast. Whether the moon is made of cheese. It doesn't matter. You will answer his questions simply and truthfully, but carefully and without interjecting your opinions. Also, you will address him as 'Baron,' but not 'Herr Baron' or any such nonsense. You don't want to sound like a bumpkin or make it appear as if the company hires the feebleminded. Is all that understood?"

"Yes," said Largo. "Speak simply and truthfully. Try not to sound like an idiot."

"Very good," said Branca. He looked Largo up and down again. "Do these things well and you'll seal your job as chief courier. Do them poorly and I'm sure I don't have to tell you the consequences."

"Not at all. I understand completely," said Largo, wishing for all the world the older man would have a heart attack on the spot.

"There's one last thing," Branca said. "If the Baron is in a talkative mood, he can go on at some length. You will stay as long as he likes, even if it's through lunch. Even if it's until the end of your shift."

"Stay as long as he likes. I have it."

"Who knows?" said Branca, going back to his desk. "If the Baron takes a liking to you, this might be your only delivery of the day. Then you can nurse that limp tonight. With Andrzej gone, I can't afford to lose any more couriers."

"I'll be fine by tomorrow," said Largo.

"And newly attired. Don't forget."

Largo pushed the jacket sleeves back from his hands. "Then can I give you this back?"

"After tomorrow you may throw the jacket away or give it to a passing donkey, for all the company cares. König doesn't need it. We won't be seeing him again."

"Yes, sir," said Largo, wanting to know more but also not wanting to know anything about the matter at all. He left the office before Branca could correct him about saying *sir* too much.

When Largo reached his bicycle, he stopped in his tracks and took a long breath, feeling a combination of terror and fury.

Someone had slashed his tires.

It would take almost an hour to fix them and get to Schöne Maschinen.

"Largo!" someone called. He whirled around, his hand going to the knife. When he saw that it was Margit he relaxed and turned his attention back to the bicycle.

When she reached his side she said, "What happened?"

"Branca insisted I wear König's jacket. I think someone objected to it."

Margit knelt and examined the tires. "They're cut all the way through. There's no fixing them."

Largo shifted the bag on his shoulder. "I don't know what to do. I'm supposed to be on my way to Schöne Maschinen already. I don't have time for this shit."

Margit stood and clapped her hands together to clear the dirt off. "Take mine," she said. "None of my deliveries are very important. I'll stay behind and get new tires from the equipment shed."

"Take your bicycle?" said Largo.

Margit shifted her hips and laughed. "Don't worry. Your masculinity will remain intact. It's a boy's bike. See?"

Largo smiled sheepishly, a little ashamed of himself. "It's not that. Won't you get in trouble if you're late on your rounds?"

"It wouldn't be the first time. This sort of thing happens to me fairly regularly."

"Your bicycle being sabotaged?"

"The tires or seat slashed. The chain broken," said Margit.

"Why? I've never seen you bother anybody."

"You also haven't noticed how some of the other couriers look at me, have you? I'm not popular."

"I mean, I've heard a few jokes here and there—"

Margit pushed Largo's bicycle against the loading dock. "Girls like me—degenerates who don't go out with boys—we're not well thought of in some circles."

Largo felt like a fool. "I'm sorry," he said. "I should have known there was more to it."

Margit wheeled her bicycle to Largo. "It's all right. We're taught what to see and not see. It's hard to break the pattern."

"It won't happen again," he said, remembering the jokes other couriers made about Parvulesco when he wasn't around. Jokes Largo never had the nerve to object to.

"That's sweet of you, but if you're really going to change, don't just do it here," said Margit. She looked out past the gate. "Do it there. Out in the world."

"I will. I promise," said Largo.

Margit drew closer and said, "I'm sorry I wasn't able to meet you last night. Things came up. It wasn't safe for either of us."

"Don't worry about it. If you'd been here we couldn't have talked anyway. There was a fight. That's what really happened to Andrzej."

Margit opened her eyes a little wider. "Did *you* fight him?"

Largo didn't like the startled way she said *you*, but he knew she was right. "No. It was Parvulesco's friend Roland."

A smile spread across Margit's face. "I bet he wasn't expecting that."

"Neither was I," said Largo. "Roland was amazing. Utterly fearless."

"That's the only way there is for us degenerates."

Largo frowned. "But Parvulesco—I mean, everybody knows he prefers other men. No one slashes his tires."

Margit said, "That's because for men and women, everything is different. We walk through entirely different worlds. Open your eyes a bit. What you see might not make you happy, but it will make you more human."

"I . . . I will," said Largo, feeling even more foolish than when he'd been dressed down by Branca. Hearing about these things from Margit, someone of about his same age and status, someone he liked, stung in a way he hadn't expected.

"Thank you," said Margit. "Now take my bicycle and get going. You're already late."

Largo looked around. "Before I go, I have to tell you something. The leaflet that Pietr gave me yesterday? Herr Branca saw it."

Margit pursed her lips, thinking. "Did you tell him where you got it?"

"No. I said I found it on the street. I tried to get it back from the trash, but it was already gone."

"I see," she said. "It's probably all right, but don't come back to the Black Palace. If you have any more deliveries there, give them to me and I'll take them."

"I'll let you know," said Largo, feeling a bit relieved. He'd dreaded the idea of returning to Machtviertel and now he had an excuse not to.

Margit said, "You should get going before Branca sees you. Good luck with the Beast today."

"The Beast?"

"Baron Hellswarth. You've never heard that name?"

"König said it once. I thought he was joking."

Margit pushed Largo toward the gate. "Now you'll get to find out for yourself."

Between Branca's orders and Margit's cryptic warning, the excitement Largo had originally felt at finally going to the armaments factory had greatly diminished. It didn't help that he was going there on a strange bicycle sized and geared for someone smaller. However, as he crossed the Ore Bridge the sun came out from behind the clouds of the belching power plants and warmed him. On his left, fog was rolling in along the bay. If he hurried, he might just make it to Schöne Maschinen before the city settled back under its normal gray shroud.

The sun was just starting to fade as Largo reached the front gate and some of the thrill at finally seeing the inside of the plant returned. Still, he couldn't quite shake what Margit had said.

"The Beast." What am I walking into?

Largo settled on the simplest plan he could think of. He would follow Branca's instructions to the letter. Listen intently, no matter how mad the Beast might be. Be polite no matter what he heard. Stay as long as the Baron wanted him there. Also, don't expect a tip. Men in as lofty a position as the Baron usually weren't aware of the concept, if they thought of money at all. It was hard to imagine. What must that be like? To snap your fingers and have tons of steel and massive war machines instantly appear at your door? No, a tip was out of the question. Largo would simply get on with his job and, if the Baron was too much to endure, he would soothe himself after work with Remy and morphia when they went clothes shopping.

Largo sat by the Schöne Maschinen gate for a moment simply taking in the place. The factory had been such a site of wonder and mystery his whole life, and now he was about to enter it. There was something almost supernatural about the moment, as if he were about to leave the solid, simple world he'd grown up in and enter another, one marked by mystery and danger. There was even a beast inside, he thought, and laughed. What the hell was he doing? This wasn't one of his mother's fairy tales. Schöne Maschinen was just another company. Just another client. Workers came and went. Materials flowed in and goods flowed out. Margit had said it: he just needed to open his eyes and see what was really there.

In this case, what was there was a massive steel gate flanked by twin stone columns at least fifty feet high. Figures were twined within the metal of the gate—victorious soldiers, scientists, and workers towered overhead, hand in hand. Above the gate were the words

Protection Progress Perfection

On the left column was a dull gray box with a small grate and a red button. Largo went to it and pushed the button. There was a dull buzz and a moment later a woman's voice said, "Yes?"

"Hello. I have a delivery for Baron Hellswarth."

"You are from the courier company?"

"Yes."

"What is your name?"

"Largo Moorden."

After a moment, the voice said, "I don't have a Largo Moorden on my deliveries list, just König. Where is he?"

Largo considered his words carefully. "I'm afraid König is no longer employed by the company. I'm very sorry for the mix-up."

"No one informed me," came the woman's voice. She sounded annoyed and frustrated. "This will take a moment. Wait there."

As Largo waited, the gate swung open and two gleaming juggernauts rolled noisily into the street. Behind them came a long flatbed truck sporting the bull crest of the War Department. Largo couldn't make out what was under the tarp on the back of the truck, but when a gust of wind lifted a section of the material, he saw something that seemed to him to resemble a large mechanical hand. With a belch of diesel smoke, the truck moved on, followed by two more noisy juggernauts. A soldier stood up out of the hatch of the closer one. Largo nodded to him, but the soldier merely stared until he lost interest and turned his gaze back to the road. As the gate swung closed, the speaker on the column crackled and the voice said, "Proceed inside and go to building three. Someone will meet you there."

"Thank you," Largo said, and he pedaled Margit's bicycle quickly through the gate before it slammed shut on him.

The factory was immense, spreading out for acres in all directions. Office buildings lined both sides of the road into Schöne Maschinen, but they were dwarfed by the numbered buildings where the factory's private foundry and assembly plants spread out in a sprawling grid. Large Proszawan flags hung on either side at the road, near the entrance to building 1. Building 3 stood to the left, so Largo turned that direction and went to a side door. He had to keep to the shoulder of the road as a steady stream of Black Widows moved from building to building carrying raw metal and heavy machine parts.

Massive I-beams and ingots of raw steel were stacked on every patch of open ground. Through one of building 3's windows, Largo could see sparks flying high into the air. A gray box was affixed to the side of building 3, but before he could press the button the side door swung open.

"Largo Moorden," said a tall woman in a dark, formal business dress.

"Yes. I'm Largo," he said.

"Of course you are. Otherwise you wouldn't have gotten this far."

Largo wasn't sure how to respond, so he said, "I have a delivery for Baron Hellswarth."

"So I understand." The woman turned away from him. Before she disappeared into building 3 she said, "Leave your bicycle there and come with me."

They entered an anteroom ringed with windows. Through them, Largo could see the immense furnaces and conveyors that moved red-hot ribbons and ingots of steel throughout the foundry. Buckets as big as tram cars poured liquid metal into molds, sending up fountains of sparks to the ceiling. A rhythmic pounding shook the ground. The roar of the machines hurt his ears.

"I am Dame Karoli," said the woman. She had to raise her voice for Largo to hear her. "I am the Baron's private secretary. If you are to be the new courier, we will no doubt get to know each other."

"Very good to meet you, Dame Karoli," said Largo. "I look forward to working with you."

She said, "You won't be working with me. You'll be working with

146

the Baron. I'm here simply to make sure you don't get lost and end up wandering into one of the blast furnaces. It would slow production and ruin the steel."

"Yes, that would be very inconvenient," said Largo. He wished König had talked more about his own deliveries to Schöne Maschinen. It would have been nice to be better prepared for the officiousness of the place. Then another thought struck him. *Perhaps König did talk about it to the wrong person and that's what got him in trouble.*

Dame Karoli walked to the entrance of the foundry floor. By the door, she reached into a pile of what looked like heavy Bakelite earmuffs and offered Largo a set. Hearing protection, he realized. Before he put them on he looked at the woman's hair. She wore it pinned up in a bun.

"Will you be wearing them too?" he said.

"Of course not," she said. "I work here. These are for our new and more"—she looked at him—"delicate visitors."

Largo drew in a breath and let it out slowly. It was like being back in Empyrean again, although this time no one was trying to throw him out—just humiliate him enough so that he would leave. Largo's fascination with Schöne Maschinen began to fade and he just wanted to get on with his job. Whatever the reason for Dame Karoli's tone, he wasn't going to give her any more opportunities to look down on him. He set the earmuffs back on the table with the others and said, "Thank you very much, but I don't want to be late getting Baron Hellswarth his package."

"Then come with me. The Baron's office is all the way at the top, overlooking the factory floor."

The noise inside the foundry was indeed staggering—a driving, grating, screeching wail that never let up. Largo had never heard anything like it, but he managed to keep an impassive expression on his face as Dame Karoli led him to a freight lift. Inside, the sound diminished from awful to merely unpleasant as they rode to the top of the building. In a way, he was glad the Baron's secretary had treated him with such derision. He was tired enough of people trying to bully him that his fear of the Beast evaporated. If he walked into the Baron's office and the man simply swallowed him whole, well, he reasoned, it meant that he wouldn't have to suffer through another meeting with Dame Karoli.

When they reached the top floor, she led him out of the lift onto a metal walkway overlooking the foundry. Largo was even more impressed looking down at the factory. And from this new angle, he noticed something that seemed peculiar. The immense space below was nearly deserted. Almost all the work of smelting, shaping, and producing finished metal was done by Maras, some of which towered three stories tall.

"Where are all the people?" said Largo.

Dame Karoli glanced down at the floor. "There are exactly as many people as are needed. Our Maras are clever. They do their work without assistance and, in some cases, can even repair themselves. We have a handful of operational managers and machinists to keep an eye on things, but soon, they too will be unnecessary."

Maras taking more jobs, he thought. How long would it be before no one needed human workers at all anymore? Then what would be left for people to do but become beggars or, as Frau Heller had intimated, become cannon fodder in a new war?

They continued across the walkway and were almost at the office doors when Largo glanced down and saw a man one floor below. He wore greasy gray overalls and had a wrench almost the length of his arm slung casually over his shoulder. The plazma light from above and the glow of the metal works below gave his skin an unhealthy, sallow look. As Dame Karoli opened the office door, the man looked up and Largo recognized him instantly. It was Pietr, the jaundiced lunatic from the Black Palace. When Pietr saw him, he put his head down and disappeared behind a large array of ducts and pipes.

Largo didn't have time to think or react as Dame Karoli ushered him into the office. His first thought was that Pietr, still concerned about his appearance at the Black Palace, had somehow followed him and broken into the factory to kill him. But that was ridiculous. How could anyone break into Schöne Maschinen?

Besides, he was dressed like a machinist. He must work here.

Largo wanted to go to Margit right then and tell her about Pietr, but he was finally in the Baron's lair. Warnings would have to wait.

When Dame Karoli closed the office door, the sounds of the foundry almost disappeared. Soundproof, Largo thought. All the better to hide the screams when the Beast ate his victims. He almost laughed. The trip into Schöne Maschinen had already been stranger than he'd ever imagined. How much odder could it get? Somehow the absurdity of it all relaxed him.

Across the room was a pair of wooden doors, large and heavy

enough to be the entrance to a cathedral. Dame Karoli knocked on one door, opened it, and stuck her head inside. "Baron? The parcel you were waiting for has arrived." A moment later she took a step back and held the door open for Largo. He didn't look at her as he went inside and she shut the door behind him.

Baron Rudolf Hellswarth and his office were utterly ordinary. The Baron stood as Largo came in, though he remained behind his desk, which was made of a dark wood with his family crest carved on the front—a bull's head over a gear and surrounded by flames. There were comfortable-looking leather chairs facing the desk and a large sofa against one wall. A dictation machine and a Trefle sat on his desk. To the Baron's right, the wall was one large window that overlooked the whole factory, yet the air smelled fresh and clean. The Baron smiled at Largo in an extremely unbeastly way. He looked like he was in his early forties, with a few strands of silver in his dark hair. He was dressed in an unexceptional dark blue pin-striped suit.

"Hello," he said. "You must be the new man. I understand you have something for me."

"Yes, sir," said Largo. He took the box Branca had given him out of his bag and handed it to the Baron. As he did so, a set of golden eyes rose from behind the desk and stared at him. A moment later, a large, shaggy hound-like chimera padded around the desk and stared at him. The creature had a long, thin head, strong legs, and a graceful, tapered body. While the Baron examined the contents of the box, the chimera came to Largo and sniffed his hand. He remained completely still. Branca hadn't given any instructions for this situation, but if he had, Largo was sure he would have been told to quietly let the creature gnaw off his hand rather than insult the Baron by screaming.

"You must be a rather special fellow," said the Baron in a joking tone.

"Sir?" said Largo.

"Kara doesn't usually care for strangers, but it appears she's taken a liking to you. You may pet her if you like."

"Thank you." Largo held out one hand tentatively and Kara pressed the top of her head into his palm. He scratched her there and behind the ears. She sat down next to him and leaned against his leg as he continued to pet her.

The Baron put the box in a drawer of his desk and said, "How about that?"

"She's lovely," said Largo. "I've never seen anything quite like her."

The Baron crossed his arms and watched the two of them. "Wonderful," he said. "We breed our eugenics to be social, but the moment you add intelligence to the mix they become unpredictable. She can't stand Dame Karoli."

Largo gave Kara an extra ear scratch for her good taste in people. "You make chimeras here?" he said.

The Baron looked out the window at the factory. "We were one of the first companies to develop the process of creating eugenic creatures. They were as important to the war effort as cannons and bombs."

"My friend Rainer told me about serving with chimeras, but I admit I thought he was exaggerating."

The Baron turned back to Largo. He said, "You didn't serve on the front lines, did you . . . ? Actually, I didn't catch your name."

He stopped petting Kara, but she remained against his leg. "Largo, sir. Largo Moorden. And no, I didn't serve at the front," he said, hoping that was all the Baron would ask about the war.

"Well, if you had, you would have seen eugenics everywhere. They fought next to the men, carried supplies, ran messages between the lines. Even their blood is compatible with ours, so they could transfuse fallen comrades."

"That's amazing," said Largo. "I had no idea."

"And we've kept on improving them. Kara here is twice as smart, twice as strong, and a thousand times more willful than the eugenics in the Great War. Aren't you, my dear?" The Baron held out his hand and Kara trotted to him, where she sat down and nuzzled his hand.

Largo said, "Most chimeras I see aren't as beautiful or friendly as Kara." He thought about the fish in the tank in Empyrean and the wolf-snake biting the Mara at Werner Petersen's party. "They're so often brutal and freakish."

The Baron looked at him. "I take it you've seen them while making your deliveries? The exotic sort that the city's nouveau riche love so much."

"Yes, Baron."

"And you don't approve?"

Largo tensed. This was exactly the kind of discussion Herr Branca had warned him about. He'd specifically told Largo not to inject opinions into any conversation. However, he'd also said to answer questions honestly. In any case, it was too late to take anything back now.

"I suppose not. It seems cruel and a waste of all the work it takes to create such amazing creatures."

Baron Hellswarth touched the back of Kara's neck and she lay down at his feet. Largo watched the man, wondering if this was where the Beast would appear and bite his head off. Finally, he said, "I'll tell you a secret, Largo. I agree with you. With the amazing range of eugenics available, why they prefer such grotesqueries baffles me."

Largo relaxed and even found himself liking the man, though in a cautious way. He'd gotten away with one slip of the tongue. He wouldn't make the same mistake twice.

The Baron sat on the edge of his desk. "However, people's thirst for ever more novel and absurd creatures helps fund research that will lead to better, smarter, and greater eugenics in the future. We're even studying how we can apply what we learn from them to ordinary people like you or me."

The Baron referring to himself as an ordinary person surprised Largo, but he wrote it off as a perverse upper-class joke.

"I'm afraid I don't understand," Largo said. "Why would you make people like chimeras?"

The Baron held up a finger. "It's not making us more like chimeras. It's taking what our eugenics teach us and applying it to the betterment of humanity. Imagine a society without disease—physical or mental. Imagine if we could eliminate the wants and needs that lead to crime. Perhaps heal the Iron Dandies. We might even put an end to war."

"Wouldn't that put you out of business?"

Baron Hellswarth shrugged. "True. But what kind of man would I be if I weren't willing to sacrifice a mere enterprise when the lives of millions are at stake? Enough of that, though. Let me ask you a few questions."

Largo prepared himself. He stood up a little straighter and ran through Branca's instructions again. Short, truthful answers, but no opinions unless they were absolutely unavoidable. In that case, keep the opinions as bland as day-old porridge.

The Baron tapped a finger on his desk. "How old are you?"

"Twenty-one, Baron."

"Do you have a girlfriend?"

"Yes, sir."

"And what is she like?"

That surprised him. Largo wasn't prepared for such personal questions, but he didn't see any choice but to answer. "She's a performer. At the Grand Dark. One of the featured players, in fact."

As he said it, Kara came and leaned against him again. Petting her was a welcome relief and distraction.

The Baron seemed to think for a moment. "Do you like your job as a courier?"

Back to business, thought Largo. *Thank God.* "Very much. I get to see people, things, and parts of the city that I'd never get to otherwise. It's fun."

The Baron squinted at him. "*Fun?* Interesting. Is that really all you aspire to?"

"Sir?" he said, knowing his answer had been wrong. The whole line of questioning made him uncomfortable.

The Baron waved off his question. "Never mind. We'll come back to that. Do you have many friends?"

This time Largo thought about his answer. "A few. Not as many as some, but more than others."

The Baron looked at him. "Was König a friend of yours?"

Careful now.

Largo said, "More like an acquaintance than a friend. But he seemed like a nice enough fellow."

"And do you, like König, carry a knife under your jacket?"

That surprised him, but he reasoned that might be the point. To test him.

All right, let me be tested.

"Yes, sir. The same one he carried, I believe."

"And you have it with you?"

"Yes."

"May I see it?"

Largo opened his jacket and handed the Baron the trench knife before he had a chance to think about it. Not thinking too much seemed to be a good idea at the moment.

The Baron stood and wandered to the window overlooking the factory, examining the knife in the light from the big furnaces. Largo thought that it looked like electric flames were dancing up and down the blade. A moment later, the Baron came back. He held the knife so that Largo could see the side of the blade.

"Very nice," he said. "It's one of ours, you know. See the bull's head seal and V along the edge? That's how you'll always know." He turned the knife so that the tip pointed at Largo's midsection. "Tell me. Have you ever used the knife?"

Don't think. Just tell the truth.

"No, Baron," said.

"Never?"

"No."

With a practiced hand, the Baron flipped the knife and handed it back to Largo, pommel end first. "How fortunate you are to have never encountered any sort of danger. You must lead a charmed life."

Largo felt nauseating embarrassment because the Baron clearly knew he hadn't been in the war at all. But he knew it wouldn't look good for himself or the company if the man thought he was a coward. "I almost used it recently," he blurted. "Last night, in fact. There was a man with some friends. They were going to attack me."

The Baron now looked at him with great interest. "And what did you do?"

Largo knew that he couldn't say, "My friend Roland saved my ass," but he had to say something believable.

Stay as close to the truth as possible.

"I suppose I used the knife in one sense, though I didn't have to stab anyone. I simply showed it to them and they backed off."

The Baron went back and sat on his desk again. He said, "So, you were in danger, but you restrained yourself and thought your way through the problem. Good for you. A cool head will take you far in this world."

"Thank you, Baron," said Largo. He felt relieved but not good, knowing he'd barely wormed his way out of the situation.

"Back to your job as a courier," said the Baron. "You say that you enjoy your job because it's fun. Is that the limit of your ambition? Fun forever without challenge?"

Damn. You're as bad as Branca. Always leading me down dangerous paths.

"I'm not sure I understand the question," Largo said, stalling.

The Baron sat back and opened his hands. "What are your goals?

Tell me this: if you could do anything you like, work anywhere, accomplish anything, what would you do?"

Kara nuzzled Largo's hand and he stroked her head. He said, "If I could do anything, I suppose I'd learn more about chimeras."

"Just learn?"

"I mean learn enough to work with them. How they're created and cared for. How, as you said earlier, they're improved and made even better than they are now."

Largo hoped that was the right answer. He'd confessed something he hadn't even admitted to Remy because it was too foolish to bring up.

The Baron took a cigarette from a box on his desk and lit it with a gold lighter that emitted not flame but a small arc of plazma. "Why don't you do it?" he said. "The university could give you a good grounding in the subject."

Largo looked down at Kara. "I have very little education, I'm afraid. My mother taught me to read and my father taught me numbers. The only books we had were ones Mother found in the trash or lifted from the market." Largo's hand froze on the chimera's head as he realized that, again, he'd said too much. *I just confessed that I came from a family of paupers, idiots, and, worse, thieves.* Branca wouldn't just fire him, he'd throttle him and toss him in the trash out back.

However, the Baron didn't seem to notice, or he didn't care. Instead he said, "Did you know that aside from producing armaments and eugenics, we're one of the largest Mara manufacturers in the country?"

Largo kept his eyes down. "No, I didn't."

The Baron puffed his cigarette and set it in an ashtray. "I only ask because we have apprenticeship programs in all of those industries. There aren't many openings, but intelligent young men with cool heads are always in demand," he said. "You'd learn the eugenic process from the bottom up. I could put in a word for you if you like."

Was this another test? Maybe to see if he was foolishly gullible, or loyal to the courier company? *Who cares?* he thought. The possibility of what the Baron said felt like the face-off with Andrzej, but in a good way. It seemed like a moment on which his whole life could pivot to a new direction. Just as he knew that he'd use the knife if Weimer or the others at work ever came at him again, Largo sensed that this was not a moment to be afraid.

"That would be incredible, Baron. Thank you."

Kara licked his hand and went back to lie down at the Baron's feet.

He said, "You understand that there's a lot to learn before you actually get to work with the eugenics themselves. There's a great deal of book study, and you'd spend your first few months in the lab mainly sweeping floors and scrubbing incubation tanks. But slowly, if you kept up with your studies, you'd be allowed to help in various procedures and taught the basics of eugenic design and function."

"I would sweep all of Lower Proszawa if you asked. I would do anything," said Largo.

The Baron smiled. "It takes years of practice to become a scribe—a somatic artisan—someone who works with eugenic creation. However, many have done it, so there's no reason that you couldn't too."

Largo stood dumbly, grasping for words. "I don't know what to say."

The Baron walked back behind his desk and sat down. "Don't say anything now. I'm sure I've kept you too long as it is. You'll have other deliveries to make."

To hell with the other deliveries, Largo thought. *I'll stand here all day and night if it will get me closer to an apprenticeship.*

"It was good meeting you," said the Baron. "Let's talk about this more on your future visits."

"Thank you. Thank you very much."

"Good day, Largo."

"Good day to you too, Baron."

Kara trotted to him for one last pet, then went back and lay down by the desk. Largo went to the outer office still excited by what had just happened. Dame Karoli eyed him like someone who suspected the fish in a butcher's window had gone bad. He almost laughed at her. Nothing could break the sense of elation he felt.

"Did you make your delivery to the Baron?" said Dame Karoli.

"Yes. Very successfully too, if I do say so myself."

"Then you're dismissed. I assume you remember the way out."

Largo pointed. "Yes. I believe I use the door."

Dame Karoli gave him a dark look. "Don't get above yourself, young man."

He gave her a broad, comical smile. "Forgive me, Dame Karoli. I meant nothing by it."

"Of course not. Go now. You're wasting my time and the Baron's air."

"I'm afraid I can't. Someone needs to sign for the Baron's delivery. Is that something I should ask him about, or is it more in line with your duties?"

Dame Karoli held out a hand and Largo gave her the receipt book. She signed the page and tossed down the book. Largo put it in his bag and gave her a little bow. "Thank you. Have a good day."

She turned to a filing cabinet and didn't reply. Largo went out along the metal walkway and pushed the button for the lift.

Have a very good day playing with papers. Someday you might have to call me Herr Moorden, professional scribe. I'll make a chimera cat like the ones at the carnival, but larger, and it will follow me around like Kara follows the Baron. It will come home with me at night and sleep at the bottom of Remy's and my bed.

The lift reached the bottom floor and Largo started out, practically floating—

Straight into Pietr's path. The man's arms were crossed and he held the large wrench against his chest.

He said, "Everywhere I go, you turn up. What are you doing here?"

Largo's good mood vanished, making him hate the man even more. He said, "I'm doing the same thing I was doing when I met you last time. Making a delivery. It's what I do. Are you capable of grasping that? I brought ink to you and a box to the Baron."

Pietr looked at him. "What kind of box?"

"I don't know. A box sort of box."

"Did you look inside it?"

"Of course not," said Largo "That's against regulations."

Pietr spit on the ground. "Naturally. A good boy like you would never bend the rules."

Largo felt the knife against his chest. He looked at Pietr's wrench. "I don't have time for this. Either hit me with that thing or get out of my way."

Pietr seemed to consider the possibility, but he finally stood aside and let Largo pass. "I don't want to see you here again."

Largo spun around. As nervous as Pietr made him, he couldn't be permitted to get between Largo and the Baron. He said, "I have duties to get back to. Why don't you go back to yours and leave me to mine?"

"This *is* mine." Pietr glanced up. "Things sometimes fall from up there, you know. Squash people flat."

"I'm going now," said Largo, knowing what it could mean to turn his back to Pietr.

Sure enough, the moment he turned around he felt a hand on his neck. He found himself lifted off the ground an inch or two and shoved toward the lift. Largo squirmed from Pietr's grasp and landed on his feet. When the big man tried to grab him again, Largo pulled the knife.

Pietr looked genuinely surprised. He stepped back, let the arm with the wrench drop to his side, and stepped back. "Don't come back here again," he said.

"You and your seditionist friends can't stop me."

"I bet we can," said Pietr as he disappeared around a corner.

Largo waited a moment before turning his back on the door. When he was certain that Pietr wasn't going to rush him from behind, he got on his bicycle and pedaled away from building 3.

Trucks, cars, and juggernauts rolled down the long driveway into and out of Schöne Maschinen. The gate was fifty yards ahead. A line of six Black Widows followed one of the trucks, crates and loads of steel on their backs. As before, Largo rode along the shoulder of the road to avoid the larger vehicles. His head pounded and he was sweating from the adrenaline rush of the encounter.

He was halfway to the open gate when he heard a loud bang and turned around to see what had happened. One of the trucks behind him had spun halfway around and crashed into the side of an automobile. Largo stopped, wondering if anyone was hurt. He was starting back toward the accident when he saw what caused it. Two Black Widows had dumped their loads and were making their way around the damaged vehicles.

Largo pulled his bicycle farther off the road to let the Widows pass, but as he moved, they moved *with* him. Puzzled, he rode slowly to the other side of the road. The Widows followed. Then he moved to the center of the road. The moment a Widow moved in the same direction, Largo had seen enough. He turned his bicycle and pedaled away as fast as he could.

Ahead, the factory gate was slowly closing. Largo rode even faster. He didn't need to look back to know that the Widows were gaining on him. As strong a rider as he was, there was no way he could match their speed. Still, there was nothing he could do but pump his legs and stop for nothing.

He made it through the gate as it was dangerously close to slamming shut. A tram full of people glided by as he sped into the street. Largo had to cut Margit's bicycle hard to the right to keep from slamming into the rear of the car. It was a slow and clumsy maneuver, one that would have been easy on his own bicycle.

The sky was clear, but it had rained recently and his back wheel slipped in a shallow puddle, almost sending him face-first onto the pavement. He regained his balance just in time to hear a loud crunch of metal from behind him. Largo glanced back and saw that the second Widow never made it out of the factory and had instead crashed into the gates. However, the first Widow was luckier. It had escaped and was quickly closing in on Largo.

Krahe Vale, the street on which Schöne Maschinen was located, was a straight, wide boulevard with nowhere to hide. When Largo reached the avenue that led to the Great Triumphal Square, he sped onto it—and still the Widow followed. As soon as the machine turned, Largo cut down a narrow side street. The heavy Widow wasn't able to turn as quickly and when it tried, it slipped on the wet pavement and slid into a stall selling yellowsheets.

After racing along two narrow blocks, Largo went down a long alley that ran by a row of squalid tenements housing foreign dockworkers. He had to dodge passersby and a horse-drawn wagon piled high with trash.

At the far end of the alley, where it opened onto the main riverfront road, he stopped. Sweating and out of breath, he gulped in lungfuls of river air that smelled of wet, rotten wood and the day's catch from the fishmonger shops.

What's happening? he wondered. He'd never seen a Widow malfunction before. If it *was* a malfunction.

Pietr. He had to have something to do with it.

Largo's hands trembled slightly, but he wasn't sure whether it was adrenaline or the fact he'd taken only a little morphia in the morning, hoping to see Remy at lunch. He was wondering briefly if he'd be able to stop long enough to take a drop when he heard screams behind him.

The Widow was at the far end of the tenement alley, racing toward him. Terrified parents grabbed children from the street, throwing themselves out of the way of the speeding machine. It sent street carts flying and smashed through the wagon, knocking the horse onto the sidewalk. Largo forgot about the morphia and rode as fast as he could onto the riverfront road.

He sped along the docks as weathered men in heavy coats hauled crates off ships to where they were loaded onto trucks by rusting Maras. Largo had to weave his way through the crowds of workers, piles of boxes, and cargo nets. The Widow, he knew, wouldn't be so careful. He heard shouts from behind him, screeching tires, and splintering wood as the charging machine ran straight through the busy dock.

Largo was getting tired. He knew he couldn't keep going at full speed for much longer. However, there were no side streets for him to veer into, just rows of warehouses on his right and moored ships on the left. His hands trembled and even though he was hot with perspiration, Largo felt an inner chill. *If only there had been a few more seconds to get the morphia*, he thought.

Judging from the sounds behind him, the Widow was trailing him by just a few yards. He looked to his right, hoping for a route that would get him off the dock, but the line of warehouses stretched into the distance. Ahead, a flatbed truck heavy with cargo pulled out of a warehouse. The dock was narrow at this point and the truck was large. It blocked the road as it maneuvered around piles of goods and machinery. Largo knew he couldn't stop or the Widow would be on him, and he couldn't ride around the truck without falling into the river or crashing into the warehouse. Still, he veered left toward the water.

At the very edge of the dock, he jerked the bicycle in a clumsy, violent arc away from the river. Largo hit his brakes but slammed into the driver's side door hard enough to knock him to the ground. He struck his head and when he tried to stand, he slid down onto his back. Largo had tricked the Widow before by turning sharply and he'd hoped it would work again, but no such luck—it ran straight at him.

The truck began rolling backward toward the warehouse. Largo grabbed the running board and the bicycle and held on, letting himself be dragged over the dock's rutted planks. The Widow reached out a spidery leg to grab him, but it was going too fast. With the truck out of the way, there was nothing between it and the water. It slid sideways off the dock—its legs ripping into the old wood as it tried to hold on—and flipped end over end. The heavy Widow vanished in a second, leaving a trail of bubbles while its legs continued to kick as it slid to the river bottom.

The driver stepped out of the truck and pulled Largo to his feet, yelling in a language he'd never heard before. He shook his head, as much to clear away the dizziness as to tell the driver he couldn't understand him. But the trucker was no longer interested in him. He grabbed Largo's shoulder and yelled, "Police!" Largo turned and saw a small group of uniformed officers running toward him.

He pushed the driver off and jumped on the bicycle. He pedaled around the truck and took off down the dock, heading for what looked like a passageway to offices a few warehouses down. The police yelled and blew their whistles. Largo hoped that they hadn't been close enough to recognize him. After the encounter with Tanz and the Sergeant back in the butchers' square, he'd had enough of bullocks for three lifetimes.

On his way back to work, Largo ducked into a bricked-over doorway in the machine breakers' quarter. Maras of all sizes, from the small delivery bread boxes to servant Maras to large earth movers, lay in pieces along the streets. Largo turned away from the machines and upended the small vial of morphia Rainer had given him. In a few seconds, his hands stopped shaking and the chill in his chest was replaced by warmth. He turned and leaned against the bricks, watching families methodically dismantling the loathsome Maras, scavenging whatever usable parts they could find to sell in the street markets. They worked quietly and steadily. Even the filthy children were serious, handling mallets and small cutting torches with ease. They ignored Largo as he let the morphia calm his system. He thought about Haxan Green and how close he'd come to being one of these children. Looking back at the docks, he half expected to see the Widow, dripping with river water, speeding toward him. But the street was empty. He thought again about what Pietr had said: "*I bet we can.*"

When Largo was younger, becoming a bicycle messenger had seemed like the grandest feat he could imagine. He'd left the Green with a respectable profession and even had a flat, as cramped and dingy as it was. But it wasn't enough anymore. He'd hoped becoming chief courier would impress Remy—and she *had* been excited for him—but how far could it take him? A job at Schöne Maschinen, though, that would change everything.

I could have a real life. Be a professional, like Remy. An artist. We'd be happy and I'd never be ashamed again.

If Pietr or one of his friends didn't kill him, of course. Still, it was worth the risk. It was worth anything.

He dropped the vial in the gutter and when he looked down he saw himself. His knuckles were scraped and he was filthy from where he'd fallen on the dock. Worse, Margit's bicycle was scratched and dented from running into the truck.

Largo got back on the bicycle wearily. He stayed to side streets as he rode back to the company. The riding was easier and there were few police. Margit was waiting for him when he arrived. She'd repaired his bicycle with two brand-new tires and smiled when she saw him. But her smile quickly faded.

"What the hell did you do to my bike?" she said. Margit looked him up and down. "And yourself? You look like shit."

"I'm sorry about your bicycle," said Largo. "It still rides perfectly. I can pay for all the repairs."

"That's not what I asked. You're too good a rider for this. What happened?"

His earlier fear bubbled up into anger. "I'll tell you what happened. Your fucking friend Pietr tried to kill me."

Margit shifted her weight uncomfortably. "What are you talking about?" she said.

"Why didn't you tell me that he worked at Schöne Maschinen? I could have looked out for him."

Margit shrugged slightly and said, "He's just a machinist. His salary helps us buy ink and paper."

"I know he's a machinist!" Largo shouted. "He threatened me with a wrench as big as you. Then he sent a couple of Black Widows after me."

Margit got closer to him. "Please lower your voice. The police might still be watching the company. What do you mean he sent Black Widows after you?"

"I don't know how he did it, but he did," Largo whispered. "Right after I scared him away the machines attacked me. He works on the machines. It was his doing."

"You scared Pietr?" said Margit, concern in her voice. "How?"

"Like this," said Largo, and he pulled out his knife. Margit calmly laid her hand over his and pushed the knife back under his coat. He slid it into its harness.

"I told you," she said. "There might be police about. Don't give them a reason to notice us. Or you."

Largo's skin was still hot from anger. He said, "I'm sorry. I'm not mad at you. This is between Pietr and me."

"No," said Margit. "Let me talk to him. If what you say is true, I'll take care of it. He won't bother you again."

Back on familiar ground with someone he liked, Largo felt his fury began to fade. He said, "All right. I trust you. But I'm telling you the truth. He did something to the Widows. They almost killed me and when they didn't, the bullocks just about got me."

"Nothing like it will ever happen again," said Margit. She got on her bicycle and tested the pedals. When they seemed to work, she rode around in a couple of tight circles. Satisfied, she got off and set it against the loading dock. "Considering what happened, keep your money. We have repair people in the group. They can fix the dents."

Largo nodded. Now that he was calmer, another thought came to him. "I'm curious. Why did you call Baron Hellswarth 'the Beast'? It was his secretary who wanted to push me into a furnace. The Baron was smart. And friendly. And . . ." He almost mentioned the apprenticeship but caught himself at the last second.

Margit leaned against the dock and put on her round dark glasses. "You're a nice guy, Largo, but you have to learn to protect yourself."

"What does that mean?"

She got on her bicycle and said, "Of course the Baron was friendly and smart. The most dangerous monsters are always the most charming. That way you won't notice as they slip you down their gullet."

Before Largo could ask her what she meant, Margit said, "I'm late with my deliveries. I'll see you later."

Largo had a dozen more questions, but she was through the gates and gone before he could get out a word. He dusted himself off and went into the office.

SERVANTS AND WARRIORS

From the supplemental section at the end of a Mara
owner's manual

Now that you have your new Hellswarth Mara maid up and running, we thought you might enjoy some fascinating facts about
the history of your new home companion.

Like many great ideas, these essential servants and warriors
began as something quite different. Maras were originally small
clockwork novelties prized by royalty and the wealthiest Proszawan families. These early Maras could each perform a single
simple task, such as serving tea, dealing cards, or imitating song-
birds.

Later, larger and more complex steam-powered Maras found
their way into the workforce, mainly on farms and in factories.
They could use their brute strength to move heavy loads or work
in areas too dangerous for human beings, such as the great furnaces at the Schöne Maschinen factory. (Since their introduction, injuries have plummeted by 84%!) More recently, with the
introduction of plasma-driven electrics and more complex control systems, Maras have moved from simple labor and into the
streets—as delivery vehicles—and our homes—as helpful servants and guardians.

Another area where Maras have become essential partners is

security. Maras work tirelessly with our brave police departments and the military, and they were decisive in aiding our victory in the Great War.

A strong military has always been a proud part of Proszawan history and the developments in martial Maras will soon be seen in our homes and city streets. New discoveries in "mechanistic intelligence" mean that Maras can be trained for more and more complicated tasks. Be on the lookout for self-driving Mara juggernauts and airships—and, soon, independent battlefield Maras. Schöne Maschinen is even investigating ways of combining Maras and chimeras into new intelligent systems that could one day replace soldiers on the battlefield and factory workers, leading to a safer and more leisure-filled world.

Thank you from everyone at Schöne Maschinen for your purchase. We're sure it will make your life more fulfilling now and for years to come. And who knows what wonders tomorrow will bring? We'll see you in the future!

CHAPTER TEN

HERR BRANCA WAS AT HIS USUAL PLACE BEHIND HIS DESK. HOWEVER, IN-stead of ignoring Largo as he filled out paperwork, he put down his pen the moment he walked in the door. "You're back," he said.

"That I am," said Largo. He took the receipt book from his bag and set it on Branca's desk and wiped some sweat from his eyes. The older man ignored the book and stared at him.

"Did the Baron challenge you to a duel?"

"Excuse me?" said Largo.

"You're a bit disheveled. I thought that perhaps Baron Hellswarth had invited you to wrestle."

Largo was exhausted and high enough from the morphia that he wasn't sure whether Branca was joking. He decided he didn't care and said, "It wasn't the Baron. He was quite fine. But on the way back a truck cut me off. I barely got out of the way in time."

Branca looked at him seriously. "Are you hurt? Did you talk to the police?"

"No," he said. "There weren't any around."

Branca opened the receipt book. "There seldom are when we most need them. How damaged are you? Can you go on your afternoon deliveries?"

Largo rubbed his shoulder where it had hit the truck. "I'm fine, sir. I can finish my rounds."

"Very good," said Branca, setting the receipt book into a desk drawer. "I don't believe that is the Baron's signature in your book. Whose is it?"

"Dame Karoli, his secretary."

"And what did you think of her?"

"She was charming."

"Was she now?" said Branca thoughtfully.

Quietly, Largo added, "Charming as a talking viper."

Branca said, "Finally. The correct answer. For a moment, I was afraid that you hadn't really gone to Schöne Maschinen."

"No, sir. I was there," he said. "It was even more impressive than I imagined inside."

"A national treasure, to be sure," said Branca offhandedly. Then he added, "A moment ago, you said that Baron Hellswarth was fine. In what sense was he fine?"

Largo wondered if this was another test. He was growing tired of them. However, there was only one way to find out. He said, "I only meant that he was very nice. We talked for several minutes. He even let me pet Kara, his chimera."

"What a special moment that must have been for all of you. What did you talk about with the Baron?"

"We talked about Schöne Maschinen and all the different things they do. Did you know that besides armaments, they produce chimeras and Maras?"

"Yes, Largo. I do possess that knowledge. So does ninety-nine percent of Lower Proszawa. Was that all you talked about?"

It occurred to Largo that this wasn't the first time Branca had asked these questions. König had been going to Schöne Maschinen for years. Branca must know a good deal about the Baron's interests. This was both good and bad. It meant he couldn't lie, but it also meant that Branca already knew most of the answers, so he didn't have to say too much.

"He asked me about myself. I suppose if I'm going to be returning to his office, he wanted to know who I was."

"And who are you?" said Branca. "To the Baron, I mean."

Largo had been so overwhelmed by the apprenticeship discussion that it was hard to remember anything else they'd talked about. "I told him that I liked my job and how exciting it was to finally see Schöne Maschinen itself for the first time."

"Is that all?"

He knew he needed to give Branca something else or the bastard would be picking at him all day. "He asked me what I would do if I could do anything."

"What did you tell him?"

Largo looked at his raw knuckles. "That I lacked a formal education and would like to do something about that."

"An education. So, you want to leave us soon? I can prepare your severance papers," said Branca.

"No, sir. That's not what I mean," Largo said. He took half a step forward. "I simply meant that I'd like to better myself."

Branca's lips moved minutely into a vague smile. "Calm yourself, Largo. I was joking. It's good that you want to expand your mind. Most other couriers simply want to drink and bed random floozies."

If it cheers them up, why not? he thought. *What do you know about happiness?*

Branca went on. "Ambition is good. The company is always looking for bright young men. A bit of schooling and soon you'll be my superior."

Maybe if I fail at everything else . . .

"I doubt that. Anyway, it was just . . . I'm not sure of the word."

"Theoretical?"

"That's it. I think that, like you, he wanted to know that I aspired to something greater."

Branca took a new receipt book from the desk. "Careful how far you climb and how quickly. You wouldn't want to end up like little Bruno Driest. Have you heard of him?"

Largo tried to place the name. "Was he another courier?"

"No. He was the progeny of a great magician. Being a child, he thought the sun was a beautiful golden apple and sought to pluck it. He flew into the sky in one of his father's machines. Do you know what happened then?"

"No, sir."

"He burst into flames and fell into the sea, never to be heard from again. You don't want that, do you?"

Was that a threat? Largo wondered. "Not at all. If the choice is between drowning and staying where I am, I'm quite happy on the ground."

"A fine code to live by," Branca said. He handed Largo the new receipt book. "Go to lunch now. In deference to your accident, take a full hour. Your afternoon deliveries are straightforward and none is urgent. You can do them when you get back. However, you might consider cleaning up in the bathroom before you leave."

"Thank you. I will," Largo said.

He put the new book in his bag and started to leave, but Branca said, "I noticed Margit changing the tires on a bicycle this morning. It looked a bit like yours."

Is the old bastard spying on us?

"Yes. My tires were flat," said Largo.

"Both of them?"

"Sadly, yes."

"How unfortunate. And how kind of Margit to help you."

"Yes, she's very nice."

"And what will you be doing for her?" said Branca.

"I'm not sure what you mean."

Branca picked up a pen and gestured with it as he talked. "Margit did you a favor. That's often a reciprocal situation."

Largo wondered what exactly he was getting at. Did Branca know something he didn't? "She didn't ask me for anything," he said.

"What a generous heart," said Branca. "Still, I'm sure any favor she might ask you in the future won't be too onerous."

He definitely knows something, thought Largo. About the leaflet? Or was he just trying to turn him against Margit? She said people at the company were out to get her. "I'm sure anything she'd ask for would be reasonable."

"She seems like a reasonable girl. Still, we must look out for our own best interests. Do you understand me?"

"Of course, sir," said Largo.

First Margit tells me to learn to take care of myself, like I'm a child. Now the fossil tells me to be afraid of Margit. It's my day for irritating advice.

Branca said, "That's all for now. Have a pleasant lunch. And watch out for trucks."

"Thank you. I will." Largo walked out before Branca could say something else stupid.

It was early enough that none of the other couriers were at the Fräulein Sabel café. Largo pushed his way through the crowd to the Trefle on the back wall. He dropped in some coins and had the operator connect him to the Grand Dark. Lucie answered.

"I'm so sorry, but Una changed the new play and everyone is in rehearsal," she said.

Largo sagged against the wall. He desperately wanted to tell someone about what Baron Hellswarth had said, and Remy was the only one he trusted. "Will she be much longer? I have an hour for lunch. I could come by."

"I'm sorry, Largo, but Una says they'll be at it all afternoon. But I do have some good news."

"Yes? What's that?"

"I'm going to be in the play too!" she said. "I've been sweeping floors and mending costumes for so long that I'd lost all hope. But today Una gave me a part. It's a small one, you understand, but I'll be in a puppet, just like Remy."

Lucie was sweet, but her moving up in her job when his chance could be years away was the last thing he wanted to hear right now. "That's wonderful. Congratulations."

"Thank you. I couldn't be more excited," she said. "In fact, I have to go. Una is calling us back to the stage."

"Good luck. Tell Remy I called."

"I will. And we'll both see you soon anyway."

"You will?"

Lucie said, "Yes. Some of us are coming along to help her pick out your new clothes."

"That sounds like fun," said Largo, wondering if he should have let the Widow finish him off after all.

"Goodbye," said Lucie.

He started to say goodbye back, but she hung up before he had the chance.

Largo walked to the bar and thought about ordering a whiskey. He wanted to see Remy, but he also wanted more morphia. The pain in his shoulder was a steady ache and he knew it would continue to get worse. He thought about the morphia he'd given Rainer, but considering his friend's condition, it wouldn't be fair to ask for it back.

He was pulling change from his pocket to pay for a drink when he decided against it. After the day he'd had, if he started drinking now he wouldn't stop. Instead, he ordered a mutton sandwich. He had his lunch at a small table in the cramped back of the café, as far as possible from other people and the world.

Branca had been telling the truth. Largo had only two deliveries in the afternoon. Both were all the way on the other side of the city but, barring another encounter with Pietr or Tanz, the rest of the day should be easy.

The first delivery was the more difficult of the two, so he did that one first. It wasn't that the address was difficult to get to, but it was an import-export company and that meant it was near the docks. After the incident with the Black Widow, he was worried he might be recognized. Largo kept his head down as he took a circuitous route that brought him through the brothel district, where he paused for a moment and watched as the police examined the prostitutes' identification papers. Any foreign ones or ones whose documents seemed suspect were deemed potential spies, loaded into juggernauts, and taken away. When a police Sergeant noticed him watching, Largo sped down a side street.

Wanting to avoid the butchers' square, he had to go along the western edge of the city, where he caught a glimpse of the carnival. He thought about the tickets at home and how happy Remy would be when he showed them to her.

Last, he cut through what was, to him, the worst part of the city—the Midden. As bad as Machtviertel was, the Midden made it look like the most refined parts of Empyrean.

The Midden was the shore on which the most dismal refuse of the war washed up. Clandestine and amateur doctors performed every sort of medical horror on the desperate and the indigent. Iron Dandies went there in hopes of new faces, but often left more hideous than before and with their money gone. Prosthetics shops hung stolen limbs outside. The ones with Mara workings twitched like they were in agony. Other shops displayed exotic statuary and strange religious icons from foreign campaigns. The most disreputable shops sold military weapons, uniforms, and medals brought there by grave robbers. The Drops was rampant in the Midden. Was this what Dr. Venohr had been talking about? Was this where the plague entered the city by way of all the misbegotten goods? Largo wondered what the merry men and women in their tuxedos and gowns in the Great Triumphal Square would think if they knew about the Midden.

When he arrived at the import-export company, he gave an envelope to a fat man named Bohm. Largo made sure he signed the receipt book, then got on his bicycle and rode away. He didn't even wait to see if Bohm would offer him a tip. More than money, he wanted to be away from the docks and the horror that was the Midden.

His last stop of the day was at *Ihre Skandale*, a yellowsheet that featured the most sensational rumors and gossip in the city. Because it printed lurid articles and photochromes of local murders, Una loved it and used the yarns as the bases for many of her plays. If he wanted to sit backstage at the theater, Largo would often have to move piles of the papers off the chairs.

Inside, he met the paper's editor in chief, Herr Ernst, a tall, thin man with ink-stained fingers. He eyed Largo as he signed the receipt book, and it made him uncomfortable.

"Going by your clothes and your knuckles it's been a rough day," said Ernst lightly.

Largo glanced at his skinned right hand. "Rougher than some. Less than others." He could tell the man was angling at something, but he couldn't decide what.

Ernst dropped the box Largo had given him on the desk and spoke thoughtfully. "König used to make our deliveries. I haven't seen you before."

Not sure how much to say, Largo replied simply, "König has left the service."

Ernst wiped some of the ink off his hands with a handkerchief. He said, "If you're the new König, you must be running all over Lower Proszawa."

Largo didn't like being called "the new König," but he let it go for the moment. "Every inch of it, sir. Wherever customers need us."

"I bet you see some interesting things on your sojourns."

"Occasionally, but I try to mind my own business."

"Of course," said Ernst. "I didn't mean to imply otherwise. The reason I'm asking, you see, is that your profession gives you a unique view of the city. One that could make you extra money. It certainly put some change in König's pocket."

Largo looked at the man with more interest. This must be what Parvulesco meant when he'd said this promotion could bring in money on the side. "König sold you stories about what he'd seen on his rounds?"

"Exactly. Now you, if you're so inclined, can do the same," said Ernst excitedly. "For instance, have you seen anything interesting to-day?"

What hasn't been interesting today? he thought. Largo looked around the office at the scattered police reports and men and women whispering into at least a dozen Trefles. More than he'd seen in one place before. "I'm not sure what would be interesting to you."

"Let's begin at the beginning. Where did you start your day?"

Largo wondered if he should tell the truth. He was leery of Ernst, but if it meant extra cash and he didn't get too specific, what harm could it do? "I was at Schöne Maschinen this morning," he said.

Ernst's expression brightened. He said, "Really now? Did you hear about what happened there?"

Largo thought for a minute and decided to see what would happen if he said just a little something. "You mean the Black Widows?"

"Yes!" said Ernst. "I don't suppose you know anything about the incident?"

He thought about Pietr. Was it possible that the bastard was going to earn him some extra coins? "I was there," he said. "I saw them escape."

Ernst grabbed Largo's arm and pulled him down into a chair beside his desk. "Tell me about it. Everything you remember."

Seeing the man's eagerness, Largo got nervous. He knew the less he told him, the better. He said, "I didn't really see very much."

"Give me a decent story and I'll give you a Valda," said Ernst.

"Right now?"

Ernst took a gold coin from his pocket and set it on the desk, far enough from Largo that he couldn't grab it and run. "Does that jog your memory? Maybe you saw more than you realized . . . ?"

Largo looked at the coin, then at Ernst, and said, "As a matter of fact, I saw quite a bit of the mayhem." He then went on to tell Ernst as much of the story as possible, careful to keep himself out of it except as an observer. When he was done, he grew nervous again. "You won't tell anyone that you got the story from me, will you?"

Over his mouth, Ernst made a motion like inserting a key into a lock and turning it. "Not a word," he said, sliding the Valda over to Largo, who put it in his pocket. "Let's come to an agreement, shall we? Any interesting, peculiar, or novel sights you come across in your duties, you observe all you can and then come here and tell me a story like you did today."

"And I'll get a Valda when I do?"

Ernst sat back in his chair. "It depends on the nature of the story and what details you have. It might not always get you a Valda, but it will always pay something. Some silver at the very least."

Largo smiled at him. "It's a deal," he said.

Ernst put his hand across the desk and they shook. "If you should ever doubt yourself about a story, especially if you should witness anything criminal, remember that *Ihre Skandale* has the largest circulation of any paper in Lower Proszawa. Giving us the story, it might have clues that the bullocks don't. You could help to solve some dastardly crimes. Think of your visits here as serving the public good."

It was a con and Largo knew it, but it was a good one and he appreciated that—as well as the money. "I always try to be a good citizen," he said.

"There you go," said Ernst. "Now why don't you get going so I can write up this beauty that you just gave me?"

"Of course." When Largo got up, he saw a pile of *Der Knochengarten* horror pulps sitting on another desk. The cover illustration was a terrifying Angel of Death with a shimmering skull peeking from his cowl, a collection of heads dangling from his honed scythe. Under it was the title "You Can't Escape the Reaper."

Ernst said, "You read *Der Knochengarten*?"

"When I can afford it."

Ernst went to the pile and tossed Largo one. "On the house," he said. "This new issue will give you the shivers. I don't think you'll be sleeping much tonight."

That made him think of Remy. He said, "That sounds all right to me."

Ernst went back to his desk and said, "Go on now. Off with you. But let's talk again soon. Here's my card. If you can't come in, you can always call me. I'll reimburse you for the Trefle charge."

Largo put the card inside *Der Knochengarten* and shoved it deep into his jacket pocket so Branca wouldn't see it. He nodded to Ernst and got on his bicycle. The ride back to the office was much less colorful than the ride to *Ihre Skandale*, but with a Valda in his pocket, it was much more pleasant.

After work, Largo met Remy at her flat on the edge of Kromium and they walked to the secondhand shops on Tin Fahrspur. Before they left, Remy said that she'd invited a couple of friends to help them pick clothes. Largo already knew that from his call with Lucie, but his heart sank a little when they reached the corner and it looked to him like she'd invited everyone she knew. Lucie and Hanna he didn't mind so much, but too-handsome Baumann was there as well. Worst of all,

Enki was joining them. *Why is he here?* Largo wondered. *He's blind, so he can't see a damn thing.*

Plus he's a loudmouthed ass.

Remy waved to the group from across the street. While they waited for a tram to pass, Largo said, "Why is Enki here? I thought you were all sick of him."

"It's true he can be a pest," said Remy with a sigh. "But he's an old friend and anyway, he sneaked off somewhere for a few days without a word. I want to find out where he went. Maybe he has a new lady love."

Only if she's blind too, thought Largo. *And deaf.*

When they reached the group, Lucie took Remy's arm excitedly. "We've been scouting good shopping prospects for you and settled on this shop."

"What's it called?" said Largo.

"We're not sure," Lucie said. She pointed above the door of a large shop a few doors down from the corner. The painted sign was so worn that the name of the shop was illegible. All any of them could make out was the painted image of a man and woman in formal attire standing on a cloud.

Baumann made a face and said, "Are they supposed to be dead?"

"No!" said Lucie. "They're happily drifting off to somewhere wonderful."

"It looks like they're floating to purgatory," said Baumann, and Lucie playfully cuffed him on the arm. "You brute," he said.

"Poor dear," said Hanna. "I know how to make it feel better." She passed him a tiny brown bottle of cocaine. He cupped a hand over his face to hide it and snorted a small amount from the back of his other hand.

"Me next," squealed Lucie. Baumann tapped out a small amount onto his hand again and she sniffed it up. "Yummy," she said, and refused to let go of his hand. To Largo it looked like he didn't mind at all. Hanna tapped out a small amount for herself and Enki. She passed the bottle to Remy and she and Largo took some. He was especially grateful since he hadn't had a chance to ask Remy for morphia before they rushed out to meet the others. The cocaine would keep him going until they could sneak away.

Enki said, "Is anyone going to tell me what the painting looks like or must I dwell in ignorance forever?" His tone surprised Largo. It was nothing like the other night at the Petersen party. He sounded almost friendly.

"It's a man and woman in lovely clothes standing on a cloud," said Remy.

"How charming," he said.

Hanna widened her eyes, pretending to be shocked. "My god. He's human after all."

In the shop, Largo tried on what seemed like an endless combination of jackets and pants until he felt like a dressing dummy. Worse, all the activity made his injured shoulder ache even more. When he complained, Enki passed him a hip flask of whiskey. After a couple of sips, trying on clothes again became pleasant, especially with the women cooing around him, telling him how handsome he looked. As they narrowed the choices, Baumann said, "I wore something like that in *Kapitan der Liebe* and women went wild."

"That decides it, doesn't it?" said Remy.

Largo looked at himself in the mirror and liked what he saw. The suit was stylish enough to not be as embarrassing as his current wardrobe, but serious enough that even a fossil like Branca had to approve of it. He bought a couple of extra shirts to go with it and as he was paying, Remy showed him a formal jacket, shirt, and tie. "You would look gorgeous in these," she said. When she checked the price tag she made a face. "But they're expensive." Largo took out his Valda and bought them without hesitation. Remy threw her arms around him and kissed him.

"We should celebrate your handsome gentleman," said Hanna.

"I agree," Remy said, and led them to a bar on the next block. Lucie used the Trefle to call Una, who joined them a few minutes later. Enki bought the first round of drinks and everybody toasted to his good health. Largo marveled at his pleasant behavior and refusal to call the bar bourgeois.

Remy said, "You've been gone for days without a word, Enki. Did you run off with a voluptuous art patron?"

"No. At least, I don't think so," he said. "The truth is, I can't remember much of anything."

"You drink too much," said Una.

"You might be right. I must have been drinking a lot to forget everything so thoroughly."

"We thought you'd abandoned us. But you've returned, and that's all that matters," said Remy.

175

"Thank you. But I want to say something. The other night, at the Petersens' party, I behaved badly. Talking about rebellion and armed revolt was stupid. Worse, if the wrong person had heard my blathering, it could have put you all in danger. I'm very sorry."

Lucie, who was sitting between him and Baumann, patted him on the shoulder.

"We were all drinking and acting foolishly. I'm sure you're forgiven," said Remy.

Hanna put down her drink and said, "You should disappear more often. It improves your disposition." Even Enki laughed at that.

A few minutes later, Largo moved his chair next to Hanna's. He said, "Do you mind if I ask you a few questions about your job?"

"Feel free," she said, curious.

"You design chimeras, right? Does that mean you work for Schöne Maschinen?"

"Yes, I do. Why do you ask?"

"I was just there and met Baron Hellswarth."

Hanna set down her cigarette. "I'm impressed. I've been there three years and have only seen him twice. What did you think of him?"

"He was very kind to me. Very smart. He let me pet Kara."

Hanna smiled. "Did you like her? I worked on Kara's development, you know. She's one of our most complex eugenics. The Baron himself directed the project."

"She was wonderful. Beautiful and very friendly."

"She doesn't like everyone, but if she liked you, she must have good taste," said Hanna. "But why are you suddenly interested in eugenics?"

Largo said, "I've always been interested. Who wouldn't be?"

Hanna puffed her cigarette. "You should let me know the next time you're at Schöne Maschinen. I might be able to give you a tour of the laboratory."

"That would be wonderful," he said. Then, more shyly, he added, "The Baron also said that you sometimes take on apprentices."

"Ah. It becomes clearer," said Hanna, patting his hand. "You don't want to spend the rest of your life running errands? Good for you. Yes, we do have an apprentice program, but why don't we take things one step at a time and I give you a tour? The work can be exciting, but it's not like we design miracles every day. There are a lot of failures and missteps."

He hadn't thought of that. "What happens to them?"

Hanna sipped her drink. "Most die quickly. Others, we have to put down ourselves. Don't worry. We're quite efficient and humane. They feel nothing."

Oh," said Largo. "I'm glad."

Hanna looked at him. "Dealing with failures is one of the first lessons you learn when working with eugenics. You have to steel your heart to it. If you can't do that . . ."

"No. I can. It's just something I hadn't thought of before."

Hanna looked at Remy, who winked at her. "She thinks I'm trying to steal you," she said. "If you weren't with Remy, I just might."

Largo flushed red. "I'm sure she isn't thinking anything like that."

"Are you blushing? Yes, under different circumstances I'd definitely eat you up."

Largo looked back at Remy, who blew him a kiss. "I'm flattered," he said softly.

Hanna brushed some hair from Largo's forehead. "You should go back to your lady love. Maybe I'll steal you both away someday," she said. "Until then, come to my lab and I'll show you what we're working on."

"I'd really appreciate it," Largo said. He held Hanna's hand as he got up.

"Now I'm the one who's blushing," she said.

When Largo sat down next to Remy she said, "What were you two whispering about?"

"I think she's planning on ravishing us both," he said.

"I've had worse offers," said Remy. "Was there anything besides pillow talk?"

"Yes. She said she might give me a tour of the chimera laboratory at Schöne Maschinen."

Remy made a face. "I'm not sure I could do that. All those strange animals."

"Yes, but some of them are beautiful."

"True. Well, if you go you'll have to tell me all about it."

"Don't worry. You'll hear everything." As pleasant as it was being with everyone, Largo wished that he and Remy were alone so that he could tell her about what the Baron had said. Instead, he whispered, "Do you have any morphia with you?"

"Of course. Do you want some now?"

"It will help me get through the rest of the evening."

"Come on," Remy said. She pulled him into a stall in the men's restroom and they put drops under each other's tongues.

When they returned to the table, Baumann said, "That must have been the quickest fuck in history." Lucie laughed and squeezed his arm.

Remy said, "It's true. Largo is that brilliant a lover."

"Lucky girl," said Una. "Now that you're so relaxed I expect an especially great performance tonight."

"I won't disappoint you."

"You never do, dear." Una looked at her watch. "On that note, ladies, it's time for us to return to the Grand Dark."

Lucie frowned and kissed Baumann passionately. Remy got up and said to Hanna, "Can I trust you with him?"

"Never," she replied.

"Take care, ladies," said Enki.

Baumann raised a glass to them as they left. He said, "I barely have time for one more drink, but plenty for a bit more of the powder. Would anyone care to join me?"

"My apologies, Largo," said Hanna. "I was in love with you a moment ago, but now I'm falling for Baumann."

"I understand," he said. "I think we're all feeling that way."

Largo spent the last of his coins on a tram home so he could protect his new clothes. In his flat, he stripped off his ragged work garb and threw it in a heap on the desk in the bedroom.

It was hard to get what Baron Hellswarth said out of his head, and Hanna's offer to show him her laboratory made it even harder. Largo put on his new clothes. He felt as if he were on the cusp of some great transformation. When he was dressed, he looked at himself in the mirror. Even in the piss-yellow light he could tell that he was changing. It made him happy that he was able to afford to buy the formal clothes because they had delighted Remy so much. Still, he needed to watch his money. But if he kept getting decent tips and could sell some stories to *Ihre Skandale*, it could help change things even faster. The thought of leaving behind everything he knew and had grown up with was unnerving, but thrilling too. What would it be like to be a whole new person? Could he do it? Then he thought of Enki at the bar.

If he can change from a horse's ass, then so can I. I just have to work harder than ever.

He thought again of Pietr.

And not die.

He wore his new suit when he rode his bicycle to the Grand Dark that night. The first play was the one he'd seen his last time in the theater, the tale of the murdered wife possessing her husband's current wife to kill him. Remy had played the murdered bride last time, but tonight Lucie took over the role. She was a passable maniac, but nothing compared to Remy. Still, it was one of her first major roles and she attacked it with passion, and Largo had to admire her for that.

The second play, *The Trench Demon*, had a similar theme, but its presentation was far more disturbing. The story was about a brave soldier who'd gone off to war in High Proszawa while his brother remained in the city. The brother had faked an injury to avoid war service and began an affair with the soldier's wife. After his death in a plague bomb attack, the soldier's ghost returned home to infect the adulterous couple with the disease that had killed him.

Una spared the audience nothing.

While the play ended in the soldier's boudoir, it began on a gruesome battlefield filled with twisted bodies covered in stage blood. The deaths of the brother and wife were prolonged and especially hideous, even by Una's standards. The flesh on their faces bubbled and smoked until it fell away, leaving just their charred, screaming skulls. Remy played the wronged soldier and Largo thought it was her most disturbing—and greatest—performance.

The audience went wild at the end of the play and gave it a standing ovation. In the lobby, patrons playfully clawed at their faces and mimed convulsions as they waited for their coats and hats. Largo didn't hear Una come up behind him.

"What did you think?" she said excitedly.

"I think you have a hit on your hands."

"I think so too. Remy was in particularly good form. Give her a kiss for me when you see her."

"I will," said Largo.

Before he could go backstage, Una added, "And go easy on her tonight. Tomorrow's crowd will be even bigger. I'll need her in good shape."

"I'll see that she gets a good night's sleep."

"Liar," said Una happily as she moved into the crowd to see off some of the Grand Dark's most important patrons.

Largo tried to congratulate Lucie on her performance, but she was already in Baumann's arms and kissing him furiously. Remy was exhausted, so he put his bicycle on the back of a Mara cab and took her home.

They didn't make it as far as the bedroom in her flat and ended up making love on the sofa in the living room. Afterward, she draped the covering over the cage in which her parakeet chirped quietly. Largo put her to bed and carefully laid out his new clothes on a chair. Remy's eyes were already heavy when he crawled into bed with her.

"I have a surprise for you," he said. "Two, actually."

"How lovely. Tell me."

"I met some people from the carnival last night and they gave me tickets."

She smiled sleepily and said, "Wonderful. I love the carnival. We should go with Lucie and Baumann. The little fool is in love and he has delightful cocaine. What's your other surprise?"

"I met Baron Hellswarth today."

She turned to him and sat up on one elbow. "Uncle Rudy? Did you boys hit it off?"

"Wait—Baron Hellswarth is your *uncle*? Why didn't you ever tell me?" said Largo.

Remy shrugged. "How much have you said about *your* family? Besides, we haven't exactly had a lot of conversations about rifles and bombs."

"What I mean is, I had no idea you were related to the Hellswarth family."

"That's how I met Herr Petersen and loads of other wealthy art patrons. I know oodles of important people," she said sleepily. "Uncle Rudy helped me get this flat. But that's not important. What did you two talk about?"

Largo told her about the possibility of his getting an apprentice-ship at the chimera laboratory. She kissed him when he was finished.

"If I'd known you were going I could have made an introduction, but it's not necessary now. You charmed him all by yourself."

Remy shivered and Largo thought about watching her convulse

during the play. He said, "How have you been feeling lately? I was so worried about you the other night."

She put her hand on his chest. "I'm fine. Dr. Venohr came by just yesterday and pronounced me fit as a fiddle."

"Is that all?"

"He gave me some silly pills. I have to take them twice a day."

"And did you take them?"

She rolled onto her back and looked at the ceiling. "Cluck cluck, mother hen. No, I haven't taken the second."

"I'll get it for you. Where's the bottle?"

"On the nightstand."

"And some water too."

"Don't fuss over me, Largo. You're no fun when you're like this."

He stopped at the bedroom door. "I tell you what. If you're a good girl and take your pill, you can have a drop of morphia before you go to sleep."

Remy clapped her hands happily. "There's my Largo. Hurry back."

He brought her the water and watched as she swallowed the pill. When she was done, he put a drop of morphia under each of their tongues. She fell back on her pillow with a blissful look on her face.

She said, "You know, Dr. Venohr works for Uncle, too. He's someone you should get to know better."

"What does he do?" said Largo.

Remy laughed. "I don't know. Some medical thing or other. We should all go out to dinner one night."

"Let's do that," said Largo eagerly, but Remy was already asleep.

Even with the morphia, talking about Baron Hellswarth got him excited again so that he couldn't sleep. He put on a robe that Remy had bought for him and went into the living room with his copy of *Der Knochengarten*. He read until his eyes got tired, but he knew that he still wouldn't be able to sleep. He put the pulp on a table and looked around the room as if he were seeing it for the first time. On the mantel and some tables were small but expensive-looking decorations. An ivory statuette of a willowy foreign goddess. Small gold bookends. A jade vase. Largo wondered which of these the Baron might have given her for Christmas or her birthday. As his mind drifted on the morphia, a darker thought came to him. What if they'd come from some random admirer? And what if that admirer had found them in the Midden?

He got up and went to examine the decorations. There was nothing special about the statuette or the bookends, but there were strange red flowers he hadn't seen before in the jade vase. He leaned in to smell them but jerked his head back. The flowers were crawling with tiny black insects. He got a rag from the kitchen and used it to toss the flowers out of a window. A few insects crawled onto the rag, so he threw that out too.

As tired as he was, Largo still couldn't sleep. He tried to read more of the pulp, but his eyes wouldn't focus. Instead, he went to the cage in which Remy's parakeet slept and pulled off the night covering. He tapped on the cage a couple of times and whistled softly. The parakeet turned and something glinted in its eyes. Largo rubbed his temples and looked again.

The parakeet is a Mara?

How had he never seen it before? But sure enough, its lens eyes rotated and stared at him. Did Remy know the bird wasn't real? She'd never mentioned it. But she'd never mentioned that her uncle was one of the most powerful men in Lower Proszawa either.

He replaced the cover over the cage and a strange thought came to him. He wondered if it was possible for someone, somewhere, to see through the bird's eyes. Largo knew that it was just a paranoid delusion brought on by reading *Der Knochengarten* so late at night, but he couldn't shake the feeling of being watched.

It took two more drops of morphia before he could fall asleep.

AT THE STREET MARKET
BY THE CROSSROADS

From *Folklore and Supernatural Belief Systems of the Lower Classes* by Johannes Schneider

Deathbed recitation of Joachim Vohrer in a state home for the destitute:

Schneider: Take your time and tell the story in your own way, Herr Vohrer.

Vohrer: All right. You have to picture the place first. In those days the market sprawled and curled around itself like a snake, forming passages where those of us from Haxan Green and other areas could come each day for food, household goods, and gossip. The market was older than anyone remembered. Before any of us were born, the land had been one of the holding pens for a vast slaughterhouse. In those days, a stray hoof or bone would sometimes ooze from the soil during the endless winter rains.

Like the city, the street market was laid out in districts. Here you would find household goods: used clothing, ramshackle furniture, morphia elixirs, and the like.

Farther on was the metal district, for cooking pots, tools, nails—and more illicit items, like knives meant for more than carving meat. There was food, mostly fish. Fishermen brought their catches to the market all day. What didn't sell became bait for the next day's haul. Off the main channel, smugglers offered their curiosities: jewelry, rugs, unstrung violins, and gleaming crystal vases—all brought in at great peril from High Proszawa, and all guaranteed to be plague-free, though no one believed the last part. Still, they did a good business.

People were sold at the market too. Young women, old women, young boys, and those who would be anything you wanted for a price worked the farthest reaches of the market in tumbledown shacks with blankets on the walls to keep down the noise. To ward off knife attacks, some pimps wore butcher's chainmail under their clothes. Everyone knew who they were because they jingled like small sleigh bells when they walked. Bullocks avoided the area unless they were in a buying mood, since they were just as likely to get their throats slit as anyone else who caused trouble.

Last was the enchanter district. It wasn't part of the main body of the market. The enchanters came and went depending on the flow of money. They did great business during the war and soon after. After that, it was a slow decline until there were only a handful of crystal gazers left. But with the Drops taking hold in the city, business was on the rise once again.

Schneider: And that's when it happened, right?

Vohrer: Yes. It was a sunny day when I went to see the enchanters, and I foolishly took the sun to be a good omen. My wife had run away soon after our son was born. It was just the two of us for years, but the flu took him and then there was just me. I didn't care about my wife—curse the slut and whoever she tormented after she deserted us. But my son . . .

I went to see the enchanters with all the household silver in my pocket. There were a dozen canvas tents at least, all inhabited by anxious women and thin men whose eyes practically burned holes in me as I made up my mind who to see. The problem was they all looked alike. The same scarves and turbans on their heads. The same astrological charts. The same promises to reveal my future, divulge my past lives, and to help find lost loved ones. It was this last offer that had brought me there, but their promises didn't help me decide as each enchanter made a better case for him- or herself and discounted his or her services while screaming over each other.

At the far edge of the group was a blue canvas tent—I remember the color distinctly. It was the color of my son's eyes. The tent wasn't the biggest or the most lavishly decorated, but the man out front caught my eye. He was fat and had black hair and a hooked nose like a raven's beak. He stood at the tent entrance calmly smoking a pipe. He didn't call to me or make outrageous promises. He merely puffed his pipe, gave me a slight nod, and stepped back through the canvas entrance. As the other enchanters shouted and offered me the moon and sky, I followed this last enchanter inside.

He sat at a small table decorated with the constellations. With his calm manner, it almost seemed as if he had been expecting me. I sat down across from him. The tent was lit by a single candle in the center of the table so that all I could see was the enchanter. He didn't have cards or a crystal ball, but merely asked me how he could help. I told him about my poor dead son, taken from me so quickly. The enchanter listened, not saying a word, just puffing his pipe. I didn't know what to make of such a quiet medium, so I put down the household silver and pushed it across the table to him. He didn't move to take it or count the contents. He merely nodded and said, "You wish to speak with him?"

"Very much," I said.

"Then you shall." He opened his hands and told me to take them in my own. His skin was soft, like a young woman's, not rough and calloused like mine. For a moment I was almost embarrassed, but then he said, "Are you ready?" and I forgot all about it.

"Yes," I said without a moment's hesitation.

He blew out the candle. The tent was completely black. I couldn't even hear the sounds of the market through the thick canvas. After a moment, the medium began to mutter softly, as if he was talking to himself. This went on for what seemed like a long time and I grew anxious that my poor son was too far away to reach. Then something happened.

Abruptly, the enchanter stopped muttering. A tiny spark of light appeared before me. It grew bigger and longer. It was an increasingly long glowing filament. I'd heard of this, didn't know its name, but recognized it right off as spirit essence. Soon, there was enough glowing filament dangling over the medium's head to outline his features. Then a voice came, high and frail, barely a whisper.

"Papa?"

Well, I almost leaped from my seat, but the enchanter held me with surprisingly strong hands. The voice came again, a little stronger this time.

"Papa?"

"Rolf?" I said.

"I'm here, Papa. Where are you?"

"Here, my boy. I'm right here."

I almost jumped from my seat when a cold, mocking voice came from behind me. *"Here, my boy. I'm right here."*

I spun around to see two of the other enchanters standing at the tent's opening. One held a small lantern in his hand. "Here's your boy, you old fool," he said, and shone the light on the medium.

He sat rock still, but with panic creeping into his eyes. From his mouth extended a length of ordinary household string that

186

had been dipped into a phosphorescent material so that it glowed. Another man stood behind him. He was dressed completely in black. All that was visible were his eyes where they peeked out of a black hood. He held a thin wire attached to the glowing string, which he had been drawing from the medium's mouth.

"My god," was all I could think to say.

The enchanters all laughed. "There's no god in here, you stupid man. Just fat Sigmund and Karl, who imagine themselves cleverer than us."

At that, I snatched my hands from the medium's grasp. I jumped up and when the medium grabbed for my silver, I shouted and punched him in his fat face. Sigmund, the medium, fell back, bleeding, while Karl disappeared out the back of the tent.

I ran outside thinking to go back into the market and buy a knife to pay back the bastard medium. But I didn't realize that I'd been shouting the whole time I pushed through the crowd. A couple of bored bullocks grabbed me and checked my breath to see if I'd been drinking. When I told them what had happened they, and what seemed like half the market, followed me to the enchanter district. The filthy bullocks just shrugged when they saw that Sigmund was gone. With no one to arrest, they wandered away. The crowd, however, didn't. I had the feeling I wasn't the first fool tricked by one of the enchanters. They quickly set fire to Sigmund's tent. The other enchanters laughed themselves silly until the crowd turned on them, scattering their cards and shattering their crystals. The bullocks stepped in only when some of the other men found my cheats and tried to toss both Sigmund and Karl into the burning tent.

While the crowd and the bullocks faced off over what to do with the enchanters, I wandered back through the market. I was in a daze and hardly remember, but I must have left because the next thing I knew I'd walked a good way toward home. I'm man enough to admit that at that point, I sat down on the side of the road and let the tears come. I'd been such a coward and a fool, so needy that I believed some sideshow bastard could bring me back my Rolf.

A moment or two later, a tiny shadow fell across me. I looked up to see a little blond girl in a dirty dress patterned with blue cornflowers. She held out a bottle. "From my father," she said. "He saw what happened. It's medicine, he said. It will help you forget."

As the child ran back to the market, I unstoppered the bottle and drank half of it. Understand, I was unused to morphia back then, so I weaved down the road and it took me twice as long as usual to get home. I went to bed and finished the bottle, feeling empty and blissful. In this state I dreamed of Rolf, of teaching him to fish and climb a tree without breaking his neck. But in the morning both my son and the blissful feeling were gone. I thought about Sigmund and his wretched partner. What a way to spend your life, cheating the broken of their money and their loved ones.

But here's the thing: even knowing that it had all been a sham, I knew that at the heart of every lie there's a little bit of truth. When I closed my eyes, I could still see the glowing filament, moving upward toward heaven, where I knew Rolf was waiting.

I never went back to another medium or enchanter, but after that day I made regular visits to the medicine stalls. The elixirs made it easier for me to see the trail of spirit essence as it spun out of the tent and into the stars. Each night I climbed the filament a little higher. Someday I know that with enough of the dream medicine, I'll climb all the way up.

Schneider: Thank you.

CHAPTER ELEVEN

EACH DAY AT THE COURIER COMPANY WAS HARDER THAN THE ONE BEFORE. IT DROVE Largo a little mad that while he was making deliveries all over the city, none was back to Schöne Maschinen. The Baron was a busy man, and with every day that passed Largo knew that he would be slipping farther and farther from the magnate's thoughts. He thought of sending the Baron something himself, just to have an excuse to go back to the factory. But what could he send that would interest a Baron? He didn't want to get to Schöne Maschinen and look stupid. Maybe Remy could arrange a meeting, or Dr. Venohr could, if the three of them had dinner? He decided to remind Remy of the idea.

His deliveries continued in their usual frustrating pattern. He'd spend days taking parcels and letters to the nicest districts in Lower Proszawa, glittering islands of endless parties, and then he'd have a series to some of the worst parts of the city. The slums were full of disease and rats. Xuxu political art and antigovernment yellowsheets were plastered on some of the buildings. Framed on the walls in the upper-class Händler merchant district were cinema notices, military recruitment posters, and colorful broadsheets touting patent medicines for the Drops. Even there, though, were signs that things weren't as they had once been. At the edges of the advertisements were the remains of previous postings—scenes of mountains and ocean cruises. Old vacation posters. Even in the rarefied worlds of Händler and Empyrean there hadn't been much pleasure travel since the war.

After another nerve-racking delivery to the docks, Largo used a shortcut that took him briefly through the Great Triumphal Square. Clouds and smoke from the factories had turned the city a uniform slate gray. Because of this, what he saw in the plaza was especially startling.

An Iron Dandy stood by the steps that led to the underground trams. When an elegantly dressed older couple emerged, the Dandy picked up a large bottle that had been sitting on the ground by his feet and followed them. When the couple reached the midpoint of the plaza, the Dandy poured the contents of the bottle over himself and struck a match.

He exploded into flame.

In the gray light, the orange-and-blue blaze created a zone of terrifying color. Everyone in the plaza froze where they were, including Largo. Making an animal scream of pain and fury, the burning Dandy ran straight at the older couple and knocked them to the ground. They struggled to get away, but he was too strong and held them tight until their clothes too were on fire. They writhed together, a human bonfire, screaming in terror and agony. A moment later, servers from one of the cafés ran to them with bottles and buckets of water. They doused the trio, but it was too late. They lay together, smoke rising from their charred bodies. The police were already blowing their whistles and running through the square before Largo could hear anything but the reverberations of their awful screams.

A crowd was quickly gathering around the scene. While the police shouted and shoved people, a louder scream came from the burned bodies. The Dandy was slowly rising to his feet, his clothes and skin scorched the color of charcoal. He lunged at one of the officers and managed to grab his leg, knocking him to the ground. The policeman kicked him in the face with his free foot and when the Dandy was upright, two of the other bullocks shot him. The crowd screamed and ran back to the edges of the plaza.

Largo didn't like being this close to the police, but he was transfixed by the awfulness unfolding before him. It took only another moment or two before armed Maras swept in to hold the crowd back. More police arrived, including the men in rubber suits he'd seen take away suspected victims of the Drops. While uniformed police wandered around the crowd taking notes as people told them what they'd seen, three black cars stopped at the edge of the plaza. They were even larger than the limousines Largo had seen at Schöne Maschinen, and they reminded him of hearses. A moment later, a juggernaut pulled up behind them.

The men who got out of the cars all wore the same long black coats and homburg hats. An armed Mara tried to prevent the dark men from entering the crime scene, but the lead man pointed a small silver box—about the size of a cigarette pack—at it. Instantly, all the Maras slumped over as if they had gone to sleep.

One of the police officers rushed to the men and saluted. The lead man merely nodded while the others fanned out among the officers, pushing them away from the burned bodies. There was a brief argument between one of the dark men and a police officer, but it was short-lived. When they parted, the officer saluted and motioned for the other officers to leave the scene. As they went, the lead dark man pointed his silver box at the Maras and they sprang to life, once again holding the crowd at bay. Largo knew that there was only one explanation for what he was seeing.

The dark men were Nachtvogel.

The only people they permitted near the crime scene were the men in rubber suits, who put the bodies in bags and carried them to the juggernaut. Largo had seen all he needed to. Bullocks were bad enough, and the corpses were nightmarish, but the sight of Nachtvogel in broad daylight truly unnerved him. He turned his bicycle and rode away from the plaza as quickly as he could.

Back at the company, Largo gave his receipt books to Branca.

"You wear your new clothes well, Largo."

"Thank you," he said, looking past Branca at a blank spot on the wall.

"Is there anything wrong?" he said. "You look a bit out of sorts."

"It's nothing. It's just that I saw something strange at the Great Triumphal Square."

"And what was that, pray tell?"

"Two carloads of Nachtvogel. One of them had a little box that turned off all the Maras in the plaza."

Branca stared at him. "Nachtvogel? Why were they in the plaza?"

"An Iron Dandy attacked an old couple. The bullocks shot him and then the Nachtvogel came and chased away the police. I've never seen anything like it."

"I should hope not. And you are all right, I take it?"

"I'm fine," said Largo. "It's just that I've never seen anybody die that horribly before."

Branca put the receipt books into his desk. "Not a pleasant sight, is it? But your emotions are normal and natural. Pity the day when witnessing another's death doesn't move you."

"I've heard that soldiers can get that way."

"Indeed they can."

Largo looked at Branca and tried to picture him in a uniform. The image was absurd, almost comical. Still, he couldn't help asking, "Were you in the war, sir?"

Branca stood still for a moment before saying, "Yes, I was. And before you ask, no, I never became so callous that death meant nothing to me. Some deaths sting more than others, but all deaths leave a mark."

Before Largo could ask anything else, other couriers began shuffling in at the end of their shifts. They handed in their books and, one by one, they left. None of them looked at him except for Parvulesco.

Largo walked outside with him. "Want to get a drink later?"

"That sounds great. Is it all right if Roland joins us?"

"Always."

"The Fräulein Sabel at seven, then?"

"I'll see you there," said Largo. He rode out with Parvulesco, but didn't take his usual route home. Instead, he turned abruptly and rode to *Ihre Skandale*.

"Sorry, but we already know about the attack at the Triumphal Square," said Ernst. "We also know who the Dandy attacked."

"Who was it?" said Largo.

"Helmut Neumann, the chairman of the plazma company."

"Do you think the Dandy knew who it was?"

Ernst tapped a pencil on his desk impatiently. "Who knows? Why? Do you know something?"

Largo put his hands in his pockets. "I'm not sure. But it looked to me like the Dandy was waiting for someone."

"Interesting," said Ernst, and he made a note on a coffee-stained pad on his desk. "Was there anything else?"

"Not really. The bullocks shoved everybody around, then shot the Dandy."

Ernst shook his head. "I'd trade one of Oskar's balls for a photo-chrome of that."

A bespectacled man at a nearby desk looked up. "What? Did you say something?"

"No, Oskar. Herr Moorden and I were just having a chat." He smiled at Largo. "I'm sorry to disappoint you. You'll just have to get here quicker with the next story."

Largo looked out the window at his bicycle. He'd come a long way for nothing. "I suppose so. The bullocks were taking chromes. Maybe you could bribe one of them."

"I've already put out the word," said Ernst. "If there isn't any-thing else, we're busy getting tomorrow's edition ready for printing."

Largo nodded. "Too bad you can't bribe a Nachtvogel. I bet they have much better chromes than the bullocks."

Ernst blinked and leaned on his desk. "Wait—there were Nachtvo-gel?"

Largo nodded. "Two cars full, and a juggernaut."

"You're *sure?*"

"They scared off the bullocks and took the bodies themselves. Ask anyone."

Ernst slapped his desk and jumped out of his chair. He looked around and threw his pencil at a man across the room. It hit him in the ear. The man yelled, "Who fucking did that?"

"I fucking did," said Ernst. He pointed at Largo. "How is it you didn't know about the Nachtvogel in the plaza today?"

The man, young and with yellowed teeth, said, "There weren't any Nachtvogel."

Ernst glanced at Largo. "You're absolutely sure?"

"Yes. They scared off the police and put the bodies in the jug-gernaut."

Ernst dropped back down into his chair and found another pen-cil. He said, "Tell me exactly what you saw."

Largo told him everything he could remember, especially how the lead man turned off all the Maras.

"That certainly sounds like the Nachtvogel," said Ernst. "You know what this means, right?"

Largo said, "No. I haven't a clue."

Ernst rocked back in his chair. "It means the Dandy *did* know who he was attacking. He was no lunatic. This was a political murder. There's no other reason the Nachtvogel would be there."

Good. That's got to be worth something, thought Largo. He said, "I didn't think your readers would be so keen on politics."

"They're not," said Ernst. He tapped his notes. "But they love a good conspiracy."

Largo took a step forward. "It seems that I didn't bring you the whole story, but did I bring you enough to count for something?"

Ernst handed him several silver coins. It wasn't as much as the Valda, but it was still good money.

"Thank you."

"No. Thank you. If my idiot writers can't get the whole story in the future, I just might have to fire them and hire you," said Ernst. "You hear that, you lazy bastards?" No one replied.

Largo put the coins in his pocket and started to leave, but Ernst put a hand on his arm. "Let me give you a story this time. People are being kidnapped right off the streets. Have you heard anything like that?"

Largo shook his head and thought for a moment about Enki's disappearance. But he'd returned on his own and, anyway, he was a drinker and had probably just blacked out. "I haven't heard anything."

"The bullocks think it's a new gang in the city. They might be grabbing people to hold for ransom. If you pick up any rumors, drop whatever you're doing and come straight here. I'll make it worth your while."

Largo liked the sound of that. "I'll bring you anything I learn."

An hour later, he was drinking and laughing with Parvulesco and Roland at the Fräulein Sabel. Largo bought the first round of drinks with his *Ihre Skandale* money and everyone was in a fine mood. However, during a lull in the conversation, Parvulesco became serious.

"You need to watch yourself," he said. "I heard that Andrzej took a runner from the hospital."

Largo said, "Arc you sure? I'm surprised he could walk after that beating."

"I must be losing my touch," Roland said.

"It gets worse," said Parvulesco. "I don't know if you noticed, but Weimer wasn't at work today. And he didn't come back from his rounds yesterday."

"Do you think he and Andrzej are up to something together?"

Largo tensed. If what Parvulesco said was right, they could have had a day and a half, perhaps two days to come up with ways to get back at him. "What do you think I should do?"

"Don't go out alone at night," Parvulesco said.

"And don't take your normal routes on the job or going home. Avoid patterns," said Roland. "It will make it harder for them to lay an ambush."

Largo gulped his whiskey. "This can't be happening right now. Things were looking up."

Parvulesco said, "I know your promotion was good news, but it's not worth getting hurt over."

"To hell with the promotion," Largo said. "I met someone who might help me leave the job altogether and start something better. A whole new life."

"Tell me about it," said Parvulesco.

"Yes," said Roland. "What kind of new life?"

Largo wasn't sure what to say. The further the meeting with Baron Hellswarth receded into the past, the more fantastic—and absurd—it seemed. *Me, working in a lab with chimeras. He was probably joking. Having fun with a gullible idiot just desperate enough to take him seriously.* Largo swirled around the last of his drink. "I can't say yet. Besides, dealing with Andrzej and Weimer is more important than mooning over something that probably won't happen."

Roland said, "You're right. Staying alive should be your only concern right now. Never go anywhere without your knife."

Largo looked at him. "Will you show me how to use it?"

He smiled. "I'm glad you finally asked. Yes. I know where we can go."

In general, Largo didn't have a fear of heights, but standing on the roof of Roland and Parvulesco's building he felt distinctly dizzy.

"It's just nerves," said Parvulesco. "You'll be fine in a few minutes."

"I'm learning to fight for my life," Largo said. "I'm not sure I'll ever be fine again."

"Calm down. We all felt that way the first time they handed us a weapon in the army," said Roland. "The basics are simple and that's all I'm going to teach you. After that, it's a matter of you practicing on your own. Got it?"

"Got it," said Largo.

"Good. Now take out the knife and stand like you're going to fight me."

Largo felt like a child brandishing the weapon, knowing that Roland could take it away from him in a second.

Roland walked around him, giving orders. "Extend your fighting arm. Get your weight onto the balls of your feet so you can move quickly. If I'm holding a knife, don't look at my hands. Look at my eyes. They'll tell you more." He went behind Largo and adjusted his hips. "Get more sideways," he said. "It makes you a smaller target. And relax."

"All right," said Largo, not believing a word of it.

Roland taught him how to thrust the knife and how to move forward and close the distance on an opponent. He showed Largo how to defend himself from another knife and the best places to punch with the spiked knuckle dusters. At the end of the lesson, Parvulesco applauded. Largo, drenched in sweat, raised his hands high over his head.

"How do you feel?" said Roland.

"I didn't fall off the roof or have a heart attack. I count that as a victory."

"Practice is the key. Do that and muscle memory will take over and you won't have to think so much."

"Practice," said Largo. "I will."

When he left, Largo took a circuitous route home. There, he toweled off, put on a clean shirt, and rode an equally absurd route to Remy's flat. They took morphia together, made love, and fell asleep. He dreamed of running after Remy through the back alleys and worst districts of Lower Proszawa. She dashed ahead of him and he had a hard time keeping up. Largo didn't know why she was running. He wanted to grab her, hold on, and tell her that everything was all right, but he couldn't. Her body was a ball of flame.

In the morning, Remy handed Largo a postcard with a picture of a beautiful woman on the front. Her body was covered by a few strands of woven silk. "Blow on it," she said. Largo did as he was told, and the silk flew aside to reveal that the woman was nude.

"A cute trick," he said. "Is she a friend of yours?"

Remy took back the card and blew on it several times. Setting it on the mantel over the fireplace, she said, "Don't be silly. It's Anita Mourlet, the Madonna of Depravity. The wickedest woman in the world."

"I've heard of her. She strips while she sings."

Remy gave him a look. "She doesn't just strip. Anita isn't some beer hall girl. She's an artist who uses her voice and body to seduce, beguile, and corrupt audiences around the world."

Largo thought for a moment. "Didn't the city fathers ban her from performing here? Something happened at one of her shows?"

Remy came back to the sofa and did a mock swoon into Largo's arms. "Yes. She practically deflowered the mayor's son during a performance at the opera house." She laughed. "Anita had half his clothes off before the bullocks rushed in and stopped the show. It was wonderful."

"If she's banned, what's the card for?"

Remy looked up at him. "She's performing here tonight. It's a secret show at the Golden Angel, one of the old theaters near the Grand Dark. There aren't any tickets. It's invitation only."

"And the card is the invitation?"

Remy sat up. "Yes, and we're going tonight. It will be the perfect opportunity for you to wear your new formal clothes. I know exactly what I'll wear. It's going to be so much fun. Maybe she'll seduce you this time."

Largo opened Remy's robe and ran his fingers over her breasts. "What would you do then?"

She put his hand between her legs. "I'd sit back and enjoy the show." Remy climbed on top of him and he used his fingers on her until she let out a little scream and fell back on the sofa. "See?" she said. "Anita is already working her wicked magic."

"If that's what her postcard can do, then I'm looking forward to the real show," said Largo.

"Meet me at the Grand Dark after the last performance. Don't wear your formal clothes there in case they get dirty. Just bring them and you can change in my dressing room."

"You have it all planned out, don't you?" he said.

"Not all," Remy said. "We have to leave something to chance. It's more fun that way."

"I agree."

He left for work soon after that. He was riding along the edge of the city, taking the long way around to the courier service, when something occurred to him.

I wonder if the knife will fit under my formal jacket?

There was no way to know until he tried it on that night. It left him anxious all day.

Remy was already dressed by the time Largo arrived at the theater. She wore a long, low-cut bloodred empire-waist gown with matching opera gloves. Her ears sparkled with diamond earrings. Around her throat was an intricately webbed crystal necklace that pulsed with pinpoints of light from tiny bioluminescent chimeras floating inside.

"What do you think?" she said.

For a moment, all Largo could do was stare. Finally, he said, "I'm speechless."

Remy gave him a peck on the cheek. "That's the right answer. And that's the only kiss you'll get right now because my lipstick is perfect and I don't want to muss.it. But don't worry. I'll make up for it later." She swatted him on the ass and said, "Now it's your turn to be beautiful. Let's see the new you."

Largo took off his work jacket and draped it over a chair back before putting on his formal clothes. Unfortunately, he couldn't wear the knife under the jacket, but he reasoned that the odds of Andrzej and Weimer sneaking into an event like this were minuscule. Still, he'd grown used to having the weight against his body and it bothered him now that it wasn't there.

As he dressed, he watched Remy making small adjustments to her outfit in the mirror. She really was the most beautiful creature he'd ever seen. He recognized the dress as one from her closet, but he'd never seen the jewelry before, though he knew she had quite a lot. The earrings were probably expensive, but her necklace looked like it must have cost a fortune. Were they more trinkets from her wealthy admirers? Largo shook his head. Even if he managed to get a job at Schöne Maschinen, would he ever be able to give her gifts like those? He put it out of his mind for now. Even though all he had was a bicycle and a shabby piss-yellow flat, Remy chose to be with him when she could have been with so many other wealthier men.

That has to mean something, he thought. *Right?*

When Largo was dressed, he looked at himself in the mirror. The clothes fit reasonably well, but something was missing. He touched his collar and said, "We forgot to get a proper tie."

"Relax," said Remy. "I remembered this afternoon and stole this from one of the puppets." She handed him a black silk bow tie.

He turned it over in his hands, then smiled at her. "Guess what I'm about to say."

Remy cocked her head at him. "That you don't know how to tie it?"

"I've never even held a real bow tie before."

She stepped behind him. "Let me show you," she said, and reached over his shoulders, sliding the tie around his neck. As she pulled it tight, Largo said, "Is this when you finally do away with me?"

Remy grinned as she cinched the tie snugly into place. "How did you know my plan?"

"It's obvious. You want my millions."

She looped the tie around into a bow and said, "And your yacht. The rule among ladies is that you poison for money, but strangle for a yacht."

When she was finished, Largo said, "Well, you missed your opportunity."

Still behind him, Remy rested her chin on his shoulder. "Who knows? Maybe I like you more than your silly boat."

Largo turned and put his arms around her. "That works out well. I like you too," he said.

She sighed. "Now I suppose no one is going to murder anyone tonight."

"Don't worry. There's always tomorrow."

"Goodie. That gives me time to plan something diabolical."

"I wouldn't want to go any other way."

Remy put a hand on his cheek. "I want to kiss you right now."

"Careful. You'll ruin your makeup."

She picked up a white fur wrap and gave it to Largo to drape around her shoulders. "Silly boy. I didn't say I was *going* to kiss you, just that I wanted to."

"Thank goodness I escaped that fate."

Remy laughed and grabbed him, kissing him deeply. When they parted, she touched his lips. "You have lipstick all over you."

"That's your fault," he said, and wiped it off with a tissue.

"No, leave it on. You look gorgeous like that."

"Another night, perhaps."

After Remy fixed her makeup they went outside to find a Mara cab. A light rain began to fall as they reached the Golden Angel, so they rushed inside.

The theater was more sumptuous than the Grand Dark, but older and more decrepit, Largo noticed. The lobby carpet was stained and paint peeled from the walls. There was also a slight smell of mildew. What impressed Largo, though, was that no one seemed to care. The crowd reminded him of the one at the Petersen party—a mix of well-dressed aristocrats and considerably scruffier artists. It didn't take long for Largo to not feel so out of place in his secondhand clothes. Remy pulled him into the theater and rushed to claim a small table for two near the stage. There was a slim vase holding a single white rose. Propped against the vase were two domino masks.

"What are these for?" he said.

"For fine gentlemen and ladies who want to be here but don't want to be recognized."

Largo held one of the small masks over his face. "Do these actually work?"

"Of course not," said Remy. "But it makes them feel better. And anyway, it's all a game. A lot of people wear them just to feel wicked."

Largo put his mask on. "How do I look?"

"Terrifying. Now take it off. I want to see your face."

Largo put the mask on the table.

"Gorgeous."

He smiled and looked around. Curtained box seats ringed the sides and back of the theater. They were decorated with paper fans and small blinking lights. Balloons and long strands of silver tinsel hung from the chandeliers overhead. Some of the balloons had fallen and people were swatting them from table to table. Largo thought that the Golden Angel looked more like a party than a theater.

A hostess in her own domino mask and silver-spangled bustier came by their table and Remy ordered absinthe and sekt. Largo whispered to her, "We should have taken morphia before we got here."

Remy looked concerned. "Do you need some?"

"I'm all right for now."

"But you'd like to feel more relaxed. Poor baby." She plucked two petals from the white rose, put one in her mouth, and gave the other to Largo. "Chew this," she said.

He squinted at the petal. "There are perfectly good masks. Why are we disguising ourselves as cows?"

"Stop stalling."

"What does it taste like?"

200

"A rose, silly. Now chew it like a piece of gum. Like me. See?"

Largo felt stupid and wondered what the joke was, but seeing Remy chew a petal with no ill effects, he did the same.

"How do you like it?" said Remy.

"Moo," he said.

A moment later, though, he began to feel something—an ease in his arms and shoulders. A pleasant looseness spread all over his body. He plucked another petal and held it up to the light. "What are these?"

Remy smiled. "Rose petals," she said. "But they've been dipped in chloral hydrate. Aren't they lovely?"

"They're not bad," he said. "And to think we've been taking morphia the old-fashioned way when we could have been dipping sausages into it."

Largo knew it wasn't that funny, but when Remy giggled drunkenly so did he. "You've drugged me and the drinks aren't even here yet."

"Don't worry," she said. "If you start to drift off I still have some of the cocaine you found in the theater."

Largo thought of his first delivery to Empyrean and the flat where a party had been going on for weeks. He looked at the rose petal, then around the theater. "Do these people live this way all the time?"

"Some," said Remy. "The lucky ones with money and nothing else to do. Why? Are you jealous?"

He thought about it and surprised himself by saying, "I suppose I am, a little. It's like another planet in here."

Remy reached out and took his hand. She said, "Not so different. Just more fun."

A bright light flashed behind them. Largo saw one of the silver-spangled hostesses taking photochromes at a table nearby. Remy squeezed his hand. "Let's get a chrome," she said excitedly. Remy waved and the woman came to their table. Remy scooted her chair close to Largo's. He opened his mouth and she pretended to feed him another rose petal. He'd never taken a chrome before and he jumped a little as the brightness of the flash caught him off guard.

He blinked at Remy. "I think I'm blind. Leave me here and save yourself."

She giggled and kissed his ear.

"I thought I recognized you two," said someone nearby. It was a man's voice, but when Largo looked up all he could see was the bright afterglow of the flash and a man-shaped shadow.

"Uncle Rudy!" shouted Remy. She jumped up and hugged the silhouette.

Largo stood too. Between the light in his eyes and the chloral hydrate in his blood, he felt a little unsteady, but he managed to stay reasonably upright. Remy took Largo's hand. "Uncle Rudy, I believe you two lovely gentlemen have met."

Baron Hellswarth put out his hand and he and Largo shook. "It's wonderful to see you again, Baron," said Largo.

"You too. But you haven't come by the factory in a while. Have you forgotten about us?"

"No, sir. I wanted to come back, but there haven't been any new deliveries to Schöne Maschinen."

The Baron waved that away. "There's no need to wait for that nonsense. Come see me on Friday and we'll talk more about your future."

"Yes, sir. Thank you, sir."

Remy looked around. "Uncle Rudy, I don't see anyone with you. Tell me you didn't come all on your own. It would be too tragic."

"Don't worry," he said. "There's a friend waiting for me in one of the boxes."

"If you're hiding her behind curtains, she must be very pretty," said Remy.

"Not compared to you, my dear," he said. "But I should be getting back. I just wanted to say hello."

The Baron kissed Remy on the cheek and wagged a finger at Largo. "Friday," he said.

"I'll be there."

Largo's eyes had cleared enough to see the Baron going back up the aisle. He dropped into his chair. A moment later the drinks arrived and Remy prepared the absinthe with the sckt. She handed him a glass and held up hers. "To the future," she said.

"To Friday," said Largo. They clinked glasses and he took a sip of his drink. The cocktail tasted somewhat peculiar as it mixed with the chloral hydrate, but nothing was going to spoil this moment. This was it, he thought. The pivot point he'd been waiting for. After all his doubts, the Baron remembered him and now he had an appointment that would change everything. He looked at Remy. "We might as well go home. There's no way this night could get any better."

"You only say that because you haven't seen Anita Mourlet yet," Remy said. She dipped a rose petal into her drink and put it in his mouth.

A moment later, the house lights dimmed and the stage lit up.

Remy squeezed his hand. "Promise that you'll forgive me if I leave you for her."

"You'll have to try harder than that to get rid of me."

"Fine. You can be our houseboy. You'll wear a gold collar and I'll lead you around on a small chain and teach you tricks."

"Only if we switch days," Largo said. "Then you'll wear the collar and I'll lead you around."

"What a lovely household we'll be," said Remy. "Even the Baron will be jealous." She settled down against him, resting her hand high on his leg.

When the theater was pitch-dark, a spotlight hit the center of the stage and Anita Mourlet walked out to thunderous applause. She had fine, perfectly sculpted features, with bright red lips and piercing green eyes. She was pretty, Largo thought, but nothing special. *Not nearly as pretty as Remy.* Still, there was something about her. He didn't want to look away, which was strange because her clothing was the opposite of what he'd expected.

Anita wore a pince-nez and a conservative man's suit. There were gasps and some nervous laughter from the audience. To Largo, she looked like any banker or salesman he'd ever seen. Remy squeezed his leg. "Isn't she marvelous?" she said.

"I don't get it. A pretty girl in a suit. What's so special?" said Largo.

Remy looked up at him. "You don't see it? She's dressed like the Minister of War."

"Of course," he said, not really seeing it at all.

The stage lights shifted, revealing a backdrop depicting an abstract version of the interior of the Golden Angel, all odd, angular shadows. Low lights played on the backdrop from behind, creating patterns like ghosts moving around the theater. As Anita began singing the first few bars of "I Sin for Pleasure," the ghosts swayed and moved together. Soon they fell to the stage and began making love en masse. Anita danced and slithered through the writing ghost forms as the song built in speed and volume.

Remy leaned forward on the table to get a better view. Largo liked Anita's voice and, yes, she was surrounded by ghosts making love, but *she* wasn't doing anything that he thought could get someone labeled as the Madonna of Depravity.

Onstage, Anita danced over to a box seat on the backdrop. The shadow of a large snake appeared there and as it crawled onto her arm, Largo realized that the snake was real. Anita draped the snake around her shoulders like Remy's fur wrap. At that moment, the song hit a crescendo and the theater lights went out for a second. When they came back up, instead of the stage ghosts, real men and women moved together, their bodies glistening with sex sweat. Even the smell of the theater seemed to change, and Largo was conscious of Remy's hand massaging his thigh.

Anita, in her Minister's suit, moved through the lovers, singing and caressing them as she went. Finally, she moved to the center of the stage and knelt down. The lovers swarmed over her, tearing at her clothes, until she was buried under a mass of nude squirming bodies. The music stopped for a moment, then exploded back, louder than ever. Anita arose from the bodies in nothing but the War Minister's pince-nez, the snake, and high heels, with a rubber cock strapped over her crotch. She was no longer singing, but the music went on, as raucous as ever.

Remy grabbed Largo's arm and said, "The Chancellor would shoot us all if he knew about this."

Largo held one of the masks over his face. "How do you know he's not here?"

Remy laughed and turned back to Anita, who wandered among the bodies, miming sex with one or two, then moving on. One of the male dancers down front wore a miter on his head. Anita held him and moved her hips as if she were fucking him from behind. The audience screamed with delight.

"The Archbishop would not be pleased," said Largo.

"How do you know?" Remy said, smiling.

Anita wrapped the snake around the Archbishop's neck, feigned an orgasm, and fell on top of him. When she grabbed the snake back and threw it into the air, it burst into flames. The audience screamed again, but more in shock than glee. The music stopped and the theater again went dark.

Largo kissed Remy's neck and the blackness seemed to go on for a long time. Then, a woman's voice rose from the dark, singing "Only the Damned Are Merry." She sang quietly at first, but as the volume increased, a spotlight came on. Anita Mourlet was at the back of the theater in an emerald corset and skirt. The theater exploded into applause.

She was bare-breasted and as she moved back to the stage, she kissed people and stole bits of their clothing—a scarf, a cigarette holder, a top hat. Audience members began to hold out their possessions for her. She ignored most, but plucked a few as she walked, always kissing the victim of her theft.

Remy gripped Largo's arm. "Make her come this way!" she said.

"How?" said Largo. "I don't have anything for her to steal."

As Anita neared the stage, she stopped to embrace a beautiful young man dressed as she was on the postcard. To Largo's surprise, Remy ran to the center aisle and got behind her. When Anita turned, she stopped. Remy took off her crystal necklace and put it around the other woman's neck. Anita bent Remy back and kissed her passionately before stepping onto the stage.

Remy ran to Largo and kissed him hard. "There," she said. "Now it's like we've both kissed her."

At that, the song ended. Anita bowed and left the stage to a standing ovation. When she was gone, the house lights came up for intermission.

Remy fell against the back of her chair, looking exhausted. Largo used a napkin to wipe lipstick from her cheek and she wiped some from his lips.

"What did you think?" she said.

"Honestly, I wasn't sure at first," Largo said. "But I think she's extraordinary."

"She is, isn't she?" Remy said. Then her face turned serious. "The way she takes our most basic instincts and turns them into art. Beautiful. Scandalous. Dangerous." Largo couldn't remember hearing Remy use the word *dangerous* about art before. She looked at him. "Tell me the truth, Largo. Do you think I'm any good as a performer?"

That caught him off guard—not because he doubted her, but because he was shocked that she doubted herself. "I think you're wonderful. There's no one at the Grand Dark who can do half of what you do."

"You're not just saying that, are you?"

"Not at all. You're the best they have."

Remy looked back at the stage. "But what am I compared to Anita Mourlet? I hide behind puppets in other people's plays. Anita holds nothing back. Risks everything for her art." She looked at Largo. "I want to be more like her. Hypnotic. Dangerous. Evil. But I don't know if I have it in me . . ."

"Of course you do. You're amazing," said Largo.

"I *want* to be. I *try* to be, but sometimes I wonder. Do I work hard enough? There are a million things more to learn about performance and I want to know them all," Remy said.

"How did Anita learn?"

Remy picked petals off the rose. "She started the way I did. But then she broke away. That's what I want to do. Break away. But not yet. There's still so much to learn at the Grand Dark. Someday, though, I want to have my own theater. Combine people and puppets together onstage. I want to write plays that don't all come from the yellowsheets."

Largo kissed her hand. "You want to be Una."

She looked at him. "In some ways. But I have to work harder. Study more. Like Anita did."

"You can do anything you set your mind to."

Remy started to put a petal in her mouth but dropped it on the table. "Do you really think so?"

"Absolutely," said Largo.

She pulled Largo closer. "I love you. Don't ever go."

"Never," he said, and touched Remy's bare throat. "I hope you didn't pay full price for that necklace. It looked expensive."

"It was, from what I understand," said Remy. "But it was worth it."

"As long as you're happy."

"I am. I truly am."

They drank and batted at balloons when they came their way. Remy hummed "I Sin for Pleasure" and looked happier than Largo had seen her since the night she'd become sick at the party.

The house lights went down again and Anita returned to the stage in a loose flowing robe. When the applause started, she held up her hands for quiet.

She said, "Thank you all for coming to our little den of iniquity. We have so much more wickedness to share with you tonight.

But first, I wanted to introduce a friend. Though she's more than a friend—she's a spiritual advisor. A few of you lucky enough might already know her name: Vera Baal. She is the greatest medium it's ever been my privilege to know. Tonight, she's agreed not only to look into the future for a few lucky members of the audience, but to speak to a deceased loved one for one special person. Please welcome to the stage Vera Baal."

There was polite applause throughout the theater. A plump middle-aged woman came out. She reminded Largo of Frau Balden, an older woman in Haxan Green who had told the children stories and taught them to pick pockets. Baal made a small bow and went to a tall chair that had been set in the middle of the stage.

Anita said, "Obviously, Vera can't read all of your futures, but those lucky few I stole from are welcome to come up and speak with her."

Remy looked at Largo, "Should I go?"

"Anita has your necklace. I say she owes you a fortune and more."

"You're right," she said, and went to the end of a small line that had already formed on the steps leading up to the stage.

Largo thought of Rainer and wished there were a way that he could be at the show too. The next time Largo saw him he'd have to ask if his friend had heard of Vera Baal.

He listened carefully. Vera had an accent that sounded as if she'd come from the eastern provinces and grown up speaking another language. But that was all that was interesting about her. Largo grew disappointed as she began reading people's futures. Vera checked their palms and their eyes, which made her look serious, but what came out of her mouth was the same tired drivel he'd heard from so-called fortune-tellers his whole life. "You'll have a happy marriage and many children"; "You'll come into money soon"; or "You will be going on a long voyage." Largo stopped listening after Vera's third boring pronouncement.

It wasn't until Remy reached her that he paid attention again.

Remy took off her gloves and gave Vera her hand. The medium looked at it, then at Remy's other hand. She studied Remy's eyes for a few seconds. Finally, Vera smiled sadly and said, "I have nothing for you, child. But you are a rare creature and you must look for happiness in that." Remy came back to the table looking puzzled.

She stared at her palms. "What do you think she meant by that?"

"I have no idea," said Largo. "Maybe we should stay after the show and see if we can talk to her."

Remy said, "All right," but Largo could tell that she'd barely heard a word he'd said. She examined her hands and Largo's, trying to find some answers. Finally, she put on her gloves and sat back with her arms folded.

"The old thing is probably a fraud," said Largo. "Just because Anita believes in her doesn't mean she isn't a fake."

"Maybe you're right," Remy said. She took Largo's hand. "In any case, let's not let it spoil the rest of the show."

Vera soon reached the end of the line. There was more polite applause as the last person went back to their seat. Anita took center stage again. She said, "Now we're in for something truly exciting. Vera will explain."

The audience murmured and rustled in their seats. Even Largo was interested.

How is the old bat going to pull this off? Force everyone to swallow rose petals and absinthe? More funny business with the theater lights?

Largo could see that Remy was interested, even though she was still smarting from Vera's strange dismissal. He decided to stay quiet, keep his doubts to himself, and let her enjoy the show. *Conjure a few good spooks and you might redeem yourself after all, Frau Swindler*, Largo thought.

Vera stood and spoke in a surprisingly powerful voice. Like with Anita, there was something strangely compelling about her now. She said, "Good evening, lovely people. Thank you for allowing me to steal a moment of your time on this fine night. As Anita has said, tonight I will attempt to communicate with the spirit of one of your deceased loved ones. Now, with a group this large, I cannot guarantee that I will succeed. I am also not sure whose spirit I will be able to find, so it would be helpful if all of you concentrated on who in the spirit realm you would most like to speak to. If I am successful, make yourself known and with luck, you will be able to ask the spirit a question or two. Thank you."

Vera sat down to the sounds of whispers and a few chuckles. After hearing her speak, Largo wasn't sure if she was a simple fraud or if she actually believed in her own nonsense. Whatever happened, he was here for Remy, who still had a confused, disappointed look on her face. He reached for her shoulder and she put her hand over his.

Anita left the stage and the spotlight narrowed onto Vera. She closed her eyes and mumbled quietly to herself. Largo leaned forward to hear better, but still could hear only a few words and phrases. He caught "Spirits of the dead, speak to me" and "Make yourselves heard." After that, Vera's voice became so quiet that all he could pick up was a steady whisper. A few more moments of this and the audience started to become restless. People even began to laugh. Largo, who couldn't help frowning, was glad that Remy couldn't see him in the dark.

With a sudden shudder, Vera threw her head back against the chair hard enough that Largo could hear the crack. A moment later, her mouth fell open and something came out of it. It was a bit like a white ribbon, but roughly and unevenly cut. The ribbon drifted from between her lips and floated into the air. It seemed endless, drifting over her head until it touched the curtains over the stage. There was a collective intake of breath at the manifestation and even Largo was mesmerized, unable to explain the trick.

Vera began to moan. A vague fog formed behind her. *Here it comes*, he thought. *The real stage trickery.*

The fog condensed into a somewhat human form, like a smeared photochrome on the front of a wet yellowsheet. Whispers and a few cries erupted from the crowd. The fog continued to contract until it took on the unmistakable form of a woman. People began to shout.

"Mother?"

"Gertrude?"

"Christa!"

Finally, the fog took on enough features to be recognizable. It was a woman, perhaps in her thirties, thought Largo. She was dressed expensively, in a formal dress with strands of pearls around her neck. Largo squinted back toward the spotlight at the top of the theater, looking for the cinema projector they must be using to make the woman appear, but could see nothing. When the spectral woman's features came into focus she spoke. She said, "Edgar? My dear? Are you there?"

"No!" someone shouted from one of the tables near the front of the stage. An old man in a tuxedo stood, pointing at Vera with a cigar. "This is wrong. Stop it immediately," he yelled.

The specter continued, "Is that you, my dear? It's been so long. I've missed you."

"Stop it!" screamed the man. "Stop this right now! Karin is dead. How dare you, you charlatan!" Two of the man's companions tried to pull the man back into his seat. Though Edgar was old, he struggled fiercely. Largo was impressed and wondered why Vera chose that particular man to hoax. Whatever the reason, it didn't seem like a good idea. He shook off his friends and threw a glass of champagne at the stage.

"Edgar, are you there? Speak to me," said the ghost.

The white ribbon no longer drifted from Vera's mouth, but hung over her head and nestled in the curtains like a peculiar cloud.

Edgar screamed, "Stop it, you whore!" and threw his cigar at Vera. It tumbled through the air well above her. Before falling, however, the hot tip grazed the edge of the ribbon and it exploded into flame. The fire shot up to where the ribbon touched the curtains and the blaze spread across the fabric as quickly as if they had been doused in kerosene. It took only a few seconds for embers from the top curtain to fall onto the sides, where they began to smolder.

Just as the flame shot up from Vera's mouth, a finger of it went down. When brightness almost reached her face, she started awake with a scream. The phantom behind her vanished instantly and she stumbled from her chair. People in the audience screamed and ran in panic for the exits. The last thing Largo saw onstage was Anita pulling Vera into the wings.

When the curtains were fully ablaze, the flames crept across the theater's ceiling. Remy coughed as Largo grabbed her hand and shouldered his way through the crowd. *She's not getting hurt because a lunatic ruined the witch's act.* For one brief second, he wondered if the old man had been part of the con too, but as the smoke made it hard to see or breathe, he knew he'd given Vera too much credit.

It was pouring rain outside. Largo tried to drag Remy away, but she stopped in the street and gazed back at the Golden Angel. Smoke was already pouring from the roof and windows on the top floor. Screaming patrons ran out of the building and many slipped and fell in the wet street. Here and there were small piles of hysterical bodies being trampled as they tried to crawl away from the theater. As much as Largo wanted to get Remy far away, he couldn't help running back to pull two women free from a pile. One had a deep gash on her forehead from where she'd fallen. Her companion used her scarf to stop the flow of blood, and Largo led them across the street. When he went back to help a man with what looked like a broken ankle, he found that Remy was already there. They got the man between them and helped him to a nearby tram bench. By then, no one else was coming out of the Golden Angel. The top floor was engulfed in flames.

"Do you think everybody got out all right?" said Remy.

Largo put an arm around her. "I'm sure they did. Look at all these people."

"You're just trying to be nice."

"No, I'm not."

"Yes, you are. And thank you."

Largo pulled her to him as sirens drew closer. Two fire squads arrived at almost the same time. People fell back to let the trucks through. Men jumped off and began pulling hoses into the street.

"Maybe we should go," said Largo. "We'll only be in the way."

Remy nodded, still staring at the flames. "You're probably right. If we walk back the way we came, we might be able to find a cab." Then she looked at Largo. "Do you think Anita got out all right?"

He gave her a thin smile. "I'm sure. Did you see her grab Baal back there? They were probably the first ones out of the building."

"Uncle Rudy!" said Remy suddenly. "Do you see him?"

"No, but I wouldn't worry. If anyone can take care of himself, it will be the Baron." He hoped for many reasons that he was right.

"We have to look for him."

As they started back toward the Golden Angel, they were blocked by a line of police officers. When Remy tried to walk through them, an officer held up his hand. "No one past this point, Fräulein."

Remy said, "But my uncle was inside."

The officer shook his head. "Locating people is what we're here for. Leave it to us."

Remy tried to argue, but the officer simply glared at her obstinance. Finally Largo pulled her away, saying, "It's no use with bullocks. We'll stay here until we see the Baron."

"Thank you."

Remy shivered and Largo put his jacket around her shoulders. He looked over the crowd and said, "All these fine ladies and gentlemen— the ones with good reputations who sneaked out tonight for a taste of the forbidden—they must be dying of embarrassment knowing the bullocks will want to question them."

More police arrived, but they wore ordinary overcoats and hats, not uniforms. *Why would they send undercover bullocks to a fire?* he wondered. "Are they here to arrest the ghost or the bastard who threw the cigar?" he whispered.

Remy shushed him. "Be quiet. We don't want to attract attention."

Largo knew she was right, but he couldn't help saying, "It's a good thing neither of us has a reputation to protect." Remy smiled and elbowed him playfully.

They stood for several boring minutes in the rain. No one questioned them. Largo thought that the firefighters and police were going well out of their way to ignore everyone. Finally, the undercover police fanned out into the crowd.

"Here we go," said Largo, and he waited for the questioning to begin. But it didn't. The undercover police began pulling people from the crowd in ones and twos and loading them into a line of Mara cabs. "What's going on?" he whispered.

"Isn't it obvious?" Remy crossed her arms. "Look who they're letting go. The Grünewalds. The Froeses. All the richest and most important people at the show. They get to go home while we have to stand here like goats."

Largo craned his neck for a better view. Remy was right. He couldn't put names to them, but he recognized several people from the covers of yellowsheets. *Lucky rat bastards*, he thought.

A woman called out to him. "Largo!" she said. He looked around and saw a well-dressed couple by the side of one of the cabs. The woman waved to him. It was Frau Heller. "Fancy meeting you here," she said. "Did you enjoy the show?"

He waved back to her. "All except the last part," he said.

She said, "Me too," as her husband pulled her into the cab. "I told you you'd look good out of those wool rags. Take care," she called.

"You too, madam."

The door shut and the cab moved off past the fire trucks.

Largo raised his hands and dropped them to his sides again as he walked to Remy. They both laughed.

"One of your customers?" she said.

"One of my first as chief courier."

"Good," said Remy. "I was about to get jealous that you were leaving me for a society lady."

"There's no chance of that. Well, very little at least."

She laughed and kissed him.

Someone grabbed Largo's shoulder and pulled him away. It took him a moment to recognize the man in the rain. It was Special Operative Tanz.

"What are you doing talking to a woman like that?" said Tanz.

"She called to me. I was just being polite," Largo said.

"I remember you from the other day. You're the one who isn't political. Who doesn't know anything about anarchist propaganda when it's on walls all over Lower Proszawa."

"I have to watch the traffic, not the walls."

"Right," said Tanz thoughtfully. He pointed to where the Hellers had stepped into their cab. "How do you know a fine woman like that?"

"I've made deliveries to her house. Well, *a* delivery."

"Was it one delivery or more? Get your story straight."

"It was just one," said Largo.

Tanz got closer. "And that lovely, important woman remembered you after one visit?"

"She told me I should change my clothes," Largo stammered.

"What? You weren't even dressed when you saw her?"

Largo remembered Tanz's games. There was nothing he could say that wouldn't be twisted against him.

"I was quite dressed," he said carefully. "She simply didn't like what I was wearing."

Tanz eyed him and said, "How long have you been sucking up to good people like that? What's your plan?"

"What? I haven't been—I have no plan. I only met her once."

Remy came over and took his arm. From behind Largo, a man said, "Might I have a word with you, Officer?" Largo turned and saw Baron Hellswarth leading Tanz away. He spoke quietly but steadily.

Remy smiled at the men. "Uncle Rudy will set him straight."

"I hope so. There's nothing you can say to that man that won't dig you in deeper."

Remy watched the two men talking. "Let him try that with Uncle Rudy."

A moment later, Tanz and the Baron returned.

"It seems that I've misjudged you," said Tanz. His face was creased into a friendly smile, but his voice was tight and strained. "The Baron here has vouched for your good character, Herr Moorden." The officer practically spit the last words. "In any case, you and the young lady are free to go."

"Thank you for understanding, Tanz," said the Baron. The officer tipped his hat, but his eyes never left Largo's. A Mara cab pulled up and Baron Hellswarth led them toward it.

Just before they stepped inside, Remy stopped. "Enki!" she yelled. Largo looked around and saw him standing alone by the edge of the crowd. She turned to the Baron. "Uncle Rudy, can we help him too? He's blind and utterly harmless, I promise you." She didn't wait for an answer but headed straight for him.

"Enki, it's me, Remy. Let us give you a ride." When she reached out to touch him, however, he fell face-first into the wet street and began to convulse violently. Blood spread around his head where he cracked his cheek on the edge of a curb. Remy reached for him again, but Largo pulled her back. Someone screamed, "It's the Drops!" and that was all it took.

The crowd reared back from them. Even the police couldn't stop the frightened mob. More screams came a few seconds later. "Here too!" The crowd lurched again. Largo saw the two women he'd helped earlier. They lay on the ground, their limbs twisting at horrible angles.

Baron Hellswarth grabbed Remy and Largo, pulled them to the waiting cab, and shoved them inside, then climbed in himself. When he was seated he shouted Remy's address into the Mara's listening tube and the cab drove away.

Remy grabbed the Baron's arm. "What about your lady friend? The one you had stashed in the theater box?"

The Baron shook his head. "I lied earlier. I was there alone. I've always wanted to see Mourlet perform, but I couldn't think of anyone in my circle who would want to go." He smiled and shook his head. "I should have known that you two would be there. Especially you, wicked girl," he said.

Remy threw her arms around him. "Thank you for saving us."

"Yes, thank you," said Largo. "That bullock has had it in for me for days. I don't even know why."

Baron Hellswarth held Remy. "Don't worry about it. I play cards

214

with his superior, the Polizeipräsident. Tanz won't be bothering you again."

"That's wonderful news, Baron."

The older man put a hand on Largo's shoulder. "When we're alone and away from the office, you may call me Rudolf." He gave Remy a squeeze. "After all, we're family here."

Remy took Largo's hand. He sat back against the seat, brushing rain out of his hair. He'd expected Anita's performance and the fire to be the strangest part of the evening. But no. Now, apparently, he was on first-name terms with a Hellswarth.

"Poor Enki," said Remy. She looked at the Baron. "Is there anything the doctors can do for him?"

"I'm sure they'll do their best," said the Baron.

Largo was certain that he knew better.

He pictured the men in rubber suits putting the Dandy from the butchers' quarter into a sealed bag. He wondered if they buried the bodies in mass graves or simply burned them.

Remy said, "When you talked to the policeman, did he say what happened to Anita and Vera Baal?"

"They got away," said the Baron. "The police are looking for them both, especially Baal. They suspect her of being an insurrectionist and the fire a deliberate attempt to murder some very important people in the theater."

Remy sat up. "They can't think Anita would be involved in something like that."

The Baron looked out the window as the rain began to abate. "Her involvement remains an open question. But you have to admit that the fact she disappeared with a terrorist is suspicious."

Remy wrapped her arms around herself. "Not Anita. I won't believe it."

"But she's just an *alleged* terrorist at this point," said Largo.

"That's true," said the Baron. "All I know is that they want to talk to her."

Remy leaned against Largo and rested her head on his shoulder. "I hope everyone made it out of the theater all right," she said.

"We all do," said the Baron.

The cab left them at Remy's building. She hugged her uncle. When Largo shook his hand he said, "Look after her tonight."

"I'll take good care of her."

Remy fumbled for her keys as the Baron rode away. "I forgot my wrap in the theater," she said. "I'm glad Uncle Rudy didn't notice. He's the one who gave it to me."

"That's too bad," said Largo. Remy shrugged.

In Remy's flat, they took morphia and Remy went straight to bed. Though exhausted, Largo once again couldn't sleep. He found the copy of *Der Knochengarten* he'd left there and read for an hour. Before he crawled into bed he stood over Remy for a few minutes. He pictured her convulsions and how much they had resembled Enki's.

But she recovered, so it wasn't the Drops.

It made sense, but the thought wasn't entirely convincing. When he got into bed, Largo put an arm around her so he could feel her breathe. He remembered what she'd said in the Golden Angel: "*I love you. Don't ever go.*"

"You too," he said.

Remy opened her eyes. "What?"

"Nothing. Go to sleep."

She held on to his arm and they stayed that way all night.

XUXU: ARTISTIC MOVEMENT OR ACADEMIC PRANK?

From *New Studies in Lower Proszawan Art* by Käthe Merg

Prior to the Great War, Xuxu was a largely unknown art movement. Founded at the Wenders School of Art in High Proszawa, in its nascent form, it was seen as pointless and frivolous, an art joke for an insular group of university students. Even the word *Xuxu* is nothing more than a meaningless sound. However, after the war, it took a form dedicated to the principle that all life and, therefore, all art is political.

Xuxu was created by a motley assortment of students, street artists, and outright criminals. Thieves, for instance, furnished many of the supplies the artists needed when they couldn't steal them from the university. Underground dealers supplied the drugs that fueled much of the movement's early work. During this period, artists collected found objects and frequently defaced accepted works of art in an attempt to break free from all tradition.

If any one person can be said to be the leader of early Xuxu, it's Volger Berk. He claimed to have created the movement's name and ethos in an act of "supernatural inspiration." However, history reveals the early Xuxu had more to do with narcotics and reading the yellowsheets for absurd stories, while also watching public walls for new government and advertising posters to mock. In many ways, Xuxu's early days were a joke wrapped inside a joke. Artists making art for other artists.

However, there was one significant idea that came from this period, that of the Pantheon of Malignance. This group of dark "gods" consisted of grotesque parodies of the Chancellor, the Archbishop, Baron Hellswarth, and various governmental secretaries who were regularly cursed and banished in quasimagical public rituals. While these performances were popular within the university, they were seldom seen by anyone but other students.

Then something important happened to Xuxu at the beginning of the Great War. While the movement remained absurdist and centered on attacking academic art, during this period all questioning of tradition was seen as unpatriotic as troops marched off to the front lines. During those years, the Xuxu movement largely fell silent except among a handful of open-minded collectors and the artists themselves. As the war went on, their meetings became more and more clandestine until they seemed to some outsiders to be possibly subversive.

Soon after Volger Berk was arrested and questioned by the Nachtvogel, he renounced the movement and it quickly fragmented into several warring schools that became ever more insular. By the end of the war, Xuxu was generally regarded to be a corpse—and an obscure one.

However, in the mass euphoria that gripped Lower Proszawa after the armistice, the repressive politics of the war years dissolved. People threw parties in the streets, social mores became more progressive, and art for its own sake came back into vogue. At the same time, the price of the war became more and more obvious. The art school that had birthed Xuxu had been destroyed. Thousands of wounded soldiers returned to the city. The economy was in tatters. Everything but heavy industry, such as Schöne Maschinen, and cheap distractions, such as the cinema and theaters like the Grand Dark, was in danger of collapsing. From these tangled ruins, a new Xuxu took form.

While the first generation ignored the presence of Maras and chimeras as bourgeois contrivances, the new Xuxu incorporated them wherever it could. The artists kept some of the magic rituals from old Xuxu and incorporated Maras, chimeras, and generals into the Pantheon of Malignance. During this period, several Iron Dandies became active members of the group, though none rose to fame because of the public's unsettled attitude toward them. Detlef Lutz was one such soldier-artist. His solo exhibition at Gallerie Buchner, which was called a sensation by many of Lower Proszawa's art critics, sold only a paltry few pieces. Hopeless and destitute, Lutz soon committed suicide in perhaps the greatest Xuxu act of them all: He'd wired a stolen Mara to bayonet maquettes of politicians in the group's magic rituals. At one performance, he stepped in front of the Mara so that his creation stabbed him in the heart. His artistic "sacrifice" was quickly incorporated into the work of other Xuxu members, many of whom made fortunes from his death. Enki Helm was one notable example.

As a child, Helm had lost his sight in an accident when a runaway juggernaut struck a tram in which he was riding. His handicap made him an object of artistic fascination, much like the disfigured Dandies, and he became a public leader in this new generation of Xuxu.

It should be noted that while Helm's work was popular

with galleries and collectors, he was never truly respected by most of the movement's other artists. Considered a curiosity and a social climber, he was not only privately laughed at but eventually added to the Pantheon of Malignance.

Whether that addition was a result of professional jealousy or a genuine distaste for Helm's work, it didn't matter. His fame continued to grow and eventually other artists had to admit that Helm's watered-down Xuxu was better than no Xuxu at all. But the laughter never stopped.

If Helm was aware of it, it was something he never acknowledged.

CHAPTER TWELVE

HIS NEW CLOTHES WERE STILL WET IN THE MORNING, SO HE LEFT THEM hanging in Remy's bathroom and put on a set of his old ones that he'd left at her flat. He took a tram to the Grand Dark and stopped outside. There was a police car across the street. He watched it long enough to make sure that it was empty before going around the theater to the stage door. It was unlocked, so he went into Remy's dressing room and changed into his new work clothes. On the way out, he walked straight into Una. She lurched back and yelled, "Shit!"

"It's all right," he said. "It's me, Largo."

There were only a few lights on backstage and Una stared at him uncertainly. "It is you," she said after a moment. "What are you sneaking around for, scaring the piss out of me?"

"I'm sorry. I left some clothes here last night and I need them for work."

"How did you get in at this hour?" said Una.

"The stage door was unlocked."

"It was? Someone is getting their ass kicked for that." She looked at the door, then back at Largo. "In the future, whether the door is unlocked or not, knock. I'm here all the time, so I can let you in. But if I'm not here or busy, you'll have to fend for yourself. I'm not running a boardinghouse."

"I understand," he said. "I'm sorry I scared you."

"Scared is only the half of it. I almost called my visitors on you."

"Visitors?"

"Never mind. I'm busy and it's time for you to go."

As he left, Largo wondered who Una would be meeting with at five thirty in the morning. He doubted that many art patrons were awake at this hour. He looked at the police car. But why would Una be talking to the bullocks at this hour? Whoever it was inside, he hoped that he hadn't gotten Remy in trouble.

Largo got his bicycle and pedaled into traffic. Last night's adventure at the theater, and now his encounter with Una, left him too tired and fed up with the world to take a circuitous path to work. With the knife back under his jacket, he thought, *Fuck Andrzej*, and rode straight to the company.

Margit wasn't at work that day, but Andrzej and Weimer were. Even though he'd arrived before the other couriers, Largo remained at the back of the room, where he could keep an eye on them. Parvulesco stood with him.

Largo said, "Have you seen Margit this morning?"

"No," said Parvulesco. "I'll let you know if I do."

"I'm worried because she told me about how some of the others don't like her."

"You think someone did something to her?"

"I don't know. I'm just worried."

From the front of the room, Branca said, "Largo and Parvulesco, will you be in conference all day or are you able to join the rest of us for your normal duties?"

"We were just discussing the weather, sir," said Parvulesco. "They say it might rain again today."

"This is Lower Proszawa. It might rain every day, or have you just arrived in our fair city? In the future I suggest you check the weather in the yellowsheets so that we might all get on with our work. Is that satisfactory for you?"

"Yes, sir. Very much."

"Delightful," said Branca. "From now on, if any of you want to know whether to wear your galoshes I'm sure our two weather mavens in the back will be happy to tell you." The other couriers laughed at Largo and Parvulesco for being singled out.

"Now, down to business," Branca continued. "Some of you may have noticed that Andrzej and Weimer have returned to the fold. While this is good news, you might also have noticed that several of your other coworkers are absent. This is unfortunate in that it means the rest of you will have to take up the slack." Voices groaned. "I know. These are difficult times for all of us. However, consider this. While you will have to take over some of your compatriots' deliveries, you will also be getting their tips." Branca looked around the room. "No more moans? Good. Then let us get started."

The couriers lined up for their first packages of the day. Largo remained at the back of the line, watching as Andrzej and Weimer left with their deliveries. When he and Branca were alone, the older man said, "You seem tense today, Largo. Is anything wrong?"

"No. I just wasn't expecting to see Andrzej back so soon."

"Yes, he was quite injured, but he's a strong young man and more dedicated to the job than I previously gave him credit for. We'll need him over these next few days, I suspect."

"Have you seen Margit?" said Largo.

"I have not, nor have I heard from her. As I said, she and several of your coworkers have chosen to be absent with no word why or when we might expect them back."

"Maybe I should check on her."

Branca looked up from his desk. "You know where she lives?"

"No. I thought that I might ask around and see if anybody else knew. Unless you want to give me her address."

"The company isn't in the business of giving out its workers' personal details."

"Naturally. I'm sure she'll show up soon."

"I wish I were as confident as you. Still, we mustn't give up hope for her swift return."

A Mara lumbered out of the back room with a package for him. "Will I be doing extra runs too?"

"I'm afraid so. However, for the chief courier, the number will be small."

"Thank you, sir."

Branca handed him a receipt book. "I haven't said it before, but you're doing a quite adequate job. Keep up the good work."

"Thank you. I will."

Largo put the book and the package in his shoulder bag and went outside. The couriers stood in a semicircle with Andrzej and Weimer in the middle. The group looked up as Largo came out. There was no way he could get to his bicycle without passing through them, so he walked down the steps as calmly as he could, trying to recall everything Roland had taught him about using his knife. But as much as he tried, he couldn't remember a word of it.

When he reached the ground, Andrzej walked briskly in Largo's direction. Something came back to him then. He turned his body almost sideways. *It makes you a smaller target*, he remembered. When he reached under his jacket for the knife, Andrzej stopped and held up his hands in front of him.

"Truce, Largo," he said. "I don't want to fight you."

"Then what are you and Weimer up to?"

"Nothing," said Weimer. He walked to Andrzej's side. "We wanted to apologize."

That caught the other couriers by surprise as much as it caught Largo. "I don't believe you," he said.

Andrzej lowered his hands. "I know. And you have no reason to. But I wanted to say that whatever happened between us before won't happen again. And that I'm truly sorry."

Largo kept his hand near the knife and said, "Why?"

"Because I had time to think about it and how stupid I was. And because I almost died. It occurred to me what a complete waste of a life it would be if I died over a ridiculous thing like an argument."

"All right," said Largo. He pointed to Weimer. "What about him? Does he suddenly want to be my friend too?"

"No," said Weimer coolly. "I know you don't trust me and I don't blame you. I doubt we'll ever be friends, but I want you to know that I'm also sorry for my behavior. And I won't bother you again."

The other couriers looked at one another, disappointed that there might not be a fight after all.

"Why should I believe either of you?' said Largo.

"I know I can't prove anything through words," said Andrzej. "So, I'll do my best to stay out of your way until you see that I mean what I said."

"Me too," said Weimer.

Largo lowered his hands from the knife. "All right. You can start by moving away from my bicycle."

Andrzej and Weimer stepped back, and the other couriers moved with them. Largo went to his bicycle, but as he got on something occurred to him. "Did either of you do something to Margit?"

"Not me," said Andrzej, seemingly confused at the accusation.

Weimer shook his head. "Me neither."

They both sounded sincere, but Largo couldn't be sure. He said, "I'm going to check on her. If I find out that either of you is lying I'll send you to the hospital myself." With that, he rode away. He wanted to turn around and see if anyone was following him, but he knew it would make him look weak. He'd threatened Andrzej and Weimer in front of witnesses. By Haxan Green rules, it meant that he couldn't back down. This wasn't at all how he wanted things to turn out, but it was too late to change that now. The difference was that this time he knew he could defend himself. Margit, on the other hand, was a different matter. The only place he knew to look for her was Machtviertel. As much as he was ready to take on Andrzej or Weimer, he wasn't sure if he could stomach another ride to the Black Palace. Pietr was a lot more frightening that a couple of bully couriers. He decided that for now he would wait and hope that she returned on her own.

Don't make me go out there, Margit. I'll buy you a whole new bicycle if something happened to yours. Just don't make me go back.

Branca had been telling the truth when he said that the couriers would be making extra deliveries. The sun was going down by the time Largo finished, but his pockets were heavy with silver and a few small gold coins, so that helped his mood considerably.

After he turned in the last of his receipt books, he went to Fräulein Sabel to call Remy on the Trefle.

Inside, raucous music was blaring from an amplified gramophone. The trip had been for nothing. He wouldn't be able to hear anything above the noise. He went into the men's room to calm his nerves, wishing he had morphia with him. On the way out, he stopped at the bar and ordered a whiskey. While waiting, he watched the happy mob that filled the café. The chairs and tables had been removed from the center of the room so that people could dance. Couples whirled around the floor. Men and women. Men and men. Women and women. They were a common enough sight, but tonight the dancers reminded Largo of the brash joy of Anita Mourlet's performance. He suddenly felt very provincial and he wasn't sure why.

As much as he had wanted to see Anita's forbidden show, he'd also been a little frightened. But of what? Maybe just the sight of a world he didn't know. He hated the idea that he'd been afraid, but for once he was being honest with himself. *So much of my life has been controlled by fear.* Fear of Remy growing bored and leaving. Fear of losing his job. Fear of not losing his job and working for the company forever. Fear of getting his life so wrong that he had to return to Haxan Green and be buried in some rich man's abandoned barn.

Does Remy see my fear, or have I fooled her? And if I have, how much longer can I keep it up? She wants to expose more of herself to the world and I want to hide. I can't go on like this, but how does someone change so drastically?

Largo decided to ask Rainer. He paid for his drink and was heading outside when he bumped into Parvulesco and Roland coming in. "Want a drink?" said Parvulesco. "It's on me. Branca was right. All those extra runs put a lot more silvers in my pocket."

Largo said, "Thanks, but I'm on my way to see a friend."

"I told Roland how you faced down Andrzej and Weimer today."

"Good for you," Roland said, "squaring off against two men like that. It was brave."

"Not really. All they did was apologize for being such a pair of bastards," Largo said.

"But you didn't know that. You were ready to fight and you stood your ground. Be proud of yourself, you dolt."

Largo thought about it. Was not accepting that he'd been brave part of his relentless fear? "I suppose. Maybe you're right."

"Of course he's right," said Parvulesco.

"Still, there was something strange about the whole thing."

"Such as?"

"Someone I know, an artist named Enki—"

"Enki Helm? The painter?" said Roland. "You know him? I love his work."

"Really? I can't stand it. Anyway, we're not really friends, but I know him a bit."

"If you can, I'd love to meet him."

Largo looked down at the street. "I'm not sure that's possible. The point I was making is that he disappeared and came back a changed man. And now Andrzej and Weimer are back and they're different too."

"Do you think it means something?" said Parvulesco.

"I don't know. But I do know that we all have to be careful. Ernst, the editor at *Ihre Skandale*, told me there's a new gang in town kidnapping people for ransom."

Parvulesco said, "It's funny you say that. A couple of men dragged me off my bike the other night. If Roland hadn't been there I don't know what would have happened."

"Do you remember what they looked like?" Largo said.

Parvulesco thought about it. "Not really. But why would someone kidnap me? Roland and I don't have any money."

"I don't know. Like I said, it's strange." He looked at Roland. "There's something else. The reason I can't introduce you to Enki is that I think he has the Drops."

"Shit," said Roland. "It feels like it's everywhere these days."

Parvulesco said, "Did you see it happen?"

"Yes," said Largo. "It was last night after Anita Mourlet's performance—"

"You know Anita Mourlet too?" said Roland, impressed. "Fuck, Largo."

"Hush," said Parvulesco.

"He fell in the street. So did a couple of women I helped after the fire," Largo said.

"You helped some women with the Drops and you're friends with Helm, who also has the Drops. Are you sure you aren't infected too?" said Parvulesco thoughtfully.

"I don't think so," said Largo. "A doctor I know told me I have a sort of immunity."

"How does he know?" said Roland.

Largo looked around nervously. *Fear again.* "It's because I take morphia."

Parvulesco looked at Roland. "I told you we should try it."

Roland rapped a knuckle on the table. "I'm not putting that in my body for any reason."

Parvulesco rolled his eyes. "Such a choirboy."

Roland said, "Tell us about Mourlet. Is she as mad as people say?"

"Madder," said Largo. "But I'll have to tell you tomorrow. I need to see my friend Rainer."

"Tomorrow then," said Parvulesco. "Have a good night. And take your own advice—be careful."

"I will."

Largo took a tram across town and rode his bicycle only the last few blocks. As he pedaled the final long street, he saw groups of old men out late whitewashing over propaganda posters. Largo touched his pocket. Even with the money, he didn't like paying the tram fare, but it was better to be safe.

Or am I wasting money by giving in to fear again? On the other hand, maybe certain kinds of fear are sensible.

It's all so fucking complicated.

He made it through the web lock on Rainer's door and went upstairs. Rainer was at a telescope, watching the north. *Always the north*, thought Largo. *He's going to go mad if he stays in here forever.*

"Hello," he called.

Rainer's voice came through the wireless horn. "Hello, Largo."

"Did I startle you?"

Rainer turned away from the telescope. "No. I know your footsteps by now."

Largo brushed some dust off the top of one of the sofas. "Do you have time to talk?"

"I have nothing but time," said Rainer. He sat across from Largo. "Was there something in particular you wanted to talk about?"

Largo plucked some lint from the top of the sofa. "There's so much going on. It's hard to know where to begin. But I was out with Remy last night and there was a fire."

"Are you both all right?"

"We're fine. But the fire wasn't the worst part. People in the crowd, including a sort of friend, collapsed with the Drops."

Rainer leaned forward, resting his hands on his knees. "That *is* serious. Sometimes I think my isolation is a gift in that it keeps me away from things like the Drops."

Your isolation is a lot of things, but it's not a gift, thought Largo. He said, "Neither of us has to worry about the Drops."

"Why is that?"

Largo told him about his conversation with Dr. Venohr.

"How funny. Morphia addiction is the trick? Of course, that presents its own problems."

"Such as?"

"There's prison, of course. And then there's living forever and watching your friends fall dead around you."

"You're morbid tonight," said Largo.

"I'm morbid every night. I just don't always get the chance to share it with others."

Rainer got a bottle of whiskey from the kitchen and poured some for each of them. Largo gulped his down while Rainer sipped his through a steel straw. Careful as he was, a little dripped from his disfigured mouth. He wiped it away with a dirty handkerchief he took from his pocket.

Reluctantly, Largo said, "I hate to ask, but can you spare a drop or two of morphia? I don't have any and can't get hold of Remy. Besides, I don't think Una wants me back at the Grand Dark tonight."

Rainer got up without a word and came back with a bottle. Largo put three drops under his tongue. He wanted more, but he didn't want to use too much of Rainer's supply.

"Feel better?" Rainer said.

"Much. Thank you."

"Good. Now, please, go on with what you were saying."

Largo said, "The Drops isn't the strangest thing going on. And maybe I'm making too much of it, but people are disappearing."

"What do you mean?"

"They're gone for a few days and when they come back they're different."

"Different how?"

Largo chuckled. "I feel strange for complaining about it. But they come back better. Nicer. Calmer. Have you ever heard of anything like that?"

"I'm afraid not," said Rainer, reaching for the whiskey.

"A man I know says that there's a gang taking people for ransom."

Rainer poured them another drink. "He might be half-right. There are gangs, but they're not looking for ransom."

Largo sat up straighter. "Then what?"

"Slaves," said Rainer, looking toward High Proszawa. "I was right. Things are happening there. Looters and grave robbers need laborers and the easiest way to get them is simply to take them."

Though he was still limp from the morphia, Largo tensed. "The last time I was here you weren't so certain about what's going on up north."

"You're not the only person I talk to."

"Who do you know who knows about slaves?"

Rainer laid a hand on one of his boards. "Sometimes the dead talk to me."

Largo relaxed. "Oh."

A rasping sound came from the wireless speaker. It was Rainer laughing. "I'm also back in contact with some people—old friends from the war who bring in contraband from the southern colonies. They talk about awful things happening in High Proszawa."

Largo sipped his drink and considered the idea. "That might explain the disappearances. But why are people different when they get back?"

"Large parts of the north are still plague zones. Disease alone could scramble their brains. The plague bombs might even be the origin of the Drops."

"Do you think the plague is catching?"

Rainer leaned back. "Who knows? It's been there for so long it might have metamorphosed."

"But why doesn't it kill the looters?"

Rainer leaned his head back. "That is an interesting question, isn't it?"

"Maybe," Largo said. "If the Drops is related to the plague, the looters must use morphia too."

Rainer laughed again. "A city of thieves and addicts," he said. "How appropriate. There you go. Mystery solved."

"Except . . . why would they bring slaves back and risk them remembering what happened? Why not just kill the ones they don't want?"

A flying Mara flashed by the window and they both turned to look.

Rainer said, "They could reason that too many permanent disappearances would draw in the bullocks. Maybe even the army. But plucking a few people off the streets and returning them? That's more of an anomaly than a reason to panic."

Largo put down his drink. "Slaves. It's horrible. Unbelievable."

Rainer held his drink in both hands. "You should have been in the war. You'd have learned that while many things are horrible, very few are unbelievable."

Largo had always been afraid to ask Rainer, but tonight was a night for overcoming fear. "Do you hate me for not going?"

Rainer looked at him. "Of course not. You were the smart one. Look at me. I was at the front fighting for God and the Fatherland. We all were. And what did we accomplish? We mutilated ourselves and destroyed High Proszawa. Yet the plague remains. The enemy remains. And we made a home for thieves and slavers. They or the plague will be on us before long."

Largo pointed to the spirit board with his glass. "Did you learn that through the boards too?"

"No. The situation is obvious."

"I'm still skeptical of your spiritual interests," said Largo.

"I know."

"But not as much as I was."

Rainer set down his whiskey. "Really? Why is that?"

Largo looked at the scratches on his knuckles from his fall on the docks. "Have you ever heard of Vera Baal?"

Rainer pointed to the wall above Largo's head. He turned and saw a leaflet with a color chrome of Vera's face.

"She's one of the best mediums in Lower Proszawa."

"I saw her last night," said Largo. "Not for long, but I saw her conjure a spirit. I didn't believe it at the time, but I don't have any other explanation."

Rainer's blue eyes locked on Largo's. "Tell me about it."

Largo told him about Anita Mourlet's performance and how she'd introduced Vera. How the spirit appeared and the white ribbon from Vera's mouth caught fire.

Rainer nodded excitedly. "The ribbon was trans zamlžení. A foreign term and difficult to pronounce, but important. It means the physical manifestation of spiritual energy. It can be very unstable."

"I wish someone had told the bastard with the cigar."

"Did people die?"

"I haven't looked at the yellowsheets," Largo said. "I'm not sure I want to know."

"You have to face these things sometime, Largo."

"I know. I promise I'll look tomorrow."

Rainer wiped his mouth with the handkerchief. "If you learn anything, let me know. In the meantime, I'll try my boards. If many died, there will be restless spirits in the city."

"What do they say to you?"

"Different things. Some tell me about their lives; others, the world. Still others don't know that they've passed on. In those cases, it's my duty to try to help them."

Largo frowned. "It sounds depressing."

Rainer moved the platen to the middle of the spirit board. "It is, sometimes."

Largo regretted not bringing food with him. He wondered if Rainer was eating. "Did you ever get your pension check?"

"Yes," he said, and clapped his hands. "Thank the Minister of War's puckered arse. Would you like a smoke to celebrate?"

Largo held up a hand. "No, thank you. I want to have my wits about me when I ride home."

"Afraid of kidnappers?" said Rainer as he lit a hashish cigarette.

"I think it makes sense. But do you? I'm serious. I'm trying to separate rational fears from irrational ones."

Rainer drew in some smoke and let it out again. "Kidnapping is a wholly rational fear right now. Do you have your knife?"

"Always."

"Are you ready to use it?"

"Yes."

"Then you're better prepared than ninety percent of the city."

That made Largo feel better. "Maybe I will have one more drink. But just a small one."

The next day, Largo bought a copy of *Ihre Skandale* from one of the kiosks in the Great Triumphal Square and read it at lunch. Six people had died in the fire at the Golden Angel.

Rainer will have plenty of spirits to talk to.

What surprised him was that there wasn't a single mention of anyone with the Drops. Surely someone as famous as Enki deserved an acknowledgment. Largo looked through the rest of the paper. It was the usual mix of lurid murders and overwrought interviews with the families of the disappeared. However, there wasn't a single mention of the Drops anywhere.

Strange. It seems like the kind of story Ihre Skandale *readers live for. I'll have to ask Ernst the next time I see him.*

When he got to the company he found that two more couriers had gone missing. It was another long day with extra deliveries for everyone. Largo liked the added money, but the only thing that made the work bearable was counting down the days until Friday, when he would meet with the Baron again.

His deliveries took long enough that he was almost late getting to the Grand Dark that evening. The theater was closed to the public, but Una and the players had invited friends to see the previews of two new plays. Largo was surprised when he spotted an older man standing by himself in the lobby.

"Dr. Venohr?"

The doctor shook Largo's hand warmly. "Good to see you under better circumstances than last time."

"It's good to see you too. How are you? Remy seems to be doing wonderfully. She said that you checked in on her the other day."

"Yes, I paid her a visit at her flat," Venohr said. "It was impossible to get her to come to my office, so I did a quick examination where she couldn't escape."

"And how did she seem?"

"In perfect form. I don't think you have any need to worry about her. But be sure that she takes the pills I gave her and doesn't miss a single dose."

"I'll make sure," said Largo. "Is she who invited you to the theater tonight?"

Venohr looked around the lobby. "Yes. I wasn't sure at first, but I don't get many invitations of this sort. It seemed like an opportunity I shouldn't miss."

"I'm sure you'll enjoy yourself. Una's plays are vivid, to say the least."

"So I've heard."

Largo lowered his voice. "Do you mind if I ask you something serious? Something medical?"

"Not at all. What is it?"

"You know about the disappearances in the city?"

"I've heard about them. Why? Do you know someone who's been abducted?"

"Three people, in fact," Largo said. "And when they came back, they were all different. Nicer. Strangely calmer. Do you know something that could account for that?"

Venohr thought about it for a moment. "I've heard such reports and discussed it with some colleagues. We think that it's purely psychological. Shock from the trauma of the abduction. Don't worry. Given time, I'm sure they'll return to their old selves again."

Largo put his hands in his pockets. "Too bad. There are a couple I like better this way."

The doctor laughed lightly. "I'm afraid I can't help you there."

"Oh well. It was worth asking."

The lights in the lobby flickered and everyone moved into the theater. Largo sat close to the stage with Venohr. The doctor had never seen puppet performers before and wanted to get a good look at how they worked.

The first play was the story Una had been so excited about—the mad scientist who put his dead lover's head onto a Mara body. In the play version of the story, the scientist's reborn lover immediately launched into an affair with his much younger and more handsome assistant. The scientist caught them and killed them both before killing himself. However, before the inevitable bloody murders, there were copious amounts of sex between both scientists and the human-Mara hybrid. Largo felt Dr. Venohr grow restless and uncomfortable during these scenes. At the end, the play received only polite applause.

During the intermission, Largo said, "Don't worry, Doctor. The plays aren't all that . . . extreme."

"You needn't worry about me. I was just caught a little off guard," said Dr. Venohr.

"What did you think of it overall?"

"I'm not sure. How about you?"

"It wasn't one of Una's best," Largo whispered. "She told me about the idea just the other day and I think she rushed to get it onstage."

"I suppose she'll try to top herself with the next play," said Venohr a bit nervously.

"With luck, she spent more time writing it."

The lights flickered and they went back into the theater. This time the doctor led them to seats in the back row.

Largo thought the second play was better than the first, but also more disturbing. It was the story of a political murder, not unlike Una's *The Erotic Underworld of Blixa Konstantin*. In the new play, Heinz, a radical who had seduced a young, aspiring actress, Ella, killed her after she failed to carry out a political murder. Afterward, he threw her body into the bay. Heinz escaped the police, but ran into a unit of armed Maras who promptly clubbed him almost to death. The beating was long and bloody. At times, Dr. Venohr covered his eyes. Just when Largo thought the play was over, an angry mob appeared onstage and decapitated Heinz. They marched offstage holding the head up high and singing patriotic songs. The applause for this play was more enthusiastic than for the first, which disturbed Largo. It seemed close enough to reality that it felt crueler than Una's usual supernatural tales. He tried to remember what story from *Ihre Skandale* it might be based on, but nothing came to mind.

Dr. Venohr didn't stay for the party after the plays were finished. They said their goodbyes and by the time Largo got backstage, it was crowded and lively. The performers were surrounded by friends and admirers. Largo ended up complimenting Una on the show out of simple politeness, and to diffuse any residual annoyance she had with him. Remy had played the innocent girl in the second play, even though Una had written the part for Lucie.

"She never turned up," said Remy. "Una even sent Ilsa to Lucie's flat, but her roommate said she wasn't there. We're all worried."

Baumann was there in an expensive new blue suit, something he'd obviously worn for Lucie. He stood alone by her dressing room and when Remy saw him, she called him over.

"Have you heard anything?" he said.

"No. I was hoping you had," said Remy.

"Not a word. I was going to take her to dinner, but I'm not sure what to do now."

"I hope she isn't hurt," said Largo, but he was thinking, *I hope she hasn't disappeared*. The thought of Lucie being forced to dig through ruins in a plague-ridden war zone was too awful to contemplate.

"Or worse," said Baumann. "I heard Enki came down with the Drops."

Remy said, "I know. We were there."

Baumann looked at her. "So it's true?"

"I'm afraid so."

Baumann absentmindedly scratched the back of his head. "I don't know what to do or think."

Largo said, "Maybe we should call the hospital. She could have simply fallen or been in a tram accident."

"That's a great idea," said Baumann. "I'll see if Una will let me use her Trefle."

When Baumann left, Remy pulled Largo into a room at the far end of the backstage area. It was full of hooded bodies. Some were clothed and some nude. They leaned against the walls and hung by hooks from the ceiling.

Remy said, "Do you like it? I like to imagine it's some madman's abattoir."

Largo went to some of the bodies and lifted their hoods. "Is this all of them? I've never seen a puppet after a show before."

"Gruesome, isn't it?"

"It is, a little." He picked up an arm from a pile of limbs in the corner and smacked Remy on the ass with it. "I feel like a grave robber on Christmas morning."

She laughed and said, "I thought you'd like it. Now come and kiss me." She took out the bottle of morphia Dr. Venohr had given them. Largo was surprised at how much they'd already used. They put drops under each other's tongues and kissed. As the warmth spread through his body, Largo pushed Remy against the wall and their kisses became more passionate. She unbuttoned her blouse and Largo kissed her breasts. Behind them, the door opened. Ilsa started in with one of the young stagehands, but stopped when she saw them.

She giggled and said, "I'm so sorry."

"We don't mind," said Remy. "Look. There are three other perfectly good walls not being used."

Ilsa grinned. "You're so silly," she said, and pulled the embarrassed stagehand outside.

"Maybe we should go back too," said Largo. "They're going to miss you and send less-attractive search parties."

Remy buttoned her blouse and said, "You're probably right. Besides, someone out there must have cocaine. We need to find them."

Largo went to get them drinks while Remy made her way around the party hunting for drugs. When he found her, she was talking to Hanna. "No one has a single bit of cocaine," she said. "Or so they claim."

Hanna said, "Baumann probably does, but I don't think this is a good time to ask."

"I hope he finds Lucie soon," said Remy. "It feels strange to hope someone is in the hospital, but what a relief it would be if she's just twisted her ankle."

"That reminds me. Should we have a drink for Enki?" Largo asked.

Hanna raised an eyebrow. "I didn't think you even liked Enki."

"I don't particularly, but I never wished the Drops on him."

"Maybe the doctors have discovered a treatment for it," said Remy.

Hanna swirled her drink. "If they had, we would know about it at the lab."

"I should have asked Dr. Venohr," said Largo.

"Was he here?" said Remy. "Why didn't he stay for the party?"

"The decapitation, I suspect. He left right after the second play. But he said hello and that you should keep taking your pills."

"The two of you. You're both mother hens."

Hanna said, "Maybe Largo is right. Maybe we should have a drink for Enki."

"And hope for the best for him and Lucie too," Largo said.

"To Enki, then," said Remy, and they all drank.

Later in the evening, Remy found a stagehand with cocaine and she and Largo made love in the puppet room—this time with the door locked.

No one heard anything from Lucie the next day. Baumann checked with both the hospital and the police, but neither could help. By now, Largo was certain that she'd been abducted. Remy burst into tears when he told her his theory. She made him promise not to mention it to anybody else. Before he left for work, he made sure that Remy took her pill.

At work, after the other couriers had left the office for their morning deliveries, Largo remained behind.

He went to Branca's desk. "Excuse me, sir," he said.

"Yes? Is there a problem with one of your packages?"

"No. They're fine. I was wondering if you might have heard anything from Margit?"

"Margit," said Branca. "She has graced us with neither her presence nor a message."

"I'm worried about her."

"Are you now? Well, I have good news for you. If she is absent without a word for one more day, she will no longer be employed here. That means she will be nothing for you to worry about."

"Is that fair?" said Largo. "Andrzej was gone for several days too."

"But we knew where Andrzej was, and his infirmities were well-documented by a doctor. Margit's absence, on the other hand, is more spectral," said Branca. He half smiled. "Perhaps she was a ghost all along and has simply returned to the grave."

Largo didn't like the easy way Branca talked about Margit being dead. "Maybe I should call the hospital."

Branca shuffled paperwork on his desk. "Don't bother. The company has already done it and there are no records of her admission."

That was a surprise, although the more Largo thought about it, the less sure he was that he believed Branca. He decided to call the hospital himself on his lunch break, but it occurred to him then that he didn't even know Margit's last name. There was no way to ask Branca for it without letting on that he didn't believe him. *Maybe Parvulesco knows*, he thought, and decided to ask him after work.

Largo said, "Thank you," and checked the address of his first package.

Before he left, Branca said, "Don't be so glum. This works out well for you too, Largo."

"How is that?"

Branca set down his pen and stacked the papers he'd been working on. "With Margit gone, you no longer have to pay back the favor you owe her."

Largo left the office without saying another word.

At lunch, he bought *Ihre Skandale* to see if Enki or the Drops were mentioned. Neither was. However, another story caught his eye. It was about the murder of a young woman by what the paper called an "anarchist mastermind." He'd evaded the police for most of the night and was killed by a police Mara in the Midden. The young woman had been popular in the district and when the police found the killer's body, it had been mutilated by the residents. Largo recognized the story immediately as the play from the previous night, but there was something wrong. According to *Ihre Skandale*, the young woman's murder had occurred around midnight and the killer didn't encounter the police Maras until almost dawn.

The party at the Grand Dark began at about ten.

So how did Una know about a murder that hadn't happened yet?

It was another dull day running letters and packages from one end of Lower Proszawa to the other. The skies remained gray and threatened rain, but it never came.

Largo's last delivery of the day was in the Granate district. He walked his bicycle along the street because it was paved with rough cobblestones that hadn't been maintained in a decade or more. The tall, narrow houses were close together. People grew vegetables in small patches of soil on the sidewalk where gardens had once stood. The district used to be home to the servants who worked for the wealthy families in Händler and Kromium. Now it was occupied by their descendants, many of whom had lost their positions to Maras and lived on minuscule government stipends and veteran pensions.

At a house whose front steps had collapsed and been replaced with an improvised stairway of wooden boxes, Largo knocked on the door. A frowning woman in curlers answered. She wore a housecoat and the skin on her face and hands was blotched red, as if she were fighting a fever.

"Frau Heckert?" Largo said. "I have a delivery for you."

Her frown turned into a broad smile. "Really? I've never had a delivery before. Who's it from?"

Largo checked the package. "I'm sorry, but the return address is smudged."

Frau Heckert put out her hands. "Never mind. Give it here."

"Would you mind signing for it first?"

She scrawled something spiky and illegible in Largo's receipt book and snatched the package away from him as if afraid he would run off with it. Chuckling excitedly, Frau Heckert tore the box open immediately. Her smile vanished and she stared at what was inside. With a rough red hand, she reached into the package and removed a small revolver. She turned it over in her hand.

"I haven't seen one of these since the war," she said. Frau Heckert held the gun out to Largo. "It doesn't bring back good memories. Do you want it?"

He took a step back. "Thank you, but we're not permitted to do that."

She frowned at the pistol and shrugged. "I suppose I could use it. Granate isn't what it used to be. Thieves. People being snatched off the street. It's madness."

"Yes, madam."

Frau Heckert opened the revolver's cylinder. "My, it's loaded and everything." She slapped the cylinder back into place and pointed the gun at Largo. Beaming at him, she said, "Ever seen the devil dance a jig?"

He froze and looked at her. "What?"

"Ever kissed a raven in the bright moonlight?"

"No, madam."

Frau Heckert laughed with a blotched hand over her mouth. "I'm just playing with you. It's something we used to say to enemy prisoners during the war, right before we executed them. It kept their minds busy while we did our business."

Largo walked down the box stairway to his bicycle. "Have a good day, madam."

"You too," said Frau Heckert. She stood in her doorway with a puzzled expression on her face. "Funny kind of gift."

Largo walked his bicycle quickly out of Granate and stopped for a whiskey and a drop of morphia before going back to the company.

That evening, Remy again played the wronged soldier in *The Trench Demon*. When the second play was over, Largo realized what he'd just seen because he'd been so preoccupied thinking about Frau Heckert and the yellowsheet story about the previous night's murder. When he ran into Una backstage, he asked her how she knew about a murder that hadn't taken place.

She said, "Don't be silly, Largo. I don't steal everything from *Ihre Skandale*. I do have a lively imagination, if I do say so myself."

"But the stories were so similar," said Largo.

"Just a coincidence," Una said. She winked at him. "Or maybe I'm clairvoyant."

He wasn't convinced, but he couldn't figure his way past her casual dismissal. "Has anyone heard from Lucie yet?"

Una walked away. "I don't know. You should ask Baumann. I hear he was out all night looking."

Largo stared as she left, startled by the callousness of her answer. After a minute, he went into Remy's dressing room. She kissed him and had him towel off the sweat that had accumulated on her back while in the galvanic suit. He mechanically began wiping her down.

"You seem distracted, darling."

"I'm worried," said Largo.

"About what?"

"The second play last night. It was about a murder that didn't happen until two hours later."

Remy took the towel and wiped her face. "That doesn't make sense. I'm sure you're getting your stories mixed up."

"I'm not. I can show you the story in *Ihre Skandale*. They match almost exactly."

"'Almost,'" she said. "That means they're not the same story."

"They're close enough for me to be worried."

Remy dropped down into a chair and began putting on her clothes. "What do you want me to do about it?"

"I'm not sure. Nothing. I don't know. But I have a terrible feeling that something is wrong at the Grand Dark. When I picked up my work clothes the other day, I ran into Una at five thirty in the morning. There was a bullock car nearby and she said she had a meeting with someone."

Remy held up her hands in a gesture of frustration. "Una sleeps in the theater sometimes when she's working late. And she meets with people when they can meet. Theater people don't keep the kind of rigid hours couriers do."

Largo frowned. "What does that mean?"

"Nothing. Please," said Remy. She put her head in her hands. "I'm exhausted. What are you telling me?"

Largo went and knelt by her chair. "That something strange happened the other night. Lucie is gone and no one cares. If it weren't for Baumann no one would even be out looking. I have a bad feeling," he said. "What if you go missing? I don't know what I'd do."

Remy sat back in her chair and looked at him in a way he'd never seen before. It was hard and cold. "Is this about our conversation at Anita's show? I want to hone my skills and become a better performer. That means I'll be working more and have less time to spend with you," she said. "Are you jealous? Are you that selfish? I'm trying to change my life."

"So am I," said Largo. "And I'm not jealous."

Remy got up and put on her coat. "You're not changing your life. Uncle Rudy is. Without him, you'll be riding that bicycle through the streets like a schoolboy when you're a hundred."

Largo was caught off guard by her anger. *Where is it coming from? This isn't like her.* It made him think of Enki and Andrzej and how they'd suddenly changed, but with Remy the shift was in the opposite direction. With her there was a new distance in her eyes, her whole manner.

"That's not true," he said. "I really want to learn and improve myself."

"Then stop being jealous of me doing the same thing!" Remy shouted.

"I promise I'm not. I'm afraid for you. Don't you understand? I think Una might be connected to a murder. Maybe even working with the bullocks."

Remy threw open her dressing room door and walked into the backstage area. "Get out! Get out of here!" she shouted. "I don't want to see you. Don't call me or come to the theater. *If* I ever want to see you again, I'll get in touch with you."

Una, Ilsa, and the other performers gathered around.

"Remy, please listen—" said Largo.

"Get out!" she screamed, and the words caught in her throat. She made a choking sound and collapsed onto the floor as her limbs went rigid and convulsed into grotesque positions. Largo and Una ran to her.

"Someone call a doctor!" Una shouted.

Largo grabbed Remy's arms and tried to keep them from twisting. Una shoved him away. "You've done enough damage for one night. Didn't you hear her? Get out and don't come back."

Largo got up and looked around. Everyone stared at him angrily. When he took a step back toward Remy, Ilsa and a couple of brawny stagehands got in his way.

"Has someone called the doctor?" shouted Una.

Something trailed from Remy's mouth. It was dark and smelled like scorched oil. He remembered the man in the butchers' quarter.

Is this why Remy was so different tonight?

When Largo tried to get back to her, one of the stagehands shoved him. Largo reached under his jacket for the knife and the stagehand backed away.

"Don't make things any worse!" shouted Una. "Just get out."

Largo closed his jacket and rode home to Little Shambles. On the way, he stopped at a shop and bought a bottle of their cheapest whiskey. He didn't wake up until the next day, when someone was pounding on the door.

CHAPTER THIRTEEN

HE WAS STILL DRESSED IN HIS CLOTHES FROM THE THEATER. LARGO OPENED the flat door an inch and five men burst in. Four were in police uniforms, but the fifth was a thin man in a gray coat. He said, "How are you this fine morning, Herr Moorden?"

Groggily, Largo said, "Tanz?"

"*Special Operative* Tanz," he said, poking Largo in the chest with each word. "Thought your friend the Baron could get rid of me, did you? Guess again."

Largo's cheap whiskey hangover made his eyes hurt and his head throb. "What do you want? I have to get to work."

The four men with Tanz fanned out behind him, their hands on their truncheons. "It seems that the Baron isn't your friend anymore. In fact, he's howling for your blood."

"What are you talking about? Why?"

"Show me your hands," said Tanz.

Largo held out his hands, palms up. Tanz flipped them over and inspected the skin. "What happened to your knuckles?"

"I fell a few days ago."

"You weren't fighting? Maybe you and your colleague Andrzej? You remember. The one who ended up in the hospital."

"No. I fell off my bicycle. What's this all about?" said Largo.

Tanz picked up the whiskey bottle from a nearby table. "Your taste in liquor is shit."

Largo gestured toward the door. "If you'd like to leave a list of better ones, please do it on your way out."

Tanz ignored him. He picked up something else from the table. "What's this?" It was a small bottle with a clear liquid inside. He shook it and looked at Largo. "This isn't morphia, is it?"

Largo froze, not knowing what to say.

Tanz handed the bottle to one of his officers. "Don't answer. You'll just lie. We'll add it to the other charges."

"What charges?"

Tanz walked around the living room, occasionally moving a yellowsheet or inspecting another bottle. "Where's your knife?" he said. "The one you threatened the stagehand with at the Grand Dark?"

Largo shook his head and immediately regretted it. "I thought he was going to attack me. I only reached for it in self-defense."

Tanz looked at him. "Then you admit that you carry a concealed knife?"

"You obviously know I do. Why are you playing these games? I don't feel well."

"Where's the knife now?"

"On the desk in the bedroom."

Tanz gestured and two of the officers went into the next room. They came back with the knife a moment later. Tanz looked impressed when he saw it. He handed it to one of the uniformed officers.

He said, "That was quite a row you had last night with your girlfriend. From what I hear, she threw you out on your ear. Humiliated you in front of all her friends."

Largo replayed the fight in his mind. It hurt more than his hangover. "It was just an argument. She was upset with something I said. I'm sure things will be fine in a few days."

"That's wonderful news," said Tanz cheerfully. Then his tone changed abruptly. "So, where is she?"

"Remy?"

"No, the fucking Archbishop. Where is she?"

Largo's heart beat faster. Remy was missing? His brain wouldn't accept the possibility. "I haven't seen her since the theater." He felt cold and his mind raced, fighting back panic.

"How are you going to work things out with her if she's gone?"

Largo tried to remember. "Have you talked to Una? She was calling a doctor after Remy got sick. Maybe he knows."

Tanz said, "I don't think a doctor will help. You see, it's not so much that she's missing as she was forcibly removed from her flat. Murdered too, I suspect."

"Murdered," Largo whispered. He tried to take a step, but his head swam and he staggered. "What do you mean Remy's murdered?"

"Her uncle—your *friend* the Baron—went to check up on her last night and her flat was, to say the least, in disarray."

The other officers chuckled at that.

"She was nowhere to be found. And here you are, brokenhearted, a knife on your desk, and enough whiskey and morphia in you to kill a black bear."

Largo tried to think. Tanz must be wrong, or it was a trick. Remy couldn't be gone.

"I love her. I wouldn't do anything to her."

Tanz turned his ear toward him. "To who?"

"Remy," said Largo.

"The missing girl?"

Largo felt a chill, but in a different way. His hands trembled ever so slightly. He glanced at the table, but the morphia was gone. "Why are you doing this to me?"

Tanz pushed Largo down into a chair. "Where were you last night after you left the theater?"

"Here."

"All night?"

"Yes."

"Then where's your bicycle?"

Largo tried to remember. "I don't know."

"I do," said Tanz. "It was found less than a block from your missing lady friend's flat. The flat that had been torn apart in a jealous rage."

That was it, then. Something really had happened to Remy. Largo put his head in his hands. "No. It wasn't me. You have to believe me."

Tanz grabbed him by the hair and held him. "I knew you were trouble that first day in the plaza."

"What are you going to do?"

"You mean arrest you?"

"Yes."

"No," said Tanz. He let go of Largo's hair and pointed over his shoulder. "He is."

One of the uniformed officers dragged Largo from the chair and threw him against the wall. While another officer held Largo's arms behind his back, he snapped heavy cuffs on Largo's wrists. They walked him into the hall and shoved and kicked him down all three flights of stairs to a waiting police van outside. Largo's neighbors watched silently as he was led away.

Largo stopped in the doorway of the police station. The interior was lit with yellow coal light, giving the grim surroundings the feel of a quarantine ward at the hospital. Tanz shoved him through a small gate and into a chair near a bored officer with a stack of old forms and a typewriter on his desk.

Tanz took off the handcuffs and slapped Largo on the back of the head. His stomach churned and he thought for a moment that he was going to vomit. Tanz said, "Give this gentleman your finest accommodations," and left without another word.

The officer at the desk looked at Largo and drew a breath. He wearily rolled a form into the typewriter and typed in the date. In the piss-colored light Largo thought he looked like he was made of old wax.

"Name?"

"Largo Moorden."

"Address?"

Largo gave it to him.

"Charges against you?"

"I don't know."

The officer drew in another breath. "They didn't tell you the charges?"

"I'm afraid not."

The officer snatched the form from the typewriter, wadded it up, and threw it in an overflowing wastebasket. "Don't lie to me. You'll make it worse for yourself."

"I'm not lying," insisted Largo. "Tanz never told me any charges."

The officer looked at him in disgust. "You can't say I didn't warn you."

Largo got up and the officer led him down a long corridor to a room that looked less like the police station and more like one of the small, shabby business offices he sometimes visited on his rounds. The officer shoved him toward a desk and said, "He's yours now."

The woman behind the desk didn't look at Largo as she slowly removed some paper and a fountain pen from a drawer. The yellow overhead light flickered and made his head worse than before.

The woman filled in something on the form. "Name?" she said.

"Largo Moorden."

"Address?"

He told her.

"Charges against you?"

"As I told the other officer, I don't know exactly."

She set down her pen. "I see. I was wondering why you were here with no paperwork." She put on a leather glove that was neatly laid out on her desk and slapped Largo hard enough that he almost fell out of his chair.

"Now, let's begin again," she said. "Name?"

It took Largo a moment before he could speak. "I already told you."

This time she punched him. There was shot or something else heavy in the knuckles of the glove. The blow knocked him to the very edge of his chair.

What is happening to me? Since last night, nothing makes sense.

"Name?" she said.

"Largo Moorden."

"Address?"

He repeated the information.

"Charges against you?"

"I don't know," he said and steadied himself for another blow. He felt weak and empty, from both fear and lack of morphia.

The woman threw down her pen. "You're not very cooperative, are you? You don't know your charges? Everyone here knows their charges. But let's try this approach: what *do* you know?"

Largo thought about it. "Nothing."

The woman rose from her chair. From the look on her face, he thought she was going to hit him again. Instead, she walked to the office door and gestured for Largo to follow. "Come with me."

She took him farther down the corridor to an even smaller office. There was only one desk and a long wooden bench. "Sit there," she said, and added, "Don't get blood on the floor. If you do, I swear you'll be licking it up."

Largo touched the side of his face and his hand came back speckled with red. He went to the bench and the woman stood by the door.

"You should have talked to me. The downstairs staff aren't as forgiving."

Feeling like a fool, Largo said, "I'm sorry."

The woman gave him one more angry glance and slammed the door. Largo heard her lock it from the other side.

This is Tanz's doing, he thought. *He's paying me back for the Baron telling him off.*

Metal blinds covered the room's single window. Gray light filtered through and hurt his eyes. In fact, he hurt all over. Largo's insides felt like ice and his hands shook. He doubled over on the bench as his stomach cramped. Blood fell onto the bench, but he didn't care. Curled in a small ball of pain, he fell into a deep, frigid sleep.

The next thing Largo was aware of was someone shaking him roughly. His eyes snapped open. It was dark beyond the metal shutters. *How long have I been here?* He looked at the man still shaking him.

The man pointed at him with a clipboard. "Who the hell are you?"

"Largo Moorden."

"How did you get in here? The door was locked."

"The woman locked it after she left me here."

"What woman?"

Largo thought for a minute. "I don't know her name. I'm not sure if she was a police officer. She wasn't in a uniform." He put his hands in his pockets to hide how much they were shaking.

The man flipped through his clipboard. "Moorden?" he said. "Fuck. You're supposed to be downstairs. They've been looking for you. You're in trouble, you ass."

"But I didn't do anything. The woman brought me in here."

The man punched him in the stomach. "Don't talk back. You'll learn that soon enough. Now get up and come with me."

Largo got to his feet slowly. He had to lean against the wall to stand. In some dim part of his mind he knew that he should be terrified by what was happening, but he was too confused and in too much pain to be afraid anymore. But he knew the fear was waiting for him, and it would be all the worse for having been held back so long.

The man with the clipboard led him farther along the corridor to a set of stone stairs that wound down to a row of underground cells so old they looked like something from one of Baumann's horror films.

Eventually, he stopped by a cell in the middle of the row. The man unlocked the door and shoved Largo inside. The only thing he could hear was the jingle of the man's keys as he locked the door. After that, it was dead silent. Largo jumped a little when he heard a moan from the other side of the cell. A badly beaten man lay on a cot in bloody clothes. There was another cot on the other side of the room, but the thin mattress had fallen to the filthy floor. Largo was shaking enough that it was hard for him to hold on to the bars on the cell door.

"Can I speak to someone?" he said.

"No. You've caused us a lot of trouble today." The man slapped Largo's hands with the clipboard. "Next time you're arrested, don't lie to everyone."

"I'm not lying. I haven't been lying."

While Largo watched, the man pulled the top form from his clipboard, wadded it, and dropped it on the floor.

"Wait. Is that my form?" said Largo. "Don't you need that? Tanz will blame me if it's missing."

The man with the clipboard went back up the stairs while Largo yelled to him. When he was gone, Largo pulled the cot mattress back onto the frame and sat down. And for the first time, he had a moment to think.

Remy is gone and everyone thinks I did it. Is she hurt? Is she dead? It can't be real. They've all made a mistake.

He closed his eyes. His head felt tight, like it was locked in a vise. His stomach cramped violently and he vomited in the corner of the cell.

One more thing I'll be blamed for.

He lay there in the dim light listening to the bloody man's ragged breathing. Eventually he fell asleep.

When Largo woke up he was in more pain than he'd ever felt before. Worse than his worst hangover, bicycle accident, or any beatings he'd taken as a child in Haxan Green. Some dim part of his mind wanted simply to die and end the pain once and for all, but even if he'd had a gun, Largo knew that his hands were too shaky for him to use it.

Sometime later, his cell door opened and someone kicked his cot. It was the first officer he'd spoken to when he'd arrived at the police station. The man looked at him angrily. Largo looked down and realized that he'd vomited on himself sometime during the night. He was lucky that he hadn't choked to death. The officer pulled a dirty towel from under the beaten man's head and threw it to Largo. "Clean up. You're being released," he said.

Largo struggled to sit up. "You found Remy? Is she all right?"

"Hurry up. People are waiting."

"Please—"

The officer casually backhanded him across the face, sending him reeling back to the cot.

"I said hurry up."

Largo cleaned himself as well as he could with the filthy towel. The officer hadn't sounded very reassuring earlier, and he was sure that meant they hadn't found Remy after all. He thought of Tanz. *This might be another one of his tricks. Tell me I'm being released and then take me somewhere even worse.* Largo didn't want to think about what worse might be.

The next few minutes were a painful blur. He stumbled up the spiral stairs and through the police station with the officer at his side. He signed a pile of forms as well as he could with his shaking hand, and with no time to read what they said—not that he could have read them anyway, with his head swimming. When they were done, the officer pushed Largo away from the desk. He stumbled and almost fell, barely managing to remain upright. Through the open door of the police station, he could see that it was raining outside. A man in a heavy coat and hat stood just to the side of the doorway.

Largo blinked a couple of times and said, "Herr Branca?"

Branca made a face at him. "Look at you, Largo. You've ruined your clothes."

He nodded shakily. "I'm sorry, sir. I'm sick."

"So I hear. Your trousers don't look so bad, but take off that filthy jacket and shirt."

Largo looked around. Police and prisoners being booked all stared at him.

"Right here?" Largo said. Then he understood what was happening but was more puzzled than frightened. "Did Tanz send you?"

Branca took off his hat and shook rain from it. "Special Operative Tanz won't be bothering you again."

Largo shivered. "Someone else said that to me once."

"Well, this time it's true. Now, take off your shirt and jacket."

He hesitated for a moment. *They already think I'm a murderer. At this point, how much worse can things get if I do what Branca says?*

He slipped off his jacket and shirt, holding them with two fingers to keep the vomit from his hands. "Where do I put them?"

Branca gestured with his hat. "Drop them on the floor. These fine gentlemen will clean them up. Won't you, gentlemen?"

"Yes, sir," said the officer who had taken Largo from his cell. He spoke very quietly.

Branca picked up a brown grocery bag from the floor and tossed it to Largo. There was a clean jacket and shirt inside. "When you've put these on, come outside to the car."

Branca put his hat on and disappeared into the rain. Largo looked around, ready for an ambush, but none of the officers made a move toward him. He put on the new clothes and went outside to the car. It was a large black sedan and it reminded him of a hearse. Branca was in the back, so Largo got in with him. It was warm inside, but the heat couldn't penetrate the ice around his bones. A moment later, the car pulled out into the street.

Branca said, "I'm disappointed in you, Largo. Those clothes were paid for with company money and therefore belong to the company. You'll have to pay them back."

"I know," said Largo through gritted teeth. "Why . . . how did you get me out?"

Branca handed him a small bottle. "Here. Use this. All that shivering is annoying."

Largo recognized it immediately as morphia. He frantically opened the bottle and put four drops under his tongue. A second later, he began to feel better. When he started to warm up and his hands had stopped shaking, he looked at Branca.

"I don't understand what's happening, sir," he said.

"Nothing could be more obvious. Rest now. We'll talk when we're back at your flat."

The neighbors stared again as Largo returned home with Branca. The driver stayed with the car.

There was a police warning glued to the door of Largo's flat. Branca tore it off and dropped it on the floor. He stood aside so that Largo could go inside first. When they were both in, Branca locked the door. Largo collapsed into a sagging chair in the corner of the room. Branca set his hat on the table with the whiskey bottle but remained standing.

Largo said, "Thank you for getting me out of there, sir."

Branca winced. "I told you once before. Stop saying 'sir' so much."

"Sorry, but I don't understand. Why would the company send you for me? You said yourself that we're both disposable."

Branca clasped his hands in front of him.

"The company didn't rescue you. *I* did. Do you know how, or can you perhaps guess why? Take your time. I find that it's better for auxiliary to work it out themselves."

Auxiliary? What does that mean?

Largo looked at the older man across the room, in his heavy black coat, and then at his matching homburg hat.

"You're not Herr Branca," he said.

"Don't be stupid. Of course I am."

"You're not the dispatcher at the company."

"I'm that too. But a person can be more than one thing at a time, can't he? Come on. You're a bright boy. Say it."

Though Largo was inside and had morphia in his system, he grew cold again. "You're the Nachtvogel."

"Very good," said Branca softly.

Largo put his hand over his eyes. "I don't understand what's happening. Why are you helping me? Tanz thinks I'm a murderer."

"That's because Tanz is an idiot and under a great deal of pressure to close the case of poor missing Remy. You were an easy and obvious catch, so he chose you."

Largo had a terrible thought. "*You* didn't hurt her, did you?"

"I assure you we didn't. We have no interest in her other than keeping Baron Hellswarth—that is to say, Schöne Maschinen—functioning and productive."

"Then who hurt her?"

"We don't know yet," said Branca. "But we know it wasn't you. And we'll soon find out."

"So you brought me home because you know I'm innocent."

"What is innocent?" Branca picked up the whiskey bottle and put it down again. "But yes—partly that, and partly because the Nachtvogel needs your services."

The fear Largo had been dreading welled up inside him. "What kind of services?"

"Nothing out of the ordinary. We simply want you to go back to work and continue in the fine manner that you've proven you're capable of."

"The bullocks took my bicycle."

Branca sighed. "We'll provide you with a new one."

Largo shook his head, trying to clear it. "Do I understand this right? The Nachtvogel wants me to be their courier?"

"That's one way to put it. But I wouldn't say it out loud if I were you. Instead, you should just say you'll be working through the company, receiving your normal pay and all the other benefits of your position," said Branca. "You see, Largo, you're what we call a 'useful fool.' You do your job well and you don't ask many questions. You're a very pliable boy. All it took to recruit you was a promotion and fifteen minutes more for lunch."

Largo said, "I didn't know I was being recruited."

"Yes, that's the 'fool' part I mentioned earlier, or weren't you listening?"

"All this time, the insults, the digging at my every action—it was all a game to you."

Branca straightened the collar of his coat. "I've had my fun, yes."

Feeling stronger, Largo sat up. "My deliveries, they weren't real deliveries, were they?"

"Some were. Others were more finely tuned to our needs. You tracked radicals for us, confirming their whereabouts. And you planted evidence on undesirables, both high and low."

Largo thought about the gun he'd taken to Frau Heckert and the ink to the Black Palace. He thought about Margit.

"Is this why you always changed receipt books?"

"Naturally. As I recall, you did ask a question about them once before. But you were also satisfied with the flimsiest of answers. As if I cared how dirty your receipt books were." He shook his head. "Your receipt books were special. We wanted your customers to touch them to obtain fingerprints. There were also quite minuscule photochrome devices in some of the books, so we were able to gather images of various suspects."

Largo wanted to say something, but the words wouldn't come.

Branca said, "I assume I don't have to tell you to keep your distance from *Ihre Skandale*? Unless there's a story we want you to give them, of course."

Something came to him. "Is Una at the Grand Dark a Nachtvogel?"

Branca brightened. "Why do you ask?"

"There was a play about a murder that hadn't happened yet."

"That was an experiment to see how smoothly we could coordinate our efforts. It wasn't bad for a first try. The next one will be better."

"Who were you murdering, the man or the young girl?"

"Very good! Both, actually. It was simpler that way."

Largo looked down at the floor. "But why the Grand Dark? They tell stories about ghosts and adulterers and mad scientists."

"Lofty political speeches and tracts aren't always the best way to move the public's mind," said Branca. "It's easier to capture the masses with a well-placed song or a laugh. With gratuitous sex or deplorable violence. Your friend Baumann is a useful fool too. A mediocre actor, he remains a star because he performs in wildly popular films that we produce."

Largo's stomach cramped again. "I'm going to be sick."

"If that's true, please do it in the bathroom. I have no desire to see or smell it."

Largo barely made it across the hall in time. There was nothing left in his stomach to bring up, so he just leaned over the toilet while his gut spasmed.

I really am a fool. I deserve this. A lifetime of fear. Of bullies. Of bullocks. Now a new war. The Drops and disappearances. But I should have been afraid of myself most of all. Tanz didn't do this to me. The Nachtvogel didn't do this.

I did it to myself.

When his stomach settled, Largo went back into his flat and sat down. "I don't want to work for you anymore."

"Oh? Would you rather be without morphia again? Would you rather go back to jail? You're suspected of murder, Largo. We're the only friends you have left."

He picked at the dried blood on his face. "I've already done things for you. Can't you just let me go?"

"No," said Branca with cold finality. "Rest for today. But be back to work at the normal time tomorrow. If you aren't there, you'll be considered an enemy of the state, and I assure you, the penalty for that is much worse than for the murder of a little rich girl."

Largo curled up in the chair.

"I'll let myself out," said Branca. "I'll see you tomorrow, Largo. One way or another."

"Wait—do you at least know if Remy is alive?"

Branca put on his hat. "You should be more concerned for your-self right now."

"Because I'm a fool," said Largo.

"A useful one. See that you remain that way," said Branca as he left.

Largo spent the day trying to make sense of what had happened. His fear of working for the Nachtvogel and his despair over losing Remy fought it out in his mind, each one overtaking the other in a horrify-ing spiral.

I'll escape. I'll wait for nightfall and go across the roofs. I can make it to the end of the block that way. Then down the fire escape and they'll never find me.

Largo laughed at himself.

I can barely walk. Which is why it won't work. They probably have an agent waiting for me on the roof right now. And if I did get away, where would I go? A few gold Valdas won't take me far.

He went to the table to get the whiskey but stopped in his tracks. His knife and harness lay on the table. He looked at them and thought about the sweet irony if he used the knife to slash his wrists. But the thought lasted only a moment. He knew he didn't have the strength of will for suicide. Not if there was any possibility of finding Remy. Largo wondered if the Nachtvogel would look for her. They might have to if they wanted to keep Baron Hellswarth from going mad. That settled it, then. He would stay alive until he learned Remy's fate.

If she's all right, I'll be here. If not, the knife or an overdose of morphia will always be waiting.

CHAPTER FOURTEEN

WHEN LARGO LEFT HIS FLAT FOR WORK THE NEXT MORNING, HE ALMOST tripped over a bicycle leaning against his door. It was lighter and better built than his previous one, which would raise questions at work, and the last thing he wanted to do at that moment was answer questions. But he didn't have any choice about what to do. He carried it down the three floors to the street and rode away. Again, his neighbors stared. *How long before they get bored with me?* He longed for another chimera stampede or a good case of the Drops. Anything to get them staring in another direction.

His back and face hurt where the police had knocked him around. The pain wasn't so bad that he couldn't work, but each stab was a reminder of how far and how quickly his life had turned into a nightmare.

He arrived at the company five minutes late and stood in the back of the room.

"I see Largo has decided to join us this morning. How kind of you," said Branca in his usual tone.

"I wouldn't be anywhere else. We're one big, happy family here, aren't we, Herr Branca?"

Branca lowered his head and said, "Even family has its limits of behavior. Remember that in the future."

"I'll write it down in one of my receipt books so I don't forget," Largo said. He wasn't even sure why he was speaking this way. The world seemed slightly unreal, and he felt drunk and reckless.

Several of the other couriers turned to stare at him, but Largo stared right back until they turned around. Parvulesco tried to catch his eye, but Largo kept his gaze firmly to the front.

Branca called the Maras from the back room to bring out the first round of letters and packages for the couriers to deliver. The office emptied quickly until it was just Branca and Largo. When he reached for his package, Branca put a hand on it.

"A word, Largo," he said.

"Of course, sir."

Branca cleared his throat. "I recognize today is a difficult one for you, and that it will take time to adjust to your new duties. Because of that, I'll forgive your little performance. However, I won't be so charitable next time. Do you understand me?"

"Yes. Completely. If I'm rude tomorrow I'm to be shot."

"I wasn't thinking of anything quite that drastic," Branca said. "In case you were wondering, what you're feeling is completely normal. You're trying to provoke a harsh response. It's called a suicidal fugue. You find yourself cornered, so you misbehave in hopes of freeing yourself through a quick and dramatic death. But I promise you that these things are never quick or dramatic. In fact, they're rather sordid." He pushed the morning's parcel into Largo's hands. "Remember what I said. Tomorrow you will be the old Largo or there will be no Largo at all."

Largo looked at the address on his delivery and pointed to his face. "The address is in Empyrean. I have a black eye and bloody cheek, courtesy of the bullocks. Don't you think that will attract attention from the district's security?"

"Leave both the municipal and private officials to me. Should you need assistance, simply call and I'll deal with it promptly."

"If you say so."

"I do say so. How do you like your new bicycle?"

Largo said, "It's very good. Better than my old one."

"Excellent. Then you'll make your rounds even faster than usual. I intend to keep you busy for these first few days. Take my advice: It's not good to think too much during this period. Neither is it good to abuse yourself. Don't drink to excess, and be careful about your morphia intake. It will be rationed and you've already seen how unpleasant it can be to lose your supply suddenly."

Largo's stomach spasmed with the memory. "Is there anything else?"

"Yes. Make sure this client holds the receipt book."

"Why does the Nachtvogel care about some cocky bluenose?"

Branca turned his gaze toward the ceiling, then back to Largo "Don't ever use the name of that organization in the office. And don't ask me about deliveries at all unless I broach the subject." He went back to his desk and picked up a pen. "Remember, we want the old Largo back. The one who asked few questions and simply did his job."

"Yes, sir."

"That's all. I'll see you when you're done."

Before going outside to his bicycle, Largo went to a stall in the employee bathroom and put another drop of morphia under his tongue. He'd already taken two drops before leaving home, but he needed something to calm his nerves after talking to Branca. As the morphia moved through his system, he felt all the usual sensations, but they weren't pleasant. He'd never thought morphia could feel this way, but he'd never imagined Remy being gone. Together, they were the real pleasure. Now morphia was merely a bitter-tasting medicine.

He put the vial away in disgust, checked his knife, and went outside.

All the couriers had left except for Parvulesco. When Largo came down the steps he said, "What the hell was that between you and Branca? And where have you been for the last couple of days? I've been worried."

"I'm fine," said Largo. "What happened with Branca is nothing. It was related to a discussion we had recently."

"You're fine?" Parvulesco said.

"Perfectly."

"Then what happened to your face? Did it come with your new bike?"

Largo took his bicycle and rolled it to Parvulesco. He said, "Stop asking questions. In fact, stop talking to me at all. It's dangerous. I don't want you getting in trouble."

Before Largo could get on his bicycle, Parvulesco grabbed his arm. "What's going on? I'm your friend. I want to help."

"Then keep your distance," said Largo. He rode away before Parvulesco could ask any more foolish questions.

Largo felt self-conscious as he rode through Empyrean. He was even more uncomfortable when he stopped at a lavender marble mansion on Ambrosiadorf and handed his receipt book to a young woman. After she signed it she gave him several small gold coins and smiled. He tried to smile back, but his face still hurt from his beating. He rode out of the district quickly, his head down, knowing that he looked like an unsuccessful thief and hoping that this early in the morning the police had other things to occupy them. He was breathing hard when he made it back to the company.

"I don't think I've ever seen you out of breath before, Largo," said Branca.

"I rode very quickly."

"You often ride quickly, and yet here you are panting like an overheated dog."

Being beaten seems to have taken a lot out of me.

"I'll be fine in a minute. Do you mind if I sit down?"

Branca gestured to a small wooden bench in the corner of the room. Largo sat, but he found that he still couldn't catch his breath. From his desk, Branca said, "Control your breathing. In through your nose and out through your mouth. You're feel better in a moment or two."

Largo tried it and, to his surprise, found that his racing heart and ragged breathing soon eased. When he felt better he went to Branca's desk. "How did you know that trick?" he said.

"You are far from the first person I've seen in the throes of panic. It's a common ailment in this transition period. Don't worry. It will wear off in a few days."

"What if it doesn't?"

"There's always medical intervention. Pills. Shots. Miracle potions."

"And if they don't help?"

Branca raised his eyes from his papers and looked at him. "You'll be fine. Otherwise we wouldn't have chosen you for this position. It's a simple matter of—"

"Controlling my breathing," said Largo.

Branca lowered his eyes back to his desk. "That's it exactly. Your next two deliveries are over there."

He put two thick envelopes and receipt books in his shoulder bag. "Are these deliveries special too?"

"From now on, assume that all of your deliveries are special. It will save us both from having to deal with a lot of pointless questions."

Largo left and continued to breathe as Branca had told him. If he did it too much it made him light-headed. However, when the fear came back and his heartbeat spiked, the breathing exercise brought it down to a normal level. *I hope Branca is right and this feeling passes. I can't do this forever,* he thought. But then a new kind of fear came to him. *How will it be when I don't feel this way anymore? When being the Nachtvogel's dog becomes my ordinary state? I'll bark, roll over, and fetch strangers who've never done anything to me. I'll be one of them.* By the time he left for his afternoon deliveries he'd dismissed the idea of killing himself with the knife, but if he could take a little less morphia each day, in time he'd save up enough to do himself in easily and painlessly. It would take a while—maybe weeks—but it was something hopeful to look forward to, and hope felt very precious right then.

A little girl answered one door he knocked on and her grandfather held the receipt book so that she could sign it. They both laughed and laughed, and Largo was almost ill from wondering what the Nachtvogel could want with them. He then made a delivery to a rest home for Dandies. Some of the men had their masks off, and as much as Largo tried not to look, he couldn't help himself. He hadn't thought any Dandy's face could be sadder than Rainer's, but he saw a dozen worse and left with his head down. His last delivery was the most unpleasant. It was a run-down print shop in the Aether district. There were antigovernment posters all over the city, but they grew in number and ferocity the closer he got to the shop. Some Dandies worked inside, and so did a few foreigners. *Which are the Nachtvogel the most interested in?* he wondered. Largo pushed the thought away. He would unquestionably go mad if he tried to guess how the secret police thought.

Several bullocks watched him ride away from the shop. His fear for the workers was replaced by a more personal anxiety. For all of Branca's boasting that he could handle the police, Largo was sure that if Tanz wanted to he could make Largo disappear as efficiently as any slaver gang from High Proszawa.

After work, Largo bought a meat pie and another bottle of whiskey from a shop and headed home. He took more morphia and listened to music on the wireless Remy had given him. He didn't want to think about her, and when her face became too fixed in his mind, he went to the whiskey and more morphia to drive her out.

Someone knocked on his door around ten that night. Unlike when

261

the police had burst in, this knock was gentle and hesitant. Largo stumbled to the door and opened it a few inches.

"Largo?" said Hanna. "My god. You look like shit."

He stood there staring at her. "What do you want?"

"May I come in?"

He looked past her down the hall but didn't see anyone. "I don't think that's a good idea," he said.

She put a hand on the doorframe. "Okay. I just came by because I wanted to tell you that I believe you. I know you couldn't hurt Remy, no matter what anyone else says."

His heartbeat began rising. Largo took a couple of gulping breaths. "Thank you. But you don't mean 'anyone.' You mean 'everyone.' They all think I killed her."

Hanna shifted her shoulder uncomfortably. "Yes. The bullocks have been all over anyone you've as much as spoken to. That Tanz character, he's quite something," she said.

Despite his breathing, Largo felt flushed. "He said that the Baron wants me dead."

Hanna pressed her lips into a thin line and nodded. "I've heard the same thing. Hardly anyone has seen him. He's either locked in his office or with Venohr."

"Dr. Venohr? He was treating Remy. Is he the Baron's doctor too?"

"No. He has a private laboratory in our section, but they're old friends. I think the Baron goes in there to talk, away from everybody else."

"I wish I could speak to Venohr," said Largo.

"That's not a good idea. Even if he believed you, he's very loyal to the Baron. He'd never go against him."

Largo rubbed sweat from his forehead. "It was just a thought."

"I'm sorry I can't bring you better news," said Hanna, looking miserable.

"That's all right. Thank you for coming. But you shouldn't come back."

Hanna looked concerned. "Are you in danger?"

"No, but I'm being watched. I don't want you tangled up in this mess."

She straightened herself. "I'm a big girl. Don't worry about me."

"Still," Largo said.

"All right, but if you need anything just call me. Do you have my number?"

"Remy gave it to me," he lied.

"All right, then. Take care, Largo," said Hanna. She touched his hand where it gripped the door. "This is going to work out. I know it is."

"Thank you. Good night."

Hanna blew him a kiss. Largo closed the door and went to bed. Through his window, he could hear the sounds of revelers down the street, a morbid reminder that, while he wallowed in misery, the rest of the city went on as it always did. And if Branca flicked a finger at him and he disappeared, it would make no more difference to the world than if he crushed a slug while riding his bicycle.

CHAPTER FIFTEEN

THE NEXT DAY LARGO MADE IT TO WORK ON TIME, BUT HE STILL STAYED AT the back of the room. He didn't want to be where anyone could look at him. His eyes were red and his head felt like concrete. He had taken a couple of drops of morphia before work and they dulled the pain, but it still lingered behind his eyes.

When the room was empty, Branca called him to his desk. "What did I tell you about drinking too much? I assume you've overindulged in morphia too."

"You're right on both counts."

"I'm not your mother, Largo. I can't make you behave, but I suggest you learn to cope with the situation in less self-destructive ways."

Largo said, "I'm destroying other people, so why not join them?"

"Don't be so dramatic. You sound like a child whose sick dog has to be put down. Sometimes things, and people, are so broken they can't be mended. It's our job to make sure these broken things don't injure other people."

"That's a very nice way to put what we're doing."

"It's true," said Branca. "Enemies of the state are your enemies too, even if you don't know it. They're enemies of your friends Remy and Parvulesco. Hanna too."

Largo looked at him. He'd been right. He was still being watched. His skin flushed, not with fear this time but with anger. He wanted to spit at Branca or, better yet, pull his knife and gut the bastard.

"You can try it, you know."

"What?"

"Why, to kill me. It's what you're thinking, isn't it? You won't be the first to have nursed the fantasy. But remember—I know you. And I know you're not going to do it."

Largo's hand drifted to his jacket. He touched the knife. Branca ignored him. He pictured the older man falling to the floor, blood streaming from his throat. Then he pictured the same thing happening to Parvulesco, Hanna, and his other friends. How many of them would the Nachtvogel hurt if he did anything foolish? Largo hated that Branca knew him so well that he could predict the limits of his actions, but it was true and he'd have to learn to live with it. He dropped his hand to his side and said, "Have you learned anything about Remy?"

"No. But we're still making inquiries. I'll let you know when we find something."

Largo considered the idea. "Why would you do that?"

Branca put his hands flat on his desk. "I know you can't comprehend it right now, but we want you to be happy. It's why I'm concerned about your self-abuse. Have you considered that you're more dangerous to yourself than I am?"

"How did you come to that conclusion?"

"Because I'm not going to throw you in front of a tram or under a juggernaut. You, on the other hand, weaving through the streets drunk or dizzy from morphia, will likely do it yourself."

Branca had a point. It had rained the night before and he'd taken a turn too quickly that morning. The bicycle slipped on the wet pavement and he almost went under the wheels of a limousine coming out of Schöne Maschinen. Instead of being scared, he'd laughed about it all the way to work. *What if that was the Baron's car? He'd missed a good opportunity for revenge.*

Branca's next question did frighten him a little. "Why were you on Krahe Vale this morning?"

Largo rubbed his aching eyes and said, "I wanted to go by Schöne Maschinen."

"Why?"

"I don't know."

"I think it's safe to assume that your appointment with the Baron has been canceled."

Can the Nachtvogel read minds too?

"I know. I just wanted to see it."

266

"Now that you have, I hope you'll be more careful in the future," said Branca.

"I intend to."

Branca picked up his pen. "Is there anything else you wanted to discuss?"

"In fact, I was curious about something," said Largo.

Branca sighed wearily. "Oh?"

"On the way to work, I rode through the Great Triumphal Square. They're erecting flagpoles around it and all down the boulevard. Do you know anything about that?"

"Why do you care? After a lifetime of political indifference are you suddenly interested in the affairs of state?"

"It just . . . felt different. The city seems strange. I saw couples coming out of the underground tram tunnels snapping at each other. Two businessmen were practically coming to blows outside Fräulein Sabel. It was too early in the morning for them to be drunk. I wondered if the flagpoles might have something to do with it."

"You have a better eye than I would have given you credit for, especially hungover."

Largo said, "Then I was right about the flagpoles?"

"In a way. The poles, and the flags that will soon fly, are to buoy people's spirits as war creeps ever closer."

"Then you really think it's going to happen."

"It's better to rally a nation for a war that doesn't happen than to be caught off guard."

Largo suddenly wanted another drink. "Then the war might not happen?"

Branca leaned on his desk, looking a bit exasperated. "No, the war will happen. It's inevitable, and it will be worse than the previous one. The enemy is making material preparations, but so are we. Now it's time to prepare people spiritually."

The easy way that Branca talked about another war left Largo numb. "I see. Thank you." He took his receipt book and a cardboard tube from the Mara.

While he was wrestling the tube into his shoulder bag, Branca said, "Do you think you'll go this time?"

Largo looked at him. "To war, you mean?"

"Yes."

"Maybe. Would you let me go if I wanted to?"

"No," said Branca.

"Then why did you ask?"

"Idle curiosity. Have a good day."

Once he had the tube in place, Largo said, "I'm doing what you want. And I promise to stop drinking. But leave Parvulesco and Hanna alone."

Branca seemed to think it over. "All right. You uphold your end of the bargain and I'll make sure no harm comes to your friends."

"Thank you."

Largo got on his bicycle and headed out of the front gates. He knew that the bargain should make him feel better, but it didn't. *I've just agreed to do anything the Nachtvogel wants. And in the end, they might still betray me. But what else is there to do?* Largo knew he wasn't a planner or schemer. He'd drifted through life too long for that. At least Parvulesco and Hanna were safe for the moment. If he had to make an even more dreadful deal in the future to protect them, he'd do that too. *This is my life now. Do as little for Branca and as much for my friends as I can. Who knows? Maybe war will be a good thing.*

He remembered a film about High Proszawa during the Great War. After the invasion, a chef took a job with the enemy, cooking for their officers. He did an exemplary job and was treated well. However, on the night of the counteroffensive from Lower Proszawa, he poisoned the entire command staff. After his capture, his interrogators asked him to name his allies. He said, "My balls and your chaos." He recalled the audience erupting into applause at that. If war came, Largo knew there would be ample chaos. What he didn't know was whether he had the balls to murder Branca before Branca murdered him.

Right now, the answer was no.

But only time would tell.

When Largo got home that night, someone was waiting for him in his flat.

From a corner of the room a shadow said, "Largo, it's me. Margit. Don't be scared."

He fell back against the wall and pulled his knife, but didn't get a good grip on it. When it fell it slid across the room. Margit picked it up and handed it back to him. "God. Are you drunk?"

"No, you startled me. And I just took a little morphia on the way upstairs."

Margit sat on the table. "I see. They're paying you in morphia. How nice it must be not having to spend your own money anymore."

Largo sat in a chair on the other side of the room. "What do you want?"

"I want you to take responsibility for what you're doing."

"Did Pietr send you to finish me off? Feel free, just don't lecture me."

Margit picked up the whiskey bottle, looked at the level of liquor left inside, and set it down again. "Feeling sorry for yourself because you were arrested? You were in and out in a day. You even got a ride home in Branca's big shiny car."

Largo pointed at her. "You've been spying on me."

"I was looking out for you. Our group has bullock contacts. We might have been able to trade something for you. Instead, you walked out the front door in a new shirt and jacket, pretty as a bride on her wedding day."

The morphia had left him tired and his brain fuzzy, but something didn't make sense. "You were looking out for me? Why?"

Margit checked her watch. "We need someone like you. You know every inch of Lower Proszawa. Most of us didn't grow up here so we have to use maps and it slows down our operations."

Largo crossed his legs. "Where are you from?"

"What does that matter?"

"Idle curiosity."

In an exasperated tone Margit said, "I'm from Goslarburg."

Largo burst out laughing. "Oh my god. You're a damn farm girl. Did you milk cows and have a favorite chicken you hid so your mother wouldn't cook it?"

Margit turned back to him. "Are you done?"

"For the moment."

"Will you help us?"

Largo tried to stand, but he couldn't. He crossed his legs instead. "This is funny, actually. Branca said you'd ask me for a favor, and here you are."

"This isn't a favor. It's an opportunity to redeem yourself. You've always been a wastrel, but you weren't a spy and a killer."

"I've never killed anyone."

"You're going to," said Margit. "All these people you've been collecting information on, what do you think is going to happen to them? The Nachtvogel doesn't give out fines. People disappear and are never heard from again."

"And that will happen to me if they find out you're here."

Margit shook her head. "Don't worry. My friend Dieter is outside and he loves pretending to have the Drops. It scared your minder right off."

"Clever, but my minder will be back tonight and then I'm sure someone else will watch me in the morning."

"The Nachtvogel only watches new conscripts for a week."

"Why only a week?" said Largo.

Margit scraped some loose paint off the table with a fingernail. "At the end of the week they decide if you're useful and obedient enough to live."

Largo laughed again. "Then my troubles should be over in a few days, one way or the other."

"And in the meantime, how many innocent people will you betray?"

He leaned forward with his elbows on his knees. "Tell me. If I don't agree to work with you, will you kill me?"

"It's been discussed."

Largo ticked off the names on his fingers. "So, you're going to kill me, the Nachtvogel is going to kill me, and Baron Hellswarth will eventually hire someone to kill me . . . Have I left anyone out?"

Margit's voice rose. "Stop feeling sorry for yourself. We've all lost friends and lovers."

"This is my first, so forgive me if I don't rally by supper."

Margit opened her hands pleadingly. "Don't you see that we can help each other?" she said. She leaned toward him. "The people who have you under their thumb are the ones we want to stop."

"You and your friends at the Black Palace are going to print tracts so withering that the Nachtvogel will simply drop dead? Now that really *is* clever."

"Stop trying to be clever yourself. We want to bring them down and the government along with them."

Largo sat stiffly. "And who will you anoint as Chancellor? Pietr?"

"Pietr is dead," said Margit quietly. "He was murdered by the bullocks two days ago while hanging posters. That's what they're doing now. If they suspect you're a dirty radical, they don't even arrest you anymore. You just get a bullet in the head. Or worse."

"What's worse?"

"They beat him to death. Cracked his head open like an egg on the curb."

Largo thought about Pietr at the Black Palace and how he'd threatened him with a wrench at Schöne Maschinen. He remembered the frantic chase along the docks. But the image of the man's head split open shook him. "That's horrible."

Margit stood up. "Yes, it is. But you can help us stop it from happening to your friends."

"Haven't you heard? I murdered Remy. I don't have friends."

"Stop it. They're using that to control you. Why do you think no one has found Remy or her body? Branca knows that as long as you think they're looking for her you'll be his errand boy."

Largo thought about it. "You think they're holding her somewhere? Do you have proof?"

"No. But it's obvious if you think about the situation with a clear head."

"No, it's not. The Baron is going out of his mind, and he's a lot more important than I am. If the government is planning for war, Schöne Maschinen has to run well. They wouldn't want to distract the man who runs it all."

A sly smile played at the edges of Margit's mouth. "How do you know he's not being blackmailed too?"

"Blackmail Baron Hellswarth? You've been reading too much of your own propaganda."

Margit checked her watch again. "It isn't safe for me to stay much longer."

Largo waved a hand at the door. "Don't let me keep you."

"I know you feel like the whole world is against you, but that's the time to act," said Margit. "If you don't want to help us, don't you at least want revenge on the people who've ruined your life?"

Largo felt light-headed, like he was falling. He held on to the arms of the chair. "I want to kill them all. The bullocks. The Maras. The Nachtvogel. Everyone in the government who's calmly planning the next war. When I close my eyes, all that's there is Remy or Branca's blood."

"Then help us."

"You didn't answer me earlier. Are you and your dozen or so friends planning on bringing down the government alone?"

"There's a lot more of us than what you saw at the Black Palace."

Largo shrugged. "Then you don't need me."

Margit stood up. "That's your final word, then?"

"I want to be left alone."

She started for the door. "That's your problem, Largo. There is no alone anymore. I hope you figure that out before it's too late."

He called after her, "Or you'll kill me like the bullocks did Pietr?"

She stopped with the doorknob in her hand. "I'm sorry I said that. I was angry. I won't bother you again."

"Why do you need me anyway? You said you have maps."

She turned to him. "The maps haven't been updated since the war. Streets have changed. Buildings have come down. We need to know how to get around the city without being seen."

Largo got up and retrieved the last of the whiskey from the table. "Where are you going that's so important?"

"Why should I tell you?"

He took a drink. "Forget it. Go away."

Margit paused for a moment. "We want to get a friend from a secret lockup in Pappengasse."

"What's the nearest street corner?"

"Pilzeberg."

He took the cap off the bottle. "That's easy. There's an old coal plant on Ott. Go in through the eastern side. Two floors down is a tunnel system that goes all over the district. Whenever it branches, stay to the left. You'll come out less than a block from the intersection."

Margit took a couple of steps toward him. "What if something goes wrong and we can't go back that way?"

"Go down Pilzeberg to the night market," he said. "Behind a little dance hall tent is a dead-end alley. There's a wall, with razor wire at the top."

"Then what use is it?"

Largo raised a finger at the ceiling. "The razor wire was put up by night market thieves. It's fake. Just rubber and Bakelite. You can climb right under it."

For the first time, Margit smiled. "Thank you."

"You're welcome. Now get out before Dieter breaks a leg. He must be getting tired of rolling around in the street."

Largo sat in the dark, wanting to finish the whiskey, but stopped himself when he remembered his deal with Branca. He turned on the wireless to listen to music, but the Foreign Minister was giving an impassioned speech.

Fuck. Can't I ever get away from you people anymore?

He turned the wireless off and fell asleep in the chair, dreaming of the Grand Dark. Remy was controlling all the puppets from backstage. They danced and caressed each other and it reminded him of Anita Mourlet. Then they fell to the floor in convulsions. Largo tried to go backstage to Remy, but he was too dizzy from morphia to move. He sat there listening to the puppets' limbs snap and break. It seemed to go on all night.

The next day, Largo delivered a notice from the tax office to a fur merchant in the Händler district and decided to stop at a nearby café for lunch. The crowd was drunk and high on cocaine, and for a moment the city felt as it had before Remy had disappeared. He was jealous of the diners' oblivious merriment. The jealousy quickly turned to anger. He was about to leave when a waiter arrived.

He ordered tea and a slice of stollen as a crowd gathered around a small truck on the other side of the plaza. A tall blond man began an impassioned speech, but Largo couldn't hear a word of it. Plus, he wasn't interested. He was thinking about Margit's visit the previous night.

What the hell did she mean by "There is no alone anymore"? Of course there is. I've never been more alone in my life. If joining her idiot's crusade is the only way to change that, I'll happily remain where I am.

The crowd by the truck was a mix of upper-class Händler residents and local shopkeepers. The speaker held a small Proszawan flag as he spoke. The group applauded politely whenever he stopped to draw a breath.

Largo was thinking about Remy again, going over different scenarios in his mind. In one, she really had been killed, but by whom? A jealous admirer who gave her a jade vase and expected her to love him for it? In another scenario, she'd been killed during an attempted kidnapping. In yet another, she'd staged the whole thing herself to get away from Largo and all the other men in her life who wanted things from her.

As the crowd grew around the truck, a rougher group from

Granate, along with some nearby laborers, joined the mix. Soon, as many people were booing the speaker as applauding. This encouraged even louder applause and hoots from one part of the crowd, which set off louder boos from the other. Largo put down his tea as the café went quiet to watch the shouting match.

Another possibility was that Remy had died from her convulsions or, worse, the Drops, and that the Baron had helped stage the violent scene to avoid a press scandal. He hadn't intended for Largo to get caught up in the mess but now that he was, the Baron had to go along with it or reveal the plot. It was almost funny. A game. *How many ridiculous scenarios can I come up with before I finish lunch or go insane?*

Largo went back to his tea and cake as the crowd outside began singing patriotic songs. As they shouted, tuneless music reached the café, and several older men stood with their hands over their hearts. Even the waiters came up front to see what was happening. One of them turned to Largo.

"Do you know what's going on? Who's angry about what?" he said.

"I don't know and I don't care," Largo said.

"Is it about the war?"

"There is no war."

The waiter held up his tray to block the view of the other diners and whispered, "That's not what I've heard. There's talk that they're already fighting along the border in the north."

"Where did you hear that?"

"Here. Bluenoses talk like the staff is deaf. It's in some of the yellowsheets too."

"I don't believe it."

The waiter lowered his tray to make another point, but a scream cut through the other noise. A fight had broken out and someone pulled the speaker down from the back of the truck. As he disappeared into the mass of bodies, the fighting spread. At the edges of the crowd, people grabbed bottles from trash bins and stole chairs from outside other cafés. The sound of breaking glass and shouts drew an even larger crowd from the nearby streets.

"Should we do something?" said the waiter.

"Such as what? Do you even know which side you're on?"

The waiter craned his head around for a better look. "I'm not sure."

"Listen to me," Largo began, but the sound of a gunshot cut him off. People at the café screamed and threw themselves to the floor.

"Did you hear that?" shouted the waiter.

"Of course, you ass," shouted Largo, crouching by the table. "Get down here."

The waiter looked around. "We have to do something. Call the bullocks."

Just as Largo grabbed the waiter's sleeve to pull him down, the side of the man's head exploded. The waiter spun onto the floor as more gunshots echoed off the plaza walls.

Two juggernauts roared to a stop outside. Police in armor and rifle-mounted Maras poured into the melee. Panicked diners ran from the café. Largo followed them and grabbed his bicycle. As he sped out of the plaza, a juggernaut coming from the opposite direction almost ran him down. He turned off the main road and took back streets all the way to the company, thinking, *Wouldn't it be funny if, after worrying about the Nachtvogel murdering me in the dead of night, I died in a fancy café with my face stuffed with cake? Branca would laugh himself sick over that.*

Largo bought a copy of *Ihre Skandale* on the way home and read it that night. Indeed, there was a lurid story on the front page strongly suggesting that there were clashes along the northern border of High Proszawa. However, there were no chromes and so few details of the supposed skirmishes that he had his doubts.

If we really are at war, wouldn't the government want everyone to know? They'd need soldiers and donations. Secret battles don't make sense. Or am I missing something? Rainer would know, but how do I get to him without drawing the Nachtvogel in his direction?

When it was dark, Largo got on his bicycle and took a long, looping route from Little Shambles to the city center. He passed through garbage dumps and along dark streets bordered on both sides by bombed-out buildings. Squatters built fires and traded stolen goods in the ruins. He worried about them noticing his new bicycle, but he kept up his speed and in his old, ragged clothes he didn't draw their attention. *I hope my minder isn't wearing a suit. They'll find his body in the dump and his clothes parceled out to a dozen or more people.*

Largo entered the Great Triumphal Square through Pillengasse, a narrow alley where food vendors dumped their unsold goods. Rats and piglike chimeras feasted on the waste.

Even with all the confusing streets he'd ridden and the sudden turns he'd made, Largo still had the nagging feeling that there were eyes on him. He didn't dare go straight to Rainer's yet. Instead, he went into Fräulein Sabel and ordered a whiskey, then huddled in the corner of the bar hoping that no one he knew would see him. He needed time to think.

Half of his whiskey was gone when Largo heard a commotion outside. His first instinct was to crouch down in case there was gunfire. Instead, the noise became rhythmic and steady. People stared out the windows as a torchlight march made its way past the café. From inside, the voices were muffled, but Largo recognized some of the chants as the same patriotic slogans he'd heard that afternoon in Händler. Running outside, he grabbed his bicycle and walked with it into the center of the march. He didn't know the words so he simply mouthed along with the chants.

A few yards past the entrance to the underground tram station, he ducked and wheeled the bicycle out of the march, turning into a narrow passage between a church and a bank. The passage was too small to even have a name, but it ended on Schimpftestrasse, well beyond the plaza. After checking that no one had followed him, Largo got on his bicycle and rode as quickly as he could to Rainer's flat. He'd thought of something exciting during the march and only Rainer could tell him if he was a fool or not.

THE WALKING WOUNDED

From "A Profile of Gemeiner Schenke: A Man, a Patriot"
by Conrad Busch for *Der Sonntagspitzel* magazine

Iron Dandies stand out the most in the mornings. Groups of them, some large and some small, meet in different parts of Lower Proszawa. They are most easily glimpsed around the humble lodgings the government provides for them as part of their wounded-soldier pension. The more able-bodied will often meet in the Great Triumphal Square. On holidays or the anniversaries of important battles they will march in formation through the square and nearby streets, often picking up donations of food and coins. At other times, ex-sailors can be seen smoking by the docks where they shipped off to battle, while infantrymen will ride the ghost trams out to the cemeteries on the edge of the city and spend the day walking between the narrow rows of headstones. It is a fine way to spend time with old comrades and is good exercise.

Civilians and soldiers who came home from the Great War relatively intact generally assume that all the Iron Dandies are bitter, sullen men. How could they not be, swaddled in their heavy coats and hidden behind steel masks, their faces ruined beyond repair? Indeed, the vast majority of Dandies suffer from sometimes prolonged periods of melancholia, but not all. And even the downhearted experience periods of pleasure. True, some complain that their housing isn't all it could be, but it's guaranteed for life and costs virtually nothing. Additionally, they receive their pensions, have their own special hospitals, and ride the trams for free. The more level-headed Dandies understand that in many ways they are better off than those able-bodied soldiers who came home after the war to find only low-wage jobs or no jobs at all. Still, some days are harder for individual Dandies than others.

In the doctor's office in the Midden, Gemeiner Schenke says, "I'll admit that I sometimes become glum when people turn away or pretend I'm not there. But those who didn't fight simply don't understand that my mask—that all of our masks—are badges of honor. And when I sometimes grow despondent, I have my comrades. We understand each other better than any family member, civilian, or intact soldier ever will. Most of all, I'm grateful for all the government has done for us."

Schenke enjoys the Mara prosthetics he received free of charge after returning from the war. Both of his arms have been replaced with elegant instruments of wood, steel, and wires, and work almost as well as his old ones. They simply need the occasional plazma recharge to keep functioning. And while some Dandies don't care for the Midden, Schenke is grateful for it because the waiting list for plazma in the military hospitals can sometimes be long. Plus, as he jokes, he isn't allowed to smoke or drink in the posh clinics. "But here in the Midden I can do whatever I like. Even bounce a pretty girl on my lap when I have money left from my pension check to pay for one."

His mind wanders occasionally as he puffs on a small cheroot. The smoke blots out the smell of the ramshackle clinic (which requested its name not be used in this profile), which is simultaneously antiseptic and slightly rank.

Schenke says, "Civilians don't grasp our situation properly.

278

Things could be much worse for us. In the barracks house, we even have pets. Lovely, fierce little brown chimeras. Kleins, we call them. They're bred down from bitva war dogs for civilians. Someday I hope to have one all to myself."

Schenke listens as the wires recharging his arms quietly crackle. He sometimes wonders how Midden doctors procure plazma, but the source is in the doctor's back room and it's forbidden for nonmedical personnel to venture back there. As tempted as he is to peek, Schenke is still a soldier at heart and understands that rules and orders exist for the greater good. And as long as the charges make his arms work, he's content with the process.

As the session draws to a close, the doctor brings him a glass of whiskey with a straw to drink it from.

"Life is fine," says Schenke. "More leisure than anything else. It's good to be home and free, with the enemy sent running."

When the session is over, Schenke pays the doctor and heads out, his arms as strong and fine as ever, even if they sometimes have a tendency to stick at the joints in cold weather. He takes a tram back home, still wistful about the strange, sometimes frightened looks he can get from other passengers. It's even worse when his presence makes children cry.

"If that's the price I have to pay to be a patriot, so be it," he says.

Never forget, dear reader: Gemeiner Schenke was a soldier, he is a patriot, and he will endure.

CHAPTER SIXTEEN

LARGO AND RAINER SAT ON HIS SOFAS SMOKING HASHISH. THEY DROPPED the ashes into the mask he used as a bowl. Rainer was silent as Largo told him about Remy's disappearance, his arrest, and the Nachtvogel.

"I'm truly sorry about Remy," said Rainer. "It's bad enough to lose someone like that, but to be accused of her murder. I can't imagine how awful it must be."

"It's not even awful anymore. I'm numb to it. To most things, really. These last couple of days I've felt like I was swimming through a dream."

Rainer took a puff of the cigarette and passed it to Largo. "What are you going to do now? Working for the Nachtvogel can't be pleasant."

Largo held the hashish for a moment without smoking it. "That's what I wanted to talk to you about. Have you heard the stories about war breaking out in the north?"

"I've read the reports in the yellowsheets."

"And?"

Rainer made a dismissive gesture with his hand. "I don't believe a word of it. Trust me, even if the border fighting started with rifles and juggernauts, the moment either side lost ground they'd bring in artillery and airships, forcing the opposing side to do the same. You'd be able to hear that kind of fighting all over Lower Proszawa."

Largo said, "Then where do the stories come from? Are the papers simply making them up? If they're real, why wouldn't the Chancellor say so?"

Largo handed the hashish back to Rainer, who took a long drag. He thought a moment and said, "After the Great War, only a lunatic would have an appetite for a new war. But if the politicians did want to launch a new campaign, claiming that Proszawa was attacked first would help sway public sympathy."

"Playing the victim," said Largo.

"Exactly. It's an old trick and it often works."

When Rainer offered Largo the hashish again he shook his head. Rainer pinched off the burning end and put the rest in the upturned mask.

"Let me ask you this," said Largo. "What if you're right and have been all along? Let's say there is no war, but things are still happening to the north. Let's say that smugglers are regularly running goods from High Proszawa and using slave labor to dig them up."

"What's your point?"

Largo put his hands down flat on the table. "What if Remy isn't dead? And she hasn't been kidnapped for ransom?"

Rainer blinked. "You think she's been taken across the bay?"

"You have to admit that it's a possibility," said Largo.

Rainer wiped some spit from his lips with a handkerchief. "A vague one at best."

"I know, but what if I'm right? The bullocks and the Nachtvogel are looking in Lower Proszawa. If she's north, I might be the only one who can save her."

Scratching his cheek, Rainer said, "Are you sure you're not just looking for a way to escape the Nachtvogel? There must be less drastic ways to do that."

"Trust me, it's not that."

"Good, because they don't forget or forgive. If you ran and ever came back they'd be waiting."

Largo shivered. It had started raining outside and the flat was close to freezing. Rainer brought Largo a blanket and put more coal in the fireplace.

"What do you think?" said Largo.

"If you don't mind my saying so, this is a surprising change in your personality. I've never seen you this brave or reckless before."

Largo looked at the cuts on his knuckles, felt the ache in his bruised face. "It's easy to be brave when there's nothing left for you to lose."

"Is that enough reason to give up everything?" said Rainer.

Largo looked at him, afraid of what he'd say. "You think I shouldn't do it?"

Rainer blew on his hands for warmth. "I didn't say that. If you'd been in the war I'd feel better about telling you to do it. You'll be going into plague zones. There are dangerous ruins and unexploded bombs. And if you find the slavers, do you think they'll simply give you Remy and let you take her home?"

"I don't know," said Largo, his mood darkening as the limitations of his idea set in. "I hadn't thought that far ahead yet. Anyway, I have no idea how I'd get there."

With his finger, Rainer moved the platen on a spirit board an inch or two. "If you're determined, I might be able to help you," he said. "My friend who brings in goods from the south knows smugglers who sometimes go north. It turns out that I know some of them from the war. I might be able to persuade one to take you. But he won't do it for free."

Largo inched forward on the sofa. "I have some money saved from work. He can have all of it." His heartbeat raced as Rainer stared at him without speaking.

Finally he said, "You're sure about this?"

"Absolutely."

Rainer poured them each a shot of whiskey. "Let me reach out and see what I can do."

"Thank you. Thank you," said Largo.

Rainer clinked his glass against Largo's and they both drank. After he wiped his lips, Rainer said, "I have some supplies you'll need for your trip." He went into the bedroom and after a few minutes came out with a small bundle, which he dropped on the table. The first thing he handed Largo was the bottle of morphia Largo had given him.

"I can't take this," said Largo. "What will you do for pain?"

Rainer held up a hand. "I'm fine. I traded one of my telescopes for an ample supply. You told me that the morphia gives you some immunity to the plague. You don't want to run out."

Largo felt a deep shame when he accepted the bottle. Rainer had lost a telescope to get his supply and now Largo might be depriving him when that ran out. He promised himself to bring the bottle back to him as soon as he got back.

"All right," he said.

Rainer tossed him one of the heavy coats the War Department gave to all the Dandies as part of their pension.

Largo said, "Winter is coming. Won't you need this?"

Rainer pointed to a similar coat hanging from a nail by the door. "I have another. And if I complain to the government enough, I might be able to get a newer one. Consider this one yours."

"I don't know what to say."

"Don't say anything. You're not nearly ready to go yet."

Rainer upended the mask bowl on the table and wiped out the ashes with his handkerchief. When it was clean, he tossed it to Largo. "Try it on," he said.

Largo felt a little dizzy and wasn't sure if it was the whiskey or Rainer's offer of the mask. As much as the Dandies were shunned, masks were also revered objects and more valuable than any medal. Largo pushed it back to him. "No. It's too much," he said.

"How do you intend to get past the Nachtvogel?" Rainer said. "Why do you think I gave you the coat? You'll become one of us. Trust me. In the mask, you can go anywhere you like and no one will look at you twice. You'll be invisible."

Largo's dizziness deepened, but he took the mask and put it on. Rainer pointed to a peeling mirror on the wall and Largo went to it. He thought, *Rainer's right. No one would ever recognize me. I can walk right by my minder.* He took the mask off and sat down again.

"There are just a couple of other things," Rainer said.

Largo set down the mask. "I can't take anything else. It's already too much."

"You aren't the experienced one here. I'll decide what you need," said Rainer firmly. "How much money have you saved?"

Largo thought about it and gave him a figure. Rainer stood up. "That's not nearly enough. Here." He took a tightly wound cylinder of bills from his pocket. Largo had never seen so much cash in one place. Rainer sat down and said, "Don't ask how I got it. Just take it and no noble arguments."

Largo nodded and put the bills in his pocket without a word. He wanted to thank him, but he could tell that Rainer didn't want to hear it.

"There's something else you'll need." Rainer opened a drawer in the table and took out a pistol. He set it on the table between them. "Do you know what this is?" he said.

"A gun, of course," said Largo, feeling even more uncomfortable than before.

Rainer picked it up by the barrel and held it out, butt first. After a moment's hesitation, Largo took it.

"Wrong. It's a Drachen semiautomatic nine-millimeter Parabellum pistol. When you shoot, aim at the torso. It's the biggest part of the body, so the easiest to hit. You're inexperienced, so don't try to shoot anyone too far away. You'll have to wait until the danger is close enough that you're sure you can hit it."

Largo turned the pistol over in his hand, already having doubts about his idea. "I've never held a gun before."

Rainer went on, "There are eight bullets in the magazine. I can give you a second magazine with eight more. Those are all the bullets I have, so don't waste them."

Largo held the gun out. "Take it back. I don't even know how it works."

"Stand up and put out your arm. Point the pistol at the window," Rainer said. Once Largo had done it, Rainer pointed along the barrel. "This is how you aim. Sight from the V in the back to the notch in the front. See it?"

"Yes."

"The safety button is on right now, so the pistol won't fire. If you want to shoot, you push down here. See?"

"Yes."

"I assume you know what a trigger is. To shoot, you use steady, even pressure. If you run out of bullets, you push this button to eject the magazine and put a new one in. Push it quickly and firmly into place."

"All right," said Largo, nervous again and feeling like a child running from danger in Haxan Green. But now he wasn't running. He said, "Is there more?"

"Yes, but that will have to do for now. Congratulations. You're not a soldier, but you are a killer. It's best to take that notion seriously."

Largo lowered the pistol. "But I don't want to shoot anybody."

"No one does until they have to," said Rainer. "If you're serious about bringing Remy home, you have to be prepared for any situation. That knife of yours is formidable, but it might not be enough." He took the extra magazine from the table and gave it to Largo. "There's one more thing," Rainer said.

"Please. No more. You've already given me too much."

Rainer went back to the sofa and Largo sat across from him. "There's something I have to say, Largo." Rainer drew in a breath. "I'm sorry that I can't go with you. I should go. I want to. Believe me. But I—I'm afraid of losing any more of myself. Some days I feel like I'm hardly here at all. Please forgive me."

Largo reached across the table and took his friend's hand. "Don't ever say that. I'm the coward. When you went away, I should have gone with you. Please forgive *me*."

Rainer put his other hand over Largo's and they stayed that way for a moment. Then Rainer said, "Will you be all right getting home with these things?"

Largo piled everything on the table, with the pistol on top. "I carry things all the time. I'll be fine."

"Let me get you a bag for all of that. Something unobtrusive."

When Rainer found one, Largo put everything inside and went to the door. "I don't know what to say. 'Thank you' feels so inadequate."

"Just come and see me when you return. Let me know that you made it back all right."

"I will," said Largo.

Rainer opened the door and patted him on the back as he left. "Tell Remy hello for me. And shoot any rat bastard who tries to stop you."

On his way home, Largo went to a night market and bought whiskey, bread, and two meat pies. They were just enough to cover the contents of the bag. He rode the rest of the way home out in the open and on main streets. If someone was watching for him, let them see him. *I was just out shopping*, he thought. *It's not my fault if your man can't keep up, Herr Branca.* He took a bite of bread on the street, then carried everything upstairs. He was equal parts excited and terrified. His life had pivoted once before, when the Baron had invited him to Schöne Maschinen, but it had all gone bad. Largo could feel the ground shift under his feet as he neared another pivot point.

Whatever I do from here, there's no going back. I'm the Nachtvogel's man forever or I'm a fugitive—and that's assuming I live to come back. Maybe Rainer was right and I am partially using Remy as an excuse to escape my life. If that's true, and if I find her, I think she'll understand and I hope she will forgive me.

He hid Rainer's bag in a hole in the wall behind his desk.

If Branca's men search the flat and find it, I'm probably dead. If I go north, I'm probably dead. If Margit's group gets fed up with me, they'll probably kill me too.

Largo sat down and ate one of the meat pies, thinking, *I'm a better fortune-teller than Vera Baal.*

He arrived at work early enough the next day that he was alone in the office with Branca.

The older man glanced up from his papers as he came in. "You're here early. And looking surprisingly healthy. What's your secret?"

Largo went to Branca's desk. "I just want to do my job and not feel like shit all the time."

Branca's lips curled downward at the ends as if he was thinking. "A commendable attitude. Did you enjoy your excursion last night?"

"I did, thank you."

"Where did you go?"

Largo tried to look relaxed and knew he was failing at it. "So I am being followed. I'll leave a trail of bread crumbs next time."

"Very amusing," said Branca. "You haven't answered my question."

He thought about the lie he'd prepared, knowing that if someone had managed to follow him he'd be caught and possibly shot on the spot. Largo said, "I went out to the Green."

Branca frowned. "Haxan Green? Were you reminiscing?"

"A bit, I suppose," said Largo. "Your life must have taken some surprising turns, Herr Branca. Don't you ever want to go back to the beginning and try to figure out how you got to where you are now?"

Branca looked at the clock. "It's not necessary. I know precisely how I came to be where I am. I worked to get here. Why? Because unlike you, I believe in what I'm doing. What have you ever believed in, Largo?"

He followed Branca's gaze to the clock. "Not a lot, I suppose. I believed in myself enough to get out of the Green. That seemed like plenty for a long time."

"And now?"

He turned back to the older man. "I think I might have aspired to more than morphia and pretty girls."

"Never fear," Branca said. He folded his hands on the desk. "You'll have ample opportunity to make yourself useful to the country. Your friends might not like what you do or how you do it, but remember that what you're doing is in their best interests."

"I'll try."

"Do and soon you won't need a minder lurking outside your door."

How many days is it until a week? Largo thought. He tried to count them, but everything since Remy blurred together.

He said, "Why doesn't your man just present himself instead of sneaking around? We could ride to work together."

"That's not how this works."

"I know why. I'm in a zoo. You want to study me in my natural environment."

Branca laughed soundlessly to himself. "I hadn't thought of it that way. That's an amusing way to put it. It's good to see your sense of humor coming back."

"It seems necessary right now."

"Soon you won't have to think about it. Your life will be your life again. You'll laugh at a funny song or weep at a sad film and all will be normal and ordinary."

What a horrible thought.

"Just keep working and don't overthink my every move. Is that it?"

"And don't try to second-guess the tasks we give you," said Branca. "What you're doing is subtler than you're aware."

"Is there anything else?"

"Drink less and don't forget to eat."

"I bought food on the way home last night."

"So I understand." Branca pressed a button on the wall that activated the Maras that would give the couriers their deliveries. "It might please you to know that you're doing relatively well. Keep it up."

"I'll do my best," said Largo.

"You'll also be pleased that you'll have an easy morning today. You'll be delivering parcels to the larger yellowsheets."

"A new story you want printed?"

Branca looked at him. "What did I just say about second-guessing?"

"Sorry."

The clock on the wall reached six as the other couriers filed in, some still eating and others with the stubs of cigarettes dangling from their lips.

Quietly, Branca said, "That's all for now. Take your morphia before you go out. I don't want you shaking in front of clients or using it in some back alley and getting knifed."

"I'll remember."

Andrzej and Weimer stood at the front of the group of couriers, looking eager and docile. Weimer nodded to Largo. He didn't return the nod but walked to the back of the room. Parvulesco was there and he stood next to him. Branca called couriers forward as the Maras brought out their parcels.

"You look better than last time," said Parvulesco.

"I have hope again."

Parvulesco smiled at him. "Then the danger is over?"

Largo leaned back against the wall. "Hardly. But I'm managing it."

"Will you tell me about it someday?"

"Someday. Until then it's still best if we're not seen together."

"All right. Roland says he's sorry about Remy."

"Please thank him for me," said Largo.

Parvulesco moved to the front of the room when Branca called his name.

Once the others were gone, Branca gave Largo five identical envelopes. After he went to the bathroom to take morphia, Largo checked the addresses. As Branca had said, they were going to all of the major yellowsheets in Lower Proszawa. *Thank you*, he thought when he found one for *Ihre Skandale*. He put it on the bottom of the pile to deliver last.

Ernst put down the receiver of his Trefle when Largo walked in. "We haven't seen you for a while," he said. "I thought you'd forgotten about us. Or did someone else offer you better money for your stories?"

"Hardly," said Largo. He handed Ernst the envelope and receipt book. "In fact, I'm not supposed to talk to you at all."

"And you're the kind of gentleman who always follows the rules."

"Only when they make sense."

Ernst said, "That's the right attitude," and handed him back the book.

Largo put it in his shoulder bag and said, "I'm going somewhere and when I get back I'm going to have a story for you."

"Where are you going?"

"I can't say, but I'll have something special for you soon."

Ernst looked at him eagerly. "We pay special money for special stories," he said.

"You'll pay a lot for this one."

"Now I'm really intrigued. Give me a hint and maybe I'll give you an advance."

Good, Largo thought. That's exactly what he'd hoped to hear. Without knowing how much the smuggler would charge for passage, he knew he needed all the money he could get. "North," he said.

"North?" said Ernst. He looked at Largo and frowned. "You don't mean High Proszawa?"

"I can't say."

The editor grinned. There was a small piece of tobacco on his front teeth. "You bring me back something good from there and I'll paper your home in cash. Here's a couple of Valdas to get you on your way."

Ernst took some coins from a desk drawer and Largo said, "Don't pass them to me."

"Is someone watching us?" Ernst said.

"Probably."

"This gets better and better. Just remember one thing for me."

"What's that?"

"I'm about to put a lot of money in your hand." Ernst grinned. "Don't die without bringing me a story."

Largo was nervous, but he didn't want to let it out enough for his minder to see, so he controlled his breathing. "Tell me off as I leave. Grab me and put the money in my pocket on the way out," he said.

Ernst came around the desk and took Largo's arm. He didn't let go until he'd shoved Largo out into the street. "Piss off, you useless mongrel. I don't want to see you here again."

Largo got back on his bicycle. "Of course, sir. I'm very sorry to have disturbed you. Have a good day."

Ernst spit in the gutter. "Fuck you, Your Highness."

Largo rode back to the company at a leisurely pace, taking main streets all the way so that his minder wouldn't lose him. Patriotic banners and posters were going up all over the city. The cafés and bars were quieter than he'd ever seen. As disturbing as the hints of war were, with new Valdas in his pocket and the meeting with Rainer still fresh in his mind, Largo felt better than he had in days.

His good mood faded in the evening when he didn't hear anything from Rainer. There was nothing the next day either. On the third evening, Largo came home grim with a bottle of good whiskey, fully intending to finish it all and damn Branca's praise about "doing well."

He flipped on the piss-yellow lights and turned on the wireless. Thankfully, what came out was music and not a speech. On the chair in the corner of the room was a dirty shirt. Largo tossed it onto the table, sat down, and opened the whiskey.

There was a square of paper lying on the floor by the door. He went to it. Unfolding the paper, Largo recognized Rainer's precise handwriting. The note read *Körpermarkt in the Midden. 10 p.m.*

At eight thirty, he moved the desk away from the wall and removed everything that Rainer had given him. Before putting on the coat, Largo strapped on the knife. He hid the bills and Valdas in one of the coat's inside pockets and put it on. The knife pressed into his side uncomfortably, but there was nothing he could do about it. He put the pistol and the extra magazine in the right coat pocket and Rainer's mask in the left. Before he headed out, he tried eating some of the bread he'd brought home three days earlier, but it was stale. Instead, he took two drops of morphia and put the whiskey and some matches in a pocket of his coat. Just before nine, he opened the door of his flat and scanned the hall. No one was there. He put on Rainer's mask as he went out and threw all three locks on his door.

For the first time, the smell of cooking fat and rotting vegetables that permeated the building didn't bother him. It was strangely comforting simply because it was familiar, and because he knew he would probably never smell it or see Little Shambles again.

Largo went up the stairs to the fourth floor until he was at a door that opened onto the roof. Nearby was an overflowing trash can and he dragged it outside with him.

The sky was clouded over and a thin mist fell. He carried the trash can to the far side of the roof. There, he poured some of the whiskey into the can and, leaning over to protect it from the rain, he lit a match and dropped it in after the liquor. The garbage burst into flame. When it was burning thoroughly, Largo threw the can off the roof. It crashed into the street and exploded, sending burning trash in every direction. The sound of the can's landing reverberated off the walls of the nearby buildings. He waited a few seconds, then ran.

In the dark, it was hard to see through the metal mask, but there was enough yellow light from the street that he made it across his roof and onto the roof of the building next door. A fire escape came down around the corner from Largo's building. He went to the edge of the roof and checked the street. Sure enough, if a minder had been watching the building, he'd run off to investigate the crash. Largo stepped over the edge and began the four-story climb to the street.

The rain made the rungs of the ladder leading down to the first landing slippery and cold. Largo's hands went numb quickly. He crept down the stairs of the next three floors as quietly and carefully as he could. The ancient fire escape shifted queasily under his weight, leaning away from the building a few inches and moving gently from side to side. Largo tried not to think about it. It wasn't hard. The rain and his fear quickly transformed into a numbness that enclosed his body and mind. The world collapsed to a single point: his careful movement down the steel stairs. One foot in front of the other.

He slipped when he reached the second-floor platform and came down hard on his side. Afraid that the residents of the flat might have heard him, Largo stepped onto the ladder that would finally take him down to the street. It was designed to lower under a person's weight, but it jammed halfway down. He looked at the street and saw that it was still empty. The jump down wasn't long, but he was directly above piles of trash that had been thrown from the building into the gutter. Instead of jumping, Largo leaned his weight on the ladder and bounced gently. There were two metallic pops, and one side of the ladder swung free of the fire escape, throwing him to the ground.

The fall knocked the breath out of him, but he rolled quickly off the trash and into the wet street, afraid the ladder might come down on top of him. It took him a moment to get back on his feet. The moment he put his full weight on his legs, he almost collapsed on his wrenched right knee. His trouser leg was torn and rain or blood or some combination of the two ran down over his ankle. Largo hid in a cellar doorway for a moment to see if his minder had heard the fall and would come to investigate. The climb had taken longer than he'd planned and the fall had slowed him down even more. He'd barely begun and he was already behind schedule. The numbness that had taken him over earlier was giving way to gnawing fear. If they caught him now, he was certain his minder or perhaps Branca himself would shoot him on sight. There was nothing left to do but move.

He limped away from Little Shambles to a nearby tram line on Shorehof. Along the way, he had to stop once to take another drop of morphia to dull the pain in his leg.

Largo started to pay for a tram ticket, then remembered that Dandies rode for free. *I have to be careful of small mistakes like that.*

The car was full, but people gave him a wide berth. *Why not?* he thought. He was filthy from wallowing in garbage and the wet street. His trousers were torn and his leg was bleeding. And there was the Dandy mask. While under normal circumstances, his look and smell might get him dirty looks and a few jeers from the other passengers, now they simply wanted to get as far away from him as possible. Even half-blind under the mask, Largo saw how resolutely the other riders looked away from him. He was more than a simple pariah. He was a reminder that coming war wouldn't be all banners and glory. It would be rent flesh and human horrors. Largo had always felt sympathy for Rainer, but now he felt a stab of the enduring loneliness that all the Dandies must experience. *How they must hate us*, he thought. *And how we deserve it.*

And Margit said there was no alone anymore.

He left the tram on bright Messerberg and limped into the unlit alleys and back streets that led to the Midden. Even though his right leg burned with each step, Largo picked up the pace, sure that if he missed the rendezvous, he'd never have another chance to get to High Proszawa.

He slipped a few times on the wet cobbles that led to the heart of the Midden. Most of the shops were closed when he arrived, their stolen and smuggled goods hidden behind windows turned gray with condensation. The only light came from a beer hall that was little more than an open garage with a few wooden planks laid atop old barrels. The dozen or so people inside went silent when he peered into the place. After an uncomfortable moment, he limped on to the Körpermarkt.

A couple of mannequin limbs and a cheap metal-and-leather prosthetic hung from an awning in the rain. He couldn't see anything inside through the mist on the windows and there was no one on the street. Largo quietly cursed himself for never getting a watch. Was it past ten? Had he missed his one chance to rescue Remy? He hated himself more at that moment than he could ever remember hating anything.

It would be perfectly like me to ruin my one chance. I should have been here an hour ago. What's a few minutes in the rain if it meant seeing her again?

The rain turned the mask icy. Largo's face went numb. His knee burned and he wondered how long he should wait before giving up, going home, and putting the barrel of Rainer's gun in his mouth. The only problem with suicide was it meant he wouldn't be there to see Branca's face when he'd spoiled all of the man's plans and Branca had to explain the mess to his bosses.

I don't imagine that the Nachtvogel forgive anyone easily, even their own. Will they execute Branca or ship him off to some new duty station even more awful than the courier service?

He hoped it was the latter and that Branca would grow old there, knowing that Largo—the useful fool—had destroyed his life.

While he was thinking this happy thought, a tall, broad man in a bowler hat came out of the beer hall and stared in his direction. After a moment, he walked slowly toward Largo, stopping a few feet away.

"Do you have any friends?" said the man in a deep, booming voice. His front teeth were all silver and glinted dully in the light from the beer hall.

For a moment, Largo wasn't sure he understood the question. Then he blurted the only thing he could think of: "Rainer."

The smuggler looked Largo up and down. "No," he said. "I don't think I can help you."

"Why? I have money."

"That's not the problem," the smuggler said. "Rainer didn't mention you were a Dandy. Some of my crew aren't the most worldly individuals. They're afraid of Dandies. They think traveling with them is bad luck. It's nothing personal, but I can't help you."

The smuggler walked away. Largo looked down the street. Several men from the bar were watching him. After his one chance to find Remy turned a corner, Largo ran after him.

"Wait!" he yelled.

The man stopped. "Are you deaf? I said I can't help you."

Largo blocked his way and slipped off the mask. The smuggler glared at him.

"Is this a joke? Why didn't you say something?"

"I couldn't back where someone might see me."

The smuggler tilted his head back slightly and looked down at Largo. "So, the bullocks want you."

"Yes."

"That will cost extra."

"I can pay."

"You understand that I make no guarantees about the trip. Sometimes there are surprise patrols and we have to turn back. There are no refunds."

"I understand," said Largo.

The smuggler started walking again. He moved quickly and Largo's limp made it hard to keep up.

"Once we get to port you can fuck off to wherever you want. Wallow in the mud and shit to your heart's content." He stopped and tapped Largo's chest with a calloused finger. "But if you're buying or trading, only bring back what you can carry yourself."

Largo said nervously, "That might be a problem."

"And why is that?"

"I might be bringing back a person."

The smuggler rubbed his chin. "So, now there's two of you booking passage."

"Maybe. But just on the way back."

The smuggler thought about it. "If you weren't Rainer's friend I'd tell you to fuck off. I'd also charge you double fare for two people. But considering you *are* his friend, I'll do it for one and a half."

"That's very reasonable."

"Do you have your own suit?"

Largo said, "What kind of suit?"

The smuggler spoke as if he were talking to a child. "We're going into a plague zone, boy. You need a sealed suit."

"Like those ones the bullocks use to move people with the Drops?"

"Those are the ones."

Largo shook his head. "I don't need one. I'm immune to the plague."

The smuggler laughed. "You're funny. I'll only charge one fare, seeing as how it's unlikely you'll be coming back."

"Then you'll take me?"

"I just said that."

"How much is it?"

The smuggler named a price. It used up almost all of Rainer's money. Largo was glad he'd taken a chance and talked to Ernst, but with so little in his pocket now he grew worried. *What if I have to bribe someone or buy Remy back? Will I have enough?*

After counting the money, the smuggler seemed satisfied. He said, "I'm Steinmetz. Let's get going. We push off the moment we get back." He started walking and, again, Largo could barely keep up.

He said, "Is it a long voyage? I've never been on a ship before."

Steinmetz clapped him on the back. "You'll love it. She's the prettiest thing you ever saw. Luxury accommodations and smooth sailing all the way."

At the end of the block sat a heavy motorcycle. Steinmetz got on and pointed for Largo to get into the sidecar. He sat down and gripped the edges tightly. "I've never been on a motorbike before either."

Steinmetz kicked the motorcycle to life. He said, "Never been on a bike. Never been on a boat. This is a grand night for you."

"I suppose so," said Largo, his stomach queasy.

"Well, hang on and keep that coat shut. On a night like this, your balls will fall off frozen and rattle around your feet."

They started to move and Steinmetz added, "And keep that mask in your pocket. The men already have doubts about bringing a stranger on board."

Largo didn't say anything as the wind and freezing rain whipped at his face. For the first time he wondered if he was making a monstrous mistake and if there was any way he could sneak back to Little Shambles and forget everything.

What if Remy really is dead and I'm throwing away my life for nothing?

What felt like another part of his mind replied, *What if she's not? What if she's just a few miles away and I leave her there? My life is already ruined. Maybe hers can be salvaged.*

Largo knew finally and with absolute certainty that he had to go through with the trip. It didn't make him feel brave or noble, simply numb again.

CHAPTER SEVENTEEN

THEY WERE MOST OF THE WAY THERE BEFORE LARGO WAS CERTAIN THAT they were going to Haxan Green. Steinmetz took them to a partially collapsed wharf not far from where his father had been murdered. Largo couldn't help looking around as frightening memories flooded him with unpleasant images. He closed his eyes for a moment and forced them away, knowing he couldn't afford to be distracted by old ghosts, his father's included.

I'm sorry, Poppa. Goodbye. Again.

He followed Steinmetz across loose, water-swollen timbers and out over the water.

"Where's the ship?" said Largo.

"It's a boat. It'll be along."

He looked over his shoulder at the deserted streets and rotting mansions. *I keep leaving here*, Largo thought. *But I never get away.*

The canal below them began to churn. Fat, gurgling bubbles burst on the surface. Something long and dull metal rose out of the water.

"It's a U-boat," Largo said.

Steinmetz looked at him. "You don't say."

The submarine looked like it had been patched in a hundred places. Looking at the welded and bolted plates, scarred metal, and rust, Largo wondered how it managed not to sink like a boulder. The hatch on top of the U-boat opened and the ghostly outline of a man emerged. He called, "Do you have the freight, Kapitän?"

"He's here," Steinmetz said. "And stuffed with cash. A veritable Christmas goose."

"We'll try not to eat him all at once."

Steinmetz laughed and led Largo across a jerry-built gangway the other man lowered from the U-boat. He said, "When you get below, watch your mouth. Not everyone is as welcoming as Pallenberg."

The hatch was narrower than Largo expected. With his bad leg and bulky coat, he was clumsy getting down the ladder and missed the bottom rung. Steinmetz had to catch him to keep him from falling onto the floor.

The interior of the U-boat was smaller than Largo had expected. It made him think of traveling in the box by his father's side. The room felt too small for his body, as if the walls were closing in on him every time he looked away.

Steinmetz said, "Here's our cargo, gentlemen. The friend of a friend from the war, so don't fuck with him too much."

There were six men, none of whom appeared happy that Largo was there. Only one had a vague smile. *That must be Pallenberg*, he thought. The interior of the U-boat stank of sweat, shit, and diesel fuel. That, coupled with the humid air, made him feel woozy, but he fought to maintain his balance and keep his face a pleasant blank.

He said, "Hello. And thank you for transporting me." None of the men replied or let up glaring.

"Enough of this merriment," said Steinmetz. He took off his coat and looked at Largo. "You can go to one of the cabins if you want, or you can stay here. Just don't get in the way."

The decision wasn't difficult. "I'll go to a room. Where are they?"

Steinmetz pointed to the stern. "Back there. The bridal suite is on the far end," he said. "You understand that if things go bad and we start to go down it means you'll be the last off."

"That sounds fair," says Largo. The crew laughed at that.

"He's a funny bastard," said Steinmetz to his men. He gave Largo a last look. "There's a bucket in the room. If you puke, do it there. If you miss, there's an extra charge for it."

"How long will the crossing take?"

Steinmetz handed his coat to one of the crewmen, who took it forward. "That depends on a lot of things. Mostly patrols. Also what route we have to take. Sometimes we have to go the long way around and there's dead ships along the bottom, so the going is slow. And then there's the minefield. That's very slow. If we're lucky, we can avoid that."

Largo felt woozy again, not from the smell but from the word *minefield*. He said, "What's the fastest we can make it across?"

"Twelve hours."

"And the slowest?"

"Assuming we don't sink, a day. A day and a half. Don't worry. We have food and water."

"But no hot showers," said smiling Pallenberg.

Judging by the smell, I believe you, thought Largo. He said, "That's all right. We both got a nice shower on the way here."

Steinmetz gave him a light shove toward the cabins. "Go back and get settled. We leave as soon as we're sure the way is clear."

Largo limped to the stern and went into the last cabin. It was smaller than the bedroom in his flat. *Which won't be my flat for much longer*, he thought. There was a narrow bunk and barely enough room on the floor to turn around. He had to keep his head down so he wouldn't bump into a cluster of pipes that ran across the ceiling. Largo hung up his wet coat and sat on the bunk, where he immediately took two drops of morphia for his leg and a third to help him calm down. There was a heavy steel clock bolted to the wall. He noted the hour so that he could time the voyage. As the morphia warmed him, Largo lay down. The boat shuddered. From somewhere behind him, engines churned. There was another shudder and he felt a strange pressure in his ears.

We're underwater, he thought. *This is really it. No turning back now.*

He closed his eyes and breathed the way Branca had taught him to calm his nerves.

He started awake without realizing he'd been asleep. The boat was quiet and there was no shudder from the engines. Largo looked at the clock. Just over eight hours had passed. His leg felt better, so he left the cabin and went forward to the control room. Steinmetz was smoking a pipe. He watched four others play a board game. Nearby, Pallenberg scanned the surface of the bay through the periscope. Largo went to Steinmetz. "Is something wrong?"

He didn't take his eyes off the game. "No. We're just waiting for a patrol to pass. There must be something going on. It's a fucking armada."

"Will we be stuck long?"

"We move when we move and not until then. Now go back to your cabin or stop bothering me."

Largo walked around the group until he could see what game the men were playing. Instead of chess or checkers, they were using a large board with a seventeen-by-seventeen grid. The men made their moves slowly, clearly used to wasting time quietly. Instead of jumping or removing each other's pieces, they added more to the board. It looked to Largo as if they were trying to surround multiple enemies at once. He'd never seen anything like it before. *It can't be from High or Lower Proszawa.* Even the game pieces were alien, a mix of small brass coins, bullets, and what looked like carved bones. One of the players looked up and when he saw Largo he motioned him over.

The man was very short and thin, with patches of sunburned skin peeling off his pale forehead and arms. He held out four coins and said something in a language Largo didn't understand. Steinmetz said, "He wants you to take the coins in one hand, throw them in the air, and catch them."

"Why?"

"It's a game."

Largo took the coins in his right hand and tossed them an inch or two in the air.

"Now close your fist," said Steinmetz.

Largo followed the instructions.

"Now blow on it."

Largo did that too.

"Now slap the coins back into Čapek's hand."

The man Steinmetz called Čapek put his hand out, palm up. Largo slapped his hand over his. Čapek and the other men peered at the coins. A broad grin spread over Čapek's bony face. Several other men laughed. Čapek held out the coins to Steinmetz, who also laughed.

"What was that?" said Largo.

"Čapek just told your fortune."

"How was it?"

Steinmetz puffed his pipe and smiled. "You're moving on to great things."

"Maybe the great beyond," said Pallenberg.

"Quiet," said Steinmetz. To Largo he said, "Don't listen to him. He's bored and just looking for a good time."

300

"I don't believe in fortune-tellers," said Largo, remembering Vera Baal sending Remy away.

"Then there's nothing to worry about, is there?" said Steinmetz.

Largo turned back to Čapek, but he'd already returned to the game. Even if Largo could ask the man a question, he couldn't understand the answer, and he didn't trust Steinmetz or any of the others to translate it properly.

"I'm going back to my cabin," said Largo, but no one answered as they'd all gone back to watching the game.

On his bunk, he was rattled and full of nervous energy. He knew the men had been teasing him, but having Steinmetz join in was unnerving. Largo understood more than ever that he really was nothing to them. Another piece of cargo to be transported or discarded. He wished he hadn't left his copy of *Der Knochengarten* in Remy's flat. It would be a welcome distraction.

He locked the cabin door. This time when he lay down on the bunk, he checked that his knife was secure in its harness. While he was willing to be the butt of some jokes if that's what it took to get him across the bay, that was the limit of his tolerance.

Anyone who thinks he can hurt me or take anything of mine will get a surprise. That goes for Steinmetz too.

Thirteen hours passed. He took more morphia, not because his leg hurt, but to calm his nerves and bolster his immunity to the plague. There was a three-month-old copy of a yellowsheet under the bunk and he read it to pass the time. He tried to picture three months ago, but couldn't. He and Remy had been happy was all he remembered. It had all felt so simple and stupid in the best possible way. Sex. Drugs. Plays at the Grand Dark. Friends. Bliss. Then he got the promotion and everything went wrong. Branca would have missed him by now and have agents out looking for him.

The Nachtvogel might be searching my flat at this moment. They'll find the hole in the wall behind my desk. I wonder what will happen to my minder?

Largo checked his pocket for Rainer's note. To his great relief it was still there. *Have I left anything behind that might lead them to my friends?* he wondered. *Of course, they would have already had a list when I got the promotion.* He wondered what else they knew about him. Then there were all the people he'd spied on without knowing about it. What was happening to them? *Is there some way I can make it up to them? What if they're dead or in prison? What can I do then?* He didn't even remember most of their names or know which of them the Nachtvogel had been watching. That was the worst part, not knowing who or how many he'd betrayed. *Even if she's doomed, maybe I should have helped Margit. Now that Pietr is gone, maybe her group is more reasonable. Or have they found a way to blame me for his death? Who is there left to trust?*

An hour later there was a knock on the door and Pallenberg came in. He tossed Largo a drab green life jacket. "Can you swim?"

"A little," said Largo. "I used to as a boy."

"Don't worry about it. Odds are we'll be blown to hell if things go shit-shaped."

"Does that mean we'll be going through the minefield?"

Pallenberg said, "We're already in it, so keep your mouth shut and don't bother anyone. You might as well come forward. It's closer to the hatch if we get a chance to swim for it."

It was quiet in the control room. Steinmetz was bent over a table covered in charts. He shouted changes in the U-boat's movement and depth to the crew. Largo looked over the Kapitän's shoulder.

"You've mapped the whole field," he said.

For a moment Steinmetz looked angry at Largo for breaking his concentration. A few seconds later he calmed down. He said, "This is from the war. We have to hope it's still correct and that none of the mines have come loose and drifted into a new position."

The boat shook violently and a metallic shriek scraped all the way down the side to the aft section.

"Don't worry," said Steinmetz. "We just kissed a dead ship. If that had been a mine we'd be talking with the devil by now."

How funny it would be to die here and now, Largo thought. *All my troubles would be over. Of course, Remy would still be in danger. And people would never guess where I'd bought it. They'd all think I'd run away. Still, there's something entertaining about the idea.*

Steinmetz barked another course correction and checked his watch, quietly counting down the seconds. After a minute he said, "Check your arses, gentlemen. I think you'll find them still firmly in place."

Largo expected a cheer or even laughter, but all he heard were sighs and men who'd been holding their breath finally exhaling. "We're through?" he said.

Steinmetz changed charts. "We're through."

"How long until we dock?"

"Another hour, maybe. We have to go upriver and hope no other bastard has sunk and blocked the way. Why don't you go back to your cabin and let us do our jobs? I'll call you when we've reached port."

Largo went to his cabin and locked himself inside. He checked over everything he'd brought with him. Money. His knife. Rainer's gun. Morphia. He wished he'd thought to bring a flashlight. High Proszawa was probably going to be on the dim side and he didn't want to stumble around blind. He hoped the storm had passed. That would give the moon a chance to come out. But moon or not, flashlight or not, he was almost there. Almost to Remy. Despite the pain in his leg and the fear that was always at the back of his thoughts, he hadn't felt so excited in days.

After a little more than an hour, someone knocked on his door. Steinmetz came in and tapped the clock bolted on the wall of the cabin. "We're here. You have eighteen hours to do whatever the hell you want. If you're not back on time, friend of Rainer's or not, we'll leave you. Understand?"

"I understand," said Largo. "The thing is, I don't have a watch."

Steinmetz said, "Rainer said you might not." He pulled a fistful of watches from his pocket and dropped them on the bunk. "Take your pick."

Largo went through the pile, not sure what he was looking for. He said, "Are all these from dead men?"

Steinmetz leaned against the cabin door. "They're not all men's, and yes."

Largo selected a watch and put it on. He followed Steinmetz forward and climbed out of the U-boat after him.

Every bit of his hope died.

Largo had known in the abstract that High Proszawa would be a ruin, but seeing it with his own eyes, one word came to mind: *wasteland*. The U-boat was docked at a ramshackle pier in a river cove, hidden from the patrols in the bay. The fresh air was a shock to his system after the stink of the submarine. It was also cold, with a chill wind blowing in from the bay. Even in his heavy coat, Largo shivered. He could hear voices and the sound of machinery, but he could see very little in the pitch dark—just vague hints of human and mechanical outlines. Then the moon emerged from behind a cloud and High

Proszawa briefly came into focus. Beyond the wharf area lay a barren expanse of mud and incinerated buildings that jutted from a frozen earth at mad angles. When the wind changed and blew from inland, it brought the scent of wet earth, but also that of a vast rot, like the offal bins in the butchers' quarter.

Below them on the wharf, Steinmetz's men fanned out in all directions, each of them wearing a rubber protective suit. Steinmetz waited on the deck. "A pretty sight, isn't it?" he said.

Largo pulled his coat tighter around him. "It isn't at all how I imagined it."

"What did you think it would be?"

"I don't know. Bombs hit some buildings near where I live. I thought it might be like that."

"Windows broken? Doors blown out, but still a city?"

"Yes," Largo said.

"Welcome to the war, my friend. The boot that grinds everything to dust."

Largo tried to imagine Rainer marching through the freezing filth with most of his face blown off. The image made Largo feel nauseated.

A cloud bank slid back in front of the moon. "Now I can't see anything. I should have brought a flashlight."

"They're not allowed," said Steinmetz. "Offshore patrols can spot them."

"Then how do you get around?"

He put on goggles and handed Largo a pair. "Try these."

Largo was blinded for a few seconds by a strange yellow light. When his vision adjusted, he could see the bustling wharf and the waste beyond lit like evening in an eerie amber glow. "What are these?" he said.

"There's wee tiny chimeras inside," said Steinmetz. "They transform darkness into light, just as long as their food lasts."

"How long is that?"

"Guess."

"Eighteen hours?"

Steinmetz said, "If you miss the pickup, you won't just be stuck here. You'll be blind too."

Largo shivered in the cold, imagining what it would be like to hunker down in the ruins of High Proszawa until he could buy his way onto another boat. "I won't be late."

"Good. Take this," Steinmetz said. He handed Largo a collapsible telescope and a sheet of paper. "The spyglass might help. It used to belong to Rainer. You can take it back to him."

"I will," said Largo. Then, "Where do they dig up things to sell in Lower Proszawa? Things like you'd find in the Midden."

Steinmetz said, "There are different crews looking for different things. That paper is a rough map of the crews I know about. Mind you, I've never been out into deep plague country, but I'm told the map is generally accurate."

"Just *generally* accurate?"

"It's what I have. Take it or leave it."

"I'll take anything right now."

Steinmetz unfolded the map and pointed northeast of the wharf. "You want to start with the curio hunters? Follow the road on the right. They're two or three hills beyond. Maybe four."

Largo looked at the map. He could read it easily in the light from the strange goggles. He started to thank Steinmetz, but the smuggler had already pulled on his hood and joined his men below. Largo folded the map carefully and put it in an inside pocket of his coat. Then he started up the road on the right.

CHAPTER EIGHTEEN

IT WASN'T THREE HILLS TO THE CURIO HUNTERS. AND IT WASN'T FOUR. After six hills and more than an hour of walking he wondered if he was already lost. After the seventh hill, he was sure of it. From time to time, the mud gave way to the cracked surface of a ruined boulevard. Hollow, broken buildings and skeletal trees loomed like screaming faces on either side of the road. Most of the time, though, he was surrounded by indefinable shapes sunk in the dirty ooze or blasted into so many pieces they were unrecognizable.

The endless wet and muck was a surprise. Largo was still wearing his city shoes. They quickly filled with freezing mud, weighing him down and making each step a chore. His right leg began to ache again.

It was over the eighth hill that he finally saw movement in the distance. Excited, Largo ran to a low cut beside a collapsed cathedral and knelt down behind what looked like the top of a juggernaut. He watched the distant scene for several minutes using Rainer's telescope.

Approximately twenty people in protective suits dug in the mud at the base of what looked like the ruins of an elegant high-rise, similar to the ones in Empyrean. Nearby were immense piles of furniture. Heaps of sofas, jumbles of bed frames, chairs, and ebony tables. On the sides were smaller masses of clocks, vases, clothing, and jewelry. Paintings were stacked next to a museum's worth of marble statues.

A thought came to Largo abruptly: Remy wasn't the only one missing. Lucie had disappeared too. What if he found both of them? What would Steinmetz say? He hoped he had enough money left.

The curio crew worked steadily, and it looked to him as if they were doing it with nothing more than shovels. He thought there was something strangely admirable about that. *The sheer force of will it must take to work by hand in these conditions. It's amazing.*

Several large doglike chimeras—as big as Baron Hellswarth's Kara—sniffed around the edges of the camp, stopping only to dig in the ground or at the side of the building. When one of them did, workers would go over to see what they'd found.

None of the chimeras had any protective covering. Largo noticed that a few of the workers had taken off their masks and were digging bare-headed. He wondered if they took the most morphia or if they were simply resigned to their fate as plague victims. Again, he was struck by the peculiar courage of the crew. With all the goods they'd accumulated, if Remy or Lucie was there, would they be willing to give them up? What if he bought their freedom but didn't have any money left for Steinmetz? He put the thought out of his mind for the moment.

This isn't the time to worry about that. One step at a time. Find them and then worry about paying their fare.

Largo watched the curio hunters for half an hour, scanning first the workers who'd removed their masks, then the ones who were still fully in their suits. He didn't spot any obvious slaves. The crew seemed to work together fairly well, he thought. No one was brutalized or punished. In fact, he saw easy conversation and even some laughter between the workers.

Maybe the slaves are inside the building. That must be the most dangerous area.

That possibility presented a whole new set of problems. He couldn't see into the building with the telescope, so how could he find any slaves without going in himself? *There's no choice*, Largo thought. *I'll have to see if there's a back entrance.*

He went around to the rear of the building in a low crouch. Once he was there, he scanned the scene with the telescope. It was similar to what he'd seen out front. Fifteen to twenty workers digging through the ruins. No one was beaten or treated badly.

No way to get in back here. Maybe I'll get lucky on the far side of the building.

Largo moved quickly, still crouching, stopping every few yards to scan the work area. It took longer than he'd hoped to get around to the side of the high-rise. The landscape was full of deep bomb craters and heaps of debris, all of which he had to circle around or risk being seen. As he went, he wondered about what to do if he found Remy or Lucie. It would be best if he could sneak them out, but with so many workers, that seemed like an unlikely solution. In that case, he'd have to bribe the scavengers.

He was moving around the rim of a crater that had blasted away most of a paved road when his back erupted in pain and he went face-down on the pavement. Warm blood trickled down his cheek where he cut it on a paving stone. He lay there stunned for a moment before someone flipped him over onto his back.

The man holding a knife to his throat wasn't wearing a protective mask. However, he was wearing a dented Pickelhaube smeared with dried mud. Officers had worn the ridiculous spiked helmets during the war. Largo wondered if the man had found it in the ruins or stolen it off a corpse. The man's face was so creased and dirty that it was impossible to guess his age. He was missing most of his front teeth, which gave him a slight lisp when he spoke.

"Who the fuck are you?" he said.

"I'm Largo. I'm not looking for trouble."

"What crew you with?"

"I'm not with a crew. I'm just looking for someone."

The curio hunter pressed the knife harder against Largo's throat. "Looking for someone? Who?"

"A woman. Maybe two women. They're both young and pretty."

"Got plenty of women in the crew, though none I'd call pretty."

"Not in your crew. I'm looking for slaves."

That seemed to puzzle the curio hunter and for a moment, he lessened the pressure of the knife. "What fucking slaves you talking about?"

"The slaves. The ones you bring in from Lower Proszawa to dig up treasure."

The hunter smiled and a drop of saliva fell from the gap in his teeth. "You're from the city?"

"Yes," said Largo. "I'm just looking for a couple of friends."

The hunter repositioned the knife so the side wasn't in Largo's throat, but the tip. "I'll tell you something, city man. We're profession-als here. We ain't got time for slaves or bluenoses. Now, answer my next question truthful 'cause it's life or death. You got any money?"

"Yes."

The hunter made a grasping gesture with his free hand. "Give it to me."

"It's inside my coat."

"Then give it slow."

Largo took the remaining bills from the inside pocket of his coat and gave them to the hunter, who looked them over and put them in a pocket of his protective suit.

"It's your lucky day, city man. This is just enough to let you off. Now, you want slaves? You go by the metal works. Those fucks'll do anything to anyone."

"Where are they?"

The hunter pointed to the west with his knife. Largo looked to where he was pointing and saw only a flat, endless mire. "I'm lost," he said. "Is there a road around to the metal works?"

"'Course. But I ain't telling you where. You so anxious? There's your way."

Largo didn't speak.

The hunter let Largo up and jammed the knife against his ribs. "Get walking. You got a long way to go."

Largo walked backward for a few yards, breaking every rule he'd grown up with. Yes, he thought, walking this way made him look weak and a bit ridiculous, but he had the sense that the old rules might not apply out here. Who cared if you looked brave or foolish here at the end of the world? All that mattered was survival, however you could manage it.

He retraced his steps around the building. It went a lot faster this time since he wasn't trying to hide. He had no idea whether to take the hunter's word for it that they didn't have any slaves, but he wasn't in a position to argue the point. The best part about heading to the metal works, he thought, was that it would put more distance between him the curio hunters.

Largo checked his map as he started across a mile-wide field of mud. The hunter hadn't been lying. The metal works were marked as due west from their camp. He put the map back in his pocket, wondering what he was going to do now with nothing but a few Valdas hidden in the back pocket of his pants. Wiping the mud from the watch Steinmetz had given him, he checked the time. More than four hours had passed and he had nothing to show for it. He wanted to run across the mud field but knew he had to be careful. There might

310

be more bomb craters and the last thing he wanted to do was fall and hurt his knee again, or drown before he found Remy.

He walked in what he hoped was a straight line west. A compass would have helped, Largo knew, but only if he knew how to use one. At places, sections of road rose from the swamp-like filth, making walking easy. But for the most part, he slogged through ankle-deep slop. Occasionally, he ended up having to push himself up when one of his legs hit a low spot and he sank up to his knee. His right leg burned with pain and the only warm part of his body was the wound in his cheek, from which blood still trickled onto his coat. Largo stopped and put two more drops of morphia under his tongue. He wanted more, but he also wanted a clear head as he made his way through the putrid marsh.

He went past armed Maras. A few were alone, but many others were in groups. Most were sinking in the mud, but some of the ones on top looked functional enough that he walked in a wide circle around them in case any of them sprang to life. He tripped and fell when he stepped on the broken rails of a tram line. At one point, he passed the lobby of a shattered hotel with a café next door. To his shock, a bottle lay face-up in the filth. Largo grabbed it and tore out the cork. He sniffed it and realized that it was wine, and a light and lovely one. He tossed the cork away and drank as he walked. After a couple of big swallows, Largo warmed up a little. He kept moving, hoping he was still headed west. He used a withered tree set between a hill and a bombed-out school building as a guide.

On his way, he saw unexploded bombs sunk nose-down in the mud. He wondered if they were ordinary ones or plague bombs. He decided that it didn't matter since if either went off it would almost certainly kill him, so he drank more wine, walked, and tried to ignore the pain in his leg.

When he reached a ruined theater, he stopped. The layout wasn't all that different from the Grand Dark. There was a wide lobby that led to a tattered, moldy curtain, which opened onto a seating area with the stage at the far end. A bomb had torn away part of the roof and the middle rows of seats were missing. He dropped into a seat at the back of the room for a few minutes, taking the pressure off his leg and trying to catch his breath. He closed his eyes, telling himself that it would be for just a minute.

Largo felt light-headed. The walls of the Grand Dark stretched for what seemed like miles so that the distant stage was barely more than a pinpoint of illumination. He tried to stand but failed on his first attempt and realized that he was feeling the effects of morphia. It must have been a very large dose to make him this disoriented, he thought. On his second try, he managed to get to his feet but kept a hand against the wall in case he lost his balance again. As he started the long walk to the stage he noticed something odd. The theater seats were all occupied by galvanic puppets, each staring straight ahead, dressed as any ordinary theatergoers who had come to see a show. He could hear faint sounds from the distant stage, but the audience was utterly silent. It was startling, then, when a head casually turned in his direction. It was a man whose face was little more than a mass of twisted meat. His cheeks were missing and his mouth was a knife slash at a severe angle up his face, leading to an empty right eye socket. Though Largo knew that it was bad luck to stare at a Dandy, he couldn't turn from the awful sight. Eventually, the scarred doll-man turned his gaze back to the stage and Largo quickened his pace along the wall, though he felt even more off-balance than before.

When he'd made it halfway to the stage, Una appeared at his shoulder and took his arm. "You're late," she whispered. "Everyone is waiting." Before he could ask her what they were waiting for, Una was pulling him to the backstage entrance. The fact that she was also a doll didn't strike Largo as strange at all, as if he'd known all along that she, like the audience, was an automaton, and that she'd designed and built herself.

It didn't surprise him that the backstage crew were also dolls. What else could they be? He looked at his hands to make sure that he wasn't a doll too, but dizzy as he was, he didn't trust himself to form a definite opinion. Through the morphia haze, the prospect of losing the last vestiges of his humanity didn't seem all that terrible.

When he finally peeked at the performance on the stage, Largo saw that Remy was there alone. It was startling when he realized that she was still herself and not a doll like everybody else. But that knowledge was tempered by the fact that her performance consisted of her writhing in the seizures that had contorted her body the last time he'd seen her. He rubbed his eyes and blinked. Even though it was Remy, her movements weren't quite human. She lay on her back and moved so quickly that she was a mere blur of motion. The music from the band was a loud, discordant drone, like screeching tram tracks. Largo pushed Una away and ran to Remy's side. By the time he reached her she was gone, vanished in a blur of twisted motion.

Alone now on the stage, he looked back into the wings and saw that they were empty. Turning to the audience, he saw Remy again. Hundreds of her. The seats that had been occupied by dolls just a moment before were now all filled with writhing and flailing Remys. The shrill music swelled in volume until he realized that the sound wasn't music at all, but hundreds of Remy doppelgängers screaming in unison. The sound rose until it bored through his head like a drill. Largo jumped from the stage into the theater and began to run.

He didn't dare look back, but he knew they were coming after him, all the Remys he couldn't save. The theater seemed endless and the morphia dizziness made him stumble against the wall. Eventually, he saw the curtain to the lobby. The shrieking voices behind him rose in pitch and volume. Just before he ran into the lobby and to safety, something landed on him from behind and he was buried in a screaming darkness . . .

Largo jerked awake sweating. He checked his watch. Another two hours had passed. He was moving too slowly, burning time he didn't have. If only the hunter had pointed him to the road. Largo had given him most of his money. He fantasized about all the ways he could get even with the man if he ever saw him back in Lower Proszawa. But the thoughts didn't last long. From the theater's stage came a low animal growl. More growls followed from the edges of the room. Largo got up and backed slowly out of the theater. The growling followed him.

When he was outside, four dark forms emerged from the shadows of the lobby. They were doglike chimeras like the ones at the curio hunters' camp, but bigger. *Bitva chimeras*, he thought. *War dogs*. Worse, they were emaciated. In the goggles' amber light, he could see their ribs and the outlines of their starving skulls. Having grown up in the Green, Largo knew one rule for facing wild dog packs: don't run unless you have somewhere safe to run to. There was nowhere for him to go in the muddy bog and he didn't want to return to the theater, knowing there might be more chimeras inside.

The pack bunched together tightly, growling and snapping, pushing him back into deeper mud. In just a few steps, he was up to his shins and barely able to move. One chimera stood at the head of the pack. *The alpha*, he thought. As it moved forward, the others followed. When it got close enough that he was certain he wouldn't miss,

Largo threw the wine bottle. It hit the chimera on its side. It yipped and jumped back a few feet, taking the pack with it. But they didn't stay back for long before they closed in on him again. He took another step back and his foot came down on nothing, sinking instead into a deep watery hole. He fell backward and the chimeras sprang in his direction.

Panicked, he thrashed around in the mud. Through the wetness, Largo felt something heavy. It was a pipe. When he got to his feet and when the alpha was just an arm's length away, he swung at it as hard as he could, slamming the metal into the side of its head. The alpha flailed for a moment and fell, but the other chimeras didn't slow. Largo ducked and covered his head, but all three landed on him at the same time, knocking him onto his knees. One bit into his bad leg and another into his left arm. The third got a death grip on his coat and was slowly pulling him down. He knew that if they got him on the ground, he was finished.

He swung the pipe at the chimera on his leg and managed to knock it off. But he couldn't reach the animal on his side. He hit the dog on his arm awkwardly. It yipped and growled but didn't let go. As he reared back for another swing, the wet pipe slipped from his fingers and flew into the dark. By then, the alpha was back on its feet. Its gait was unsteady, but it came right at him.

There was a familiar pressure under his arm as the chimera on his side tried to pull him down, but for a second his panic lessened enough that he was able to think again. Largo reached under his coat and pulled out his knife.

He stabbed the chimera on his arm first and caught it in the throat. It fell thrashing into the mire. He caught one diving for his leg, driving the blade deep into its spine. Rather than fight the chimera that was trying to pull him over, he threw his weight forward and got an arm around its neck. He stabbed it blindly, over and over again. It snarled and yipped, its jaws snapping. But it finally let go of him and fell over.

Largo was facedown in the filth when he heard the alpha behind him. He tried to stand, but the mud held him firmly in place. All he could manage to do was roll over onto his back and hold the knife out just as the alpha slammed into him. Its teeth closed on his injured arm, but the bite wasn't as vicious as he'd expected. Then he saw that his knife was halfway into the animal's chest. Largo let the chimera hold on as he pushed the blade in up to the hilt.

The chimera didn't make a sound. When its bite loosened, it tried to grab him again, but couldn't. Soon it slumped over beside Largo in the quagmire. He lay on the ground for several minutes, trying to catch his breath. When he could move again, he dragged himself out of the deep mud to where he could stand. The chimeras lay around him in a semicircle and when he was certain that they were all dead, he put his knife away. Sure that the noise would have attracted any other chimeras hiding nearby, he went back into the more solid ground of the theater and fell into one of the seats.

All that waste. Creatures like that born in laboratories, bred to do nothing but kill. My chimeras would be different. They would have been, at least. Smart, beautiful, and surprising. Like Remy.

He was bleeding from his arms, leg, and side, but he decided the injuries weren't bad enough to stop his search. Mostly, he was in pain. He took four drops of morphia and lay back in the theater seat, trying to gather himself. However, the act of getting out the morphia made him remember something. He reached into his right coat pocket and found Rainer's pistol. *I could have stopped the chimeras before they even touched me*, he thought. Then he began to laugh.

When Largo opened his eyes, he realized that he'd fallen into an exhausted sleep.

Goddammit.

He started to check his watch but he knew it would only frighten him. Whatever else happened, he had to keep looking. Once he got to his feet, he found the withered tree between the hill and school and headed for it once more.

Less than an hour later, he realized that the hill he'd used as a sightline wasn't really a hill at all. It was the top of a deep bunker. When he reached the edge, he fell onto his stomach and peered down inside.

It was an astonishing sight. Spread out in the interior of the bunker were orderly rows of trucks, juggernauts, and cannons. Workers cannibalized broken equipment and used the parts to repair other vehicles and weapons. Disassembled bombs lay in pieces along one wall near rows of war Maras. Another Mara emerged from the back of the bunker, but not like any Largo had seen before. It was immense, as tall as a two-story building and as broad as a juggernaut. Workers directed it to a wrecked truck, which it picked up and moved across the bunker as easily as an adult picking up a child's doll. *Where do they get the power to run all this?* he wondered. As he moved around the edge of the bunker, he got his answer. Inside the ruined school, and under layers of cargo nets, were a series of huge plazma generators.

Largo went back to the bunker and watched the people at work. There were no slaves down there, he was certain. *These people are well trained.*

What was also interesting was that, aside from hard hats, very few of the workers wore any protective clothing at all. Largo was certain that a group this organized wouldn't work without suits because of laziness or neglect. *They know something*, he thought. Had the plague transformed into something milder, as Venohr had said? Or was it something worse? Maybe the plague stories were a ruse. A bedtime story to scare away the bay patrols and the curious. In the Green, they'd used stories about ghosts and cannibals to keep out snoops from other districts. Were these people doing the same thing?

It seemed to Largo that a group as organized as the metalworkers wouldn't bother with slaves at all. Clearly they had power and plenty of Maras. Any work that people didn't want to or couldn't do, they could teach an automaton to perform. Besides, after the fiasco with the curio hunters and his new injuries, the idea of sneaking in somewhere so well run felt suicidal.

He took out the map and looked for other camps. There were two more to the north along a nearby road. He limped along the road, but the going was slow and he didn't want to take any more morphia and risk falling asleep again. Gritting his teeth, he walked on, amusing himself by imagining Branca trying to explain his disappearance to his bosses. Maybe he'd claim that Largo had been carried off by slavers too. Would the Nachtvogel believe a story like that? He doubted it and was delighted by the idea of Branca desperately sending more and more minders into the city to find him. *Soon there won't be any ordinary people left. Just bullocks and the Nachtvogel scouring the morphia dens looking for me.*

His good mood made the walk to the first camp easier, but it died quickly when he saw that the place was deserted. Following the map farther north he found the remains of the second camp. It was nothing but charred timbers; burned and decomposing bodies were scattered in the muck. The nose and rear fins from a bomb—recently exploded, judging by the smell—lay among the carnage. Other unexploded bombs were strewn in the mud nearby. Nothing moved and the place stank of rot and decay. Largo checked his watch. Thirteen hours had passed.

How long was I in the fucking mud back there?

The map showed more camps farther north and some back east toward the curio hunters. But he knew that on foot, and moving slowly, he'd never find them and make it to the wharf in time. There was only one more camp he might be able to reach, and he'd have to hurry to get there and back to the boat.

To Largo's great surprise, the last camp was even stranger than the metal works. And the smell was staggering.

A large crew of men were digging up a vast cemetery. They tore open the ground with excavating equipment and stacked dead bodies in piles twenty feet high in some places. Trucks laden with more corpses rolled down nearby roads and dumped their cargo before turning around and heading out again.

None of the workers wore protective suits, though most wore gloves and breathing masks to keep out the stink. Largo covered his own face with his sleeve to keep from vomiting. The crew seemed well organized and he didn't see any women at all. *No Remy or Lucie*, he thought. *At least not here.*

Largo made his way around the edge of the camp to one of the roads where the trucks were bringing in bodies and followed it into the wilderness. He was off Steinmetz's map now and traveling blind.

The road curved through the remains of a district of the city. The pavement had been torn off the top, revealing bricks underneath. Largo walked past toppled high-rises and empty shopping districts. The walls of the standing structures were pitted with bullet holes and bomb damage. Crushed trucks and burned-out juggernauts lay everywhere. He followed the muddy tire tracks deeper into the ruins.

Just past a bleak stand of scorched trees, Largo found the corpse truck. The workers looked like the ones he'd seen at the larger camp. They all were men and wore breathing masks, except when they had to talk to one another. Smaller vehicles brought in more loads of bodies and dumped them by the corpse truck.

Largo had never thought about the sheer number of people who must have died here during the war. The population of Lower Proszawa was over a million and High Proszawa had been easily twice as large. That, coupled with all the soldiers, meant that he might be surrounded by a million or more corpses.

But why would anyone want them?

Before he had a chance to speculate, a familiar sight caught his eye. While workers loaded bodies onto pallets that were taken to the large corpse trucks, what actually moved the bodies was a long line of Black Widows. They were covered in filth but unmistakable. Largo hid behind the trees, watching the smooth precision of the workers and the Widows. *More professionals*, he thought. Like all the other equipment, the corpse truck was covered with muck and ooze. But the receptacle on the back was high enough that the mud only went halfway up. There was a design visible just above the dirt line. It was a bull's head over a gear, surrounded by fire. Largo tapped his goggles to make sure they were working properly, but when he looked again, the design hadn't changed. It was the carving he'd seen on the front of Baron Hellswarth's desk, his family crest and the emblem of the armaments company.

He made his way back to the cemetery as quickly as he could and hid by the side of the road. Black Widows unloaded pallets of bodies while Schöne Maschinen trucks and excavators moved through the graveyard with practiced precision.

Are they all stolen? he wondered. *They have to be. What could it profit the Baron to be involved with grave robbery?* It was too vile to think about.

Largo sat down on the muddy road. Fourteen hours had passed and he still needed to get back to the U-boat. He was freezing and covered from head to toe in mud and probably worse. He was exhausted and bleeding. And he'd accomplished nothing more than wasting his time and Rainer's money, dooming himself with the Nachtvogel, and perhaps losing any chance he had to find Remy.

Was this all a folly of ego? he thought. *I'm no hero. Look at me, lying in the mud like a child. Worse, Branca was right. I'm a fool, and not even a useful one.*

He put three drops of morphia under his tongue and headed south along the road, hoping he wasn't too late to get back onto Steinmetz's boat. He had no idea what would happen once they reached Lower Proszawa. All Largo was sure of was that he wanted—he *needed*—to get out of High Proszawa as quickly as possible.

He made it back to the wharf with half an hour to spare. He couldn't find Steinmetz or any of his crew, so he went and sat on a crate on the side of the cargo area. He'd be clear of workers and machinery there, plus he was somewhat isolated and that was exactly what he wanted. The thought of having to explain his trip to anyone made him feel angry and sick. The amber chimera light from the goggles was beginning to give him a headache, so he closed his eyes. Several minutes had passed when he felt something sharp in his side. When he opened his eyes, he saw the man with the ridiculous helmet from the curio hunter camp. A woman in a protective suit hung on his arm. She said, "I told you we'd find him here."

The curio hunter pressed his knife into Largo's side and said, "Thought you'd got away from us, didn't you?"

Largo knew he should be scared. He wanted to be scared, but all he felt was exhaustion and indifference. He said, "I didn't get away. You let me go."

Red-faced, the woman slapped the curio hunter. "You let him go, you simpleton?"

"I took his money," he said.

The woman pointed at Largo. "He's a city man," she said. "City men have lots more stuff than just money."

The hunter turned to him angrily. *The idiot is blaming me for his beating,* Largo thought. *Wonderful.*

He said, "Is she right, city man? What else you got?"

The woman slapped him again. "Don't ask his permission. Just search him," she yelled.

The hunter wheeled around to the woman. As he spoke, he emphasized each word by gesturing with the knife. "I fucking told you not to hit me like that, Marta, I fucking told you."

She got closer, sneering at him. "What you going to do, dummes junge?"

"Don't call me that," he growled.

"You child!" she yelled.

"Stop it!"

All the fear and fury Largo had bottled up for days overwhelmed him. He bolted from the crate and grabbed the hunter's knife hand. They fell to the ground, fighting all the way. The hunter thrashed and spit at him, but Largo managed to stay on top and pin the other man with his weight. Still, the hunter was able to bend the wrist holding the knife and jam the tip into the back of Largo's hand. He screamed and drove his knee into the other man's crotch. While the hunter was stunned, Largo, furious now, pulled his own knife. The hunter punched him in the side of his head and tried to gouge his fingers into Largo's eyes. Without planning, without thinking, working simply from pain and rage, Largo drove his knife into the hunter's ribs. When he realized what he'd done, he expected the man to scream. Instead he went rigid and let out a ragged, gasping breath. He struggled against Largo for a few more seconds, but there was no strength in it. Finally, he lay still.

The back of Largo's head exploded in pain.

He staggered and fell onto his back, blinded for a moment. When he was able to see again, he found Marta on top of him with a club in her hand. She was going through his inner jacket pockets. After a moment, she pulled something out and squealed with delight. Largo swung his arm up and punched her in the jaw with the knife's spiked knuckle duster. She fell off him, screaming. He tried to grab her, but she was too fast. Holding a hand to her bloody face, Marta ran around the side of the crates—and straight into Steinmetz. But she spun past him and disappeared into the crowd of wharf workers.

Steinmetz leaned over and helped Largo to his feet. "Lucky you I went looking for your silly arse. These two just about cut your trip short."

Largo fell back against the crates. He put away the knife and checked his pockets. The gun, telescope, and mask were still there, as were the Valdas in his back pocket. *The morphia*, he thought. *She got my morphia*.

Steinmetz pressed his ear to the hunter's chest.

"Is he all right?" said Largo.

"That's the wrong question, boy. Are *you* all right?"

Largo rubbed the back of his head and checked his bloody hand. The cut was long but shallow. Still, there was a lot of blood.

After his burst of anger, Largo felt dead inside. His body ached, but he seemed to have no opinion about it. Largo said, "He's dead, isn't he?"

Steinmetz knelt by the body. "He won't dance at your wedding, that's for sure."

Largo looked around the busy wharf. "Is there someone we should tell? What do we do?"

The smuggler grabbed Largo's sleeve and pulled him down beside the hunter's body. "What we do is we don't say anything to anyone. From what I saw, the prick deserved what he got. And seeing as I helped a little there at the end, I propose that we do a divvy."

"A divvy?"

Steinmetz went through the hunter's pockets and laid everything he found on the ground between them. There was a large pile of cash, more than the bills Largo had lost. *They must dig up money in the ruins*, he thought. *Pluck it from the pockets of the dead.* There were diamond bracelets and other loose jewels. There was also a round steel ball, like a pockmarked pomegranate.

"What's that?" said Largo.

Steinmetz picked it up. "This, my friend, is as insidious a toy as there ever was. It's a plague grenade."

Largo almost said that he no longer believed in the plague, but he didn't care one way or another about it anymore. All he said was "How strange."

"Strange and valuable," said Steinmetz. "You took the brunt of the beating, so you choose first. What do you want?"

Largo looked at him. "We're just going to steal it all?"

"He's not going to the bank anytime soon, don't you think?"

The light in the goggles dimmed slightly. The eighteen hours were up. *Time to go home*, he thought.

"Well?" said Steinmetz impatiently.

"Can I have the money?" said Largo. "You can have everything else."

The smuggler pushed the cash to Largo. He put the grenade in his pocket and handed Largo a small diamond bracelet. He said, "If I took all of them, I'd feel like I'd taken advantage of you."

Largo looked at it. The stones sparkled in the light. He held it out to Steinmetz and said, "I don't know what I'd do with it."

Frowning, Steinmetz said, "You're not much of a negotiator, are you? Listen, this mysterious person you were looking for. Was it a woman?"

"Yes," said Largo.

"And you didn't find her?"

"No."

"There you go," Steinmetz said. "She's probably waiting for you in the city. You can give it to her when you see her. But don't tell her you tried to give it away. She'll think you're as mad as you are dumb."

Largo put the bracelet in his pocket with the cash. Too tired to argue, he said, "I'm sure you're right."

"Let's get to the boat before somebody sees us."

"Do we just leave the body here?"

"Unless you want to take him home as a souvenir."

Steinmetz pulled Largo to his feet and they walked to the U-boat. The rest of the crew were lounging on the gangway, but when they got a look at the blood on Largo's face and hands, they stepped out of his way. He went straight to his cabin, took off his wet coat, and threw it on the floor with the goggles. Dropping his weight onto the bunk, he lay down. Every inch of him ached. With his knife, he cut out some of the coat's lining and used it to wrap his bleeding hand. If the chimera bites were bleeding too, he thought, there was nothing he could do about it. He was going to get the bunk bloody.

If Steinmetz gets angry, he can take back the damn bracelet. What am I supposed to say when Remy asks where I got it? "It's a funny story, dear. You see, I murdered a man for it."

Soon Largo heard the engine grind to life and his ears popped. He relaxed a little, knowing they were on their way. He felt a kind of dull relief as they left High Proszawa behind. He thought of the colorful banners in Lower Proszawa and the patriotic songs people would be singing to rouse themselves for the glory of a new war. He touched the gash on his cheek and fantasized about murdering all of them— stabbing them like he had the curio hunter and then listening to the last breaths leaving their bodies. He wanted to show them the cruel stupidity that he'd seen and shove their faces in it. Instead, he closed his eyes, and when he opened them again, several hours had passed and Steinmetz was standing in his cabin doorway.

CHAPTER NINETEEN

MIND IF I COME IN?" HE SAID.

Largo sat up on the bunk. "Of course not. I think I was asleep."

"Having strange dreams? That will happen," said Steinmetz. "Killing isn't easy, especially the first time. But you'll get over it."

"I'm not sure I want to."

"It can't be helped. Now it's all horror and nightmares. In a month, the memory will begin to lose focus. In a year, it will feel like it happened a lifetime ago. In two years, it won't even have happened to you. It will be a story you read in a yellowsheet or saw in the cinema."

The idea of forgetting about the curio hunter troubled Largo, but he nodded, knowing that Steinmetz was trying to help him. "That will be a relief," he said.

The smuggler had a small medical kit with him. "Is there one damn inch of you that isn't bloody?" he said. "I don't know if I have enough bandages to swaddle you like a baby, but I have alcohol so you can clean your wounds."

Largo wiped his hand and cheek. It stung like fire, but the pain was good. He felt like he was waking up into his body again. By the time he was finished with the chimera bites and the knot on the back of his skull, his head began to clear. He said, "That feels better."

"I'd offer you morphia, only we're out. But I can offer you some whiskey."

"I could use a drink."

"Come to the control room, then. There's plenty."

The smuggler opened the door. There was a clean pea coat hanging from a pipe outside the cabin. "That's yours, if you want it," he said.

"Another present from a dead man?"

"It is indeed."

"You can have it."

"Keep it," said Steinmetz. "It's bad luck to trade a dead man's things too many times."

"I'll remember that."

"Before we go up, strap on that knife of yours. Between that and the bloody bandages, none of the men will be giving you grief again."

"That would be nice," said Largo.

Several whiskeys later, Largo went back to his cabin. It was cold in the U-boat without Rainer's coat, so he put on the pea coat Steinmetz had left for him. He soon fell into a deep, black sleep. There was no Remy or Lucie or home. There was just the darkness and the rumble of trucks. Largo opened his eyes, half-awake. He knew that the constant mechanical sound was really the U-boat's engine pushing them under the bay, but all he could think of was an endless procession of dirty trucks.

He woke up to Steinmetz shaking his shoulder. The smuggler said, "Get your gear together. We've landed."

Largo got up and transferred everything from Rainer's coat into his new one, then headed for the control room. He felt cold and his hands trembled slightly. He needed morphia.

Pallenberg was waiting at the bottom of the ladder. "I don't suppose you want to sell that knife of yours?" he said.

Largo shook his head. "No. It's a gift from a dear friend. I'm looking forward to returning it to him."

When he started up the ladder, Pallenberg grabbed his shoulder. "I'll give you a good price for it."

Largo shoved him away. "Touch me again, my fine brother, and you'll get the knife, but not how you'd like."

Pallenberg stepped around to the far side of the ladder and backed away. He said, "It was just an idea."

Largo went up the ladder quickly, suddenly wanting to be outside. His stomach cramped, but not too badly. Still, he knew that if he didn't get morphia soon, he'd be helpless.

It was a chilly night on the canal along Haxan Green. Largo

walked down the gangway and stood next to Steinmetz. He said, "I suppose you'll want a ride back into the city."

"I'd appreciate it. I can pay."

"Don't bother. There's someone I want to surprise with a ruby or two. What about you?"

Largo thought about it for a moment. "I'm not sure what I'm going to do," he said. Then, "Can you drop me in the Midden?"

"That shit pile? Why there? Nothing is open at this hour."

"There's just something I have to do."

Steinmetz walked to the shed where he'd left the motorcycle. "Let's go, then. While you're wandering those sorrowful streets, I'll be slipping into clean sheets with a close friend."

The memory of Remy stabbed him, or it might have been the chimera bite in his side. Still, Largo smiled. "I hope you both have a fine night."

The trip to the Midden was faster without the rain. When they reached the outskirts, Largo climbed out of the sidecar and shook Steinmetz's hand.

"Thank you for everything. I might be dead without you."

Steinmetz laughed. "From the look of you, all you did up there was almost die. Did you find anything you were looking for?"

Largo thought about it. "I know that Remy isn't up there. I know that alive or dead, she's in Lower Proszawa. That's not much, but it's something."

"Take care, Largo," said the smuggler. "And tell that bastard Rainer that I took good care of you."

"I will."

Steinmetz gunned the motorcycle and sped away. Largo fell against the side of a building. He didn't have to pretend to be all right anymore. His hands shook violently and he felt cramped and cold. The ache in his right leg returned, so he limped down the Midden's main street until he came to the office of one of the district's charnel house doctors. After a quick look around, Largo broke a pane in the office's front door and let himself in.

The room was lit only by the moon. He wished he still had the amber goggles. The office stank like the back of a butcher shop. A day ago, that would have bothered him, but the smell was nothing compared to High Proszawa.

He moved around the office, hunting for morphia. By the door to a back room, he found a locked cabinet. He smashed it open with the knife and took a handful of boxes to the front window so he could read the labels. When he didn't find any morphia, he dropped the boxes on the floor and went back for more.

His second trip was luckier. He found a large box with several vials of morphia inside. Largo put the knife back in its harness and began to open one.

From the back of the office, someone shouted, "Who's there? Don't move, you bastard."

He froze. All he could see was a shadow with an axe in its hand. It seemed to be looking around.

"What's that in your hand? Give it to me," shouted the shadow.

Largo clutched the morphia to his chest. He couldn't run and he couldn't reach his knife.

The shadow advanced a step. "Don't worry, thief," it said. "I'm a doctor. I know where a chop will hurt the most."

When the shadow took another step, Largo pulled Rainer's pistol from his pocket and fired once into the floor. He said, "Put down the axe."

The shadow dropped it.

Largo was shaking all over. His stomach knotted and he almost doubled over. "I'm sorry, but I don't know where else to get it," he said. "I have money, though." He put the morphia into his jacket and took out some bills. "Tell me how much."

The shadow had its hands in the air. "Keep your money. Take what you want and go."

"But I can pay you."

"Please, just go."

Largo put the bills back in his pocket. A small crowd had gathered outside, drawn by the sound of the gunshot. Before he went out, Largo put on Rainer's mask. He pointed the pistol at the curious group and they backed away.

"Farther," he said.

When he was satisfied that they had moved far enough away, he ran to the end of the street and stumbled out of the Midden as quickly as he could.

He rounded another corner and ducked into an alley that looked to him like where the residents of the district burned trash. He climbed over mounds of ashes, half-burnt furniture, and torn military posters until he was hidden from the street.

Hunkering down on the dirty ground, Largo tried to catch his breath. He listened as some of the crowd from the doctor's office walked by the alley discussing what they should do if they caught him. When the street was quiet again, he took the mask off and opened a morphia vial. Because his hands were shaking, he missed his mouth entirely and lost some down the front of his coat. Eventually, he managed to put four drops under his tongue. The relief was immediate and warming. But he still felt awful.

Look at me. I can't go on like this. Morphia will kill me if I don't stop. On the other hand, why bother living? In the past day I killed a man and almost shot another. There's nothing left of me. I'm gone.

Rather than making him depressed, in a strange way, the thought energized him. Remy's disappearance and the Nachtvogel were a gun to his head. In High Proszawa, he'd pulled the trigger.

I can do whatever I have to now. There are no reasons for fear or limits anymore. I'm free.

Largo put the mask back on and went to the other end of the alley. The street was clear, so he walked out of the Midden and back to the tram line on Messerberg. Though the tram ran all night, at four A.M. it came only on the half hour. He took off the mask and waited in a small commuter shelter on the curb, considering his options. He couldn't return to his flat. The Nachtvogel would be watching it. He couldn't go to Remy's flat because another tenant would likely see him and report him to the police. So where else could he go?

When the tram arrived twenty minutes later, Largo had an idea. He stepped into a deserted car and took off his pea coat. His pants and shoes were caked in dried mud, but he was able to wipe most of the ashes off his coat by the time the tram reached the center of the city. He put the mask back on and headed for the bars and dance halls along the edge of Kromium. There, he found a Mara cab and gave it an address across town. Sitting in the soft back seat he felt safer than he had in days. He watched Lower Proszawa slide by outside. Police and armed Maras pushed through the night crowds. Red-faced men gave impassioned speeches to cheering crowds. Largo felt as far from his home as a gull blown out to sea.

It was five in the morning when he knocked on the door.

A moment later, Roland opened it and frowned at what he saw. "Yes? Can I help you?" he said.

Largo took off the mask and said, "It's me. Largo. I know it's a ridiculous hour, but can I come in?"

Roland's face relaxed and he said, "Of course."

When he was in the flat he heard Parvulesco call from the bathroom. "Who is it?"

"Largo," said Roland. "And he seems to have joined the navy."

Parvulesco rushed into the living room with shaving cream on half of his face. "What are you talking about?"

Largo said, "He's joking. The coat was a gift. Mine was unsalvageable."

"Where have you been the last couple of days?" said Parvulesco. "Branca has been going mad. Barking at everyone. He almost hit Andrzej yesterday. Not for screwing up, but for being too nice."

"Do you mind if I sit down?" said Largo, suddenly exhausted.

Roland cleared a place on their sofa, which was covered in books and yellowsheets. "Make yourself comfortable."

Largo sat down and put his head in his hands. Parvulesco sat next to him. "Are you all right? I have to admit that this is unexpected after you telling me to stay away."

"I know," Largo said. "And I still mean it. We can't be seen together. But don't worry. No one saw me come here."

"What have you been up to?" said Roland. "Why do you look like warmed-over hell and why are you wearing that absurd coat?"

Largo laughed. "Because I've been to sea," he said. "On a U-boat."

"What the hell are you talking about?"

"It's true. I was on a smuggler's ship to High Proszawa. I just got back a couple of hours ago."

"High Proszawa? Are you serious?" said Parvulesco.

"Completely," Largo said. He looked at Roland. "I'm sorry."

"About what?" said Roland.

"The war. I never imagined that it could be that horrible. Hundreds of bodies everywhere. Some in the mud. Some stacked up like logs outside a country cabin."

Roland looked at him for a moment, his eyes moving from the bloody rips in Largo's coat to his crudely bandaged hand. "You mean it, don't you? You were really there."

Largo rubbed the knot on the back of his head. He meant to say, "Yes," but instead blurted, "I killed a man."

Parvulesco whispered, "What?"

Roland grabbed a chair and pulled it to the sofa. "Tell me exactly what happened."

Largo told them about the curio hunters' camp and how later, the hunter had been waiting for him with Marta. He showed them the wound on his hand where the hunter had stabbed him.

"It sounds like self-defense to me," said Roland. "Did anyone see you do it?"

"Just the woman," Largo said. "And she's not quite in a position to be calling the bullocks."

"Then you're probably all right. I doubt your smuggler friends will be alerting the authorities either."

Largo felt a great relief at confessing to the killing, at least to Roland. Now someone who understood and whom he trusted knew. But he wasn't sure how Parvulesco would take the news.

"What the hell were you doing there in the first place?" Parvulesco said.

He almost didn't want to answer. It seemed so mad now, like something a lunatic might do. "I was looking for Remy. I'd heard that slavers sometimes kidnapped people and brought them north. But it's a lie. There's no one there who doesn't want to be."

Parvulesco looked at Roland and then at the clock on the wall. "Listen, I have to get to the company. Will you be here when I get back?"

Largo looked up. "If you'll let me."

Roland put the chair back across the room. "Of course you can stay. But I have to go to work too."

"There's food and beer in the icebox," said Parvulesco, heading back to the bathroom. "Make yourself at home. I want to hear everything tonight."

Largo sat back on the sofa and took another drop of morphia. When Parvulesco was leaving, Largo handed him the box with the rest of the vials. "Will you get rid of these for me? I'll keep using it if I have it, and I want to stop."

"What do you want me to do with it?"

"Throw it away. Give it to a friend. Sell it. Just, please, get it away from me."

He headed out. Roland gave Largo a key and said, "If you go out, be sure to wear the mask."

"I will," Largo said.

"Good. We'll see you tonight."

Largo went to the window and watched them go. There was such ease in the way they left, each off to his own job—a certainty of return. Each knew that the other would be back later that evening. Watching them, Largo felt a tightness in his chest, and it had nothing to do with wanting morphia. He pictured dozens of mornings with Remy. A kiss or a touch of the hand, and the same certainty that they'd be back together soon. It hurt so much knowing that the last time they'd left each other, Remy had hated him. It was a hate that under normal circumstances they would have fixed and made right. As much as he knew that he would keep looking for her, Largo was certain that he'd never see her again.

Parvulesco and Roland's flat was larger than his. Their living room was half again the size of the one in Little Shambles. And they had their own private bath. Largo went into it and washed his face and hands. Though he'd wiped his coat clean, there were ashes in his hair and his hands were sooty enough that he had to wipe a black ring from the sink when he finished washing. He looked at himself in the mirror. The lacerations on his face and hand would definitely leave scars. There were dry islands of blood on his shirt around the chimera bites. His pants were torn and stiff with blood and dried mud. His shoes and socks were unsalvageable. *With the mask I'm anonymous, but I'll draw attention anywhere I go in these clothes*, he thought. After debating it for another minute or so, Largo put on his mask and went out.

He took a tram to Tin Fahrspur and went to the shop he'd visited with Remy and the others to buy his new work clothes. A young woman gasped when she saw him and Largo noticed other shoppers watching him out of the corners of their eyes. He didn't waste a lot of time deciding on what to buy. He grabbed a plain white button-down shirt, black work pants, and a pair of boots.

As he was paying, someone bumped into his shoulder. Largo turned and found himself face-to-face with Andrzej. Weimer was by the door looking at vests.

"I'm so sorry, sir," said Andrzej. He took a step back. "Please forgive me."

In a low, gruff voice Largo said, "It's all right." He pushed past him and hurried for the door.

"Thank you for all you've done," Andrzej called.

At the entrance, Weimer held out his hand to shake. Largo nodded to him, but didn't put out his hand. He hurried from the shop, wondering if Branca was grooming one of them to be the new head courier. Maybe he was grooming both, his new useful fools.

Largo went straight back to Parvulesco and Roland's flat, stopping only to buy a bottle of whiskey at a nearby shop.

Back inside, he changed into the new clothes, tying the old ones in the brown paper in which the clerk had wrapped his new ones. He took the bundle to a garbage chute down the hall and threw it in. His hands were shaking but he wasn't sure if it was from lack of morphia or seeing Andrzej and Weimer.

The imbeciles are like ticks. You don't see them until they're burrowing into your skin. Am I ever going to get free from Branca and his parasites?

Largo sat down on the sofa and opened the whiskey, wishing he never had to leave the flat again.

THE WONDERS OF THE SOUTH

From a prewar Lower Proszawa tourist brochure

Explore Lovely Heldenblut Bay!

Are you looking for a cheerful and relaxing excursion for the entire family? Come to Lower Proszawa's greatest attraction, Das Kaas Wunder Urlaubsort.

More than a simple hotel or theme park, it's a complete entertainment experience.

Our 100-room lodge features five dining rooms and even a theater where guests can revel in performances by Lower Proszawa's most talented singers and dancers.

Do you prefer fun in nature? Try the resort's outdoor water park with wading pools for the children, and for the adults, we have both cold and heated pools fed by the healthful waters of the bay.

Spend the day plying the placid bay waters on a sailboat and see sights from a vantage point no landlubber can experience. For those who prefer to remain on shore, we offer horseback tours of the nearby hills.

For the children we have play and crafts areas watched over by education professionals. And just for the little ones, don't forget our chimera zoo. Under the watchful eyes of trained animal handlers, they can interact with and learn about these gentle wonders of modern science.

Our Mara staff is available to you 24 hours a day, whether you require nanny services, a middle-of-the-night snack, or a drink from our prize-winning wine cellar.

Stay a day, a week, or more. Das Kaas Wunder Urlaubsort exists only to entertain fun-seeking, adventurous families along the vibrant and unspoiled waters of Heldenblut Bay, one of the natural marvels of the Proszawan world.

CHAPTER TWENTY

THAT EVENING, LARGO TOLD PARVULESCO AND ROLAND EVERYTHING THAT had happened in High Proszawa. The only thing he left out was the incident in the doctor's office in the Midden. It felt too raw and shameful.

Roland said, "I'd heard rumors of looters, but never anything about the scale of it. Or the grave robbing. Were they taking valuables from the bodies?"

"If they were, I missed it," said Largo. "I'm afraid that once I saw the corpses I couldn't think at all for a while."

"Don't feel bad. It happened to all of us. Nothing normal prepares you for that kind of death."

"Are you sure about the plague?" said Parvulesco. "Maybe you should go to a hospital for a checkup."

Largo took a sip of his whiskey. "Whatever plague there was, it's not there now. I'm certain of it. I wish I could talk to Dr. Venohr."

"Why?"

"He thinks the plague is the source of the Drops. I wish I could tell him he was wrong and that he needs to look elsewhere if he's trying to cure it."

Parvulesco said, "How are you feeling?"

Largo pulled his coat around himself. "All right. I'm cold, but the whiskey warms me up. And it helps numb the cramps."

"Is there anyone you want us to let know that you're back and safe?" said Roland.

A tremor passed through Largo's hands and he almost dropped his glass. "No one. It's too dangerous. I shouldn't even be here. Tonight I'll go to one of the rooming houses for Dandies."

"As sick as you are?" said Parvulesco.

"How long before the withdrawal eases?" Roland said.

"A day or two."

"All right," said Parvulesco. "If you still want to go, you can go then."

Largo gulped more whiskey, as it felt like his insides were turning to ice. "Thank you. I don't know how I can repay you."

"You've already paid me plenty," said Parvulesco. "After you disappeared, Branca made me head courier. I'm making almost twice my normal pay."

"And a longer lunch hour," said Roland.

"That too!"

Largo looked at Parvulesco. "There's something you need to know about the head courier position. You're a Nachtvogel spy."

Parvulesco went pale. "What?"

"It's true. They want you to collect fingerprints and photos. You'll also be delivering packages the Nachtvogel can use as an excuse to arrest people."

"Is that what you were doing?"

"I didn't find out until later. But you know now, at the beginning. You can do something about it."

"That's easy," said Parvulesco. "I'll do something stupid and get demoted."

"That's not a good idea. Branca's smart and he knows you are too. He'll suspect something if you're suddenly bad at your job."

"Then what should I do?"

"You could quit," said Roland.

Largo said, "I don't think that's a good idea either."

"You two aren't very much help, are you?" said Parvulesco.

Largo thought for a minute. "Get hurt. Fall off your bicycle. Pretend you ran into a truck. Anything that will keep you off your feet long enough that Branca has to appoint a new head courier."

"But that person will be a spy too," said Roland.

"True, but there's nothing you can do about it," said Largo. He tried to pour more whiskey but couldn't hold his glass still. Parvulesco poured for him. "All you can do now is not get in any deeper with the Nachtvogel. If you pretend you're hurt badly enough it will give you an excuse to quit in a week or two."

"All right," said Parvulesco uncertainly. "I don't like it, but I suppose it's the only way out."

"I'm surprised Branca didn't appoint someone meaner, who wouldn't care about spying on people, like Andrzej or Weimer," said Largo.

"I think he wanted to, but since they've been back, aside from being nicer, they're both dumber. They make mistakes all the time. I'm surprised Branca hasn't fired them."

After thinking about it Largo said, "Maybe they're spies too and Branca can't afford to fire them. Branca will have a reason and it will be something awful."

Parvulesco looked at Roland. "Instead of having lunch, would you like to run me off the road tomorrow?"

Roland raised his eyebrows. "I think Largo's point is that you don't have to actually be hurt. You can pretend to be hurt."

"That's a much better idea. I like that," said Parvulesco.

"It might not be a bad idea to have a black eye or at least some scrapes," said Largo.

"Damn. You're right. Roland, instead of running me off the road, would you give me a boxing lesson?"

"That I can do," Roland said. "There are lots of ways to cause bruises that won't hurt too much."

"Are there any that don't hurt at all?"

Roland shook his head. "I'm afraid not."

Parvulesco sighed and poured himself some of Largo's whiskey. "Serves me right for being ambitious."

"Have you seen Margit?" said Largo.

"Not since before you left. No one's heard a word."

Between the cramps and chills, Largo felt a spasm of guilt. Maybe instead of running off on a fool's errand up north, he should have stayed and helped her. Not joined her group, but given her ideas on how to get around the city undetected. *Maybe I should go back to the Black Palace*, he thought. *Though, if she's not there, I might not get a warm welcome*. Still, after what he saw in the north, if her cabal was trying to stop the war, he knew he had to take the chance.

When I'm past the worst of the sickness, I'll go to them.

They talked into the night until Largo couldn't fight the withdrawal any longer and vomited in the bathroom. He told them, "I'm going to get worse tonight and unpleasant to be around."

"We should be going to sleep soon anyway," said Roland.

Parvulesco said, "Are you sure you don't want someone to sit up with you?"

Largo tried to speak, but the cramps doubled him over. When he could talk again he said, "I'll be fine. I've been through this before. I just need time to get the morphia out of my system."

"All right. If you need help, just knock on our door."

"I will. Don't worry."

After they went to bed, Largo's symptoms grew worse. After almost vomiting on his new clothes, he stripped naked and curled up on the floor of the small bathroom. He spent the remainder of the night crawling back and forth between the toilet and the shower. Occasionally he turned on the water, both to clean himself and to get warm.

In the morning, Parvulesco helped him from the bathroom to the sofa and covered him with a blanket. He slept most of the day, with periodic desperate trips to the bathroom. By the time Parvulesco and Roland came home, he felt better enough to even consider eating.

"What should I make?" said Parvulesco.

"Nothing," said Largo. "Let me at least buy you dinner. I passed a hofbräu nearby. I'll go and bring food back here."

"Why don't I go with you?" said Roland.

"No. I'll be slow, and besides, aren't you supposed to give Parvulesco a boxing lesson?"

Parvulesco let his head drop slightly. He said, "I was hoping everyone would forget about that."

"I didn't," said Roland. "Let me get some gloves and we'll go up to the roof."

"You're too good to me," Parvulesco said, making a sour face.

Largo got dressed and put on the mask. He had to stop twice on the way to the hofbräu, but the fresh air felt good. The walk back was easier, and he made it without stopping. As he climbed the stairs to the flat on the second floor, Largo heard shouts.

At the top of the stairs, he saw two police officers leading Parvulesco and Roland from their flat in handcuffs. Two more officers came out, followed by Special Operative Tanz.

He said, "We know he's been staying with you. Where is he?"

"I told you, we haven't seen him in days," shouted Parvulesco.

"Shut up," said Tanz. "We know he's been here."

"Whoever told you that is lying," said Roland.

Largo started down the hall toward the group. When Roland and Parvulesco saw him, Roland shook his head slightly. *He wants me to walk by*, thought Largo.

Tanz looked at him. "Mind your own business, Dandy," he said. Then, "Have you seen anyone with these Eierschlürfers?"

Largo shook his head.

"Where are you going?"

Largo pointed to the next floor.

Tanz moved his head in the direction of the stairs. "Then get going and not a word of this to anyone."

Largo walked to the stairs. He looked at Parvulesco and Roland, hoping to catch either's eye, but they stared straight ahead. Largo's stomach felt like it would float up his throat and choke him. As he took the first step up he heard, "You two, take them away. You other two wait here in case he comes back."

Largo missed the step and fell against the railing, feeling sick and dizzy. The bag tumbled from his hands. He couldn't walk any farther. As he stumbled against the wall Parvulesco and Roland were being led away.

Tanz stared at him. "I told you to move on. Or are you deaf as well as ugly?"

Largo's head spun. He put a hand on the wall to steady himself. With his other hand, he pulled Rainer's pistol and shot Tanz in the face.

When he fell, the officers with Parvulesco and Roland dragged them downstairs. The other two policemen fumbled to pull their pistols and Largo shot them both. He ran for the stairs when he heard another loud *bang* and his left shoulder felt like it was on fire. One of the officers he'd shot was on his knees in the hall firing at him. Largo ducked and shot back. The officer fell back against the wall and dropped his gun. Largo ran down the stairs. But he was too late.

A police juggernaut was speeding away from the building. Largo thought about shooting at it, but he knew he'd be more likely to hit someone in the street. Rather than wait for more police to arrive, he went back inside the building's vestibule and took Parvulesco's bicycle. He could feel blood trickling down his shoulder and his arm was numb. It was difficult steering the bicycle with one hand, but he had no choice. He went through a small park nearby and took an employees' path behind the greenhouses. It let him out on a suburban street. He rode through the quiet avenues until he turned abruptly, taking narrow lanes out of the district until he reached Lysergsäurehof.

Rainer's elaborate gate had been torn off and lay in pieces on the ground. There was an X of police warning tape over the open door and a Health Department quarantine poster on the wall. It read DISEASE ZONE. ENTRY IS FORBIDDEN. In smaller lettering underneath it said, *For your safety, report all suspected cases of the Drops to the Health Department immediately.*

Largo left the bicycle behind a line of dying shrubs and crawled under the police tape. He crept up the stairs as quietly as he could.

Rainer's flat had been ransacked. Much of the furniture was overturned. The drawers in all the cabinets and cases had been pulled out. Rainer's telescopes and star charts were gone.

If the bullocks want to convince people Rainer died from the Drops, they'll have to do better than this.

The spiritualist posters were still on the wall, but Rainer's medium boards were in pieces on the floor. Largo went to the wall, tore off the photo of Vera Baal, and crumpled it in his hand. Above it was a colorful poster for someone called the Astonishing Szamanka. He ripped it in half. To his surprise, there was another poster underneath. He pulled down the rest of the Astonishing Szamanka and found a parody of a government recruitment placard. The image was the same brave soldier in uniform as on the official posters, but where it should have read *To War! To War! Destroy the Enemy or Be Destroyed!* the word *Enemy* had been replaced with *Politicians.* There was a small target symbol in the bottom right corner of the poster. Largo remembered it from the leaflet Pietr had given him. *Rainer had joined the radicals*, he thought. *Right to the end, he was braver than me. An older brother I could have looked up to. Now he's surely dead. Where was I when he needed me? Chasing my own tail through the mud.*

Largo took off the mask and pea coat and went into Rainer's bathroom. He didn't dare turn on the lights, but illumination from the nearby harbor lit the room with a faint glow. The bullet had only grazed his shoulder and hadn't gone in. Still, a piece of his flesh the size of his little finger was missing. He found gauze and used it to pack the wound. With one hand, he clumsily wrapped his shoulder in a bandage. He was sweating by the time he was finished and beginning to feel nauseated again. The adrenaline that had moved him across the city was fading quickly. He vomited and went back to the living room.

Whoever had searched the flat had sliced open Rainer's mattress with a knife, but his blankets were undamaged. With his good arm, Largo dragged them into the living room, lay down on the single intact sofa, and pulled the blankets on top of him. However, his shoulder hurt too much for him to sleep. He went back into the bathroom, but the only painkiller he could find was morphia. So that he wouldn't be tempted, he poured it into the toilet. There was a half-full bottle of whiskey in one of the cupboards. He took it back to the sofa and sipped it until the pain faded.

Largo awoke to the sound of rain on the windows. His head pounded and his shoulder ached.

Maybe the whiskey wasn't the best idea. When he stumbled into the bathroom this time he could finally see the contents of Rainer's medicine cabinet clearly. There was a nearly full bottle of aspirin, which he took to the kitchen. When he couldn't find any water, he washed down a handful of the pills with another sip of whiskey.

It could have been the withdrawal symptoms or the frigid bay air, but the room felt icy. While he'd been afraid to light a fire at night when it might be seen, now that it was daylight he piled kindling and wood in the fireplace and lit them. Even when the wood caught, it took a few minutes for the heat to penetrate his body. He dragged one of the blankets from the sofa and sat by the fire until he was warm enough to think clearly.

The bandage on his shoulder was soaked through with blood. Once he was warm enough, he got the gauze and bandages and rewrapped it. The wound hurt more now than it had last night and the simple act of wrapping it made him unsteady.

When Largo was warm and the dizziness had passed he realized he was desperately hungry. *When was the last time I ate?* he wondered. In the kitchen, he found a tin of crackers and some cheese in an ice chest. After wolfing half of it, he put the rest away for later and sat by the fire.

With food in his stomach and the aspirin dulling the pain in his shoulder, he thought over his options and came up with one that didn't require him making the journey all the way to Machtviertel.

As Largo waited for nightfall, he tried to think of anything but Remy, but images of their time together—and their final fight—always came back and pushed all other thoughts out of his head. His memories of High Proszawa weren't any better. For all that had happened to him, all that truly mattered to him at this point were the piles of corpses and the fact that he was now a murderer. *Four times a murderer, in fact. I can never take that back. The only thing that can possibly make up for it is finding Remy and saving Parvulesco and Roland.* He checked his watch. It was still several hours until dark. He lay back down on the sofa and found a spiritualist magazine. When he couldn't stand any more of the talk of ghosts and visitations he threw it into the fire.

He slept for much of the afternoon. When the sun set he took more aspirin and changed his bandage. There were several clean shirts in Rainer's closet. He chose a black one that would hide blood if he started bleeding again. A heavy coat hung from a hook inside the closet door. He transferred everything into the new coat and threw the pea coat in the fire so that it couldn't be traced back to Steinmetz.

At least I can keep one person out of this mess.

Largo felt much better after the long nap. He even could use his left arm if he was careful. After dousing the fireplace embers, he put on the mask and left the flat, careful to duck under the police tape on his way out. Parvulesco's bicycle was still behind the withered bushes. A car drove past him as he rode out of Lysergsäurehof, but he kept riding, even when someone shouted at him.

"You there," a man called. "Stop where you are."

He didn't need to see their uniforms or their guns. Largo recognized the tone of the man's voice.

Bullocks. Shit.

Swerving left, he went down a walkway too narrow for the car to follow. He could hear it backing up as he rounded another corner that took him along a line of loading areas for trucks going to and from the shipping companies that used to dot the district. He was running parallel to the main road so that if the police were following him or trying to cut him off, he'd be able to see them.

Largo hit his brakes when he came to the end of the loading area. There were no side streets here, just an open lane that led to a roundabout. He waited for the police car to pass him on the main road, then sped through the long turn behind it, heading for the center of the city, with its side streets and dark alleys. However, someone in the police car must have seen him go by because it turned off the round-about and sped toward him. Largo slowed just enough for them to get within a few yards of his back wheel. Then he veered quickly to the right and right again, retracing his steps back toward Lysergsäurehof. The police car tried to follow him, but fishtailed on the wet pavement.

By the time he headed back out of the district, he'd lost the car. He still wanted to head deeper into the city but knew he couldn't do it in a straight line. *They might have sent out my description on the wireless.* He had no choice but to take a circuitous route around the city, similar to the way he'd gone when he thought Andrzej and Weimer were going to ambush him.

After he passed a second police car, Largo grew nervous. Neither of them had followed him, but he wanted to get off the road as quickly as possible. A Dandy on a bicycle was a rare enough sight that he knew he'd stand out anywhere he went. He turned north, and when he saw lights ahead he pedaled straight for them.

THE SHAPE OF THE WORLD

From *Noble Aspirations and Hard Realities: Life in Lower Proszawa* by Ralf Moessinger, author of *High Proszawa: A Dream in Stone*

Seagulls wheel over Heldenblut Bay. They squawk and call to each other, soaring higher than the flying Maras. But there is a commonality in their actions. They are all looking down at the *things* moving over and just under the surface of the water.

Subtle changes in wind patterns nudge the birds and the flying eyes first in one direction, then another. From the ground, passersby who look up often note this and feel sympathy for both the gulls and the winged contraptions. "They're trapped," the observers say.

But if the observers continue to watch, they notice something quite different. What at first appear to be random turns and pivots are anything but. The gulls and Maras aren't battling the wind—they are allied with it. For long periods, they ride on the gusts like ships on the sea, hardly flapping their wings except when using them to turn and dive. And when either group, the feathered or the mechanistic, is done with their time in the sky, they glide off for their home perches, whether out at sea or on a government ship in the south bay. The observers shake their heads and feel sorry for them while at the same time sure of their own superiority. On the ground, they are free to go wherever they want, whenever they want. They aren't slaves to the whims of the air, they declare. Which is true enough. But if they were to look further, the observers will see how they are also trapped, and by something more prosaic and sinister.

When I first spoke to Sabine Galeen, she planned to leave Lower Proszawa and raise her infant son with family in the western colony of Veidtland, away from the debauchery of the city. She had a small family inheritance and since her husband had been killed in the war, she had his pension. However, it wasn't enough to afford airship tickets, so after submitting the forms for their travel papers, she began looking for a boat on which to book passage.

Before the Great War, luxury liners, fishing trawlers, sailboats, and freighters plied the waters around both High and Lower Proszawa. Goods moved in and out of the cities continuously, ferried in from the colonies and carrying goods out to allies around the world. However, the situation changed on the day the first shots of war were heard, and nothing on the water had been quite right since.

Heldenblut Bay, with its rivers and tributaries, became a battlefield during the war, and even the armistice hasn't healed all of its wounds. Just below the surface of the waters surrounding High and Lower Proszawa lie the broken hulks of military and merchant ships. Along with them in the deep water, rolling this way and that like sluggish seaweed, are underwater mines weighted to the bay floor.

This treacherous array of war machines makes travel by all but the smallest boats precarious at best. Lower Proszawa's own merchant ships chance the waters on a regular basis because the city needs constant replenishment, but sea travel as the city once knew it has virtually disappeared. And because it's surrounded on three sides by unfriendly neighbors, Lower Proszawa resembles nothing less than an island prison.

In subsequent interviews, Frau Galeen revealed that her first attempt to obtain travel papers was refused because of a clerical error. Assured that it would take months to correct and resubmit the papers, she bribed the forms solicitor, who delivered them in a few weeks. After that, she managed to find passage on a freighter carrying a dangerous load of coal oil to one of the colonies. However, when she and her child arrived at the ship on the day of their departure, they were refused admittance because her cabin had been given to a city official and his family. According to Frau Galeen, it took her two weeks of searching to find the correct office where she could be reimbursed for the ticket.

By then, winter was approaching and the seas were becoming more treacherous. Frau Galeen said that she finally booked passage on an old steamer that would take weeks to reach Veidtland. However, as the ship made its way into port in Lower Proszawa, it struck a mine and sank. The freight company declared bankruptcy and this time she wasn't able to recoup the price of her ticket. With her options—and money—running low, she and her son returned to the little house she shared with her late husband's family in Granate. There she remains to this day, like so many others, a hostage in her home country—and out a considerable amount of her inheritance.

Each day, the yellowsheets carry stories trumpeting government solutions to the travel and supplies situation, each more fantastic than the next. Undersea railways and ocean-spanning pneumatic tubes. Long-distance airships and freighters that can travel vast distances without a single human aboard, controlled only by Maras with what they term "mechanistic intelligence."

Frau Galeen devours the stories with a mix of envy and excitement. She wants the future to happen immediately so that she and her son can be on their way and out of the crowded little house. The yellowsheets assure her that these and other wonders are just around the corner and that there is nothing stopping this glorious new world now that Lower Proszawa is finally and forever at peace.

Yet she and so many others remain waiting for a miracle to save them. According to Frau Galeen, the most maddening part of her story is that there are a handful of ships that still carry citizens in and out of Lower Proszawa every day. But, as she puts it, "Like so many of the best things in life, they're reserved for our betters."

To a degree, she's right. By and large, the few passenger ships still operating carry the same wealthy High Proszawan refugees who came south at the beginning of the Great War. Some of the elegant neighborhoods they've built in Lower Proszawa are turning into ghost towns as whispers of war begin anew. Where will they go? Some, ironically, to Veidtland, the very place Frau Galeen has dreamed of for so long. The good news is that the government has begun a lottery whereby a limited number of free ship tickets will be available to the general public. Frau Galeen has already registered and, as of this writing, is waiting to hear if she'll be one of the fortunate ones. We can only wish her good luck. Perhaps the glorious future that she's dreamed of for so long is just around the corner.

CHAPTER TWENTY-ONE

IT WAS THE CARNIVAL. THERE WERE TENTS, A FERRIS WHEEL, AND A MID-way where couples and families played games of chance. Largo remembered the pretty dancer who gave him free tickets. He'd left them in his flat. *I wonder if a bullock or Nachtvogel pocketed them to come here with a lover.* He left Parvulesco's bicycle at a nearby stand. At a small kiosk, Largo took out some money to buy a ticket, but the man inside waved him through.

Largo nodded in thanks. As he walked into the crowd he felt a sudden relief. People looked away and let him pass, even through the most crowded parts of the midway. He was completely exposed but utterly anonymous.

On the far side of the midway was a pen full of chimeras and he went there as quickly as he could without attracting attention. Some of the small catlike animals rubbed against the wire around the enclosure and changed colors. There were larger chimeras too. He recognized the doglike horse creatures that had knocked him down in the street—how long ago had it been? Time seemed so elastic now. Along the fence were thin deerlike creatures with antlers that sprouted flowers. When anyone petted them, the deer giggled like little girls and playfully bounded away. Largo was happy for the first time in days, but at the same time he felt his heart breaking. He'd never get to study animals like this. Never learn the chimeras' secrets.

I came so close. I might have worked with Hanna in her lab. The Baron said to call him Rudolf. I was going to be somebody.

Two of the giggling deer came to him and he rubbed their soft ears. Out of the corner of his eye he saw two police officers standing by the fence, laughing at the creatures. One took a swat at a passing dog-horse but missed. Largo left the deer and went quietly the other way out of the enclosure.

He hoped to lose himself in the crowd but on his way, Largo spotted a fortune-teller's tent. There were spirits and strange runes painted on the sides, and lanterns around the entrance. A painted placard read MADAME TAJEMSTVÍ. He thought of Rainer. Would he be amused or angry to see his beloved spiritualism turned into something so tawdry? Largo peered inside the entrance, but it was too dim to see much from the outside. He was about to leave when the two police officers from the chimera pen started in his direction. Instead of trying to make it to the midway, Largo went into the tent and sat down at a small table with a crystal ball in the middle. A moment later, an old woman in a peasant dress came out from behind a curtain and sat across from him.

"Good evening, kind sir," she said. "How may I help you tonight?"

Largo looked back at the entrance. "I . . . I don't know. Is it all right if I just sit here for a minute and think about it?"

In a soothing tone she said, "Of course. Take your time. But remember that Madam Tajemství doesn't judge and has had many requests over the years, from the everyday to the astoundingly exotic."

Something about the woman's voice made him look at her harder. She did look old, but he began to suspect it was at least partly makeup, and her hair was wrong. It hung around her shoulders. However, he couldn't shake the feeling that he knew her. He leaned across the table for a better look and she moved back a few inches.

"Is there anything wrong?" she said in a wary tone.

Largo sat back and said, "I know you. You're Vera Baal."

The fortune-teller slapped the table once and said, "Fuck." She got up, closed the tent flaps over the entrance, and sat back down. From a deep pocket in her dress she pulled a cigarette case and lit one from a nearby candle. "You don't look like a bullock. How much do you want to keep your mouth shut? I'm not a rich woman."

He waved a hand at her. "I don't want anything."

Vera smoked and stared. She pointed to his mask. "I just tell fortunes, you know. I'm not a witch. I can't help you with your face."

Largo took off the mask and set it on the table.

A wry smile creased her face. "Interesting. It looks like we're all hiding from someone."

"It does, doesn't it?" he said, smiling back at her. "You don't know me, but I saw you perform with Anita Mourlet."

Vera crossed her arms. "The fire wasn't my fault," she said tightly.

"I know. I saw the drunk throw his cigar into the . . . what's the word?"

"Trans zamlžení," she said, still wary. "It's a tricky substance. Very volatile. The fool could have killed everyone in the theater."

Largo said, "It's unfair that everyone blames you. Isn't there anyone who can tell the bullocks it wasn't your fault?"

Vera shook her head. "People have, but it's the nature of our time for them not to believe a word. I'm a foreigner and there were a lot of important people there to see Anita. Bluenoses, industrialists, politicians. In the current climate, it's easier for the bullocks to arrest than to waste time investigating crimes."

Largo remembered lying in agony in the cell with the beaten man. "I was in jail a week ago."

"Then you understand why I would rather avoid the place."

He nodded. "It was horrible. No one seemed to know what they were doing and I got the feeling it was deliberate."

Vera pushed the cigarette case across the table. He shook his head politely. She said, "How did you get out?"

That wasn't a question he expected. Largo was tired of lying all the time, but he didn't want to tell her everything. He said, "Someone I know had connections I wasn't aware of."

Vera gestured with the hand holding the cigarette. "Then why are you wearing that mask? Isn't your friend protecting you?"

Largo leaned on the table, remembering Branca calmly explaining to him that he was a Nachtvogel agent. "He wanted me to do things I didn't like. We had a falling-out."

Vera tapped out some ashes into her hand and tossed them under the table. "It happens," she said. "Angels don't always stay angels."

"He was never an angel. Just the opposite. But why are you still here? Shouldn't you have left the city?"

Vera nervously cut and recut a tarot deck as she spoke. "It's not that easy. My name is everywhere. If I tried to use my travel papers the bullocks would be on me in a second."

"If you could leave, where would you go?"

She said, "Among other considerations, somewhere no one has ever heard of Lower Proszawa, the Great War, or the Nachtvogel."

Largo tried to picture it. "You'll have to go very far away for that."

"That's the idea."

"It's a good one. I like it," he said. "But how will you do it if everyone is looking for you?"

Vera put the cigarette in her mouth and held up a finger. "Ah, but no one is looking for Madame Tajemství. I just need travel papers."

He remembered Margit and the printing press at the Black Palace. "I know someone with a printing press, but I don't know if she can do that kind of thing."

Vera cut the cards again and held them out to Largo. "Touch the deck," she said. He tapped it with his index finger. She began laying out a hand. "Don't worry about me," she said. "I have friends too. They'll help me."

Largo looked back over his shoulder, half expecting the police to come charging in with their pistols drawn. He said, "Why are you working? Shouldn't you be in hiding?"

"I need money to pay for the papers and for passage. I need money so I can eat."

Largo held his hands on the table. "I've got money," he said. "I'd let you have some, but I need it to help friends in jail."

Vera moved the cards around. "Why would you do that? You don't even know me."

"I'd like to leave too, but I'm looking for someone. Once I find her, I don't know what will happen. There are people after me and I don't know anyone who can help me, much less get me travel papers."

"So that's it, then." Vera looked down at the cards she'd laid out. "You're either a nice young man or just a fool."

That made him laugh. "I've been called the second a lot lately."

"I'm not surprised. What's your name?"

"Largo."

Baal pinched off the burning end of her cigarette and tossed it on the floor. She put the rest back in the silver case. She half turned in her chair and said, "Anita. Come out and meet Largo."

A moment later, Anita Mourlet emerged from behind the curtain where Vera had first appeared. Largo stood up. This close, she was even more beautiful than he remembered. But she was smaller than he'd thought she'd be. After the performance at the Golden Angel he'd thought of her as a giant, but she was no taller than Remy. "I saw you at the theater. You were amazing," he said.

She wore a short cream-colored coat trimmed with a black fur collar. Largo was surprised at how plainly she was dressed. Anita said, "I've had better nights, but thank you."

"My girlfriend is a performer too," Largo said. "After your show, I think she's a little in love with you."

Anita mock-frowned. "Just a little? How sad. Is she with you tonight?"

Largo looked at a candle rather than the women. Talking about Remy was easier that way. "No. She's gone. Vanished. The bullocks say she's dead, but I don't believe it," he said. "She's the reason I have to stay in the city."

Anita picked up the mask and held it over her face. Vera said, "Is she the reason you have to wear the mask?"

"Yes, just like you changed your hair and name," said Largo.

Vera looked up at Anita. "Do you think your friends might be able to help this young man?"

She set down the mask and frowned. "I don't know. Things are difficult right now and they get worse every day."

Largo stared at her, not sure if he'd heard correctly. "You're with the radicals?" he said.

"Don't use that word," said Anita. "That's the government's word. We simply want to stop another slaughter."

"I would never have guessed."

"I want to keep it that way, so I'd appreciate it if you didn't mention it to anyone."

Largo held up his hands. "I'm hiding from the world behind a Dandy mask. Who would I tell?"

Anita nodded at the tent entrance. "Did you see any bullocks outside?"

"A few."

"Damn them. I have to get out of here and meet some people in the movement."

"But she's a bit recognizable," said Vera. "You see the problem."

Largo still couldn't believe that he was sitting across from Anita Mourlet. What would Remy say? He knew in an instant.

Help her.

353

"I know every alley and back street in the city. I can get you where you need to be."

Anita nervously toyed with the edge of her fur collar. "The police would spot me the minute I went outside."

Largo held up the mask. "Not if you wear this." He handed it to her.

"What about you?" Anita said.

"I doubt regular patrol bullocks know what I look like," he said. "Try it on. Maybe you can pretend to be blind?"

"Maybe," said Anita.

Largo thought it over. "If I keep my head down and you're a blind Dandy, no one will look at us twice."

Vera looked from Largo to Anita. She said, "In the absence of a good idea, it's not a bad one." She went into the back of the tent and came back with a cane, which she handed to Anita. "Here. Swing this around in front of you when you walk."

Vera tossed Largo a leather hat with ear flaps. "You look like a fisherman. A bit. Anyway, it will help cover your face."

Anita put a hand on Vera's arm. "I'm scared, Vera. Can't I just stay here?"

"And if the bullocks decide to start searching tents, what then? You'll be safer in the city, away from the carnival."

"Can I trust him?"

"I think so. And the cards said yes."

Largo stood up. "I wouldn't hurt you."

Anita let go of Vera's arm. "If she says it's all right, then I believe you."

"Before we go, I have a question for you, Vera," said Largo. "When you were telling fortunes at the Golden Angel, you refused to tell Remy's. Why?"

"That was your girlfriend?" said Vera. "I'll tell you the truth as best I can, though I'm not sure I can explain. But . . . she was an empty vessel."

Largo looked at her. "What does that mean?"

"I looked for a person to read, but there was no one inside her."

"I still don't understand."

Vera shrugged. "Neither do I, but here's the interesting thing. She's not the first I've seen like that. There are others."

"Are you saying she's dead? A ghost?"

"No," said Vera. "She's as alive as you or I, but she's . . . empty. I can't explain it any better than that."

Anita came around the table to Largo's side. She said, "Please, can we go? I'm frightened and I have to get across the city."

Largo was both scared and frustrated. *An empty vessel.* He pointed to Vera. "I'm coming back and we're going to talk about this more."

"Don't come back unless you're wearing the mask. And bring my hat with you."

"I promise." Largo took the mask from Anita's hands and put it over her face. "Are you ready?"

She took a breath and said, "Yes."

"Wait a minute, you dunces," said Vera. "She can't go out in that coat. Dandies don't wear mink collars."

Anita looked at Largo. He said, "Take off your coat and leave it here. Put on mine."

"It's freezing outside. What will you wear?"

"I'll be all right."

"Both of you stay here," said Vera. She left the tent, closing the flap when she was outside.

It struck Largo again that he was standing next to the real Anita Mourlet. Remy would love this so much. *At least I'll have one good story to tell when I find her.* He looked at Anita. "Where am I taking you?"

"I'm staying with friends in Granate. Do you know how to get there?"

"With my eyes closed."

"Good," Anita said from behind the mask. "I'm smiling now. You can't see it, but I am."

Vera returned a couple of minutes later with a long oilskin jacket in her hands. She tossed it to Largo. "Try this on."

Largo put it on, trying to move his injured shoulder as little as possible.

"You're bleeding," said Anita.

"Yes. A bullock took a shot at me yesterday. He mostly missed."

"You need to have that looked at."

"You can take him to dinner with the grandest doctor in Lower Proszawa," said Vera. "But later. Right now, you both have to leave."

Largo flexed his arms in the jacket. It was too large for him, but it was warm. "How much was it? I can pay you back," he said.

Vera batted away the comment. "It belongs to Scheffler the strong man, and it didn't cost a cent. I'll tell him his fortune tomorrow and make it a happy one. He'll be delighted."

The two women embraced and Anita kissed Vera on her cheeks. She said, "Remember, you're blind. Let Largo lead you."

Anita nodded and held out her arm. Largo looped his around hers. "Here we go," he said.

They paused for a moment outside the tent while Largo looked around for the police. When he didn't see them, he tugged Anita forward. "Don't forget to swing the cane," he said.

Together, they walked slowly through the crowd to the front gate. As always with the mask, few people looked at them. At the edge of the carnival, three police officers were smoking and talking to the man in the ticket kiosk. Largo felt Anita's arm tense against his. He patted it and kept them walking at an even pace. As they approached the exit one of the officers stepped back, blocking the way out. Largo realized that he'd left Rainer's pistol in the side pocket of his coat. With Anita wearing it, there was no way he could get to it in time if the police tried to stop them. Her arm squeezed him even harder. It felt as if she was trying to pull away and run. Largo held her tight.

The police were still there when they reached the exit. Largo had no choice but to say, "Excuse me, Officer," to the one blocking their way. *Stupid bastard bullock*, he thought, but he smiled as the officer turned. He frowned at Largo, then stepped out of the way when he saw Anita in the mask.

"Sorry," he said. "Have a good night."

"Thank you. You too."

Anita gasped when they'd moved a few yards from the entrance. "It feels like I've been holding my breath for an hour."

"You're all right now. It's just a little farther to my bicycle."

Anita went rigid against him and stopped. "A bicycle? You don't have a car?"

"I'm sorry. All I have is a bicycle."

"Oh god," she said. "Can you ride it with two people?"

"I'm a courier. I carry packages all the time. A person is no problem."

"I suppose there's no choice now. I couldn't make it back to Vera's tent without having a heart attack."

"Me neither," said Largo. "Trust me. This will be fine."

"How long will it take to Granate?"

"If I go the direct route, a half hour at the most."

"I suppose that's all right," said Anita.

"We'll be fine. But I should take this." Largo took the pistol from the coat and put it in his oilskin jacket.

Anita let out a breath. "Oh god."

It was harder biking them to Granate than Largo had thought it would be. Not that Anita was large, but between her in Rainer's heavy coat and him in the strong man's jacket, the balance was all wrong. Plus, there was his injured shoulder. Instead of taking a half hour, it took forty-five minutes to reach the address in Granate. Largo was out of breath when they got off the bicycle, and the wetness on his arm told him that his shoulder was bleeding again. He walked Anita to the door of the little house.

She gave him back the mask and said, "I don't know how to thank you." Then a little guiltily she added, "I'd invite you in, but my friends don't like new faces."

"I understand. But do you mind if we switch coats? There are things in that one I need."

When they traded coats, Anita asked, "What's that under your arm?"

"A trench knife," said Largo.

Anita looked at him. "You're more formidable than I gave you credit for at first, Herr Largo."

He took the pistol out of the jacket, checked the magazine, and put it back in his coat pocket. "I'm not entirely sure how I should take that," he said.

"It was an attempted compliment. Sorry if I mangled it. I'm still a little shaky from the carnival and the bike ride."

"If you say it was a compliment, I'll take it that way. Have a good evening with your friends."

He started away, but Anita put a hand on his shoulder. "Do you have a place to stay tonight?"

"I was going to try one of the Dandy rooming houses."

"Listen," she said. "We should be done by midnight. Come back then and you can stay here."

Largo took a step back, thinking of Parvulesco and Roland. "Thank you, but that's not a good idea. They raided the last place I stayed."

Anita took out her keys. "Bullocks don't come to Granate unless there's a fire," she said. "Besides, one of our people is an operative.

He lets us know if there's trouble." She took a key off the ring and put it in Largo's hand. "Come back after midnight. I guarantee you it's more comfortable here than a five-to-a-room flophouse."

Largo looked at the key. The offer really did sound better than a night in a freezing tenement. "I'll think about it," he said finally. Then he laughed.

"What's so funny?" Anita said.

"Me staying under the same roof as Anita Mourlet," he said. "Remy would be so jealous."

She smiled and said, "I'll see you later."

Riding away from the house was considerably easier than getting there had been. He had several hours to kill before he could return—if he decided to return at all. The metal mask still froze his face, but now it smelled of perfume, which was alternately delightful and depressing. Delightful because it reminded him of Remy and depressing for the same reason.

What if she really is dead? This might be the last time I'm ever close enough to a woman to smell her living presence.

After riding to the familiar streets of central Lower Proszawa, Largo found that the weight of the mask was beginning to drive him a little mad. He wanted to rip it off and throw it in the bay or onto one of the patriotic bonfires burning throughout the city. However, he grew nervous as he pedaled the streets. Lurking on many corners were a new kind of armed Mara. They were the largest he'd ever seen, easily a head taller than the tallest man. People spoke to them and they seemed to respond, pointing as if they were giving directions, sometimes holding children while parents and men from the yellowsheets took photochromes. Largo looked up to see flying Maras gliding quietly overhead, little stars observing everything below. He thought of the glass lens eyes of the parakeet in Remy's flat. Had someone been watching them through those?

As he rode, he caught fragments of speeches and cheering crowds. Eventually, he didn't ride around the mobs but through them. He would make his way from the edge of the throng to the center in a series of long loops, eventually riding around the speaker several times before pushing out of the crowd again. He would applaud the speaker or pump his hand in the air or shake hands with strangers, all of whom thanked him for his various sacrifices. He bumped into police officers more than once. Most were apologetic, but the more he rode and the wilder the streets became, the less polite the police became. One grabbed him and almost pulled him off his bicycle.

"Show me your papers, Dandy," he yelled. Largo patted his pockets and shrugged as if he couldn't find them. The officer was on the verge of arresting him when the crowd closed in, shouting and shoving him. It was clear that the crowd wasn't going to let the officer complete the arrest. As they circled the officer and held his arms, they stepped away from Largo, creating a small corridor he could ride through. He put his head down and veered out of the swarm, heading across town.

That was stupid, he thought. However, the sense of desolation brought on by the perfume wouldn't quite let go. *If I'm going to die or get caught tonight, there's something I have to do. One last thing.*

He took a familiar route to the theater district. Soon he saw the bright lights of the marquee.

THEATER OF THE GRAND DARKNESS

Ilsa wasn't in the box office, which was disappointing. Largo didn't want to spend his last night with strangers. The young freckled woman who sold him his ticket said, "You've missed the first performance, but you're in time for our new show, *The Ghastly Fall of the Boudoir Butcher.*"

He nodded to her and went inside. The second show hadn't started, but most of the theatergoers remained in their seats rather than gathering in the lobby to drink, chatting away, fueled by the performance and cocaine. In fact, the theater was strangely subdued as the patrons stared straight ahead at an empty stage. Largo shifted in his seat in the back row, feeling the weight of the knife against his side and the pistol in his pocket. The strange crowd reminded him of docile Andrzej and Weimer.

He touched his chest as his heart raced. *This was a bad idea*, he thought. *Who are these people? Do they all have the Drops? Are things really getting that out of hand?*

Largo was getting up to leave when the curtains opened on the stage and the band began to play. He'd come to the Grand Dark hoping to taste Remy's world one last time, but all he felt was confusion and fear. The last things he remembered about the theater were Remy's collapse. Screams. Threats. He wanted to run from the place, but he thought, *Where would I go? I was almost arrested once to-night. I can't let that happen again.* The sense of panic faded as he went through Branca's breathing exercise. He glanced around to see if anyone had noticed him, but everyone stared straight ahead at the stage like mannequins.

The galvanic puppets emerged from the wings, moving in their ghostly way as the music swelled. Miserable and unable to move, Largo settled back and watched with everyone else.

The Ghastly Fall of the Boudoir Butcher was about a rising young actress and her cruel lover who spent her money on drugs and other women. Worse than that, he was a murderer who killed for mobsters and later for foreign agents. The lover was able to cover up his crimes and move easily through the city because he worked as a bicycle messenger.

God—it's me and Remy. Una's made us into something horrible. But why?

When the lover killed another woman, who refused his advances—*She looks like Lucie*—her ghost returned to warn the actress. But it was too late. The lover was on the run from the police and when she confronted him about the murder, he threw acid in her face. Her death was long and gruesome even by Grand Dark standards. Even the passive audience gasped. Largo closed his eyes and held on to his seat as the puppet shrieked in agony. When he looked again, the actress's neighbors, who had heard her screams, held the murderous courier and made him drink the remainder of the acid. He screamed in agony as his entrails spilled onto the stage in a sudden red gush. When the audience rose to applaud, Largo put his head down and pushed his way outside.

Fortunately, it was after eleven. He bought a small bottle of whiskey and drank it as he rode back to Granate. It was well after midnight when he arrived at Anita's house, so he let himself in with the key. She was waiting for him in the living room with a glass of wine.

"I had a feeling you were smart enough to come back," she said. "How was your evening?"

"Aside from seeing my girlfriend's murder and my own, it was lovely. How was yours?"

CHAPTER TWENTY-TWO

LIKE MANY OF THE OLD SERVANT HOUSES IN GRANATE, THIS ONE WAS somewhat narrow, with a steep staircase to an upper floor. The place hadn't been kept up very well by the owner. However, the mismatched furniture in the living room looked sturdy. A few family photos rested on the mantel above the fireplace. He wondered who'd lived there before.

Largo sat down and explained what he'd seen and heard over the last few hours.

"Do you think it was a threat?" said Anita.

"I don't know. The whole thing has me puzzled."

"You think the writer can see the future?"

"No, but I'm sure Una has been talking to the bullocks."

"Then you'll have to be more careful."

"I think it's a bit late for that."

The room was warm. Largo took off his coat and put it over the back of his chair.

Anita said, "You don't look good. How do you feel?"

He leaned on the table. His whole left side was numb. "I had some whiskey, so I'm a little light-headed."

Anita touched his sleeve. "You're also bleeding. Take off your shirt so I can see your shoulder."

The order made him feel very tired. He said, "In the last few days I've been shot, beaten, and attacked by chimeras. I'm not pretty to look at."

Anita got up and went into the next room. She said, "The request wasn't about your beauty, but your health. Now take your damn shirt off."

He did it but as he pulled the shirt over his head, the numbness in his left arm was replaced by a sharp stabbing pain.

Anita returned with a small white metal box and a needle and thread. After she removed his bloody bandages, she took a bottle from the box and poured a small amount of a clear liquid onto Largo's shoulder. "This will help with the pain," she said. "You can also drink wine, if you like."

Largo looked at his shoulder. It was swollen around the wound, which was deep and red. "Do you have whiskey?" he said.

"Not a drop," said Anita.

"Never mind then. I'll be fine." He watched her thread the needle and use it to sew the wound closed. Even with the anesthetic, he winced each time the needle punctured his skin. Largo looked at Anita. "You're a singer, a dancer, and now a doctor too?"

"No, but I know how to mend costumes. These stiches won't be attractive, but they should stop the bleeding."

He changed his mind and gulped down the glass of wine, hoping it would dull the pain a little more. "Not bleeding would be a nice way to spend a night."

"You've been on the run for a while, then?"

He almost laughed. "Only a few days. But they've been eventful."

"When was the last time you slept in a proper bed?"

"What month is it?"

Anita gave him a little smile. "There's a guest room upstairs. You can sleep there."

"What if I bleed on the sheets?"

"Trust me, you wouldn't be the first," she said. "The movement has used this house for quite a while."

"Then I accept your invitation. Did your meeting go well?"

Her smiled faded. "Yes and no. The more dangerous things become, the more reckless some in the group feel."

Largo winced when the needle went through a particularly painful spot. "I know how they feel. I did some irrational things while I was out. But I also saw some things. Bigger Maras and flying Maras right over the center of the city."

"I'm sure," said Anita. "The flying ones have always been there, just not so obviously. Did you get close to the big Maras? They don't just say

'Yes, ma'am' and 'No, ma'am' anymore. They're smart. They think. And they aren't even the most dangerous things. We've heard about new weapons using plazma power. New, vicious bitva dogs. Flying transports."

Largo poured himself more wine. "What's a flying transport? Like an airship?"

"It's smaller and much faster. They can drop men as well as bombs."

"The world has gone completely insane," he said.

Anita squinted as she worked on his shoulder. "Not the whole world," she said. "That's why some of us are trying to get out of Lower Proszawa. Some just want to run. But others want to go where they can help."

A little woozy, Largo said, "Which are you?"

"I honestly don't know yet. How about you? What would you do if you could leave?"

Largo said, "I don't even know if the city is worth saving. It used to be all parties, but if you'd seen the mobs I saw tonight, you might feel the same way."

"I do some days," she said. "Others days I'm not so sure."

Largo gulped more wine. He didn't know what was more depressing, thinking about the mobs or the idea that even if he and Remy could leave Lower Proszawa they still might not be able to get away from its madness. He said, "I know a radical group. They print leaflets and put up posters. What good are leaflets against an army?"

"You might be surprised," said Anita, nodding her head.

"I doubt it," he said. "I take it that your situation is like Vera's. You can't travel under your own name?"

"Exactly. That's why I'm staying. It's safer to hide here than to try to leave without new papers and a plan. But with luck, my friends can get them for Vera and me."

"I'm glad," said Largo.

"They might even be able to help you."

He looked at her but caught a glimpse of his bloody, half-closed wound and turned away. "Why would your friends do that?"

Anita spoke cautiously. "You helped me. Maybe you can be one of the ones who helps from afar."

He took a breath. "I don't even know if I want to leave."

"Don't be stupid. Of course you do," she said. "You're just being melodramatic because of your lost love."

Largo tried to think about it, but between the liquor, the pain, and the warmth of the room, he had trouble forming complete thoughts. "Is that what you think it is? Melodrama?"

Anita used gauze to wipe blood off his shoulder. "What I mean is that you need a plan too. What if you find her? You're a wanted man. Will you hide in her broom closet for the rest of your life? And what if you don't find her? What if, and I'm sorry to say it, she's dead? What then? Will you give yourself up to the bullocks? Let them shoot you? Suicide is easy. Living is hard."

He let his head fall back. He wanted to applaud. "You really are a good performer. That was a lovely speech."

"Thank you. But I meant it," she said. "You should leave, with or without your lady friend."

"I'll think about it."

Anita stopped sewing for a moment and wrote something on a piece of paper. She slid it into his shirt pocket. "Put this somewhere you won't lose it."

"What is it?"

"The Trefle number here," she said. "When you've made your choice, call me. We need all the help we can get."

"So do I."

Anita cut the thread with a small pair of scissors. "There. You're going to have a lovely scar to make up stories about."

Largo looked at his shoulder. The wound was closed neatly, but it still looked swollen and awful. "Thank you."

As she put the needle and medical supplies away, Anita said, "What will you do now?"

"Before anything else, I need to get some friends out of jail."

She came back to the table and poured them more wine. "And how will you do that?"

"There's someone who can help me. He has no choice."

"And if he doesn't?"

"I'll kill him."

Anita raised her glass in a toast. "See? You're already a soldier in the fight."

He looked at her. His shoulder felt tight around the stiches. "Is that what I am?"

"You're part of the battle whether you know it or not."

"I don't want to be a soldier."

"No one does," said Anita. "What do you want to be?"

Largo scratched his wounded cheek. "It sounds stupid now."

Anita leaned forward. "Even better. Tell me."

Why not? All she can do is laugh, he thought. "I wanted to be a scientist and make chimeras. Not the kind for war. Beautiful ones like they have at the carnival."

She didn't laugh but rather looked at him with a sad smile. "Maybe you'll get that chance someday. But you have to live, first."

At the moment, both ideas seemed rather ridiculous. He picked his shirt up from the floor and Anita helped him put it on. "Are you afraid all the time?" he said.

"No. Are you?"

"I was. For my whole life I was afraid of everything. But since I came back to the city it's not the same. Yes, I'm still afraid at times, but now it's different. Some moments I feel like a ghost. Like I died but I'm still here. There's not enough of me left to be afraid for."

"That sounds very sad," Anita said. "But you can use that feeling. Go and find the man who can help your friends. Go and look for your lover. But then call me. We can work together."

He applauded lightly, but it made his shoulder hurt, so he stopped. "Another good speech. Remy was right."

"About what?" she said with a half smile.

"She wanted to be more like you. I think she'd want to even more now."

Anita pushed some hair out of Largo's face. "You look tired. The stitches are likely to hurt tonight. Do you want some morphia?"

His whole body tensed at the sound of the word. "I would love some, but no. Giving it up almost killed me."

"See? You are brave."

He rubbed his eyes with the back of his hand. "Do you mind if I go to sleep now?"

"Not at all," she said. "I'll show you to your room." She led him up a short flight of stairs to a door at the end of the hall. "If you need anything, I'm just down the hall."

"Thank you for everything."

"Thank you for saving me tonight."

"Good night," he said.

Anita kissed him on the cheek. "Good night, Largo."

He awoke in the late morning with his shoulder throbbing. He'd bled very little in the night, but his head ached from all the whiskey and wine. Anita gave him aspirin and cooked some bacon and toast. They ate together and he felt much better with food in his stomach.

While Anita made calls on the Trefle, Largo tried to read some of her group's pamphlets but quickly became bored. All the radicals sounded alike to him. *"Down with the government." "Up with the people." "Destroy this." "Empower that." They sound like angry children.* He wanted to at least admire their sincerity but it all sounded like pipe dreams. The bullocks and the Nachtvogel. The bastard Maras. They were everywhere and as the war drew nearer, they'd only become more ruthless.

In the evening, he put on the mask and oilskin coat and rode Parvulesco's bicycle to the company, where he waited for Branca to leave. It was after seven when Largo saw him get into a small black sedan and drive away. He followed him across the city to the working-class suburbs outside of the Klinge district. They were nicer than Granate, but not by much. If Branca were just a low-level supervisor and not a Nachtvogel bastard it might be sad to see him here, thought Largo. Branca's warning about their position in the company on the first day of his promotion made more sense than ever. Largo had never felt so "utterly disposable" in his life.

The building was a seven-story tower block. After Branca went inside, Largo checked the mail boxes in the lobby and found the flat number on the fourth floor. There was a lift, but it was blocked by an *Out of Service* sign. He walked upstairs and took out Rainer's pistol. After checking that there was no one around, he knocked on the door. A moment later, Branca opened it.

"Ah, Largo. I'd been expecting you at some point," he said. "The mask is a nice touch. Do come in."

Branca's blasé tone was unnerving, but he knew that it was supposed to be, so he pushed the feeling away and concentrated on his reason for coming.

He took off the mask and entered the flat, keeping the pistol aimed at Branca. "Sit down," Largo said. He quickly checked the bedroom, kitchen, and bathroom.

"I assure you we're alone," Branca said. He was still standing by the door.

"I told you to sit down," said Largo.

"I heard you quite well. It's that I don't feel like sitting at the moment. You, however, should feel free to get comfortable. I heard that one of Tanz's men shot you the other night."

"It was just a graze. Hardly anything."

"Pity. Your death would simplify so many things."

"How did the bullocks know I was back?"

Branca gave him a pitying look. "After all you've seen, you're still naïve," he said. "Never trust a smuggler when he smells an easy profit."

Steinmetz. Branca is right. I should have known better.

The older man went on, "I see you were wise enough to change clothes. One of the bullocks you shot lived long enough to describe his assailant as a Dandy in a pea coat. The police, literal-minded dullards that they are, are looking for that exact thing. It must be such a relief that you're safe from them."

"But not from the Nachtvogel."

"I'm afraid not."

Largo leveled the pistol at Branca's head. "I want you to tell the police to release Parvulesco and Roland."

"Don't be absurd. Why would I do that?"

"I'll shoot you if you don't."

"My superiors would shoot me if I followed the orders of someone as obviously deranged as you, and I would deserve it," Branca said. "Your problem has always been that you don't look beyond the tip of your nose. You'll see Parvulesco and his friend again. And very soon, too."

The way Branca said it made Largo nervous. "But it won't be them, will it? It will be someone nicer and duller and easier to order around."

Branca pointed at him. "This is exactly what I mean by the tip of your nose. You worry about your friends when you should be worried for Lower Proszawa and, really, the world."

After the ride, the pistol was heavy in his hand. "What are you talking about?"

"Your friends will return changed because there's no choice but to change them," said Branca.

"There's always a choice."

"Not in their case, I'm afraid." Branca leaned against the wall and put his hands in his pockets. "Aren't you going to ask me about Remy? If she's alive and if so, where she is?"

Largo's face flushed. "Then you know?"

"Of course I know. I've known all along."

"Then you were lying earlier. Why should I believe you now?"

The older man shrugged slightly. "Believe what you want, but if you want to know where she is all you have to do is ask me."

He eyed Branca. Largo knew that he was being led into some kind of trap. *But what else can I do but go along with it right now?* "Where is she?"

Branca's smile was wide and friendly. "She's neither here nor there. She never was. Remy Berber never existed."

Largo lowered the pistol a few inches. "I don't understand what that means," he said, not believing but frightened all the same.

Branca went to a small table by the wall and picked up his cigarettes. He lit one. "I know this will be difficult to hear, but you must listen to me, Largo. She is not and never was your paramour."

He raised the pistol again. "Of course she was. We practically lived together."

"But you didn't. Do you know why?"

"Tell me, but don't lie."

"I don't have to," said Branca, smiling brightly. "The truth is too delightful."

"Tell me."

Branca straightened a little. "She wasn't your paramour because she wasn't *real*. Remedios Berber was a Mara created by Baron Hellswarth and Schöne Maschinen."

Largo closed his eyes for an instant and opened them. He felt very cold inside, as if he were going through withdrawal again. "You're lying. I told you not to lie."

The older man held out his hands before him. "I'm not lying, Largo. She was a Mara given to you by the Baron."

Even though he knew he was being lied to, Largo felt dizzy. "Why would he do that?"

"He used you for the same reason I used you. You were foolish enough to be useful."

"But why make her for *me*?"

"He didn't make her for you," said Branca. "With our help, he merely sent her to you. You were the perfect test subject for integrating somewhat intelligent automata into ordinary society."

Largo's shoulder throbbed and his knee ached again after all the riding. Through gritted teeth he said, "No. You're just trying to confuse me. *Where is Remy?*"

Branca didn't seem to hear him. He said, "Intelligent automata are being eased into the populace all the time now. You must know this. We've worked with them."

"You mean Andrzej and Weimer? They were real people."

"I'd argue that those creatures were never real people, but never mind. They're definitely not people anymore."

"Why would someone even dream of doing something like that?"

Branca gestured toward the window. "Look at the world, Largo. Humans are soft, pliant organisms. They're chaotic, easily confused, and, more often than not, violent when provoked by ideas they don't fully understand. Like you," he said. Branca frowned and crushed out his cigarette in an ashtray. "The changes I mentioned are a question of evolution and survival. Are we to allow arbitrary and self-destructive genetic impulses to control history or are we going to take back civilization and the future? Science has given us the tools to make a rational choice."

What Branca was saying didn't make sense. Nothing made sense anymore. "What's rational about what you're saying?"

When Branca spoke, it was if he were addressing a group of new couriers, explaining their duties in the simplest language he could use. "While the general public accepts that the Great War was a stalemate, people who truly understand these things know that, in fact, we lost. One only has to look at High Proszawa to know that. This cannot be allowed to happen again. The enemy didn't invade, but they will not be so kind to us a second time. Make no mistake, Largo. We are on the brink of extinction as a nation and a species."

Largo glanced at the window. He said, "These so-called soft, pliant organisms you talk about changing are human beings. Real people with real lives."

"Of course they are," said Branca. "Human, that is. But real lives? What does life even mean now? Endless, self-destructive decadence? The grotesque poverty of the poor too dim-witted or drunken to pull themselves out of the gutter? The whole system in which we live is teetering on the edge of collapse. The point of our work is to uplift the human condition. In its current form, it's woefully out of date."

"You're a murderer."

"No more than you. I'm sure Special Operative Tanz would agree."

Branca waited for Largo to say something and when it didn't happen, he continued. "Think of me as a simple greengrocer. When an apple goes soft or a head of lettuce wilts, I remove it so that it can be replaced with one that's more palatable and nutritious for the body."

Largo looked around the room. His face was hot and his shoulder hurt. "If you're telling the truth, the people you bring back aren't people. They're machines."

Branca spoke eagerly. *Proudly*, thought Largo. "These are early days. The techniques will be refined and more of the original flesh in those we're replacing will be preserved. Defects in the system, such as Remy's convulsions and the Drops, will disappear. Eventually we may be able to correct humanity's self-destructive tendencies in the womb. A perfect species born to perfect lives. Until then, we work with Dandies and marginals such as Andrzej and Weimer—people who will be little missed."

The pistol grew heavy again. Largo hurt all over and wished he had just a drop or two of morphia.

"What about Remy and Enki Helm?" he said. "A lot of people will miss them."

Branca made a sour face. "The real Helm was a subversive. A civilized Helm was a bold experiment. If he hadn't malfunctioned he might have changed many minds with his newly enlightened attitude."

Largo hesitated. "And Remy?" It was hard even to say her name.

"Creating her was the decision of Baron Hellswarth and Schöne Maschinen. And a visionary one, if you ask me. But they have their own reasons and it isn't necessary for them to explain them to those of us tasked with carrying them out."

"Don't talk about her like that!" Largo yelled.

Branca sighed. "If you wish."

Largo couldn't speak for a moment. It was too much to take in. Why would Branca tell him such a strange and elaborate lie when it was simpler to just say "She's dead" or "I'll take you to her" and kill him along the way? If Branca was playing a game, it was one in which the rules weren't clear to Largo.

"By the way," Branca said, "Una Herzog sends her regards."

"What do you mean?" said Largo, startled by the name.

"I never asked you about the play you mentioned earlier. The evil anarchist ripped apart by a mob. Did you enjoy it?"

"Why are you asking about that? What does it have to do with me?"

370

"I would think it was tailor-made for your tastes."

Largo looked at Branca. "Una really is one of you then. A Nachtvogel."

Branca glanced at his watch briefly as if he was growing bored. "No. But she's a patriot who will do anything to protect the country."

Largo thought about the play. "How did she know about a murder that hadn't happened yet?"

Branca chuckled. "You know, in an earlier draft of the play the radical was a bicycle messenger who bore a startling resemblance to you. It was amusing, but I talked her out of it."

"You didn't answer my question."

"She didn't foresee a murder, Largo. We arranged for a killing that matched the rough outline of her play."

"But why would you do that?"

"It was a test," Branca said. "You see, it's not enough to make people pliant if their brains are still as confused and corrupt as before. We need to delve deeper into the workings of their minds. Una's play was simply an experiment in memory."

"But how can they remember something that hasn't happened?"

Branca raised a finger in the air. "That's the crux of the experiment. Can we make people understand that what they remember isn't what their flawed brains tell them, but what *we* tell them? If we say that a certain murder occurred at such-and-such an hour and they recall something different, how many will remember what we want them to?"

"How many?" said Largo.

"Most, at this point. With refinement and diligent effort, soon it will be all."

"Nothing you say or do makes any sense, you know that, don't you?"

"You're becoming desperate, Largo. Why don't you put down the gun and we can discuss your future?"

"No. You're going to try to confuse me," he said. Wanting to get some control over the conversation, his mind settled on something and he said, "Why is Hellswarth digging up corpses in High Proszawa?"

Branca cocked his head. "I have no idea what you're talking about," he said. "My interests lie with the redemption of the citizens of Lower Proszawa, not tidying up graveyards."

"Redemption? You're kidnapping and killing them."

"Studying them and, where appropriate and possible, improving them."

Largo was sweating. He shifted his weight. "When were you going to do it to me?"

"Not for some time. You were too valuable to the Nachtvogel the way you were."

"But you would have done it."

Branca opened his arms as if giving a benediction. "Look at yourself, Largo. You're a curious case. You've lasted much longer in the wild than I expected, but let's be honest with one another. You must know that if any creature in Lower Proszawa needs redemption, it's you."

He took a breath. "If Hellswarth took Remy, where is she now?"

"You'll have to ask the Baron about that," said Branca. "But don't despair. I have some good news for you too."

Largo grew wary again. "What's that?"

"It's two things, actually." Branca ticked them off on his fingers. "The first is that the police have dropped all charges against you where it comes to your lady love Remy's murder. One cannot murder a machine."

Largo took an angry step forward. "Stop saying that."

Branca remained calm. "Don't you want to know the second bit of good news? I'll tell you anyway. Since you've returned to us, it will no longer be necessary to use the evidence I have here to frame you as part of the gang of kidnappers." Branca patted a small parcel wrapped in butcher paper.

"The kidnappers don't exist," Largo said.

"The public and the police believe they do. We've used the yellow-sheets quite effectively to convince them."

"What did you mean by 'returned to us'? Do you really expect me to go back to my old job and spy on people?"

Branca reached for his cigarettes again. "I don't expect you to, but I was hoping I could convince you."

The dizziness returned. Largo wanted to be out of the flat as soon as possible. He said, "Leave the cigarettes alone. Stop moving your hand."

The older man ignored him. By the time he realized that Branca had a hidden gun in his hand, Largo had no choice. He shot Branca three times. The older man fell against the wall, leaving a blood trail behind as he slid to the floor. Largo grabbed the butcher paper parcel and put on his mask. People were just coming into the hall as he ran down the stairs.

He got on the bicycle and rode away from the building, taking the quickest route out of the central city on the road to Machtviertel. The whole way there the same words spun around in his head over and over again.

He was lying. It's a trick. Remy is real and alive. He was lying. It's a trick. Remy is real and alive . . .

When Largo reached Machtviertel, he changed the pistol's magazine the way Rainer had showed him. He left his bicycle by the collapsed light tower and took off the mask. The crows were still there, but instead of being asleep like sensible birds, they squawked and pecked at his hands and scalp as he made his way to the Black Palace. He swung at them with his good arm, but they were too fast and after a few steps he ended up running for the Palace's entrance. Before he got inside, however, he heard someone calling his name.

"Largo! What are you doing here?" It was Margit and she was running to him across blocks of broken concrete and coal dust.

"I'm looking for you," he said. "I need your help."

Margit's expression was a combination of anger and confusion. "What are you talking about? Come inside before someone sees you."

As he followed her to an abandoned train roundhouse Largo said, "You're not in the Palace anymore?"

"The bullocks raided it. We had to move over here."

Largo tripped on a concrete boulder. "Branca might have gotten the information from my delivery," he said guiltily. "The raid might be my fault."

"Yes, it might," said Margit flatly. "So don't mention it when we get inside."

The exterior of the roundhouse was streaked with wet dust and the bricks were pitted with age. All the windows had been covered from the inside with tar paper. Margit led him around to a door that was secured with a padlock and loose chain. "We leave the door like this so the building still looks empty. You have to crouch to get in."

Maneuvering through the doorway hurt, and he was gritting his teeth when he got inside. Taking a minute to catch his breath, he looked around. The interior of the roundhouse was frigid and smelled of cigarette smoke and the thick reek of coal oil from empty barrels along one wall. Largo was startled by the number of people. There must have been at least fifty. The crowd was separated into several smaller groups, some warming themselves by a small coal furnace, others gathered around tables covered in maps and blueprints, while still others worked, unloading rifles and ammunition from crates. Largo noticed the noise level in the room drop when he entered. "This is a lot more people than you had last time," he said.

"What you saw was just our printing facility," said Margit.

A man in an old army coat pointed at Largo. He said, "Is he the one who brought the ink? Did he sell us out?"

A tall woman with a balaclava pulled down around her neck said, "Pietr warned us about you."

Several people started in his direction. Largo pulled out his pistol and held it down by his side. When Margit saw it, she put her hand over his and pushed the gun back into his pocket. She spoke to the others, saying, "Leave him alone. He helped us rescue our people in Pappengasse."

"What does he want?" said the tall woman.

Margit looked at him. "Yes, Largo. What do you want?"

"The police have arrested Parvulesco and Roland. I want you to get them out of jail. I can pay you." He took all of the money from his pocket and held it out to Margit.

"Fuck him," said the man in the army coat.

The tall woman said, "Don't let him go."

Margit held up a hand and they both stopped. She looked at Largo and said, "Now that you're back, maybe you can help us. We want to get into Schöne Maschinen, but we can't very well go in the front door. How can we get there without being seen?"

Largo let his hand with the money drop to his side. "You can't. All you can do is get close to it. Then you'll have to cross open ground from a power station."

Margit took a step closer. She spoke quickly. "All right. How do we get close?"

Largo held out the money again. "Free Parvulesco and Roland and I'll tell you."

She gave him an exasperated look. "We don't want your money," she said. "Listen, if you don't help us a lot of people could get killed."

Largo pocketed the cash. "Then *you* help me."

Margit raised her arms in a gesture of frustration. "What's wrong with you?"

When he spoke, Largo kept his hand on the pistol in his pocket. "I've been strange places the last few days. I've seen people picking the dead clean. I've seen trucks full of corpses. I've been attacked by bitva chimeras. I've murdered people. And I came here because someone told me that Remy isn't real. That she was a Mara and that we were an experiment. I don't know what or who to believe anymore. I want revenge, but I don't even know who to go after first."

"Who said that Remy isn't real?" said Margit, frowning.

"Branca. The Nachtvogel."

She peered at the group, then back to Largo. "They don't know anything. Hellswarth tells the government what he wants and they tell the Nachtvogel. It's true that the city is full of strange automata. But Remy isn't one of them."

"How do you know?" said Largo warily.

"Pietr wasn't our only informant inside Schöne Maschinen."

"Who's the other?"

"I can't tell you, but I know this much: Baron Hellswarth would never hurt Remy."

He gripped the pistol harder. "Why?"

Margit took Largo's arm and pulled him aside. "Because he's in love with her."

"You're mad," he said.

"The Baron has been in love with her since she was a teenager. Yes, she has admirers who give her baubles, but who do you think gives her the money for such a nice flat? All those jewels and her Trefle? Do you think she earns all that from a small theater like the Grand Dark?"

"How do you know all this?" Largo looked at her hard, suspicious. The night had already been full of lies.

"It's our job to know people in power's dirty little secrets. It makes them easier to blackmail."

Nervously, he asked, "Was Remy in love with the Baron?"

"Of course not. But he's Baron Hellswarth, and after the Chancellor, he's one of the most powerful men in Lower Proszawa. Do you think she could simply send him away like a schoolboy with a crush?"

Largo thought back to the Golden Angel. "That night in the car," he said. "They seemed so close."

"People do a lot of unpleasant things out of fear, especially women," Margit said. "But you know a lot about fear too, so you must understand."

"Yes," he whispered.

"Besides, according to our informant, the Baron has been doing things to Remy. Experiments."

Largo's stomach tightened. "What kind of experiments?"

"I don't know, but he and Venohr have been experimenting with hybrids. Humans and Maras. Humans and chimeras."

He remembered Una's play about the mad scientist creating a human-automaton lover, and Remy talking about getting a vitamin shot—one that had her memorizing her scripts faster. And Venohr had known about it. "Hanna said that Venohr has a private laboratory in Schöne Maschinen. If Remy is alive, she could be there."

Margit looked at the other people in the roundhouse, then back to Largo. "It's possible. But we have to get inside to find out."

"I'll take you there," said Largo. "But under one condition."

Her face became hard. "What kind?"

"I want to go inside with you."

She relaxed again. "All right, but understand, we won't leave an inch of the place standing."

Largo looked around. "You're not going to bring down Schöne Maschinen with those few guns over there."

She nodded. "I know. We'll use this." She went to a table and brought back what looked like a rectangle of yellow clay the size of a bar of soap.

"What's that?" said Largo.

"Amatol," Margit said. "It's an explosive from the war." She took the clay bar back and said, "See? We've come a long way since the day you got ink on your fingers."

He remembered letting Branca get away with the leaflet and the guilt he felt earlier came back. "I'll help you get in, but you have to let me get Remy out before you destroy the factory."

She glanced at the floor and said, "I can't guarantee that. We'll wait as long as we can, but when the explosions start there's no stopping them."

"When do you want to do it?" Largo said.

"Tonight, if possible."

Largo peered at the group. There were a lot of them. They had

376

guns and a large pile of the yellow bars. *They might actually be able to accomplish something.* He said, "I know how to get you there. But you have to get Parvulesco and Roland first."

Margit thought for a minute. "If the police took them in as radicals they'll be in the same jail you gave us the directions to the other night."

"Good. Once you have them, call me." Largo found some paper and a pencil on a nearby table. He scrawled something and handed it to Margit. "Here's the Trefle number where I'm staying."

Margit folded the paper and put it in her pocket. "What if we can't get them? Will you still help us?"

He stared at her. "You worked hard to get your own people out of jail. Get mine and I'll take you anywhere you want to go."

She walked Largo to the door and said, "We'll call you as soon as we have them."

As he crouched to get under the chain, Largo said, "Thank you."

He put on the mask and rode back to Granate. He'd hoped to take the time alone to think things through clearly, but his mind was spinning. Was Remy real or not? Who should he believe, Branca or Margit?

Either of them would say anything to get what they want. But if there's still a chance of saving Remy, I have to take it.

CHAPTER TWENTY-THREE

HE HAD SOME SOUP AND WINE WITH ANITA WHILE HE WAITED. LATER, SHE read a book of ghost stories she'd found in one of the bedrooms. Largo tried reading a children's book about the history of chimeras, but he couldn't concentrate. A few minutes after two in the morning the Trefle buzzed. Anita answered and handed it to Largo.

"Hello?" he said.

The line crackled. "We have them." It was Margit.

"Let me talk to Parvulesco."

A moment later he heard a familiar voice. "Largo? Is that you? Margit told us you arranged this."

"Are you and Roland all right?"

"Roland fought back, so he got it worse than I did, but we'll both live."

Largo cursed under his breath, then said, "I'm so sorry about what happened."

"I'm glad you got away," said Parvulesco. "Otherwise, we might have been in there forever."

"Are you somewhere safe?"

"We're with Margit by the Black Palace."

Largo said, "Stay there and tell Roland I'm sorry too. If it's any consolation, those bullocks won't be bothering anybody again."

"How do you know?"

"I killed them."

He heard Parvulesco gasp. "What?"

"Put Margit back on the line."

A moment later he heard "Well?"

"Thank you for saving them."

"You're welcome. Now how do we get into Schöne Maschinen?"

"I'll take you there myself. Where should we meet?"

"The Great Triumphal Square," said Margit.

"When?."

"At three A.M. sharp."

"I'll see you there."

At three A.M., Largo leaned against the railing by the underground tram station pretending to drink whiskey through a straw the way he remembered Rainer doing it. The all-night cafés and restaurants were doing a brisk business. People went in and out of the underground station. The new Maras stood on each corner. Largo walked by them and listened. In kind, clear voices they gave travelers directions and answered questions about the state of the war in the north. "We're winning on all fronts" was always their reply.

When he saw Margit, Largo went back to the tram station. She made a face when she saw him. "Are you drinking?"

"No, but I have to look like I'm doing something," he said. "There are more of the new Maras than before."

"Yes. They're dangerous, but it's easy to distract them. Some of our people will stay behind and talk to them while we leave. Give me some."

"It's okay for you to drink?"

"We might all die tonight. I deserve a fucking drink."

Largo passed the bottle to Margit. She removed the straw and took a sip.

"How long before all your people arrive?"

"They're here already."

Largo looked around. The crowd in the square looked the way it did on any other night. He said, "Tell them to go through the passage between the church and the bank. They'll come out on Schimpfte-strasse. Across the street and to the left is a market bazaar. It's dark at this hour, so no one will see us. We can move from there to the power station."

Margit walked away and seemed to ask an elderly man the time. When she came back, the old man moved off into the crowd.

"Berthold will pass the word. Let's go."

Largo and Margit went through the passage to the bazaar arm in arm. The bazaar was an open-air mall closed on three sides. It was very quiet once they were away from the street.

While they waited, Largo looked at Margit. He said, "Are you supposed to shoot me before I get you into Schöne Maschinen or after?"

She squinted at him. "Neither. We're not the bullocks or the Nachtvogel. We're trying to stop that sort of thing, not perpetuate it."

Three women and a man soon arrived.

"Are all of your people so broadminded?" said Largo.

"I'll take care of them," said Margit. "You just do your job."

Largo threw the whiskey into a trash barrel and took off the mask. "I don't suppose I'll be needing that tonight."

As more people arrived, Margit said, "Assuming we live, what will you do tomorrow? Or have you thought that far ahead?"

Largo checked his watch. The more time passed, the more nervous he became. "If you're going to tell me to join your group you're too late. Someone already gave me that speech and she was better at it than you."

"What did you say?"

"Nothing matters until Remy is safe."

Slowly, more people arrived.

"You'll have to leave the city."

"I know. Chances are you will too, don't you think?"

"I hope not, but I might," Margit said.

"Don't go north. I've been there."

"You?" she said incredulously. "You've been to High Proszawa? No wonder you're so bent."

"You know about it, then?"

"We have contacts there, too. Despite what you might have seen, it's not all chaos."

"Have you been there yourself?"

"No."

"Until you have, don't tell me about it," Largo said.

People streamed into the bazaar steadily now. They stood in small groups, all staring at Largo and Margit.

"There are places to hide up north," she said.

"When Remy and I leave it will be to somewhere far away."

"Then you're still a coward and wastrel."

He looked at her. "I'm told people can help from other places than Lower Proszawa."

She made a face. "Don't tell me that's your plan."

Largo looked right back at her. "Isn't that your plan if you fuck off north to play in the mud with your friends?"

"There's plenty more than mud up there."

Largo noticed people checking their weapons. He took out his pistol and nervously looked at the magazine again. It was full.

Margit said, "You actually look like you know what you're doing."

"I've only ever changed the magazine once."

She turned to the group. "Don't tell any of the others."

Largo put the pistol away. "If the people I know can get travel papers for Remy and me I'll owe them, so I'll have to do something to repay them."

"Your enthusiasm is inspiring."

A few more stragglers entered the bazaar. It was filling up.

Largo said, "If Remy is inside and Hellswarth has done something to her, I might kill him before you do. Branca is dead, by the way."

Margit bounced anxiously on the balls of her feet. "You did that?"

"It's not like he didn't deserve it."

"Just be careful where you point that gun tonight." When the last people arrived, Margit motioned them over.

"I've been in the munitions building, but not the others," said Largo. "Which is the eugenic one?"

"Building one. The laboratories are on the second and third floors."

"All right."

When the group surrounded them, Margit said, "I think we're ready. Where do we go now?"

"This way," Largo said. "And be quiet. There's no one around, but it's very dangerous."

"Dangerous how?"

"You'll see soon enough."

They moved in small groups through unlit alleys and behind warehouses well off the main streets. Eventually, they came to one of the neighborhoods that had been hit by bombs during the war. There was a high brick wall with an iron gate blocking the way in. Signs warning of unexploded bombs were plastered all over the walls. There was a cold gust of rain and a mist began to fall.

"Are those signs real?" said the tall woman in the balaclava.

Largo said, "Yes. And we have to get moving before the ground turns to mud."

"Fuck," she said. "Why is this even here?"

Largo pointed to the ruin. "The government left it. It's like a minefield to keep people like us from the power plant."

"But you know the way," said Margit.

"Of course," said Largo. "Now come on. We have to hurry."

"The gate is locked," said tall woman. "How do we get inside?"

Largo leaned into the gate with his shoulder. It slid open. He turned to the others and said, "The lock has been broken for years."

They passed through an old neighborhood that at one time had been as elegant as Kromium. Now whole sections of the streets had collapsed into bomb craters and the buildings were falling in on themselves. Margit was by Largo's shoulder. He said, "Pretty much all of High Proszawa looks like this, only sunk in mud and bones."

"Then you weren't in the right parts. Some are intact. The ones built underground."

"You mean the steelworker area," Largo said.

Margit's head spun in his direction. "You've seen it?"

"I saw them. It looked like they were getting ready to start their own war."

She shook her head. "They're a defense force to hold off any army that attacks from High or Lower Proszawa."

"Who's in charge? They had a lot of government equipment."

"It's all salvaged from the wreckage."

"Is that where you'll go after this?"

Margit shrugged. "I might. As I said, I don't want to leave the city."

Largo nodded. "Good. Stay here no matter what."

"I might not have a choice."

"Then I feel sorry for you."

At the end of a long boulevard they came to a thirty-foot-high brick wall. The mist turned to rain.

Largo said, "It's taller than it was before. They must have reinforced it."

"Wonderful," said the woman.

"How do we get through it?" said Margit.

"Don't worry," said Largo. "We were never going to climb it. I'm just worried that if they used heavy equipment they might have shifted things in the bomb field."

"Bomb field?" the tall woman said. "Margit, he's leading us into a trap."

Largo said, "Don't worry. I know the way."

Margit held on to the tall woman's sleeve. "Mia, we've come too far to turn back now."

"Fuck."

Largo pointed. "There's a metal fence at the other end. It was down, but they might have repaired it. You have tools for that, right?"

"Of course," said Margit.

They turned right along the wall and came to an open field of dirt, craters, and bomb casings protruding from the ground at crazy angles.

Largo said, "Let me go into the field first, then have people follow one by one, stepping in the footprints of the person before them."

"I'll go next," said Margit.

"Don't worry. I won't run away. You can't run here."

Margit turned to Mia. "Pass the word down the line."

"Right," she said, and moved off.

"While she does that, I'm going to get started," said Largo. "Let me get at least twenty paces ahead before you follow."

"Why?" said Margit.

He looked into the minefield. "Because if I'm wrong and a bomb goes off you might live."

Margit followed his gaze. "You're sure this is the only way to the power station?"

"If you don't want to be seen."

She nodded. "All right. Go."

Largo laid his arms across his chest so there was less chance of touching anything. The stitches in his shoulder felt tight. He walked slowly, counting his steps, not thinking except to chart the turns and straightaways with numbers. The ground under his feet began to soften as the rain fell. He thought, *On the one hand, people will be able to see my footprints better. On the other hand, there will be more chances to slip.* He wanted to tell them to be extremely careful, but there was no point in that. *It's better to get through quickly before the ground gets any softer.*

At one point, his right shoulder brushed a tail fin. *That's new.* He adjusted his step a few inches to the left. The roofs and outside stairways on some of the buildings were newly collapsed. *Damn it. They probably did use machinery on the wall. I hope Margit and the others have a light step.*

A few more minutes and he was through. He looked back and saw Margit following him just a few steps behind. When she was close, Largo reached out and pulled her from the field. He said, "I told you to wait."

"I couldn't. Waiting for you to blow up was driving me crazy."

He looked back to the trail. "There are a couple of places where the bombs have shifted. I tried to adjust my step, but no one better rush."

Margit wiped rain from her face. "There's nothing we can do about it now."

"Who has the tools to get us through the wire fence?"

"Dieter. He'll be along soon."

"We should go through as soon as possible so we don't bunch up here."

"You're right."

"And in case some of the others don't make it," he added.

"Yes."

Mia came through next. Dieter, a plump young blond man with freckles, arrived after another minute. Margit immediately sent him to work on the fence with bolt cutters.

When it was open, the four of them crept through to the other side and waited. Twenty people arrived. Thirty. People smoked and talked quietly. Then the ground shook and the sky lit up like a bloody dawn as something exploded. A second explosion knocked them to the ground. A third explosion quickly followed, then everything went quiet. Everyone got to their feet.

Largo went to Margit. "We have to keep going. They'll have heard the explosions all over the city."

Margit craned her neck for a better look. "I can see the factory on the other side of those buildings. Can we get to the plant without being seen?"

Largo shook his head. "There are plasma tanks that will block the view most of the way, but there's a small open field at the end."

Margit took a few steps. "Let's go before someone comes to investigate."

Mia said, "This might be a blessing. The explosion could be a distraction."

"I hope you're right," said Margit.

When they reached the edge of the field, Largo said, "Do you have enough people left to destroy the factory?"

Margit adjusted her coat. "I don't know. We have guns and plenty of amatol. We have to try."

"Listen to me first. Once we're inside, there's no way out anymore except through the front gate."

"We'll worry about that later."

"I hope you're ready. There are a lot of guards ahead."

"Will the guards see us coming?"

Margit checked her watch. "We made it just in time for the shift change. With luck they'll be too distracted by the explosions."

"Let's fucking go," Mia said.

Margit was the first person into the field. Mia and Dieter were next. Finally, Largo pulled his pistol and ran after them. To his amazement, they all made it across alive. He leaned against a wall, panting, more out of nervousness than anything else.

"We're going for the munitions. Be fast or you'll get left behind," said Margit. She handed Largo two of the yellow cakes of amatol. "If you get a chance, leave these in the labs."

"Gladly," said Largo.

"They have timers set for one minute. Just push the button and get out of there."

"Good luck."

"You too," said Margit.

Largo ran alone to building 1.

His shoulder and leg ached. He wished he had some morphia, as much for his nerves as the pain.

The interior of building 1 was surprisingly ordinary. It looked like a dozen different bland medical offices where he'd delivered parcels— how long ago was it? It felt like years. Most of the lights were off in the lobby. There was a reception desk, but no one was there. Largo went straight to the lift, which opened right away. He pushed the button for the second floor and held his pistol at chest level in case there were any guards.

But there weren't. The whole building was dimly lit and nearly silent. There was a sign across from the lift. It said BIOLOGIE EIN-SATZGRUPPE. The second floor was laid out in a straight line running to the left and right of the lift. Largo went to the right and opened each door he came to. There were offices with desks and Trefles, small examination rooms, and closets full of medical supplies, but nothing that looked like a laboratory. He went the other way down the corridor and found the same frustrating configuration of offices and closets.

In the distance, he heard gunshots and an explosion.

When he turned a corner at the end of the corridor he came to a windowless door marked FORSCHUNGSLABOR #2—PRIVAT. Largo tried the door, but it wouldn't budge.

There was another explosion nearby that shook the building. It was followed by several rapid bursts of gunfire.

Largo stepped back and fired at the lock twice. This time when he pulled, the door opened.

Inside was a brightly lit laboratory divided into two sections. The main room held two long black worktables covered with microscopes, test tubes, and glass and metal devices he couldn't hope to identify. *I was supposed to be here*, he thought. *This was supposed to be my world*. But Branca and the Baron had snatched it away.

The building shook again. The orange and blue light of fires filtered into the room through the windows.

The second room of the laboratory looked like an operating room. There was a metal table with a large, bright light overhead. Near the table, used surgical instruments lay on a tray with specks of fresh blood around the rim. Largo noticed that the metal table was damp, as if it had recently been used.

He heard a crash in the other room.

A man in a white lab coat had jumped out from under one of the worktables, knocking over some equipment. He ran for the laboratory door.

"Stop," shouted Largo. When the man didn't, he shot at the door. The man stopped and put his hands over his head. "Turn around."

The man turned. He was bald and had a great gray beard. "Dr. Venohr?" said Largo.

Venohr looked relieved and put his arms down. He said, "Largo, what are you doing here? Have you gone mad?"

Largo went to him and pointed the pistol at the doctor's head. He said, "Where is Remy? Is she alive?"

Venohr put his hands back up. "Yes. Please calm down."

"Is it really her? Not a Mara?"

Venohr waved his hands. "We made a Mara, but only so people wouldn't miss her," he said. He lowered his hands and clasped them in front of him. "She was magnificent—a Mara-eugenic hybrid grown from just a few cells of Remy's flesh. The first of her kind."

Largo pushed the doctor against the door. "Take me to her."

Venohr shook his head as if trying to clear away an unpleasant thought. "Forget her!" he shouted. Then more quietly, "She's *contaminated*."

The way he said it infuriated Largo. He grabbed Venohr and pushed him onto a laboratory stool. He kept the pistol pointed at the doctor and said, "What does 'contaminated' mean?"

The doctor put his head in his hands. "The Mara was never the goal," he said. "The Baron wanted *her*. We extracted a quantity of her essence—"

"Essence? What do you mean?"

"Flesh. Blood. Cells." Venohr looked at him in mild disgust. "Do you even know what cells are? You ignorant boy."

Largo gestured with the pistol. "Go on."

"We fused her essence with that of a eugenic and the Baron infected her with it."

Outside, there were more explosions and gunfire. Venohr cringed at the noise. Largo said, "The Baron wants to make Remy into a chimera?"

"No," said the doctor. "Well, a bit. You see, by taking a bit of the eugenic's essence he hoped he could tame her. Make her pliable." Venohr smiled nervously. "Make her love him."

Largo felt cold inside, almost like morphia withdrawal. "Did it work?"

Venohr said, "To some degree. It wasn't clear if the procedure was entirely successful."

Largo thought about everything he could remember from the last couple of weeks. He said, "Kara, the chimera in his office—is part of that Remy?"

"Yes," said Venohr eagerly. "Gorgeous, isn't she? The Baron used a small quantity of Remy's essence in making Kara."

Largo remembered petting her. "He said Kara didn't like most people. But she liked me."

"Yes, and it infuriated him."

Largo pressed the gun to Venohr's temple. "Kara isn't all that's left of Remy, is it?"

The doctor frowned. "Don't be stupid. She's still herself, just, you see, different. She's unlikely to even recognize you."

"Take me to her."

One of the windows exploded, showering the room in glass. Largo ducked and Venohr crouched on the floor. "I can't," he said. "The Baron took her away days ago."

"Where?"

Venohr got up on his knees. "He wouldn't tell me. He said somewhere familiar where she'd be safe and happy."

"Home?"

"No," said Venohr conspiratorially. "He's afraid of the police discovering our work. They're cretins. They wouldn't understand at all."

Largo said, "Which work? Kidnapping people or changing them into your puppets?"

Venohr slowly stood back up. "You of all people should understand that we're helping them. Think of it. No more morphia addicts. No more bullies or sexual degenerates. A country free of all aberrant behavior."

"So you can rule them."

Venohr looked offended. "So we can *survive*. Do you think we can win the war with those hordes in the streets?" With the window gone, the gunfire outside was louder than ever. The doctor glanced at Largo's pistol. "Please don't kill me."

Largo remembered the night at the Golden Angel when Vera had said that Remy was an "empty vessel." *She could have meant the Mara Remy. Or the one transformed by chimera essence.* He grabbed Venohr's lab coat. "Too many people have lied to me tonight. Show me the other lab. I want to make sure she's not there."

With Venohr in front, they went into the corridor. Largo said, "Why is Schöne Maschinen digging up bodies in High Proszawa?"

Venohr stopped and spun around to look at him. "How do you know about that?"

"I was there. I saw it with my own eyes."

The doctor turned away and shook his head. "I don't want to talk about it."

Largo hit him with the butt of the pistol.

Venohr stumbled against the wall with a hand on the back of his neck. He said, "We need the bodies. The city needs them."

"Why?" shouted Largo.

The doctor took his hand from behind his head and checked it for blood. "We hoped that when we took people from the streets and transfigured them into Maras there would be enough, but there simply wasn't. That's why we need more bodies."

"Enough of what?"

"Trans zamlžení, of course," said Venohr. "Where do you think plazma power comes from? The sky?"

Largo stood still for a moment, trying to process the thought. He remembered trans zamlžení drifting from Vera's mouth as the spirit appeared. The Golden Angel burning. "*A tricky substance*," she'd said. "*Very volatile.*" He looked at Venohr and said, "Isn't trans zamlžení part of a person? Their spirit? You're . . . you're burning people for fuel?"

The doctor stood up from the wall as if offended. "We're harvesting a vital element from corpses that don't need it anymore."

"Yes," said Largo. "But you're also *making* a lot of the corpses you're draining."

Venohr lunged at Largo and shoved him against the wall. As he ran down the corridor for the lift, Largo shot twice. The second shot knocked Venohr onto the floor. He shouted, "You hit my leg!"

"You're lucky I'm not a better shot."

Largo took out one of the amatol cakes, pushed the timer button, and threw it into Venohr's laboratory. Then he went to Venohr and pulled him into the lift.

"What was that you threw?" said the doctor.

"You'll see."

The lift took them to the third floor. Just as the door opened, the building rocked with an explosion. Venohr looked at Largo. "My god. What have you done? All my notes were in there."

"Good."

Largo pushed the limping Venohr into the third-floor laboratory, where he tumbled onto his back, holding his bloody leg. The room looked almost exactly like the one on the second floor. And like that one, it was empty.

"See? I was telling the truth. Let me go," Venohr said.

"Not until you tell me where Remy is."

"Don't you understand?" Venohr shouted. He held his hands out like claws. "She's polluted. Not even human anymore. She might be insane, harbor diseases or worse."

Largo said, "You said the technique might not have worked."

"I was being modest." Earnestly, he added, "Help me and we can find her together."

Largo shook his head. The dead feeling settled into him again. "You've done enough for Remy." He felt Venohr's belt until he found a set of keys. He tried several in the laboratory lock before finding one that worked.

Venohr said, "Please. Together we can save her."

"Goodbye, Doctor." He pushed the timer on the second bar of amatol and tossed it on the floor with Venohr. On his way out he locked the door and broke off the key.

Largo was physically and mentally exhausted. He pushed the button for the lift and when the doors opened a woman stood there with a gun in her hand. He raised his and they both stood that way for a few seconds. Then he said, "Hanna?"

She lowered her pistol and hugged him. "Margit told me you were working with the group," she said. "I thought you might need some help."

"You're the other contact in Schöne Maschinen," he said. "It never crossed my mind."

"Imagine my surprise when Margit told me you were coming tonight. But what are you doing in the labs?"

An explosion sent them sprawling against the wall. "We should leave," said Largo. "I'll explain things on the way."

Hanna pressed the lift button for the first floor. Nothing happened. She motioned to Largo and they went down the stairs. As they went she said, "You're looking for Remy, aren't you?"

"Yes. Do you know where she is?"

"No. I was hoping she'd be in Venohr's laboratory."

"I was just there. It's empty," said Largo. "But I have an idea where she might be."

Someplace she's safe and happy.

When they got outside, the sound of gunfire and the *whump*s of explosions were even louder. The ground shook and the air was acrid with smoke. Men and women with rifles ran past them. Stumbling at the rear was a small blond woman holding her side with a bloody hand. "Margit!" called Hanna.

They ran to her as she fell onto the pavement. Hanna opened Margit's jacket. "You're hit," she said.

Margit shook her head and winced. "It's not that bad. I think it just broke some ribs."

"You need to get out of here," said Largo.

"We're leaving," Margit said. "The whole munitions building will blow soon. Help me to one of the juggernauts."

Largo and Hanna got on either side of Margit and carried her to a line of transport vehicles by building 1. The rear of a juggernaut was open and people were scrambling inside. They set Margit on the floor. A dozen scared, pale fighters sat around them. Dieter was behind the controls at the front of the juggernaut.

"Is this everyone?" said Largo.

"All that are left," said Mia.

Dieter extinguished the light and turned the juggernaut around. A moment later they sped down the driveway to the front gate of Schöne Maschinen. Largo moved up front. "Won't the guards follow us?" he said.

"Let them try. We booby-trapped their vehicles."

They burst through the gate without stopping as bullets peppered the juggernaut's rear. From behind them came the sound of more explosions as the juggernauts blew up. Largo knelt beside Dieter and directed him along a circuitous path to Machtviertel.

Using only shadows and memory to direct them, to Largo the trip seemed to take hours.

When they arrived, Largo looked at the sky. "Won't the flying Maras have followed us?"

"Let them," said Mia. A moment later, the roundhouse where they'd met earlier exploded into flames. "We're done with this place."

The healthy people moved the injured ones from the juggernaut into a yellowsheet delivery van. Largo helped to carry Margit. As the van sped onto the main road away from Machtviertel Hanna examined her. Largo said, "Will she be all right?"

"I think so," said Hanna.

Margit said, "There's an underground hospital in Kromium. They can help us. Did you find Remy?"

"No, but I think I know where she is. I'm going to have to leave when we get back to the city."

"Do what you have to," Margit said. She squeezed Largo's hand. "Welcome to the real war."

He shook his head. "I'm no soldier."

"Look around. Look at Hanna. We all said the same thing."

He watched Hanna get a medical kit from a corner of the van and pack gauze into Margit's wound. "Thank you for letting me come with you," he said.

Margit closed her eyes. Largo looked at Hanna. She said, "Margit will be all right. I promise."

There was a toolbox in the back of the van. He opened it and took out a crowbar. "Do you mind if I take this?" Largo said.

"Go ahead," said Margit. "Find Remy."

When they were back in the city, the van stopped just long enough for Largo to get out of the back. Hanna held out a hand to him and said, "Give Remy my love."

While the earlier rain had cleared, a dense fog had settled over the city. Largo waved to Hanna as the van dissolved into the mist.

He walked to the Great Triumphal Square and hailed a Mara cab. When it asked where he wanted to go he said, "The Grand Dark."

THE CORRUPTER OF INNOCENCE, ACT 1

Discarded draft of a new play by Una Herzog

CHARACTERS

HEINZ: A drug-addicted bicycle messenger and anarchist.
ELISE: An innocent young actress and Heinz's lover.

*Heinz comes home to their cramped and filthy flat
after a meeting with his anarchist cell.
He is unshaven and in a foul mood.*

ELISE
How was your meeting, my love?

HEINZ
Don't ask stupid questions. Did you do it?
Elise looks frightened.

ELISE
I couldn't. Don't be mad. I know he's a
politician, but he's an old man with a family.
Heinz slaps her viciously.

HEINZ

Fool! All it would have taken was one thrust of
the knife. The Party will have my head for this.

ELISE

Can't someone else do it?

HEINZ

We're all being watched. It had to be you.
(Bitterly) An innocent lily of the field. Too bad
she's an idiot too.

ELISE

I'm sorry. Here's the knife back.
Elise meekly puts it on the table. Heinz shoves her
away violently.

ELISE

Would you like some tea? I just made it.

HEINZ

No.

ELISE

A drink?

HEINZ

No! I have to think.

ELISE

Here's some tea in case you change your mind.
She wanders their dirty flat picking up his clothes,
which he has carelessly strewn everywhere. Heinz
clearly sees her as little more than a servant.

ELISE

I didn't see your bicycle this morning.

HEINZ

I had to sell it for morphia, you cow. The
bottle is in the bedroom. Bring it to me.
Elise cowers in the corner of the room.

ELISE

My mother's bad back . . . her poor twisted hands
from years of work . . . She was in so much pain.

HEINZ

What are you telling me?

ELISE

I gave it to her.

HEINZ

All of it?

ELISE

I'm sorry.

HEINZ

How dare you? First you won't do your duty to the
Party and now you starve me of my one pleasure in
life? You're not even a good fuck anymore.

ELISE

Please! I try so hard.
What can I do to make it up to you?
Heinz throws the tea in Elise's face. She screams as

397

it burns delicate flesh. (Speak to technicians about
erupting into boils and scars)

HEINZ

How can you make it up to me? I'll show you!
Heinz grabs the knife from the table.

HEINZ

You can die, you whore!
Heinz stabs her. She screams in agonizing
death throes. *(Draw these out. Show the*
audience what a monster he is.)
When Heinz sees what he's done, ever the
coward, he drops the knife and flees, his shirt
and hands covered in Elise's blood.
Fade to black.

CHAPTER TWENTY-FOUR

THERE WASN'T A BUILDING IN THE CITY TALLER THAN A SINGLE STORY TO-night. Anything above that was swaddled in vapor, turning Lower Proszawa into something old, liminal, and unfinished. The cab had to creep slowly through the gloom. Largo grew frustrated, then furious at their progress.

"Can't you go a little faster?" he said into the cab's speaker tube.

It replied, "Apologies, mein Herr, but under the circumstances that isn't permitted."

Largo leaned back into the seat as the fog settled farther down onto the road so that the buildings became vague outlines. *That could be a bank*, he thought. *Or a restaurant. Or an elephant.* Street lamps and crossing lights were hazy stars that passed overhead. He checked his watch. It was just after five A.M. The city would be waking up soon and he wanted to be done with things before there were people in the street.

Finally the cab slowed and stopped. There was nothing outside but a solid bank of gray.

"The Grand Dark," said the Mara. Largo threw money at the driver and stepped out of the cab. He tripped over the curb trying to get his bearings, but finally saw the dark marquee above him. He went around the side of the building, now happy for the fog since it would obscure his presence.

It took a moment to find the stage entrance. When he did, he pried open the door with the crowbar from the van. After what felt like an hour, there was a pop as the lock broke and the door swung open.

The backstage area was pitch-black. Largo fumbled along the wall until he found a light switch. When he could see where he was, he rushed to Remy's dressing room and found it padlocked shut. He used the crowbar to wrench the lock out of the door and went inside. But she wasn't there. The room was a shambles, with clothes and furniture thrown onto the floor. He went back out and checked the other dressing rooms one by one. There were no people anywhere, but the furniture and clothes in the other rooms were neatly arranged and in their proper places.

Largo checked the closets and the storage room where the props were kept. Nothing. Next to the plazma area where the electrics were housed, he entered the room where they stored the puppets and galvanic suits.

In the dim light from backstage, he remembered how Remy had once called it a madman's abattoir. Human forms—some clothed and some nude—hung lifeless from hooks in the ceiling. He flipped the light switch, but it didn't work. Using the crowbar, he pushed a few of the puppets out of the way and went deeper into the room. There was nothing. He was heading back to the stage area when he heard a sigh.

Largo whirled around. "Remy? Is that you?"

A small plazma lamp went on. A man's voice calmly said, "Come in, Largo. Put down the crowbar."

He set the crowbar on the floor and pushed puppets out of the way until he came to an open area at the back of the room. Remy was asleep on a cot. Next to her was a small table with the plazma lamp and a plate with food scraps on it. Near the lamp were several small vials and a syringe. Largo started toward Remy, but the Baron stood next to her with an oddly shaped pistol in his hand. Largo had never seen anything like it before. "Stop where you are," Hellswarth said.

Largo watched Remy's chest slowly rise and fall as she slept. "What have you done to her?"

"Remy is fine," said the Baron. "She just needs rest."

Largo pointed to the syringes. "I mean the other things," he said angrily. "If you love her, how could you use her like that?"

"She was sick."

"Because she loved me and not you."

The Baron looked down at Remy. "Partly. But I'm fixing her, just like I fix any other broken mechanism."

"Don't talk about her like that."

The Baron said, "I cured her morphia addiction. You should thank me for that, at least."

Largo felt the pistol in his pocket but knew he couldn't get to it without being shot first. "You didn't cure her for her own sake or you would have done it before. You did it to make her a better pet."

Hellswarth gestured with the pistol. "And what were you doing by giving her morphia in the first place?"

Largo took another step closer. The Baron raised the gun higher. "I never kidnapped her. I never filled her with whatever filth it is you and Venohr made."

Baron Hellswarth didn't resemble the man Largo had seen at the factory or the Golden Angel. It looked like he hadn't shaved or combed his hair in days. He said, "You saw Venohr? Where is he?"

Largo gave him a satisfied smile. "Dead at Schöne Maschinen."

The Baron's jaw clenched for a second. "That's too bad. We were going to do great things. Still, I can carry on without him."

"I destroyed his notes. If there was a copy at the factory, it's gone too."

Hellswarth frowned and stared down at Remy.

Largo looked at him, wanting to say something. All he could think of was "That's a strange gun you have there, Baron."

He held it up so that Largo could see. It was matte black and instead of a barrel it had two thin electrodes, about five inches long. "It's new. It shoots plasma instead of bullets."

"I've heard about those."

"Now you can see how it works," said Hellswarth. He inclined his head toward the door. "Go outside, Largo. Remy is only half-asleep. I don't want to kill you in front of her."

With nothing to lose anymore, Largo went and knelt next to Remy. He held her hand for a moment, kissed it, and laid it back across her.

"Get up," said the Baron. "I'll shoot you here if I have to."

Largo got up, keeping his eyes on Remy. When he turned to go, he swept his hand across the table, knocking the lamp toward Hellswarth. It landed at his feet and burst into flame. Burning plazma splashed onto the Baron's trousers and jacket. He tried to shoot at Largo, but he couldn't hold his hands steady. Instead, a jagged bolt of white light blew a hole in the ceiling as the Baron spun to the floor, trying to put out the flames.

Largo grabbed Remy and was trying to pull her to her feet when something slammed into him from behind, knocking him on top of her. He turned and ducked just in time as the crowbar smashed into the wall, scattering plaster and brick dust. As Una raised the crowbar over her head again, Largo grabbed her. She missed his head and her arm swung over his shoulder so that he caught most of the blow on his back. "Shit!" he yelled and tried to push her off, but she was surprisingly strong and wouldn't let go. They swung around the room as Una slammed the crowbar into Largo's back over and over.

There was another bolt of light, and then another. "Move, Una!" shouted the Baron. The two of them swung around again, and this time Largo was the one who wouldn't let go. The next shot caught Una in the small of the back. She didn't scream, but lit up a bright, searing red for a moment as her body burned from the inside. The stench of her glowing flesh was awful. It was like being back in High Proszawa.

Largo shoved her off and grabbed his pistol. Baron Hellswarth's face and arm were badly burned and his hand trembled as he tried to aim. Largo pulled the trigger on his gun, but it merely jumped in his hand as it jammed.

The Baron shot again, but the bolt hit a puppet, igniting it. Largo kicked the burning doll at Hellswarth and ran behind it, tackling him as he jumped out of its way. When they hit the floor, the Baron's pistol went spinning into the dark. He held on to Largo, punching him in the ribs and face. Largo grabbed the Baron's throat and squeezed until the man's grip loosened just enough that he could get his knife and slash out with it. He left a deep gash in the Baron's injured arm.

The flames from the burning puppet set two others on fire.

As Largo pulled the Baron upright, they knocked a tool tray off the wall. When he tried to stab him again, Hellswarth grabbed a hammer and swung it at him, hitting Largo's arm hard enough that the knife fell to the floor. Before he could grab it, the Baron found his pistol. There was a shriek as Remy threw herself on top of him, digging her teeth into his gun hand. He swore and dropped the pistol. As he shoved Remy off, Largo grabbed the knife and swung the spiked handgrip into the Baron's burned face. He staggered and fell by the open door. Remy thudded to the floor on her back. Largo grabbed her, but when he turned to the Baron he was gone.

Several puppets were burning and the room began filling with smoke. Largo pulled Remy up and dragged her out, kicking the door closed behind them.

Remy was unsteady on her feet and looked around the backstage area as if she'd never seen it before. But when she saw Largo, she said his name. "Is it really you?"

"It is," he said. She grabbed him around the neck and hugged him tight.

Smoke crept from under the puppet room door and ceiling as the fire spread. "We've got to go," he said.

Remy held on to his face. "Good. I don't like it here anymore."

He took her hand and they ran out the stage door. Smoke followed them as they made it to the curb. Remy shivered. Largo draped his coat around her shoulders and put on the metal mask.

Remy laughed and said, "You look silly."

"Boo."

Largo held her by the shoulders and they walked back toward the center of the city. Behind them, the fog flickered with orange light as the fire spread and the Grand Dark burned.

They soon found a cab and Largo had it take them to the edge of Granate. They walked the rest of the way to Anita's house. As they went, the fresh air seemed to help revive Remy. "Where are we?" she said.

"We're going to stay with a friend for a while," said Largo.

Remy stopped and took his mask off. "I need to see your face again. It is you, isn't it?" she said.

"It is," he said. "I promise."

Remy looked at the buildings and trailed her hands through the fog, making it swirl around her fingers. She said, "I think I was in the hospital."

"It was like a hospital, but you're all better now."

"Good. I didn't like it there."

"You won't ever have to go back," Largo said.

He took her hand and they began to walk again. "Uncle Rudy said I was sick. And he told me you were dead," she said. Remy looked thoughtful and serious.

Largo put an arm around her. "We're both all right now. He won't bother you again."

Remy rested her head on his shoulder. She said, "I'm very tired."

"We're almost there. A special friend is waiting for you."

"Who?"

"It's a surprise."

It took Remy a few minutes to accept that she was really sitting by a fire with Anita Mourlet.

"I gave you a necklace at the Golden Angel," Remy said.

Anita smiled. "Yes. Largo told me."

"And then you kissed me."

"I remember."

Remy held her hand as if trying to convince herself that, like Largo, she was real. He was worried about her. Remy's eyes were unfocused and she seemed sedated. *What was he giving her back there?*

Largo told Anita what had happened and said, "We have to get out of the city. If the Baron is still alive, he's going straight to the bullocks." He sat next to Remy and she took his hand too. He said, "The problem is that all the money I have in the world is in that coat. I don't know how we're going to live."

Remy, who had been resting her head on Anita's shoulder, sat up and said blearily, "There's my money."

"What money?" said Largo.

"All the money and jewels Uncle Rudy gave me. I didn't want them so I put them in a box in the closet."

Anita looked at him. "A Baron's money and trinkets could go a long way to getting you started."

Remy looked from Anita to Largo. She frowned and gripped his hand tighter. "Don't go," she said pleadingly.

Largo kissed her hand. "I have to, but Anita will take care of you while I'm gone."

Anita smiled and put an arm around Remy. "It's true. I will."

"You're both very sweet," said Remy, and she closed her eyes. She seemed to fall asleep sitting up.

Largo whispered, "Do you have a gun?"

"The group took them all when they left," she said. "What happened to yours?"

"I lost it. My knife too," he said. He got up and put on the bulky oilskin coat. "I'm not very good at playing the hero."

"I think you're doing fine," said Anita. "So does Remy, I suspect."

Largo took a tram to the artists' quarter in Kromium. It was almost dawn, but the sky was still a solid gray canopy overhead. A fine mist came down, the precursor to more rain.

From the outside, Remy's building looked deserted. As with Rainer's flat, there was police tape over the entrance and Health Department quarantine posters out front. Largo ducked under the tape and went inside.

He listened for the sounds of people coming awake, but there was nothing. *They cleared the whole building for one woman's disappearance*, he thought. *The Baron must be terrified someone might find out what happened. Maybe that means somewhere deep down inside he's still human.*

There was hardware for a padlock on the door to Remy's flat, but no lock. Largo pushed the door open. A light went on, blinding him for a moment.

"There you are," said the Baron. "Let's see if we can get things right this time."

When his eyes adjusted to the light, Largo saw Hellswarth sitting stiffly on the black sofa. He was covered in livid patches where the fire had burned deeply into his face and arm. On a table in front of him were piles of cash and jewels, and a large glass of whiskey. Next to that was a large box full of letters. The Baron pointed a pistol at him, an ordinary one this time.

Largo said, "You have a lot of guns, Baron."

He winced. "I make them, you imbecile. My family has made them for four hundred years."

"You won't be making them again for a while."

"I suppose not." The Baron gestured with the pistol. "Put your hands up, by the way." Largo did as he was told.

The Baron picked up a handful of letters. "I wrote her one a week for years, telling her how I felt. All she did was stuff them in a box." The Baron shook his head. "What did you do to her? She loved me so much when she was a girl."

Largo frowned at him. "She was a child then. Remy loves me now."

The Baron's lips grew tight. "She might think so for the moment, but I'll fix that."

"Venohr told me what you did to her. But it didn't work."

Hellswarth gave him a broad, knowing grin. "Yes, it did. I checked her blood. She isn't herself anymore. She's becoming something else. Something brand-new."

"It doesn't matter," said Largo. "She's not yours and she never will be. If she wants me to go she'll be the one to tell me, not you."

The Baron brightened. "Maybe we should both let her go together. What do you say? A suicide pact?"

Largo ignored him. "Those burns look like they hurt."

"They do."

"Your face is never going to be the same. Maybe you should be the one wearing a mask. Would you like mine?"

The Baron opened his mouth, winced, then opened it again. "You're an arrogant little prick, aren't you?"

Largo looked at the ceiling for a second. He hurt all over and the oilskin coat was making him sweat. "Remy loves me and we destroyed your life's work tonight. If anyone is leaving it should be you."

"I could call the police, you know. I'm sure they'll be happy to torture Remy's whereabouts out of you."

That was a more frightening possibility than being shot, but he knew he couldn't show it. The Green came out once more—no backing down, no showing fear.

"Do it, my fine brother. She's with people who know how to make things happen. By the time the bullocks finish with me, Remy will be long gone and there's nothing you can do about it." Largo added, "Plus, there's the matter of her hating you."

"I'll make her love me."

"You're a pathetic old man."

"Not so old," said the Baron.

His first shot knocked Largo to his knees. He knelt there, gripping the edge of the table with both hands. Strangely, he didn't feel any pain from the wound, just the wind knocked out of him. The Baron had paused for a moment, seemingly to enjoy Largo's gasping breath. Before he could get off another round, Largo tightened his grip on the table and jumped up, using it as a battering ram. They fell onto the sofa, rolled, and together they tumbled to the floor. The Baron shot again, but Largo had a grip on his gun hand. Seeing that there was still a little whiskey in the Baron's partially overturned glass, he grabbed it and threw it at Hellswarth. The Baron screamed as the liquor burned into his eyes and the wounds on his face. Stumbling to his feet, he shot two more times blindly, trying to wipe his eyes clean with his sleeve. Largo threw himself at him, knocking the Baron onto his back. But the older man was stronger than Largo had counted on. The Baron worked his gun hand free and pistol-whipped him. Largo's vision went red for a second. His weight shifted. When his head cleared, the Baron was on top of him with the gun to his temple. Largo reached out blindly and his hand fell on some envelopes. He grabbed a handful and shoved them in Hellswarth's face.

"Look at all of them. Remy buried your letters like the trash they are," he said.

"You don't know anything, boy."

"I know the real Remy, which you never will." Largo pressed his head against the muzzle of the pistol. "Go ahead. Kill me. Start a war. Burn the world. She'll never love you and you know it."

For a moment, the Baron seemed to consider the words. The pistol drifted away an inch or two. It was enough. By pure instinct, Largo grabbed the Baron's gun hand and bit down as hard as he could. Hellswarth screamed as Largo shifted his weight and broke free. When the Baron tried to get up, Largo clumsily threw himself on top of the man, pinning him to the floor in the middle of the pile of discarded letters. The Baron's gun hand was pointed at the ceiling and Largo kept a tight grip on it.

"It's over," he said. "Schöne Maschinen. Your eugenics. Remy. Listen, Baron. Can you hear the car taking her away from you forever?"

The Baron's eyes were hard but wet. *From pain or from losing Remy?* Largo wondered. A small knot of fear scratched at the back of his skull, but he remained indifferent to it. It was just another kind of pain in a body that hurt all over. Whatever happened now, Largo was sure that the Baron wouldn't find Remy. That was all that mattered.

Hellswarth struggled under him for a moment, trying to maneuver the pistol. Largo dropped all of his weight down on the man, forcing his hand down. The Baron never looked away from Largo's eyes.

He kept steady pressure on the Baron's arm. Soon the weapon was almost level with the older man's head. Seeing it, Largo froze, not sure what to do. Kill him? Leave him alone in his misery? None of the choices made sense. Nothing made sense anymore. He pictured Remy at the Grand Dark. He saw himself cowering from bullies in Haxan Green. The theater, the squalid streets that shaped him, both places were poison, but for a moment Largo wasn't sure if he was strong enough to break away.

He kept pressure on the pistol.

How many people have I killed already?

He looked down at the Baron. The hand not holding the pistol clutched at his letters to Remy. His face was red, and not just from the burns. Tears fell from his eyes. He spoke very quietly.

"Remy might not be mine, but remember this: She's not yours either. She's something no one has ever seen before."

Largo thought about what Dr. Venohr had said: *"She's still herself, just, you see, different."*

"What do you mean?" he said, pressing down on Hellswarth. "What did you do to her?"

The Baron said, "I made her perfect." He jerked his body violently to the side and pressed his head against the pistol.

The sound of the gun going off sent Largo rolling onto the floor. Hellswarth's blood covered the letters. Largo looked away. Getting up, he staggered to the bathroom to wash the filth off of his face. He found a fresh hole in the side of the oilskin coat and understood how the Baron had missed shooting him earlier: the garment was bulky enough that the man had aimed off center, hitting the material and not Largo.

I owe Vera a drink. Many, many drinks.

He left the love letters on the floor with the dead man who wrote them and filled the box with the cash and jewels. Before he left, he spotted his copy of *Der Knochengarten*. He'd used Ernst's business card for a bookmark. Largo went to Remy's Trefle and told the operator the number. The line rang several times before Ernst answered.

"It's me, Largo," he said.

"Largo," said Ernst blearily. "I thought you might have been eaten by sea monsters. Do you have my High Proszawa story?"

"I have a better one. I know you enjoy a good scandal."

"It'd better be very good if you're going to cheat me out of High Proszawa."

He gave Ernst Remy's address. "Get here as fast as you can. You'll find Baron Hellswarth and the sad truth about a national hero. Be sure to take lots of chromes."

"Are you serious?"

Largo looked down at the Baron's body.

"Deadly."

"I'm on my way."

He put on the mask, tucked the box under his arm, and left Remy's flat for the last time.

At the nearest tram station, a drunken mob was tearing down the signs, singing patriotic songs, fighting, and pissing on the tracks. Cars had been overturned. A few were on fire. In the distance stood a group of police, but they weren't foolish enough to approach the revelers.

Above the thick clouds overhead, something rumbled. Not thunder, but something ringed with lights. *One of the new airships?* Largo wondered. The mob cheered its passing.

This is who we are now. We drank and played to celebrate the end of the last war and now we're doing it again, but to ring in the new one. It's horrible, but at least we're our own fools and not Hellswarth's, the Nachtvogel's, or anyone else's.

The idea was small comfort, but it would have to be enough for the moment.

He took side streets all the way on his long walk back to the house in Granate.

CHAPTER TWENTY-FIVE

WHEN HE LET HIMSELF INSIDE, HE FOUND REMY AND ANITA CURLED UP asleep together on the sofa. He woke them and showed them the box of jewelery and cash. Remy picked up a diamond necklace and held it around her neck for a few seconds before throwing it on the table.

Anita sat down next to Largo. "You're limping. Bleeding again too, I bet."

He let his head fall back. "I don't suppose you have any thread left?"

"I'll get the box."

Remy held his hand as Anita mended his shoulder.

"I have good news," she told him. "My friends know that you helped in the attack on Schöne Maschinen tonight. They're willing to get travel papers for you both—if you'll help them."

Largo thought about it for just a second. "We will. From afar," he said.

Anita continued sewing. "Where will you go?"

He looked at Remy. "Where do you want to go?"

She shook her head, more awake than before but still fighting through cobwebs. "I don't know," she said. "I still feel like I'm dreaming. Where do you think we should go?"

Largo thought about it for a moment. "What did Vera say? Somewhere no one has ever heard of Lower Proszawa, the Great War, or the Nachtvogel."

Anita sighed. "It sounds lovely. Let's all go."

Largo turned to Remy. "Does that sound all right?"

"I'm really not dreaming?" she said.

"Not even a little."

They waited in the house for two days. Anita received calls on the Trefle at all hours of the day and night. Afterward she would sometimes seem happy, but at other times nervous. Largo asked her what the calls were about, but all she would say was "They're doing their best, but some of the border crossings have been closed." When he asked her what that meant for them, Anita wouldn't answer.

They kept the lights off at night. Crowds marched in and out of Granate. There were parties in the street outside, with people singing old folk songs. At some point, someone would start a bonfire and the songs would turn patriotic and angry.

On the third day, their food ran out. Largo volunteered to go to a nearby market, but Remy insisted that she should do it.

"Are you sure?" he said. "It's only been a few days."

She took some cash from the box Largo had brought back from her flat. "I'm much better now," she said. Largo had to admit that in the past day or so, she'd come around to seeming like the old Remy again. "Besides, I'm tired of people fussing over me like I was a laboratory rat. I'm capable of walking to the market and back."

"I'm sorry," said Largo. "I didn't mean—"

Remy took his hand. "It's all right. It's just that I'm so angry all the time and I don't even know exactly why. I can't remember much about what happened to me."

"Maybe that's for the best," said Anita.

"No. I want to know everything. Now that I'm better you'll tell me, right, Largo?"

He sat down at the battered living room table. "If that's what you want."

"I do."

"All right."

After she left the house, Largo watched her go down the block from behind the curtains until she was out of sight. Anita sat on the sofa with a cigarette. "You're worried about her."

"She might have a condition."

"What kind?"

"I don't know."

"Does she need a doctor?"

Largo dropped onto the end of the sofa. "She had a doctor. That's the problem. I don't know if she'll ever trust one again."

"What happened to her?"

"They experimented on her. The doctor and her uncle. Don't ask me what kind of experiments because I don't know."

Anita frowned. "That's horrible."

Largo bounced a fist lightly off the arm of the sofa. "They won't hurt anyone again."

Waving some smoke away, Anita said, "Is that why there was blood on your hands the other night?"

Largo looked at his palms. "I thought I'd washed it off."

"You got most of it, but not all."

He drew in a long breath. "I hate this place."

Anita puffed the cigarette. "You're sure it's all right for Remy to travel?"

"Is there any choice? Besides, Remy is strong."

"I didn't doubt that for a minute. I'll help you keep an eye on her."

"I'd appreciate that."

Remy soon returned with wine, cheese, and bread. She turned an envelope over in her hands. "It was on the floor when I came in. Someone must have slipped it under door."

"May I see it?" said Anita. Remy gave it to her and she ripped it open. There was a small slip of paper inside.

Largo stood up. "What does it say?"

Anita smiled broadly and held the note out to them. "Be ready tonight."

The rest of the day seemed to crawl by. One or all three of them would run to the curtains every time there was a loud noise, but it was always the revelers or groups of serious young men waving bats and axe handles like rifles. It was dark by seven. They picked at the bread and cheese, but the bottle of wine they drained long before sunset. Just after eight o'clock there was a knock at the door.

Unsure if it was the right caller, Largo brought a butcher knife from the kitchen and stood just to the side of the entrance so that whoever was outside wouldn't see him. Anita put on her brightest stage smile and opened the door. She stood there for a moment, just long enough for Largo to grow tense. Finally, he heard a woman's voice.

"I was told there were three of you."

Anita stood back and let the other woman in. Largo lowered the knife but didn't put it down until he saw her face. The woman closed the door and looked at him. "Hello, Largo. Going to carve the armistice goose?"

He tossed the knife on the table. "Margit. It's nice to see you."

"You too."

She wore a loose cap, a dirty coat, and coveralls, like a mechanic. There was a worn valise in her right hand. In the living room, she pulled a packet of papers from inside her coat and dropped them on the table. "That's everything you need. Travel papers. Identification. Transport tickets."

While Anita and Remy looked them over, Largo said, "You look a lot better. The last time I saw you I thought you might not make it."

She took off her cap and ran a hand through her short blond hair. "I told you it looked worse than it was. I hear that you've been busy."

"Busy how?"

From inside her coveralls, Margit pulled a copy of *Ihre Skandale*. The chrome on the top of the front page showed an apparently lifeless hand lying atop a pile of bloody letters. Below it the headline read NATIONAL HERO OR NATIONAL DISGRACE? Largo set the paper down on the table.

"Aren't you going to read it?" said Margit.

"I'll read it as we travel. By . . . ?"

"Ship. You're going on a sea voyage."

Largo tried to picture being out at sea. "I've never been on a ship before. Not one that went on top of the water, at least."

She pointed to the yellowsheet. "Thank you for taking care of that particular problem for us."

"I didn't do it for any revolution."

"I know. But it still helps."

He looked at her. "I didn't know that you were in Anita's group."

Margit shook her head. "We weren't originally, but since Schöne Maschinen burned, the remaining groups have banded together."

He couldn't think of anything else to say in response, so he just left it with "Well, thank you for the papers."

She put the valise on top of the table. "There are clothes in here for all of you. A suit for you and dresses for them. If we're going to get you onto a ship, you have to look the part."

Largo opened the valise and spread the clothes on the table.

"Don't admire them too long," said Margit. "Your ship sails in just over two hours, so you'll need to move."

No one bothered going to one of the bedrooms. They changed right where they stood. Anita and Remy went to the bathroom to do their makeup. When they came down, Largo barely recognized Anita. She'd done something to her face. She looked like herself, but much older and worn. The women carried suitcases with them.

"Is there anything in them?" said Largo.

"Whatever was in the closets," said Anita.

Remy said, "After all, we have to look like travelers."

They gathered up the travel papers and the bags, but Margit didn't move. She looked at Largo. "I know Anita's loyalties, but did you mean it about being willing to help from afar?"

"I did."

"Me too," said Remy.

"It will be dangerous."

"More dangerous than walking through a minefield with a gaggle of lunatics?"

Margit nodded, a faint smile on her lips. "They're more or less the same, I suppose." Then she looked serious again. "Anita is your contact. We'll get in touch with her at the right time."

"I understand."

"Then let's go. There's a car outside. Turn off the light as we leave. No one needs to see our faces."

They drove in a large, heavy sedan. The man at the wheel didn't speak to them. Margit was up front with the driver. Largo, Remy, and Anita were in the back. Margit turned to Remy. "Do you know how to fire a pistol?"

She shook her head. "No. I haven't even held one since I was a little girl."

"That's all right." Margit took out two small pistols and handed them to Largo and Anita. "I know these two can shoot."

Remy raised her eyebrows at Anita. "Will you teach me how to shoot?"

"Of course," she said.

"What about me?" said Largo. "I've shot a gun."

"You can come along too," said Remy. "We'll have a picnic and kill the leftovers."

Margit glanced at Largo and turned back around in her seat.

They drove through heavy traffic along Krahe Vale. At one point, their way was blocked by reserve soldiers and Dandies marching in formation before a cheering crowd. At the Great Triumphal Square people hurled rocks through the windows of shops and cafés owned by foreigners. Young men and women sat drinking atop war memorial statues, shooting fireworks and pistols into the air.

"This is shit," said the driver. "We'll never make it in time."

Largo leaned up behind him. "Turn left here into that side street. There's an alley that runs parallel to the main road for the port."

The driver looked at Margit. She nodded and said, "Listen to him." The driver turned and they left the cheers and explosions behind.

The road was blocked twice more on the way to the port, but Largo told the driver how to circle around the obstructions. They made it to the port with just under an hour before the ship was to set sail. However, once there, another traffic jam made its appearance. The police had set up a checkpoint at the entrance to the port. They were checking the papers of everyone coming into the area. Largo spoke to Margit. "Is this normal?"

"Don't worry," she said. "Your papers have all the right stamps, and mine and Erich's are good. It's just a question of how slow these fucking bullocks are."

"They seem to be taking their sweet time."

"Don't talk when we get there. We're your loyal servants seeing you off on your trip. You're our posh bastard bosses. Understand?"

"Completely," said Largo. He sat back, but made sure the safety switch on his pistol was off.

It was fifteen long minutes before they reached the police line.

"Everyone's papers," said a bored officer.

Margit leaned past Erich. "Good evening, sir. It's just our employers who are traveling. We're simply giving them a ride."

"Traveling or not, if you're on the dock, I need to see your papers."

"Of course, sir."

Margit and Erich handed their identity papers to the officer, but he didn't check them or hand them back. He stepped to the rear of the car and rapped lightly on Anita's window with a knuckle. Anita rolled it down. "Good evening," she said icily, playing an upper-class snob. Largo kept his pistol by his side.

"Papers, Fräulein," said the officer.

Anita opened her handbag, but before she could hand them to the officer he looked at the three of them and said, "What's the nature of your travel?"

"It's a family matter," said Margit. "Their grandmother is gravely ill."

"A grandmother," said the officer. He shook his head. "Why are all you bluenoses such cowards?"

Largo put his finger on the trigger.

The officer pulled out a small flashlight and shone it in their eyes. "There's a war coming and you're pissing off to grandmama's house?"

Anita took her papers from her handbag and slapped them into the officer's hand without a word. He waited for Largo's and Remy's before looking at them. With all of their papers in his hand, he went to a senior officer, who shone his own light on them. Largo leaned across Anita, the pistol just below the level of the door window. Margit reached back and grabbed his arm. "Sit back and don't do anything unless I tell you. Understand?"

Remy pulled him back into the seat. He said, "He won't be the first bullock I've killed."

Erich half turned in Largo's direction. Margit shook her head. "Calm down, Largo. No one is dying tonight," she said.

Largo watched the officers go through their papers. The senior officer pointed to them and said something loud and rapid. He pointed back to their car and the officer came back, handing everything to Anita. He touched the brim of his hat. "Sorry to have delayed you. I shouldn't have spoken out of turn before. I'm sorry for your loss, but we'll get the bastards, don't worry."

"Thank you, Officer. Have a good evening," said Anita, as icy as before. She rolled up her window without looking at the man. The officer waved them around the other traffic and they quickly found themselves close to the front of the line.

Largo held on to his pistol and looked around. "What the hell was that?" he said.

"I told you the papers were good," said Margit. "Erich and I might be working-class trash, but you three are foreign representatives for Schöne Maschinen."

Largo thought the idea over for a moment and finally put the pistol back in his pocket. There was a kind of awful, beautiful symmetry to the idea that they worked for Schöne Maschinen. And it was at least partially true, he thought. *None of us would be here if it weren't for Baron Hellswarth.*

Erich pulled them into a parking spot about fifty yards from the ship. It was immense, full of lights and movement. Like the tallest building in Lower Proszawa laid on its side, Largo thought. He'd seen chromes of other ships, but this one looked different. The prow was strangely shaped. It bulged in the front, hanging like a belly over the water. What looked like black portholes ringed the bulge. Dozens of flying Maras circled overhead.

Anita said, "I've traveled all over the world and I've never seen a ship like this. What the hell is it?"

Margit got out of the car and retrieved their bags from the trunk. "You built it," she said. "Schöne Maschinen. Your employer, remember? It's a Mara ship. They're building dozens of them for the navy. They say it practically sails itself."

"Will the navy's version fight all by itself?" said Largo.

"We'll find out soon enough. Apparently they're sending several north right now for tests. You're getting out of here just in time."

Largo put a hand on Margit's arm. "I meant what I said earlier. We're going to send all the help we can."

"I know you will," she said. "Just don't go shooting every bullock who gives you a funny look. You'll run out of bullets."

He nodded. "How are Parvulesco and Roland?"

"Fine. They're with us now. They said I should give their 'sodomite sister' their regards. What's that about?"

Largo smiled. "A joke from a long time ago. Back when I was frightened of my own shadow."

"I'd say you've gotten over that."

"I still get scared."

"We all do. You just learn to live with it and keep moving."

Remy came over and put her arm around him. He kept his eyes on Margit. "Will I see you again?"

"I don't know. I hope so."

"Me too. I'd give you a goodbye hug, but—"

"I know," she said with a light laugh. "The bosses don't hug the help."

Erich walked up behind her and said, "Can we go? All these bullocks make my arse ache."

Remy tugged Largo's arm. "It's time for us to go too."

Anita took off Margit's hat and ran a hand through her short hair. "I don't mind saying goodbye to the help," she said. She gave her a kiss on the lips and headed for the ship with Margit's hat on her head. Largo and Remy followed.

When they were on board, Largo looked out over the crowd, hoping to catch a last glimpse of Margit and Erich before they left. However, everything below him was a madhouse—a teeming mass of hundreds of people all jostling to get themselves and their luggage aboard first. The ship sailed right on time. It was called *Ulfsaxa*, the name of a folktale goddess married to Saldr, the god of war. While he was all bluster and confidence, she was smarter. The goddess of guile and subterfuge. Largo asked Remy and Anita, "Do you think that's a good omen?"

Anita crinkled her nose. "I don't believe in omens."

"I do," said Remy. "And it's a very good one."

They sailed through Heldenblut Bay until they reached the open sea. It was considerably colder on the open water. All three of them shivered. "Let's go inside," said Remy.

"Just one more minute," said Largo. "It's funny. I don't even know where we're going."

"I'll tell you when we get somewhere warm. I'm freezing my tits off right now," said Anita.

They started inside, but Largo turned abruptly and walked to the railing at the edge of the deck. He looked down into the black water. Though it was churning against the hull of the ship, to him it looked strangely calm. When he was certain that no other passengers were looking, he took the pistol from his pocket and dropped it overboard. Part of him was frightened watching it disappear into the black, but he felt exhilarated too. Fear would come again, he knew, but it would not overwhelm him. Not now.

You just learn to live with it and keep moving.

The three of them went inside, letting the goddess of guile lead them out to sea and into a dark, new night.

ACKNOWLEDGMENTS

Thanks to my agent, Ginger Clark, and everyone else at Curtis Brown. Thanks also to my editor, David Pomerico, and the whole team at HarperCollins. Thank you to Borderlands Books, San Francisco's great science fiction and fantasy bookstore, for their kindness over the years. As always, thanks to Nicola for everything else.

MORE FROM RICHARD KADREY

SANDMAN SLIM SERIES

Sandman Slim
"An addictively satisfying, deeply amusing, dirty-ass masterpiece." —William Gibson

Kill the Dead
"Sandman Slim is my kind of hero."
—Kim Harrison

Aloha From Hell
"Richard Kadrey's 'Sandman Slim' series is one of my favorite sets of fantasy books from the last few years..." —John Scalzi

Devil in the Dollhouse
James Stark, a.k.a. Sandman Slim, has a new job, but being the new Lucifer in town gives fresh meaning to the word "Hell." Especially when he hears of hideous massacres near a haunted fortress out on Hell's frontier.

Devil Said Bang
Combining outrageously edgy humor with a dark and truly twisted vision, Kadrey once again delivers a masterful amalgam of action novel, urban fantasy, and in-your-face horror.

Kill City Blues
Kadrey returns to his bestselling Sandman Slim series with a high-octane fifth adventure.

The Getaway God
Sandman Slim must save himself—and the entire world—from the wrath of some enraged and vengeful ancient gods in his sixth high-octane adventure.

Killing Pretty
Sandman Slim investigates Death's death in this hip, propulsive urban fantasy through a phantasmagoric LA rife with murder, mayhem, and magic.

The Perdition Score
Sandman Slim returns in a stunning, high-octane thriller filled with the intense kick-ass action and inventive fantasy.

The Kill Society
Fury Road becomes a battle between Heaven and Hell in the ninth book in Richard Kadrey's bestselling Sandman Slim series.

Hollywood Dead
Life and death takes on an entirely new meaning for half-angel, half-human hero James Stark, aka, Sandman Slim, in this insanely inventive, high-intensity tenth supernatural noir thriller.

Ballistic Kiss
Sandman Slim is back in Los Angeles and kicking more supernatural ass in this inventive, high-octane page-turner.

ANOTHER COOP HEIST

The Everything Box
"A rolling bouncy-house of a caper tale,...abounds with quick-witted characters, snarky dialogue, and surreal analogies. "
—Christopher Moore, New York Times bestselling author of Lamb, A Dirty Job, and The Serpent of Venice.

The Wrong Dead Guy
In this fast paced sequel to The Everything Box chaos ensues when Coop and the team at DOPS steal a not-quite-dead and very lovesick ancient Egyptian mummy wielding some terrifying magic.

OTHER NOVELS

Dead Set
A wonderful stand-alone dark fantasy in which a young girl is caught between the worlds of the living and the dead.

Metrophage
Los Angeles in the late 21st century—a segregated city of haves and have nots, where morality is dead and technology rules. A small group of wealthy seclude themselves in gilded cages. Beyond their high security compounds lies a lawless wasteland where the angry masses battle hunger, rampant disease, and their own despair to survive.

The Grand Dark
"The Grand Dark is a miracle of the old and the new: a tale of weimar decadence that is also a parable for our New Gilded Age [...] It's a fun and terrifying ride, gritty and relentless, burning with true love and revolutionary fervor." —Cory Doctorow